Ruskin Bond's first novel, *The Room on the Roof*, written when he was seventeen, won the John Llewellyn Rhys Memorial Prize in 1957. Since then he has written several novellas (including *Vagrants in the Valley*, *A Flight of Pigeons* and *Delhi Is Not Far*), essays, poems and children's books, many of which have been published by Penguin India. He has also written over 500 short stories and articles that have appeared in a number of magazines and anthologies. He received the Sahitya Akademi Award in 1993 and the Padma Shri in 1999.

Ruskin Bond was born in Kasauli, Himachal Pradesh, and grew up in Jamnagar, Dehradun, Delhi and Shimla. As a young man, he spent four years in the Channel Islands and London. He returned to India in 1955 and has never left the country since. He now lives in Landour, Mussoorie, with his adopted family.

ALSO BY RUSKIN BOND

Fiction
The Room on the Roof & Vagrants in the Valley
The Night Train at Deoli and Other Stories
Time Stops at Shamli and Other Stories
Our Trees Still Grow in Dehra
A Season of Ghosts
When Darkness Falls and Other Stories
A Flight of Pigeons
Delhi Is Not Far
A Face in the Dark and Other Hauntings
The Sensualist
A Handful of Nuts

Non-fiction
Rain in the Mountains
Scenes from a Writer's Life
The Lamp Is Lit
The Little Book of Comfort
Landour Days
Notes from a Small Room

Anthologies
Dust on the Mountain: Collected Stories
The Best of Ruskin Bond
Friends in Small Places
Indian Ghost Stories (ed.)
Indian Railway Stories (ed.)
Classical Indian Love Stories and Lyrics (ed.)
Tales of the Open Road
Ruskin Bond's Book of Nature
Ruskin Bond's Book of Humour
A Town Called Dehra

Poetry
Ruskin Bond's Book of Verse

CLASSIC

RUSKIN BOND

COMPLETE AND UNABRIDGED

PENGUIN BOOKS

PENGUIN BOOKS

USA | Canada | UK | Ireland | Australia
New Zealand | India | South Africa | China

Penguin Books is part of the Penguin Random House group of companies
whose addresses can be found at global.penguinrandomhouse.com

Published by Penguin Books India Pvt. Ltd
7th Floor, Infinity Tower C, DLF Cyber City,
Gurgaon 122 002, Haryana, India

Penguin
Random House
India

This omnibus edition first published by Penguin Books India 2010

The Room on the Roof first published by André Deutsch 1956; *Vagrants in the
Valley* first published by IBH Publishing Company, Bombay, as *The Young
Vagrants* 1981; *Delhi Is Not Far* first appeared in *Delhi Is Not Far: The Best of
Ruskin Bond* published by Penguin Books India 1994; *A Flight of Pigeons* first
published in Viking by Penguin Books India 2002; *The Sensualist and A Handful
of Nuts* first published as part of Strangers in the Night: Two Novellas 1996

15 14 13 12 11 10 9 8 7

ISBN 9780143414667

Typeset in PalmSprings by SÜRYA, New Delhi
Printed at Repro India Ltd, Navi Mumbai

www.penguinbooksindia.com

CONTENTS

THE ROOM ON THE ROOF

Chapter One

The light spring rain rode on the wind, into the trees, down the road; it brought an exhilarating freshness to the air, a smell of earth, a scent of flowers; it brought a smile to the eyes of the boy on the road.

The long road wound round the hills, rose and fell and twisted down to Dehra; the road came from the mountains and passed through the jungle and valley and, after passing through Dehra, ended somewhere in the bazaar. But just where it ended no one knew, for the bazaar was a baffling place, where roads were easily lost.

The boy was three miles out of Dehra. The further he could get from Dehra, the happier he was likely to be. Just now he was only three miles out of Dehra, so he was not very happy; and, what was worse, he was walking homewards.

He was a pale boy, with blue-grey eyes and fair hair; his face was rough and marked, and the lower lip hung loose and heavy. He had his hands in his pockets and his head down, which was the way he always walked, and which gave him a deceptively tired appearance. He was a lazy but not a tired person.

He liked the rain as it flecked his face, he liked the smell and the freshness; he did not look at his surroundings or notice them—his mind, as usual, was very far away—but he felt their atmosphere, and he smiled.

His mind was so very far away that it was a few minutes before he noticed the swish of bicycle wheels beside him. The cyclist did not pass the boy, but rode beside him, studying him,

3

taking in every visible detail, the bare head, the open-necked shirt, the flannel trousers, the sandals, the thick hide belt round his waist. A European boy was no longer a common sight in Dehra, and Somi, the cyclist, was interested.

'Hullo,' said Somi, giving his bell a tinkle. The boy looked up and saw a young, friendly face wrapped untidily in a turban.

'Hullo,' said Somi, 'would you like me to ride you into town? If you are going to town?'

'No, I'm all right,' said the boy, without slackening his pace, 'I like to walk.'

'So do I, but it's raining.'

And to support Somi's argument, the rain fell harder.

'I like to walk in the rain,' said the boy. 'And I don't live in the town, I live outside it.'

Nice people didn't live *in* the town . . .

'Well, I can pass your way,' persisted Somi, determined to help the stranger.

The boy looked again at Somi, who was dressed like him except for short pants and a turban. Somi's legs were long and athletic, his colour was an unusually rich gold, his features were fine, his mouth broke easily into friendliness. It was impossible to resist the warmth of his nature.

The boy pulled himself up on the cross-bar, in front of Somi, and they moved off.

They rode slowly, gliding round the low hills, and soon the jungle on either side of the road began to give way to open fields and tea-gardens and then to orchards and one or two houses.

'Tell me when you reach your place,' said Somi. 'You stay with your parents?'

The boy considered the question too familiar for a stranger to ask, and made no reply.

'Do you like Dehra?' asked Somi.

'Not much,' said the boy with pleasure.

'Well, after England it must seem dull . . .'

There was a pause and then the boy said, 'I haven't been to England. I was born here. I've never been anywhere else except Delhi.'

'Do you like Delhi?'

'Not much.'

They rode on in silence. The rain still fell, but the cycle moved smoothly over the wet road, making a soft, swishing sound.

Presently a man came in sight—no, it was not a man, it was a youth, but he had the appearance, the build of a man—walking towards town.

'Hey, Ranbir,' shouted Somi, as they neared the burly figure, 'want a lift?'

Ranbir ran into the road and slipped on to the carrier, behind Somi. The cycle wobbled a bit, but soon controlled itself and moved on, a little faster now.

Somi spoke into the boy's ear, 'Meet my friend Ranbir. He is the best wrestler in the bazaar.'

'Hullo, mister,' said Ranbir, before the boy could open his mouth.

'Hullo, mister,' said the boy.

Then Ranbir and Somi began a swift conversation in Punjabi, and the boy felt very lost; even, for some strange reason, jealous of the newcomer.

Now someone was standing in the middle of the road, frantically waving his arms and shouting incomprehensibly.

'It is Suri,' said Somi.

It was Suri.

Bespectacled and owlish to behold, Suri possessed an almost criminal cunning, and was both respected and despised by all who knew him. It was strange to find him out of town, for his interests were confined to people and their privacies; which privacies, when known to Suri, were soon made public.

He was a pale, bony, sickly boy, but he would probably live longer than Ranbir.

'Hey, give me a lift!' he shouted.

'Too many already,' said Somi.

'Oh, come on Somi, I'm nearly drowned.'

'It's stopped raining.'

'Oh, come on . . .'

So Suri climbed on to the handlebar, which rather obscured Somi's view of the road and caused the cycle to wobble all over the place. Ranbir kept slipping on and off the carrier, and the boy found the cross-bar exceedingly uncomfortable. The cycle had barely been controlled when Suri started to complain.

'It hurts,' he whimpered.

'I haven't got a cushion,' said Somi.

'It is a cycle,' said Ranbir bitingly, 'not a Rolls Royce.'

Suddenly the road fell steeply, and the cycle gathered speed.

'Take it easy, now,' said Suri, 'or I'll fly off!'

'Hold tight,' warned Somi. 'It's downhill nearly all the way. We will have to go fast because the brakes aren't very good.'

'Oh, Mummy!' wailed Suri.

'Shut up!' said Ranbir.

The wind hit them with a sudden force, and their clothes blew up like balloons, almost tearing them from the machine. The boy forgot his discomfort and clung desperately to the cross-bar, too nervous to say a word. Suri howled and Ranbir kept telling him to shut up, but Somi was enjoying the ride. He laughed merrily, a clear, ringing laugh, a laugh that bore no malice and no derision but only enjoyment, fun . . .

'It's all right for you to laugh,' said Suri. 'If anything happens, I'll get hurt!'

'If anything happens,' said Somi, 'we *all* get hurt!'

'That's right,' shouted Ranbir from behind.

The boy closed his eyes and put his trust in God and Somi— but mainly Somi . . .

'Oh, Mummy!' wailed Suri.

'Shut up!' said Ranbir.

The road twisted and turned as much as it could, and rose a little only to fall more steeply the other side. But eventually it began to even out, for they were nearing the town and almost in the residential area.

'The run is over,' said Somi, a little regretfully.

'Oh, Mummy!'

'Shut up.'

The boy said, 'I must get off now, I live very near.' Somi skidded the cycle to a standstill, and Suri shot off the handlebar into a muddy side-track. The boy slipped off, but Somi and Ranbir remained on their seats, Ranbir steadying the cycle with his feet on the ground.

'Well, thank you,' said the boy.

Somi said, 'Why don't you come and have your meal with us, there is not much further to go.'

The boy's shyness would not fall away.

'I've got to go home,' he said. 'I'm expected. Thanks very much.'

'Well, come and see us some time,' said Somi. 'If you come to the chaat shop in the bazaar, you are sure to find one of us. You know the bazaar?'

'Well, I have passed through it—in a car.'

'Oh.'

The boy began walking away, his hands once more in his pockets.

'Hey!' shouted Somi. 'You didn't tell us your name!'

The boy turned and hesitated and then said, 'Rusty . . .'

'See you soon, Rusty,' said Somi, and the cycle pushed off.

The boy watched the cycle receding down the road, and Suri's shrill voice came to him on the wind. It had stopped raining, but the boy was unaware of this; he was almost home, and that was a miserable thought. To his surprise and disgust, he found himself wishing he had gone into Dehra with Somi.

He stood in the side-track and stared down the empty road; and, to his surprise and disgust, he felt immeasurably lonely.

Chapter Two

WHEN A LARGE WHITE butterfly settled on the missionary's wife's palatial bosom, she felt flattered, and allowed it to remain there.

Her garden was beginning to burst into flower, giving her great pleasure—her husband gave her none—and such fellow-feeling as to make her tread gingerly among the caterpillars.

Mr John Harrison, the boy's guardian, felt only contempt for the good lady's buoyancy of spirit, but nevertheless gave her an ingratiating smile.

'I hope you'll put the boy to work while I'm away,' he said. 'Make some use of him. He dreams too much. Most unfortunate that he's finished with school. I don't know what to do with him.'

'He doesn't know what to do with himself,' said the missionary's wife. 'But I'll keep him occupied. He can do some weeding, or read to me in the afternoon. I'll keep an eye on him.'

'Good,' said the guardian. And, having cleared his conscience, he made quick his escape.

Overlunch he told the boy, 'I'm going to Delhi tomorrow. Business.'

It was the only thing he said during the meal. When he had finished eating, he lighted a cigarette and erected a curtain of smoke between himself and the boy. He was a heavy smoker. His fingers were stained a deep yellow.

'How long will you be gone, sir?' asked Rusty, trying to sound casual.

Mr Harrison did not reply. He seldom answered the boy's questions, and his own were stated, not asked; he probed and suggested, sharply, quickly, without ever encouraging loose conversation. He never talked about himself; he never argued: he would tolerate no argument.

He was a tall man, neat in appearance; and, though over forty, looked younger because he kept his hair short, shaving above the ears. He had a small ginger toothbrush moustache.

Rusty was afraid of his guardian.

Mr Harrison, who was really a cousin of the boy's father, had done a lot for Rusty, and that was why the boy was afraid of him. Since his parents had died, Rusty had been kept, fed and paid for, and sent to an expensive school in the hills that was run on 'exclusively European lines'. He had, in a way, been bought by Mr Harrison. And now he was owned by him. And he must do as his guardian wished.

Rusty was ready to do as his guardian wished: he had always obeyed him. But he was afraid of the man, afraid of his silence and of the ginger moustache and of the supple malacca cane that lay in the glass cupboard in the drawing-room.

Lunch over, the boy left his guardian giving the cook orders, and went to his room.

The window looked out on the garden path, and a sweeper boy moved up and down the path, a bucket clanging against his naked thighs. He wore only a loincloth, his body was bare and burnt a deep brown, and his head was shaved clean. He went to and from the water-tank, and every time he returned to it he bathed, so that his body continually glistened with moisture.

Apart from Rusty, the only boy in the European community of Dehra was this sweeper boy, the low-caste untouchable, the cleaner of pots. But the two seldom spoke to each other, one was a servant and the other a sahib and anyway, muttered Rusty to himself, playing with the sweeper boy would be unhygienic ...

The missionary's wife had said, 'Even if you were an Indian, my child, you would not be allowed to play with the sweeper boy.' So that Rusty often wondered: with whom, then, *could* the sweeper boy play?

The untouchable passed by the window and smiled, but Rusty looked away.

Over the tops of the cherry trees were mountains. Dehra lay in a valley in the foothills, and the small, diminishing European community had its abode on the outskirts of the town.

Mr John Harrison's house, and the other houses, were all built in an English style, with neat front gardens and nameplates on the gates. The surroundings on the whole were so English that the people often found it difficult to believe that they lived at the foot of the Himalayas, surrounded by India's thickest jungles. India started a mile away,where the bazaar began.

To Rusty, the bazaar sounded a fascinating place, and what he had seen of it from the window of his guardian's car had been enough to make his heart pound excitedly and his imagination soar; but it was a forbidden place—'full of thieves and germs' said the missionary's wife—and the boy never entered it save in his dreams.

For Mr Harrison, the missionaries, and their neighbours, this country district of blossoming cherry trees was India. They knew there was a bazaar and a real India not far away, but they did not speak of such places: they chose not to think about them.

The community consisted mostly of elderly people, the others had left soon after Independence. These few stayed because they were too old to start life again in another country, where there would be no servants and very little sunlight; and though they complained of their lot and criticized the government, they knew their money could buy them their comforts: servants, good food, whisky, almost anything—except the dignity they cherished most . . .

But the boy's guardian, though he enjoyed the same comforts, remained in the country for different reasons. He did not care who were the rulers so long as they didn't take away his business; he had shares in a number of small tea-estates and owned some land—forested land—where, for instance, he hunted deer and wild pig.

Rusty, being the only young person in the community, was the centre of everyone's attention, particularly the ladies'.

He was also very lonely.

Every day he walked aimlessly along the road, over the hillside; brooding on the future, or dreaming of sudden and perfect companionship, romance and heroics; hardly ever conscious of the present. When an opportunity for friendship did present itself, as it had the previous day, he shied away, preferring his own company.

His idle hours were crowded with memories, snatches of childhood. He could not remember what his parents were like, but in his mind there were pictures of sandy beaches covered with sea shells of every description. They had lived on the west coast, in the Gulf of Kutch; there had been a gramophone that played records of Gracie Fields and Harry Lauder, and a captain of a cargo ship who gave the child bars of chocolate and piles of comics—*The Dandy, Beano, Tiger Tim*—and spoke of the wonderful countries he had visited.

But the boy's guardian seldom spoke of Rusty's childhood, or his parents, and this secrecy lent mystery to the vague, undefined memories that hovered in the boy's mind like hesitant ghosts.

Rusty spent much of his time studying himself in the dressing-table mirror; he was able to ignore his pimples and see a grown man, worldly and attractive. Though only sixteen, he felt much older.

He was white. His guardian was pink, and the missionary's wife a bright red, but Rusty was white. With his thick lower lip and prominent cheekbones, he looked slightly Mongolian, especially in a half-light. He often wondered why no one else in the community had the same features.

*

Mr John Harrison was going to Delhi.

Rusty intended making the most of his guardian's absence: he would squeeze all the freedom he could out of the next few days; explore, get lost, wander afar; even if it were only to find new places to dream in. So he threw himself on the bed and visualized the morrow . . . where should he go—into the hills again, into the forest? Or should he listen to the devil in his heart and go into the bazaar? Tomorrow he would know, tomorrow . . .

CHAPTER THREE

IT WAS A COLD morning, sharp and fresh. It was quiet until the sun came shooting over the hills, lifting the mist from the valley and clearing the blood-shot from the sky. The ground was wet with dew.

On the maidan, a broad stretch of grassland, Ranbir and another youth wrestled each other, their muscles rippling, their well-oiled limbs catching the first rays of the sun as it climbed the horizon. Somi sat on his veranda steps; his long hair loose, resting on his knees, drying in the morning sun. Suri was still dead to the world, lost in blanket; he cared not for the morning or the sun.

Rusty stood at the gate until his guardian was comfortably seated behind the wheel of the car, and did not move until it had disappeared round the bend in the road.

The missionary's wife, that large cauliflower-like lady, rose unexpectedly from behind a hedge and called, 'Good morning, dear! If you aren't very busy this morning, would you like to give me a hand pruning this hedge?'

The missionary's wife was fond of putting Rusty to work in her garden: if it wasn't cutting the hedge, it was weeding the flower-beds and watering the plants, or clearing the garden path of stones, or hunting beetles and ladybirds and dropping them over the wall.

'Oh, good morning,' stammered Rusty. 'Actually, I was going for a walk. Can I help you when I come back, I won't be long . . .'

The missionary's wife was rather taken aback, for Rusty seldom said no; and before she could make another sally the boy was on his way. He had a dreadful feeling she would call him back; she was a kind woman, but talkative and boring, and Rusty knew what would follow the garden work: weak tea or lemonade, and then a game of cards, probably beggar-my-neighbour.

But to his relief she called after him, 'All right, dear, come back soon. And be good!'

He waved to her and walked rapidly down the road. And the direction he took was different to the one in which he usually wandered.

Far down this road was the bazaar. First Rusty must pass the rows of neat cottages, arriving at a commercial area—Dehra's

Westernized shopping centre—where Europeans, rich Indians, and American tourists en route for Mussoorie, could eat at smart restaurants and drink prohibited alcohol. But the boy was afraid and distrustful of anything smart and sophisticated, and he hurried past the shopping centre.

He came to the Clock Tower, which was a tower without a clock. It had been built from public subscriptions but not enough money had been gathered for the addition of a clock. It had been lifeless five years but served as a good landmark. On the other side of the Clock Tower lay the bazaar, and in the bazaar lay India. On the other side of the Clock Tower began life itself. And all three—the bazaar and India and life itself—were forbidden.

Rusty's heart was beating fast as he reached the Clock Tower. He was about to defy the law of his guardian and of his community. He stood at the Clock Tower, nervous, hesitant, biting his nails. He was afraid of discovery and punishment, but hungering curiosity impelled him forward.

The bazaar and India and life itself all began with a rush of noise and confusion.

The boy plunged into the throng of bustling people; the road was hot and close, alive with the cries of vendors and the smell of cattle and ripening dung. Children played hopscotch in alleyways or gambled with coins, scuffling in the gutter for a lost anna. And the cows moved leisurely through the crowd, nosing around for paper and stale, discarded vegetables; the more daring cows helping themselves at open stalls. And above the uneven tempo of the noise came the blare of a loudspeaker playing a popular piece of music.

Rusty moved along with the crowd, fascinated by the sight of beggars lying on the roadside: naked and emaciated half-humans, some skeletons, some covered with sores; old men dying, children dying, mothers with sucking babies, living and dying. But, strangely enough, the boy could feel nothing for these people; perhaps it was because they were no longer recognizable as humans or because he could not see himself in the same circumstances. And no one else in the bazaar seemed to feel for them. Like the cows and the loudspeaker, the beggars were a natural growth in the bazaar, and only the well-to-do—sacrificing a few annas to placate their consciences—were aware of the beggars' presence.

Every little shop was different from the one next to it. After the vegetable stand, green and wet, came the fruit stall; and, after the fruit stall, the tea and betel-leaf shop; then the astrologer's platform (Manmohan Mukuldev, B.Astr., foreign degree); and after the astrologer's the toy shop, selling trinkets of gay colours. And then, after the toy shop, another from whose doors poured clouds of smoke.

Out of curiosity Rusty turned to the shop from which the smoke was coming. But he was not the only person making for it. Approaching from the opposite direction was Somi on his bicycle.

Somi, who had not seen Rusty, seemed determined on riding right into the smoky shop on his bicycle. Unfortunately his way was blocked by Maharani, the queen of the bazaar cows, who moved aside for no one. But the cycle did not lose speed.

Rusty, seeing the cycle but not recognizing the rider, felt sorry for the cow, it was sure to be hurt. But, with the devil in his heart or in the wheels of his machine, Somi swung clear of Maharani and collided with Rusty and knocked him into the gutter.

Accustomed as Rusty was to the delicate scents of the missionary's wife's sweet peas and the occasional smell of bathroom disinfectant, he was nevertheless overpowered by the odour of bad vegetables and kitchen water that rose from the gutter.

'What the hell do you think you're doing?' he cried, choking and spluttering.

'Hullo,' said Somi, gripping Rusty by the arm and helping him up, 'so sorry, not my fault. Anyway, we meet again!'

Rusty felt for injuries and, finding none, exclaimed, 'Look at the filthy mess I'm in!'

Somi could not help laughing at the other's unhappy condition. 'Oh, that is not filth, it is only cabbage water! Do not worry, the clothes will dry . . .'

His laugh rang out merrily, and there was something about the laugh, some music in it perhaps, that touched a chord of gaiety in Rusty's own heart. Somi was smiling, and on his mouth the smile was friendly and in his soft brown eyes it was mocking.

'Well, I am sorry,' said Somi, extending his hand.

Rusty did not take the hand but, looking the other up and down, from turban to slippers, forced himself to say, 'Get out of my way, please.'

'You are a snob,' said Somi without moving. 'You are a very funny one too.'

'I am not a snob,' said Rusty involuntarily.

'Then why not forget an accident?'

'You could have missed me, but you didn't try.'

'But if I had missed you, I would have hit the cow! You don't know Maharani, if you hurt her she goes mad and smashes half the bazaar! Also, the bicycle might have been spoilt ... Now please come and have chaat with me.'

Rusty had no idea what was meant by the word chaat, but before he could refuse the invitation Somi had bundled him into the shop from which the smoke still poured.

At first nothing could be made out; then gradually the smoke seemed to clear and there in front of the boys, like some shining god, sat a man enveloped in rolls of glistening, oily flesh. In front of him, on a coal fire, was a massive pan in which sizzled a sea of fat; and with deft, practised fingers, he moulded and flipped potato cakes in and out of the pan.

The shop was crowded; but so thick was the screen of smoke and steam, that it was only the murmur of conversation which made known the presence of many people. A plate made of banana leaves was thrust into Rusty's hands, and two fried cakes suddenly appeared in it.

'Eat!' said Somi, pressing the novice down until they were both on the floor, their backs to the wall.

'They are tikkees,' explained Somi, 'tell me if you like them.'

Rusty tasted a bit. It was hot. He waited a minute, then tasted another bit. It was still hot but in a different way; now it was lively, interesting; it had a different taste to anything he had eaten before. Suspicious but inquisitive, he finished the tikkee and waited to see if anything would happen.

'Have you had before?' asked Somi.

'No,' said Rusty anxiously, 'what will it do?'

'It might worry your stomach a little at first, but you will get used to it the more often you eat. So finish the other one too.'

Rusty had not realized the extent of his submission to the other's wishes. At one moment he had been angry, ill-mannered; but, since the laugh, he had obeyed Somi without demur.

Somi wore a cotton tunic and shorts, and sat cross-legged, his feet pressed against his thighs. His skin was a golden brown, dark on his legs and arms but fair, very fair, where his shirt lay open. His hands were dirty; but eloquent. His eyes, deep brown and dreamy, had depth and roundness.

He said, 'My name is Somi, please tell me what is yours, I have forgotten.'

'Rusty . . .'

'How do you do,' said Somi, 'I am very pleased to meet you, haven't we met before?'

Rusty mumbled to himself in an effort to sulk.

'That was a long time ago,' said Somi, 'now we are friends, yes, best favourite friends!'

Rusty continued to mumble under his breath but he took the warm muddy hand that Somi gave him, and shook it. He finished the tikkee on his leaf, and accepted another. Then he said, 'How do you do, Somi, I am very pleased to meet you.'

Chapter Four

THE MISSIONARY'S WIFE'S HEAD projected itself over the garden wall and broke into a beam of welcome. Rusty hurriedly returned the smile.

'Where have you been, dear?' asked his garrulous neighbour. 'I was expecting you for lunch. You've never been away so long, I've finished all my work now, you know . . . Was it a nice walk? I know you're thirsty, come in and have a nice cool lemonade, there's nothing like iced lemonade to refresh one after a long walk. I remember when I was a girl, having to walk down to Dehra from Mussoorie, I filled my thermos with lemonade . . .'

But Rusty had gone. He did not wish to hurt the missionary's wife's feelings by refusing the lemonade but, after experiencing the chaat shop, the very idea of a lemonade offended him. But he decided that this Sunday he would contribute an extra four annas to the missionary's fund for the upkeep of church, wife and garden; and, with this good thought in mind, went to his room.

The sweeper boy passed by the window, his buckets clanging, his feet going slip-slop in the watery path.

Rusty threw himself on his bed. And now his imagination began building dreams on a new-found reality, for he had agreed to meet Somi again.

And so, the next day, his steps took him to the chaat shop in the bazaar; past the Clock Tower, past the smart shops, down the road, far from the guardian's house.

The fleshy god of the tikkees smiled at Rusty in a manner that seemed to signify that the boy was now likely to become a Regular Customer. The banana plate was ready, the tikkees in it flavoured with spiced sauces.

'Hullo, best favourite friend,' said Somi, appearing out of the surrounding vapour, his slippers loose, chup-chup-chup; open slippers that hung on to the toes by a strap and slapped against the heels as he walked. 'I am glad you come again. After tikkees you must have something else, chaat or golguppas, all right?'

Somi removed his slippers and joined Rusty, who had somehow managed to sit cross-legged on the ground in the proper fashion.

Somi said, 'Tell me something about yourself. By what misfortune are you an Englishman? How is it that you have been here all your life and never been to a chaat shop before?'

'Well, my guardian is very strict,' said Rusty. 'He wanted to bring me up in English ways, and he has succeeded ...'

'Till now,' said Somi, and laughed, the laugh rippling up in his throat, breaking out and forcing its way through the smoke.

Then a large figure loomed in front of the boys, and Rusty recognized him as Ranbir, the youth he had met on the bicycle.

'Another best favourite friend,' said Somi.

Ranbir did not smile, but opened his mouth a little, gaped at Rusty, and nodded his head. When he nodded, hair fell untidily across his forehead; thick black bushy hair, wild and uncontrollable. He wore a long white cotton tunic hanging out over his baggy pyjamas, his feet were bare and dirty; big feet, strong.

'Hullo, mister,' said Ranbir in a gruff voice that disguised his shyness. He said no more for a while, but joined them in their meal.

They ate chaat, a spicy salad of potato, guava and orange; and then gol-guppas, baked flour-cups filled with burning syrups. Rusty felt at ease and began to talk, telling his companions about his school in the hills, the house of his guardian, Mr Harrison himself, and the supple malacca cane. The story was listened to with some amusement: apparently Rusty's life had been very dull to date, and Somi and Ranbir pitied him for it.

'Tomorrow is Holi,' said Ranbir,'you must play with me, then you will be my friend.'

'What is Holi?' asked Rusty.

Ranbir looked at him in amazement. 'You do not know about Holi! It is the Hindu festival of colour! It is the day on which we celebrate the coming of spring, when we throw colour on each other and shout and sing and forget our misery, for the colours mean the rebirth of spring and a new life in our hearts ... You do not know of it!'

Rusty was somewhat bewildered by Ranbir's sudden eloquence, and began to have doubts about this game; it seemed to him a primitive sort of pastime, this throwing of paint about the place.

'I might get into trouble,' he said. 'I'm not supposed to come here, anyway, and my guardian might return any day ...'

'Don't tell him about it,' said Ranbir.

'Oh, he has ways of finding out. I'll get a thrashing.'

'Huh!' said Ranbir, a disappointed and somewhat disgusted expression on his mobile face. 'You are afraid to spoil your clothes, mister, that is it. You are just a snob.'

Somi laughed. 'That's what I told him yesterday, and only then did he join me in the chaat shop. I think we should call him a snob whenever he makes excuses.'

Rusty was enjoying the chaat. He ate gol-guppa after golguppa, until his throat was almost aflame and his stomach burning itself out. He was not very concerned about Holi. He was content with the present, content to enjoy the newfound pleasures of the chaat shop, and said, 'Well, I'll see . . . If my guardian doesn't come back tomorrow, I'll play Holi with you, all right?'

Ranbir was pleased. He said, 'I will be waiting in the jungle behind your house. When you hear the drum-beat in the jungle, then it is me. Then come.'

'Will you be there too, Somi?' asked Rusty. Somehow, he felt safe in Somi's presence.

'I do not play Holi,' said Somi. 'You see, I am different to Ranbir. I wear a turban and he does not, also there is a bangle on my wrist, which means that I am a Sikh. We don't play it. But I will see you the day after, here in the chaat shop.'

Somi left the shop, and was swallowed up by smoke and steam, but the chup-chup of his loose slippers could be heard for some time, until their sound was lost in the greater sound of the bazaar outside.

In the bazaar, people haggled over counters, children played in the spring sunshine, dogs courted one another, and Ranbir and Rusty continued eating gol-guppas.

*

The afternoon was warm and lazy, unusually so for spring; very quiet, as though resting in the interval between the spring and the coming summer. There was no sign of the missionary's wife or the sweeper boy when Rusty returned, but Mr Harrison's car stood in the driveway of the house.

At sight of the car, Rusty felt a little weak and frightened; he had not expected his guardian to return so soon and had, in fact, almost forgotten his existence. But now he forgot all about the chaat shop and Somi and Ranbir, and ran up the veranda steps in a panic.

Mr Harrison was at the top of the veranda steps, standing behind the potted palms.

The boy said, 'Oh, hullo, sir, you're back!' He knew of nothing else to say, but tried to make his little piece sound enthusiastic.

'Where have you been all day?' asked Mr Harrison, without looking once at the startled boy. 'Our neighbours haven't seen much of you lately.'

'I've been for a walk, sir.'

'You have been to the bazaar.'

The boy hesitated before making a denial; the man's eyes were on him now, and to lie Rusty would have had to lower his eyes—and this he could not do . . .

'Yes, sir, I went to the bazaar.'

'May I ask why?'

'Because I had nothing to do.'

'If you had nothing to do, you could have visited our neighbours. The bazaar is not the place for you. You know that.'

'But nothing happened to me . . .'

'That is not the point,' said Mr Harrison, and now his normally dry voice took on a faint shrill note of excitement, and he spoke rapidly. 'The point is, I have told you never to visit the bazaar. You belong here, to this house, this road, these people. Don't go where you don't belong.'

Rusty wanted to argue, longed to rebel, but fear of Mr Harrison held him back. He wanted to resist the man's authority, but he was conscious of the supple malacca cane in the glass cupboard.

'I'm sorry, sir . . .'

But his cowardice did him no good. The guardian went over to the glass cupboard, brought out the cane, flexed it in his hands. He said, 'It is not enough to say you are sorry, you must be made to feel sorry. Bend over the sofa.'

The boy bent over the sofa, clenched his teeth and dug his fingers into the cushions. The cane swished through the air, landing on his bottom with a slap, knocking the dust from his pants. Rusty felt no pain. But his guardian waited, allowing the cut to sink in, then he administered the second stroke, and this time it hurt, it stung into the boy's buttocks, burning up the flesh, conditioning it for the remaining cuts.

At the sixth stroke of the supple malacca cane, which was usually the last, Rusty let out a wild whoop, leapt over the sofa and charged from the room.

He lay groaning on his bed until the pain had eased.

But the flesh was so sore that he could not touch the place where the cane had fallen. Wriggling out of his pants, he examined his backside in the mirror. Mr Harrison had been most accurate: a thick purple welt stretched across both cheeks, and a little blood trickled down the boy's thigh. The blood had a cool, almost soothing effect, but the sight of it made Rusty feel faint.

He lay down and moaned for pleasure. He pitied himself enough to want to cry, but he knew the futility of tears. But the pain and the sense of injustice he felt were both real.

A shadow fell across the bed. Someone was at the window, and Rusty looked up.

The sweeper boy showed his teeth.

'What do you want?' asked Rusty gruffly.

'You hurt, chotta sahib?'

The sweeper boy's sympathies provoked only suspicion in Rusty.

'You told Mr Harrison where I went!' said Rusty.

But the sweeper boy cocked his head to one side, and asked innocently, 'Where you went, chotta sahib?'

'Oh, never mind. Go away.'

'But you hurt?'

'Get out!' shouted Rusty.

The smile vanished, leaving only a sad frightened look in the sweeper boy's eyes.

Rusty hated hurting people's feelings, but he was not

accustomed to familiarity with servants; and yet, only a few minutes ago, he had been beaten for visiting the bazaar where there were so many like the sweeper boy.

The sweeper boy turned from the window, leaving wet fingermarks on the sill; then lifted his buckets from the ground and, with his knees bent to take the weight, walked away. His feet splashed a little in the water he had spilt, and the soft red mud flew up and flecked his legs.

Angry with his guardian and with the servant and most of all with himself, Rusty buried his head in his pillow and tried to shut out reality; he forced a dream, in which he was thrashing Mr Harrison until the guardian begged for mercy.

Chapter Five

In the early morning, when it was still dark, Ranbir stopped in the jungle behind Mr Harrison's house, and slapped his drum. His thick mass of hair was covered with red dust and his body, naked but for a cloth round his waist, was smeared green; he looked like a painted god, a green god. After a minute he slapped the drum again, then sat down on his heels and waited.

Rusty woke to the sound of the second drum-beat, and lay in bed and listened; it was repeated, travelling over the still air and in through the bedroom window. *Dhum!* . . . A double-beat now, one deep, one high, insistent, questioning . . .

Rusty remembered his promise, that he would play Holi with Ranbir, meet him in the jungle when he beat the drum. But he had made the promise on the condition that his guardian did not return; he could not possibly keep it now, not after the thrashing he had received.

Dhum-dhum, spoke the drum in the forest; dhum-dhum, impatient and getting annoyed . . .

'Why can't he shut up,' muttered Rusty, 'does he want to wake Mr Harrison . . .'

Holi, the Festival of Colours, the arrival of spring, the rebirth
of the new year, the awakening of love, what were these things
to him, they did not concern his life, he could not start a new life,
not for one day ... and besides, it all sounded very primitive,
this throwing of colour and beating of drums ...

Dhum-dhum!

The boy sat up in bed.

The sky had grown lighter.

From the distant bazaar came a new music, many drums and
voices, faint but steady, growing in rhythm and excitement. The
sound conveyed something to Rusty, something wild and
emotional, something that belonged to his dream-world, and on
a sudden impulse he sprang out of bed.

He went to the door and listened; the house was quiet, he
bolted the door. The colours of Holi, he knew, would stain his
clothes, so he did not remove his pyjamas. In an old pair of
flattened rubber-soled tennis shoes, he climbed out of the window
and ran over the dew-wet grass, down the path behind the
house, over the hill and into the jungle.

When Ranbir saw the boy approach, he rose from the ground.
The long hand-drum, the dholak, hung at his waist. As he rose,
the sun rose. But the sun did not look as fiery as Ranbir who, in
Rusty's eyes, appeared as a painted demon, rather than as a god.

'You are late, mister,' said Ranbir, 'I thought you were not
coming.'

He had both his fists closed, but when he walked towards
Rusty he opened them, smiling widely, a white smile in a green
face. In his right hand was the red dust and in his left hand the
green dust. And with his right hand he rubbed the red dust on
Rusty's left cheek, and then with the other hand he put the green
dust on the boy's right cheek; then he stood back and looked at
Rusty and laughed. Then, according to the custom, he embraced
the bewildered boy. It was a wrestler's hug, and Rusty winced
breathlessly.

'Come,' said Ranbir, 'let us go and make the town a rainbow.'

*

And truly, that day there was an outbreak of spring.

The sun came up, and the bazaar woke up. The walls of the houses were suddenly patched with splashes of colour, and just as suddenly the trees seemed to have burst into flower; for in the forest there were armies of rhododendrons, and by the river the poinsettias danced; the cherry and the plum were in blossom; the snow in the mountains had melted, and the streams were rushing torrents; the new leaves on the trees were full of sweetness, the young grass held both dew and sun, and made an emerald of every dewdrop.

The infection of spring spread simultaneously through the world of man and the world of nature, and made them one.

Ranbir and Rusty moved round the hill, keeping in the fringe of the jungle until they had skirted not only the European community but also the smart shopping centre. They came down dirty little side-streets where the walls of houses, stained with the wear and tear of many years of meagre habitation, were now stained again with the vivid colours of Holi. They came to the Clock Tower.

At the Clock Tower, spring had really been declared open. Clouds of coloured dust rose in the air and spread, and jets of water—green and orange and purple, all rich emotional colours—burst out everywhere.

Children formed groups. They were armed mainly with bicycle pumps, or pumps fashioned from bamboo stems, from which was squirted liquid colour. The children paraded the main road, chanting shrilly and clapping their hands. The men and women preferred the dust to the water. They too sang, but their chanting held a significance, their hands and fingers drummed the rhythms of spring, the same rhythms, the same songs that belonged to this day every year of their lives.

Ranbir was met by some friends and greeted with great hilarity. A bicycle pump was directed at Rusty and a jet of sooty black water squirted into his face.

Blinded for a moment, Rusty blundered about in great confusion. A horde of children bore down on him, and he was subjected to a pumping from all sides. His shirt and pyjamas, drenched through, stuck to his skin; then someone gripped the end of his shirt and tugged at it until it tore and came away. Dust was thrown on the boy, on his face and body, roughly and with full force, and his tender, underexposed skin smarted beneath the onslaught.

Then his eyes cleared. He blinked and looked wildly round at the group of boys and girls who cheered and danced in front of him. His body was running mostly with sooty black, streaked with red, and his mouth seemed full of it too, and he began to spit.

Then, one by one, Ranbir's friends approached Rusty.

Gently, they rubbed dust on the boy's cheeks, and embraced him; they were like so many flaming demons that Rusty could not distinguish one from the other. But this gentle greeting, coming so soon after the stormy bicycle pump attack, bewildered Rusty even more.

Ranbir said, 'Now you are one of us, come,' and Rusty went with him and the others.

'Suri is hiding,' cried someone. 'He has locked himself in his house and won't play Holi!'

'Well, he will have to play,' said Ranbir, 'even if we break the house down.'

Suri, who dreaded Holi, had decided to spend the day in a state of siege; and had set up camp in his mother's kitchen, where there were provisions enough for the whole day. He listened to his playmates calling to him from the courtyard, and ignored their invitations, jeers, and threats; the door was strong and well-barricaded. He settled himself beneath a table, and turned the pages of the English nudists' journal, which he bought every month chiefly for its photographic value.

But the youths outside, intoxicated by the drumming and shouting and high spirits, were not going to be done out of the pleasure of discomfiting Suri. So they acquired a ladder and made their entry into the kitchen by the skylight.

Suri squealed with fright. The door was opened and he was bundled out, and his spectacles were trampled.

'My glasses!' he screamed. 'You've broken them!'

'You can afford a dozen pairs!' jeered one of his antagonists.

'But I can't see, you fools, I can't see!'

'He can't see!' cried someone in scorn. 'For once in his life, Suri can't see what's going on! Now, whenever he spies, we'll smash his glasses!'

Not knowing Suri very well, Rusty could not help pitying the frantic boy.

'Why don't you let him go,' he asked Ranbir. 'Don't force him if he doesn't want to play.'

'But this is the only chance we have of repaying him for all his dirty tricks. It is the only day on which no one is afraid of him!'

Rusty could not imagine how anyone could possibly be afraid of the pale, struggling, spindly-legged boy who was almost being torn apart, and was glad when the others had finished their sport with him.

All day Rusty roamed the town and countryside with Ranbir and his friends, and Suri was soon forgotten. For one day, Ranbir and his friends forgot their homes and their work and the problem of the next meal, and danced down the roads, out of the town and into the forest. And, for one day, Rusty forgot his guardian and the missionary's wife and the supple malacca cane, and ran with the others through the town and into the forest.

The crisp, sunny morning ripened into afternoon.

In the forest, in the cool dark silence of the jungle, they stopped singing and shouting, suddenly exhausted. They lay down in the shade of many trees, and the grass was soft and comfortable, and very soon everyone except Rusty was fast asleep.

Rusty was tired. He was hungry. He had lost his shirt and shoes, his feet were bruised, his body sore. It was only now, resting, that he noticed these things, for he had been caught up in the excitement of the colour game, overcome by an exhilaration he had never known. His fair hair was tousled and streaked with colour, and his eyes were wide with wonder.

He was exhausted now, but he was happy.

He wanted this to go on for ever, this day of feverish emotion, this life in another world. He did not want to leave the forest; it was safe, its earth soothed him, gathered him in so that the pain of his body became a pleasure . . .

He did not want to go home.

Chapter Six

❦

Mr Harrison stood at the top of the veranda steps. The house was in darkness, but his cigarette glowed more brightly for it. A road lamp trapped the returning boy as he opened the gate, and Rusty knew he had been seen, but he didn't care much; if he had known that Mr Harrison had not recognized him, he would have turned back instead of walking resignedly up the garden path.

Mr Harrison did not move, nor did he appear to notice the boy's approach. It was only when Rusty climbed the veranda steps that his guardian moved and said, 'Who's that?'

Still he had not recognized the boy; and in that instant Rusty became aware of his own condition, for his body was a patchwork of paint.Wearing only torn pyjamas he could, in the half-light, have easily been mistaken for the sweeper boy or someone else's servant. It must have been a newly-acquired bazaar instinct that made the boy think of escape. He turned about.

But Mr Harrison shouted, 'Come here, you!' and the tone of his voice—the tone reserved for the sweeper boy—made Rusty stop.

'Come up here!' repeated Mr Harrison.

Rusty returned to the veranda, and his guardian switched on a light; but even now there was no recognition.

'Good evening, sir,' said Rusty.

Mr Harrison received a shock. He felt a wave of anger, and then a wave of pain: was this the boy he had trained and educated—this wild, ragged, ungrateful wretch, who did not know the difference between what was proper and what was improper, what was civilized and what was barbaric, what was decent and what was shameful—and had the years of training come to nothing? Mr Harrison came out of the shadows and cursed. He brought his hand down on the back of Rusty's neck, propelled him into the drawing-room, and pushed him across the room so violently that the boy lost his balance, collided with a table and rolled over on to the ground.

Rusty looked up from the floor to find his guardian standing over him, and in the man's right hand was the supple malacca cane and the cane was twitching.

Mr Harrison's face was twitching too, it was full of fire. His lips were stitched together, sealed up with the ginger moustache, and he looked at the boy with narrowed, unblinking eyes.

'Filth!' he said, almost spitting the words in the boy's face. 'My God, what filth!'

Rusty stared fascinated at the deep yellow nicotine stains on the fingers of his guardian's raised hand. Then the wrist moved suddenly and the cane cut across the boy's face like a knife, stabbing and burning into his cheek.

Rusty cried out and cowered back against the wall; he could feel the blood trickling across his mouth. He looked round desperately for a means of escape, but the man was in front of him, over him, and the wall was behind.

Mr Harrison broke into a torrent of words. 'How can you call yourself an Englishman, how can you come back to this house in such a condition? In what gutter, in what brothel have you been! Have you seen yourself? Do you know what you look like?'

'No,' said Rusty, and for the first time he did not address his guardian as 'sir'. 'I don't care what I look like.'

'You don't . . . well, I'll tell you what you look like! You look like the mongrel that you are!'

'That's a lie!' exclaimed Rusty.

'It's the truth. I've tried to bring you up as an Englishman, as your father would have wished. But, as you won't have it our way, I'm telling you that he was about the only thing English about you. You're no better than the sweeper boy!'

Rusty flared into a temper, showing some spirit for the first time in his life. 'I'm no better than the sweeper boy, but I'm as good as him! I'm as good as you! I'm as good as anyone!' And, instead of cringing to take the cut from the cane, he flung himself at his guardian's legs. The cane swished through the air, grazing the boy's back. Rusty wrapped his arms round his guardian's legs and pulled on them with all his strength.

Mr Harrison went over, falling flat on his back.

The suddenness of the fall must have knocked the breath from his body, because for a moment he did not move.

Rusty sprang to his feet. The cut across his face had stung him to madness, to an unreasoning hate, and he did what previously he would only have dreamt of doing. Lifting a vase of the missionary's wife's best sweet peas off the glass cupboard, he flung it at his guardian's face. It hit him on the chest, but the water and flowers flopped out over his face. He tried to get up; but he was speechless.

The look of alarm on Mr Harrison's face gave Rusty greater courage. Before the man could recover his feet and his balance, Rusty gripped him by the collar and pushed him backwards, until they both fell over on to the floor. With one hand still twisting the collar, the boy slapped his guardian's face. Mad with the pain in his own face, Rusty hit the man again and again, wildly and awkwardly, but with the giddy thrill of knowing he could do it: he was a child no longer, he was nearly seventeen, he was a man. He could inflict pain, that was a wonderful discovery; there was a power in his body—a devil or a god—and he gained confidence in his power; and he was a man!

'Stop that, stop it!'

The shout of a hysterical woman brought Rusty to his senses. He still held his guardian by the throat, but he stopped hitting him. Mr Harrison's face was very red.

The missionary's wife stood in the doorway, her face white with fear. She was under the impression that Mr Harrison was being attacked by a servant or some bazaar hooligan. Rusty did not wait until she found her tongue but, with a new-found speed and agility, darted out of the drawing-room.

He made his escape from the bedroom window. From the gate he could see the missionary's wife silhouetted against the drawing-room light. He laughed out loud. The woman swivelled round and came forward a few steps. And Rusty laughed again and began running down the road to the bazaar.

*

It was late. The smart shops and restaurants were closed. In the bazaar, oil lamps hung outside each doorway; people were asleep on the steps and platforms of shopfronts, some huddled in blankets, others rolled tight into themselves. The road, which during the day was a busy, noisy crush of people and animals, was quiet and deserted. Only a lean dog still sniffed in the gutter. A woman sang in a room high above the street—a plaintive, tremulous song—and in the far distance a jackal cried to the moon. But the empty, lifeless street was very deceptive; if the roofs could have been removed from but a handful of buildings, it would be seen that life had not really stopped but, beautiful and ugly, persisted through the night.

It was past midnight, though the Clock Tower had no way of saying it. Rusty was in the empty street, and the chaat shop was closed, a sheet of tarpaulin draped across the front. He looked up and down the road, hoping to meet someone he knew; the chaat-walla, he felt sure, would give him a blanket for the night and a place to sleep; and the next day when Somi came to meet him, he would tell his friend of his predicament, that he had run away from his guardian's house and did not intend returning. But he would have to wait till morning: the chaat shop was shuttered, barred and bolted.

He sat down on the steps; but the stone was cold and his thin cotton pyjamas offered no protection. He folded his arms and huddled up in a corner, but still he shivered. His feet were becoming numb, lifeless.

Rusty had not fully realized the hazards of the situation. He was still mad with anger and rebellion and, though the blood on his cheek had dried, his face was still smarting. He could not think clearly: the present was confusing and unreal and he could not see beyond it; what worried him was the cold and the discomfort and the pain.

The singing stopped in the high window. Rusty looked up and saw a beckoning hand. As no one else in the street showed any signs of life, Rusty got up and walked across the road until he was under the window. The woman pointed to a stairway, and he mounted it, glad of the hospitality he was being offered.

The stairway seemed to go to the stars, but it turned suddenly to lead into the woman's room. The door was slightly ajar; he knocked and a voice said, 'Come ...'

The room was filled with perfume and burning incense. A musical instrument lay in one corner. The woman reclined on a bed, her hair scattered about the pillow; she had a round, pretty face, but she was losing her youth, and the fat showed in rolls at her exposed waist. She smiled at the boy, and beckoned again.

'Thank you,' said Rusty, closing the door. 'Can I sleep here?'

'Where else?' said the woman.

'Just for tonight.'

She smiled, and waited. Rusty stood in front of her, his hands behind his back.

'Sit down,' she said, and patted the bedclothes beside her.

Reverently, and as respectfully as he could, Rusty sat down. The woman ran little fair fingers over his body, and drew his head to hers; their lips were very close, almost touching, and their breathing sounded terribly loud to Rusty, but he only said, 'I am hungry.'

A poet, thought the woman, and kissed him full on the lips; but the boy drew away in embarrassment, unsure of himself, liking the woman on the bed and yet afraid of her ...

'What is wrong?' she asked.

'I'm tired,' he said.

The woman's friendly smile turned to a look of scorn; but she saw that he was only a boy whose eyes were full of unhappiness, and she could not help pitying him.

'You can sleep here,' she said, 'until you have lost your tiredness.'

But he shook his head. 'I will come some other time,' he said, not wishing to hurt the woman's feelings. They were both pitying each other, liking each other, but not enough to make them understand each other.

Rusty left the room. Mechanically, he descended the staircase, and walked up the bazaar road, past the silent sleeping forms, until he reached the Clock Tower. To the right of the Clock Tower was a broad stretch of grassland where, during the day, cattle grazed and children played and young men like Ranbir wrestled and kicked footballs. But now, at night, it was a vast empty space.

But the grass was soft, like the grass in the forest, and Rusty walked the length of the maidan. He found a bench and sat down, warmer for the walk. A light breeze was blowing across the maidan, pleasant and refreshing, playing with his hair. Around him everything was dark and silent and lonely. He had got away from the bazaar, which held the misery of beggars and homeless children and starving dogs, and could now concentrate on his own misery; for there was nothing like loneliness for making Rusty conscious of his unhappy state. Madness and freedom and violence were new to him: loneliness was familiar, something he understood.

Rusty was alone. Until tomorrow, he was alone for the rest of his life.

If tomorrow there was no Somi at the chaat shop, no Ranbir, then what would he do? This question badgered him persistently, making him an unwilling slave to reality. He did not know where his friends lived, he had no money, he could not ask the chaat-walla for credit on the strength of two visits. Perhaps he should return to the amorous lady in the bazaar; perhaps . . . but no, one thing was certain, he would never return to his guardian . . .

The moon had been hidden by clouds, and presently there was a drizzle. Rusty did not mind the rain, it refreshed him and made the colour run from his body; but, when it began to fall harder, he started shivering again. He felt sick. He got up, rolled his ragged pyjamas up to the thighs and crawled under the bench.

There was a hollow under the bench, and at first Rusty found it quite comfortable. But there was no grass and gradually the earth began to soften: soon he was on his hands and knees in a pool of muddy water, with the slush oozing up through his fingers and toes. Crouching there, wet and cold and muddy, he was overcome by a feeling of helplessness and self-pity: everyone and everything seemed to have turned against him; not only his people but also the bazaar and the chaat shop and even the elements. He admitted to himself that he had been too impulsive in rebelling and running away from home; perhaps there was still time to return and beg Mr Harrison's forgiveness. But could his behaviour be forgiven? Might he not be clapped into irons for attempted murder? Most certainly he would be given another beating: not six strokes this time, but nine. His only hope was Somi. If not Somi, then Ranbir. If not Ranbir ... well, it was no use thinking further, there was no one else to think of. The rain had ceased. Rusty crawled out from under the bench, and stretched his cramped limbs. The moon came out from a cloud and played with his wet, glistening body, and showed him the vast, naked loneliness of the maidan and his own insignificance. He longed now for the presence of people, be they beggars or women, and he broke into a trot, and the trot became a run, a frightened run, and he did not stop until he reached the Clock Tower.

CHAPTER SEVEN

THEY WHO SLEEP LAST, wake first. Hunger and pain lengthen the night, and so the beggars and dogs are the last to see the stars;

hunger and pain hasten the awakening, and beggars and dogs are the first to see the sun. Rusty knew hunger and pain, but his weariness was even greater, and he was asleep on the steps of the chaat shop long after the sun had come striding down the road, knocking on nearly every door and window.

Somi bathed at the common water-tank. He stood under the tap and slapped his body into life and spluttered with the shock of mountain water.

At the tank were many people: children shrieking with delight—or discomfort—as their ayahs slapped them about roughly and affectionately; the ayahs themselves, strong, healthy hill-women, with heavy bracelets on their ankles; the bhisti—the water-carrier—with his skin bag; and the cook with his pots and pans. The ayahs sat on their haunches, bathing the children, their saris rolled up to the thighs; every time they moved their feet, the bells on their ankles jingled; so that there was a continuous shrieking and jingling and slapping of buttocks. The cook smeared his utensils with ash and washed them, and filled an earthen *chatty* with water; the bhisti hoisted the water-bag over his shoulder and left, dripping; a piedog lapped at water rolling off the stone platform; and a baleful-looking cow nibbled at wet grass.

It was with these people that Somi spent his mornings, laughing and talking and bathing with them. When he had finished his ablutions, dried his hair in the sun, dressed and tied his turban, he mounted his bicycle and rode out of the compound.

At this advanced hour of the morning Mr Harrison still slept. In the half empty church, his absence was noted: he seldom missed Sunday morning services; and the missionary's wife was impatiently waiting for the end of the sermon, for she had so much to talk about.

Outside the chaat shop Somi said, 'Hey, Rusty, get up, what has happened? Where is Ranbir? Holi finished yesterday, you know!'

He shook Rusty by the shoulders, shouting into his ear; and the pale boy lying on the stone steps opened his eyes and blinked in the morning sunshine; his eyes roamed about in bewilderment, he could not remember how he came to be lying in the sunshine in the bazaar.

'Hey,' said Somi, 'your guardian will be very angry!'

Rusty sat up with a start. He was wide awake now, sweeping up his scattered thoughts and sorting them out. It was difficult for him to be straightforward; but he forced himself to look Somi straight in the eyes and, very simply and without preamble, say, 'I've run away from home.'

Somi showed no surprise. He did not take his eyes off Rusty's nor did his expression alter. A half-smile on his lips, he said, 'Good. Now you can come and stay with me.'

Somi took Rusty home on the bicycle. Rusty felt weak in the legs, but his mind was relieved and he no longer felt alone: once again, Somi gave him a feeling of confidence.

'Do you think I can get a job?' asked Rusty.

'Don't worry about that yet, you have only just run away.'

'Do you think I can get a job?' persisted Rusty.

'Why not? But don't worry, you are going to stay with me.'

'I'll stay with you only until I find a job. Any kind of job, there must be something.'

'Of course, don't worry,' said Somi, and pressed harder on the pedals.

They came to a canal; it was noisy with the rush of mountain water, for the snow had begun to melt. The road, which ran parallel to the canal, was flooded in some parts, but Somi steered a steady course. Then the canal turned left and the road kept straight, and presently the sound of water was but a murmur, and the road quiet and shady; there were trees at the roadsides covered in pink and white blossoms, and behind them more trees, thicker and greener; and amongst the trees were houses.

A boy swung on a creaking wooden gate. He whistled out, and Somi waved back; that was all.

'Who's that?' asked Rusty.

'Son of his parents.'

'What do you mean?'

'His father is rich. So Kishen is somebody. He has money, and it is as powerful as Suri's tongue.'

'Is he Suri's friend or yours?'

'When it suits him, he is our friend. When it suits him, he is Suri's friend.'

'Then he's clever as well as rich,' deduced Rusty.

'The brains are his mother's.'

'And the money his father's?'

'Yes, but there isn't much left now. Mr Kapoor is finished . . . He looks like his father too, his mother is beautiful. Well, here we are!'

Somi rode the bicycle in amongst the trees and along a snaky path that dodged this way and that, and then they reached the house.

It was a small flat house, covered completely by a crimson bougainvillaea creeper. The garden was a mass of marigolds, which had sprung up everywhere, even in the cracks at the sides of the veranda steps. No one was at home. Somi's father was in Delhi, and his mother was out for the morning, buying the week's vegetables.

'Have you any brothers?' asked Rusty, as he entered the front room.

'No. But I've got two sisters. But they're married. Come on, let's see if my clothes will fit you.'

Rusty laughed, for he was older and bigger than his friend; but he was thinking in terms of shirts and trousers, the kind of garments he was used to wearing. He sat down on a sofa in the front room, whilst Somi went for the clothes.

The room was cool and spacious, and had very little furniture. But on the walls were many pictures, and in the centre a large one of Guru Nanak, the founder of the Sikh religion: his body bare, the saint sat with his legs crossed, the palms of his hands touching in prayer, and on his face there was a serene expression: the serenity of Nanak's countenance seemed to communicate itself to the room. There was a serenity about Somi too; maybe because of the smile that always hovered near his mouth.

Rusty concluded that Somi's family were middle-class people; that is, they were neither rich nor beggars, but managed to live all the same.

Somi came back with the clothes.

'They are mine,' he said, 'so maybe they will be a little small for you. Anyway, the warm weather is coming and it will not matter what you wear—better nothing at all!'

Rusty put on a long white shirt which, to his surprise, hung loose; it had a high collar and broad sleeves.

'It is loose,' he said,'how can it be yours?'

'It is made loose,' said Somi.

Rusty pulled on a pair of white pyjamas, and they were definitely small for him, ending a few inches above the ankle. The sandals would not buckle; and, when he walked, they behaved like Somi's and slapped against his heels.

'There!' exclaimed Somi in satisfaction. 'Now everything is settled, chaat in your stomach, clean clothes on your body, and in a few days we find a job! Now is there anything else?'

Rusty knew Somi well enough now to know that it wasn't necessary to thank him for anything; gratitude was taken for granted; in true friendship there are no formalities and no obligations. Rusty did not even ask if Somi had consulted his mother about taking in guests; perhaps she was used to this sort of thing.

'Is there anything else?' repeated Somi.

Rusty yawned. 'Can I go to sleep now, please?'

Chapter Eight

Rusty HAD NEVER SLEPT well in his guardian's house, because he had never been tired enough; also his imagination would disturb him. And, since running away, he had slept very badly, because he had been cold and hungry and afraid. But in Somi's house he felt safe and a little happy, and so he slept; he slept the remainder of the day and through the night.

In the morning Somi tipped Rusty out of bed and dragged him to the water-tank. Rusty watched Somi strip and stand under the jet of tap water, and shuddered at the prospect of having to do the same.

Before removing his shirt, Rusty looked around in embarrassment; no one paid much attention to him, though one of the ayahs, the girl with the bangles, gave him a sly smile; he looked away from the women, threw his shirt on a bush and advanced cautiously to the bathing place.

Somi pulled him under the tap. The water was icy cold and Rusty gasped with the shock. As soon as he was wet, he sprang off the platform, much to the amusement of Somi and the ayahs.

There was no towel with which to dry himself; he stood on the grass, shivering with cold, wondering whether he should dash back to the house or shiver in the open until the sun dried him. But the girl with the bangles was beside him holding a towel; her eyes were full of mockery, but her smile was friendly.

At the midday meal, which consisted of curry and curds and chapattis, Rusty met Somi's mother, and liked her.

She was a woman of about thirty-five; she had a few grey hairs at the temples, and her skin—unlike Somi's—was rough and dry. She dressed simply, in a plain white sari. Her life had been difficult. After the partition of the country, when hate made religion its own, Somi's family had to leave their home in the Punjab and trek southwards; they had walked hundreds of miles and the mother had carried Somi, who was then six, on her back. Life in India had to be started again right from the beginning, for they had lost most of their property: the father found work in Delhi, the sisters were married off, and Somi and his mother settled down in Dehra, where the boy attended school.

The mother said, 'Mister Rusty, you must give Somi a few lessons in spelling and arithmetic. Always, he comes last in class.' 'Oh, that's good!' exclaimed Somi. 'We'll have fun, Rusty!' Then he thumped the table. 'I have an idea! I know, I think I have a job for you! Remember Kishen, the boy we passed yesterday? Well, his father wants someone to give him private lessons in English.'

'Teach Kishen?'

'Yes, it will be easy. I'll go and see Mr Kapoor and tell him I've found a professor of English or something like that, and then you can come and see him. Brother, it is a first-class idea, you are going to be a teacher!'

Rusty felt very dubious about the proposal; he was not sure he could teach English or anything else to the wilful son of a rich man; but he was not in a position to pick and choose. Somi mounted his bicycle and rode off to see Mr Kapoor to secure for Rusty the post of Professor of English. When he returned he seemed pleased with himself, and Rusty's heart sank with the knowledge that he had got a job.

'You are to come and see him this evening,' announced Somi, 'he will tell you all about it. They want a teacher for Kishen, especially if they don't have to pay.'

'What kind of a job is without pay?' complained Rusty.

'No pay,' said Somi, 'but everything else. Food—and no cooking is better than Punjabi cooking; water—'

'I should hope so,' said Rusty.

'And a room, sir!'

'Oh, even a room,' said Rusty ungratefully, 'that will be nice.'

'Anyway,' said Somi, 'come and see him, you don't have to accept.'

*

The house the Kapoors lived in was very near the canal; it was a squat, comfortable-looking bungalow, surrounded by uncut hedges, and shaded by banana and papaya trees. It was late evening when Somi and Rusty arrived, and the moon was up, and the shaggy branches of the banana trees shook their heavy shadows out over the gravel path.

In an open space in front of the house a log fire was burning;

the Kapoors appeared to be giving a party. Somi and Rusty joined the people who were grouped round the fire, and Rusty wondered if he had been invited to the party. The fire lent a friendly warmth to the chilly night, and the flames leapt up, casting the glow of roses on people's faces.

Somi pointed out different people: various shopkeepers, one or two Big Men, the sickly looking Suri (who was never absent from a social occasion such as this) and a few total strangers who had invited themselves to the party just for the fun of the thing and a free meal. Kishen, the Kapoors' son, was not present; he hated parties, preferring the company of certain wild friends in the bazaar.

Mr Kapoor was once a Big Man himself, and everyone knew this, but he had fallen from the heights; and, until he gave up the bottle, was not likely to reach them again. Everyone felt sorry for his wife, including herself.

Presently Kapoor tottered out of the front door arm-in-arm with a glass and a bottle of whisky. He wore a green dressing-gown and a week's beard, his hair, or what was left of it, stood up on end and he dribbled slightly. An awkward silence fell on the company; but Kapoor, who was a friendly, gentle sort of drunkard, looked round benevolently and said, 'Everybody here? Fine, fine, they are all here, all of them ... Throw some more wood on the fire!'

The fire was doing very well indeed, but not well enough for Kapoor; every now and then he would throw a log on the flames until it was feared the blaze would reach the house. Meena, Kapoor's wife, did not look flustered, only irritated; she was a capable person, still young, a charming hostess, and, in her red sari and white silk jacket, her hair plaited and scented with jasmine, she looked beautiful. Rusty gazed admiringly at her; he wanted to compliment her, to say, 'Mrs Kapoor, you are beautiful', but he had no need to tell her, she was fully conscious of the fact.

Meena made her way over to one of the Big Men, and whispered something in his ear, and then she went to a Little Shopkeeper and whispered something in his ear, and then both the Big Man and the Little Shopkeeper advanced stealthily towards the spot where Mr Kapoor was holding forth, and made a gentle attempt to convey him indoors.

But Kapoor was having none of it. He pushed the men aside and roared, 'Keep the fire burning! Keep it burning, don't let it go out, throw some more wood on it!'

And, before he could be restrained, he had thrown a pot of the most delicious sweetmeats on to the flames.

To Rusty this was sacrilege. 'Oh, Mr Kapoor ...' he cried, but there was some confusion in the rear, and his words were drowned in a series of explosions.

Suri and one or two others had begun letting off fireworks: fountains, rockets and explosives. The fountains gushed forth in green and red and silver lights, and the rockets struck through the night with crimson tails; but it was the explosives that caused the confusion. The guests did not know whether to press forward into the fires, or retreat amongst the fireworks; neither prospect was pleasing, and the women began to show signs of hysterics. Then Suri burnt his finger and began screaming, and this was all the women had been waiting for; headed by Suri's mother, they rushed the boy and smothered him with attention; whilst the men, who were in a minority, looked on sheepishly and wished the accident had been of a more serious nature.

Something rough brushed against Rusty's cheek.

It was Kapoor's beard. Somi had brought his host to Rusty, the bemused man put his face close to Rusty's and placed his hands on the boy's shoulders in order to steady himself. Kapoor nodded his head, his eyes red and watery.

'Rusty ... so you are Mister Rusty ... I hear you are going to be my schoolteacher.'

'Your son's, sir,' said Rusty, 'but that is for you to decide.'

'Do not call me "Sir",' he said, wagging his finger in Rusty's face,'call me by my name. So you are going to England, eh?'

'No, I'm going to be your schoolteacher.' Rusty had to put his arm round Kapoor's waist to avoid being dragged to the ground; Kapoor leant heavily on the boy's shoulders.

'Good, good. Tell me after you have gone, I want to give you some addresses of people I know. You must go to Monte Carlo, you've seen nothing until you've seen Monte Carlo, it's the only place with a future ... Who built Monte Carlo, do you know?'

It was impossible for Rusty to make any sense of the conversation or discuss his appointment as Professor of English for Kishen Kapoor. Kapoor began to slip from his arms, and the boy took the opportunity of changing his own position for a more comfortable one, before levering his host up again. The amused smiles of the company rested on this little scene.

Rusty said, 'No, Mr Kapoor, who built Monte Carlo?'

'I did. I built Monte Carlo!'

'Oh yes, of course.'

'Yes, I built this house, I'm a genius, there's no doubt of it! I have a high opinion of my own opinion, what is yours?'

'Oh, I don't know, but I'm sure you're right.'

'Of course I am. But speak up, don't be afraid to say what you think. Stand up for your rights, even if you're wrong! Throw some more wood on the fire, keep it burning.'

Kapoor leapt from Rusty's arms and stumbled towards the fire. The boy cried a warning and, catching hold of the end of the green dressing-gown, dragged his host back to safety. Meena ran to them and, without so much as a glance at Rusty, took her husband by the arm and propelled him indoors.

Rusty stared after Meena Kapoor, and continued to stare even when she had disappeared. The guests chattered pleasantly, pretending nothing had happened, keeping the gossip for the next morning; but the children giggled amongst themselves, and the devil Suri shouted, 'Throw some more wood on the fire, keep it burning!'

Somi returned to his friend's side. 'What did Mr Kapoor have to say?'

'He said he built Monte Carlo.'

Somi slapped his forehead. *Toba!* Now we'll have to come again tomorrow evening. And then, if he's drunk, we'll have to discuss with his wife, she's the only one with any sense.'

They walked away from the party, out of the circle of firelight, into the shadows of the banana trees. The voices of the guests became a distant murmur: Suri's high-pitched shout came to them on the clear, still air.

Somi said, 'We must go to the chaat shop tomorrow morning, Ranbir is asking for you.'

Rusty had almost forgotten Ranbir: he felt ashamed for not having asked about him before this. Ranbir was an important person, he had changed the course of Rusty's life with nothing but a little colour, red and green, and the touch of his hand.

Chapter Nine

AGAINST HIS PARENTS' WISHES, Kishen Kapoor spent most of his time in the bazaar; he loved it because it was forbidden, because it was unhealthy, dangerous and full of germs to carry home.

Ranbir loved the bazaar because he was born in it; he had known few other places. Since the age of ten he had looked after his uncle's buffaloes, grazing them on the maidan and taking them down to the river to wallow in mud and water; and in the evening he took them home, riding on the back of the strongest and fastest animal. When he grew older, he was allowed to help in his father's cloth shop, but he was always glad to get back to the buffaloes.

Kishen did not like animals, particularly cows and buffaloes. His greatest enemy was Maharani, the Queen of the Bazaar, who, like Kishen, was spoilt and pampered and fond of having her own way. Unlike other cows, she did not feed at dustbins and rubbish heaps, but lived on the benevolence of the bazaar people.

But Kishen had no time for religion; to him a cow was just a cow, nothing sacred, and he saw no reason why he should get off the pavement in order to make way for one, or offer no protest when it stole from under his nose. One day, he tied an empty tin to Maharani's tail and looked on in great enjoyment as the cow pranced madly and dangerously about the road, the tin clattering behind her. Lacking in dignity, Kishen found some pleasure in observing others lose theirs. But a few days later Kishen received Maharani's nose in his pants, and had to pick himself up from the gutter.

Kishen and Ranbir ate mostly at the chaat shop; if they had no money they went to work in Ranbir's uncle's sugarcane fields and earned a rupee for the day; but Kishen did not like work, and Ranbir had enough of his own to do, so there was never much money for chaat; which meant living on their wits—or rather, Kishen's wits, for it was his duty to pocket any spare money that might be lying about in his father's house—and sometimes helping themselves at the fruit and vegetable stalls when no one was looking.

Ranbir wrestled. That was why he was so good at riding buffaloes. He was the best wrestler in the bazaar, not very clever, but powerful; he was like a great tree, and no amount of shaking could move him from whatever spot he chose to plant his big feet. But he was gentle by nature. The women always gave him their babies to look after when they were busy, and he would cradle the babies in his open hands, and sing to them, and be happy for hours.

Ranbir had a certain innocence which was not likely to leave him. He had seen and experienced life to the full, and life had bruised and scarred him, but it had not crippled him. One night he strayed unwittingly into the intoxicating arms of a local temple dancing-girl; but he acted with instinct, his pleasure was unpremeditated, and the adventure was soon forgotten—by Ranbir. But Suri, the scourge of the bazaar, uncovered a few facts and threatened to inform Ranbir's family of the incident; and so Ranbir found himself in the power of the cunning Suri, and was forced to please him from time to time; though, at times such as the Holi festival, that power was scorned.

On the morning after the Kapoors' party Ranbir, Somi, and

Rusty were seated in the chaat shop discussing Rusty's situation. Ranbir looked miserable; his hair fell sadly over his forehead, and he would not look at Rusty.

'I have got you into trouble,' he apologized gruffly, 'I am too ashamed.'

Rusty laughed, licking sauce from his fingers and crumpling up his empty leaf bowl.

'Silly fellow,' he said, 'for what are you sorry? For making me happy? For taking me away from my guardian? Well, I am not sorry, you can be sure of that.'

'You are not angry?' asked Ranbir in wonder.

'No, but you will make me angry in this way.'

Ranbir's face lit up, and he slapped Somi and Rusty on their backs with such sudden enthusiasm that Somi dropped his bowl of aloo chhole.

'Come on, misters,' he said, 'I am going to make you sick with gol-guppas so that you will not be able to eat any more until I return from Mussoorie!'

'Mussoorie?' Somi looked puzzled. 'You are going to Mussoorie?'

'To school!'

'That's right,' said a voice from the door, a voice hidden in smoke. 'Now we've had it . . .'

Somi said, 'It's that monkey-millionaire Kishen come to make a nuisance of himself.' Then louder, 'Come over here, Kishen, come and join us in gol-guppas!'

Kishen appeared from the mist of vapour, walking with an affected swagger, his hands in his pockets; he was the only one present wearing pants instead of pyjamas.

'Hey!' exclaimed Somi, 'who has given you a black eye?'

Kishen did not answer immediately, but sat down opposite Rusty. His shirt hung over his pants, and his pants hung over his knees; he had bushy eyebrows and hair, and a drooping, disagreeable mouth; the sulky expression on his face had become a permanent one, not a mood of the moment. Kishen's swagger, money, unattractive face and qualities made him—for Rusty, anyway—curiously attractive . . .

He prodded his nose with his forefinger, as he always did when a trifle excited. 'Those damn wrestlers, they piled on to me.'

'Why?' said Ranbir, sitting up instantly.

'I was making a badminton court on the maidan, and these fellows came along and said they had reserved the place for a wrestling ground.'

'So then?'

Kishen's affected American twang became more pronounced. 'I told them to go to hell!'

Ranbir laughed. 'So they all started wrestling you?'

'Yeah, but I didn't know they would hit me too. I bet if you fellows were there, they wouldn't have tried anything. Isn't that so, Ranbir?'

Ranbir smiled; he knew it was so, but did not care to speak of his physical prowess. Kishen took notice of the newcomer.

'Are you Mister Rusty?' he asked.

'Yes, I am,' said the boy. 'Are you Mister Kishen?'

'I am Mister Kishen. You know how to box, Rusty?'

'Well,' said the boy, unwilling to become involved in a local feud, 'I've never boxed wrestlers.'

Somi changed the subject. 'Rusty's coming to see your father this evening. You must try and persuade your pop to give him the job of teaching you English.'

Kishen prodded his nose, and gave Rusty a sly wink.

'Yes, Daddy told me about you, he says you are a professor. You can be my teacher on the condition that we don't work too hard, and you support me when I tell them lies, and that you tell them I am working hard. Sure, you can be my teacher, sure . . . better you than a real one.'

'I'll try to please everyone,' said Rusty.

'You're a clever person if you can. But I think you are clever.'

'Yes,' agreed Rusty, and was inwardly amazed at the way he spoke.

*

As Rusty had now met Kishen, Somi suggested that the two should go to the Kapoors' house together; so that evening, Rusty met Kishen in the bazaar and walked home with him.

There was a crowd in front of the bazaar's only cinema, and it was getting restive and demonstrative.

One had to fight to get into this particular cinema, as there was no organized queuing or booking.

'Is anything wrong?' asked Rusty.

'Oh, no,' said Kishen, 'it is just *Laurel and Hardy* today, they are very popular. Whenever a popular film is shown, there is usually a riot. But I know of a way in through the roof, I'll show you some time.'

'Sounds crazy.'

'Yeah, the roof leaks, so people usually bring their umbrellas. Also their food, because when the projector breaks down or the electricity fails, we have to wait a long time. Sometimes, when it is a long wait, the chaat-walla comes in and does some business.'

'Sounds crazy,' repeated Rusty.

'You'll get used to it. Have a chewing-gum.'

Kishen's jaws had been working incessantly on a lump of gum that had been increasing in size over the last three days; he started on a fresh stick every hour or so, without throwing away the old ones. Rusty was used to seeing Indians chew paan, the betel-leaf preparation which stained the mouth with red juices, but Kishen wasn't like any of the Indians Rusty had met so far. He accepted a stick of gum, and the pair walked home in silent concentration, their jaws moving rhythmically, and Kishen's tongue making sudden sucking sounds.

As they entered the front room, Meena Kapoor pounced on Kishen.

'Ah! So you have decided to come home at last! And what do you mean by asking Daddy for money without letting me know? What have you done with it, Kishen bhaiya? Where is it?'

Kishen sauntered across the room and deposited himself on the couch. 'I've spent it.'

Meena's hands went to her hips. 'What do you mean, you've spent it!'

'I mean I've eaten it.'

He got two resounding slaps across his face, and his flesh went white where his mother's fingers left their mark. Rusty backed towards the door; it was embarrassing to be present at this intimate family scene.

'Don't go, Rusty,' shouted Kishen, 'or she won't stop slapping me!'

Kapoor, still wearing his green dressing-gown and beard, came in from the adjoining room, and his wife turned on him.

'Why do you give the child so much money?' she demanded. 'You know he spends it on nothing but bazaar food and makes himself sick.'

Rusty seized at the opportunity of pleasing the whole family; of saving Mr Kapoor's skin, pacifying his wife, and gaining the affection and regard of Kishen.

'It is all my fault,' he said, 'I took Kishen to the chaat shop. I'm very sorry.'

Meena Kapoor became quiet and her eyes softened; but Rusty resented her kindly expression because he knew it was prompted by pity—pity for him—and a satisfied pride. Meena was proud because she thought her son had shared his money with one who apparently hadn't any.

'I did not see you come in,' she said.

'I only wanted to explain about the money.'

'Come in, don't be shy.'

Meena's smile was full of kindness, but Rusty was not looking for kindness; for no apparent reason, he felt lonely; he missed Somi, felt lost without him, helpless and clumsy.

'There is another thing,' he said, remembering the post of Professor of English.

'But come in, Mister Rusty . . .'

It was the first time she had used his name, and the gesture immediately placed them on equal terms. She was a graceful woman, much younger than Kapoor; her features had a clear, classic beauty, and her voice was gentle but firm. Her hair was tied in a neat bun and laced with a string of jasmine flowers.

'Come in ...'

'About teaching Kishen,' mumbled Rusty.

'Come and play carom,' said Kishen from the couch. 'We are none of us any good. Come and sit down, pardner.'

'He fancies himself as an American,' said Meena. 'If ever you see him in the cinema, drag him out.'

The carom board was brought in from the next room, and it was arranged that Rusty partner Mr Kapoor. They began play, but the game didn't progress very fast because Kapoor kept leaving the table in order to disappear behind a screen, from the direction of which came a tinkle of bottles and glasses. Rusty was afraid of Kapoor getting drunk before he could be approached about the job of teaching Kishen.

'My wife,' said Kapoor in a loud whisper to Rusty, 'does not let me drink in public any more, so I have to do it in a cupboard.'

He looked sad; there were tear-stains on his cheeks; the tears were caused not by Meena's scolding, which he ignored, but by his own self-pity; he often cried for himself, usually in his sleep.

Whenever Rusty pocketed one of the carom men, Kapoor exclaimed, 'Ah, nice shot, nice shot!' as though it were a cricket match they were playing. 'But hit it slowly, slowly ...' And when it was his turn, he gave the striker a feeble push, moving it a bare inch from his finger.

'Play properly,' murmured Meena, who was intent on winning the game; but Kapoor would be up from his seat again, and the company would sit back and wait for the tune of clinking glass.

It was a very irritating game. Kapoor insisted on showing Rusty how to strike the men; and whenever Rusty made a mistake, Meena said 'thank you' in an amused and conceited manner that angered the boy. When she and Kishen had cleared the board of whites, Kapoor and Rusty were left with eight blacks.

'Thank you,' said Meena sweetly.

'We are too good for you,' scoffed Kishen, busily arranging the board for another game.

Kapoor took sudden interest in the proceedings, 'Who won, I say, who won?'

Much to Rusty's disgust, they began another game, and with the same partners; but they had just started when Kapoor flopped forward and knocked the carom board off the table. He had fallen asleep. Rusty took him by the shoulders, eased him back into the chair. Kapoor's breathing was heavy; saliva had collected at the sides of his mouth, and he snorted a little.

Rusty thought it was time he left. Rising from the table, he said, 'I will have to ask another time about the job . . .'

'Hasn't he told you as yet?' said Meena.

'What?'

'That you can have the job.'

'Can I!' exclaimed Rusty.

Meena gave a little laugh. 'But of course! Certainly there is no one else who would take it on. Kishen is not easy to teach. There is no fixed pay, but we will give you anything you need. You are not our servant. You will be doing us a favour by giving Kishen some of your knowledge and conversation and company, and in return we will be giving you our hospitality. You will have a room of your own, and your food you will have with us. What do you think?'

'Oh, it is wonderful!' said Rusty.

And it was wonderful, and he felt gay and light-headed, and all the troubles in the world scurried away. He even felt successful: he had a profession. And Meena Kapoor was smiling at him, and looking more beautiful than she really was, and Kishen was saying: 'Tomorrow you must stay till twelve o'clock, all right, even if Daddy goes to sleep. Promise me?'

Rusty promised.

An unaffected enthusiasm was bubbling up in Kishen; it was quite different to the sulkiness of his usual manner. Rusty had liked him in spite of the younger boy's unattractive qualities, and now liked him more; for Kishen had taken Rusty into his home and confidence without knowing him very well and without asking any questions. Kishen was a scoundrel, a monkey—crude and well-spoilt—but for him to have taken a liking to Rusty (and Rusty held himself in high esteem), he must have some virtues . . . or so Rusty reasoned.

His mind, while he walked back to Somi's house, dwelt on his relationship with Kishen; but his tongue, when he loosened it in Somi's presence, dwelt on Meena Kapoor. And when he lay down to sleep, he saw her in his mind's eye, and for the first time took conscious note of her beauty, of her warmth and softness; and made up his mind that he would fall in love with her.

CHAPTER TEN

MR HARRISON WAS BACK to normal in a few days, and telling everyone of Rusty's barbaric behaviour. 'If he wants to live like an animal, he can. He left my house of his own free will, and I feel no responsibility for him. It's his own fault if he starves to death.'

The missionary's wife said, 'But I do hope you will forgive him if he returns.'

'I will, madam. I have to. I'm his legal guardian. And I hope he doesn't return.'

'Oh, Mr Harrison, he's only a boy . . .'

'That's what you think.'

'I'm sure he'll come back.'

Mr Harrison shrugged indifferently.

*

Rusty's thoughts were far from his guardian. He was listening to Meena Kapoor tell him about his room, and he gazed into her eyes all the time she talked.

'It is a very nice room,' she said, 'but of course there is no water or electricity or lavatory.'

Rusty was bathing in the brown pools of her eyes.

She said, 'You will have to collect your water at the big tank, and for the rest, you will have to do it in the jungle . . .'

Rusty thought he saw his own gaze reflected in her eyes.

'Yes?' he said.

'You can give Kishen his lessons in the morning until twelve o'clock. Then no more, then you have your food.'

'Then?'

He watched the movement of her lips.

'Then nothing, you do what you like, go out with Kishen or Somi or any of your friends.'

'Where do I teach Kishen?'

'On the roof, of course.'

Rusty retrieved his gaze, and scratched his head. The roof seemed a strange place for setting up school.

'Why the roof?'

'Because your room is on the roof.'

*

Meena led the boy round the house until they came to a flight of steps, unsheltered, that went up to the roof. They had to hop over a narrow drain before climbing the steps.

'This drain,' warned Meena, 'is very easy to cross. But when you are coming downstairs be sure not to take too big a step because then you might bump the wall on the other side or fall over the stove which is usually there . . .'

'I'll be careful,' said Rusty.

They began climbing, Meena in the lead. Rusty watched Meena's long, slender feet. The slippers she wore consisted only of two straps that passed between her toes, and the backs of the slippers slapped against her heels like Somi's, only the music—like the feet—was different . . .

'Another thing about these steps,' continued Meena, 'there are twenty-two of them. No, don't count, I have already done so . . . But remember, if you are coming home in the dark, be sure you take only twenty-two steps, because if you don't, then'—and she snapped her fingers in the air—'you will be finished! After twenty-two steps you turn right and you find the door, here it is.

If you do not turn right and you take *twenty-three* steps, you will go over the edge of the roof!'

They both laughed, and suddenly Meena took Rusty's hand and led him into the room.

It was a small room, but this did not matter much as there was very little in it: only a string bed, a table, a shelf and a few nails in the wall. In comparison to Rusty's room in his guardian's house, it wasn't even a room: it was four walls, a door and a window.

The door looked out on the roof, and Meena pointed through it, at the big round water-tank.

'That is where you bathe and get your water,' she said.

'I know, I went with Somi.'

There was a big mango tree behind the tank, and Kishen was sitting in its branches, watching them. Surrounding the house were a number of litchi trees, and in the summer they and the mango would bear fruit.

Meena and Rusty stood by the window in silence, hand in hand. Rusty was prepared to stand there, holding hands for ever. Meena felt a sisterly affection for him; but he was stumbling into love.

From the window they could see many things. In the distance, towering over the other trees, was the Flame of the Forest, its flowers glowing red-hot against the blue of the sky. Through the window came a shoot of pink bougainvillaea creeper; and Rusty knew he would never cut it; and so he knew he would never be able to shut the window.

Meena said, 'If you do not like it, we will find another . . .'

Rusty squeezed her hand, smiled into her eyes and said, 'But I like it. This is the room I want to live in. And do you know why? Because it isn't a real room, that's why!'

*

The afternoon was warm, and Rusty sat beneath the big banyan tree that grew behind the house, a tree that was almost a house in itself; its spreading branches drooped to the ground and took new root, forming a maze of pillared passages. The tree sheltered scores of birds and squirrels.

A squirrel stood in front of Rusty. It looked at him from between its legs, its tail in the air, back arched gracefully and nose quivering excitedly.

'Hullo,' said Rusty.

The squirrel brushed its nose with its forepaw, winked at the boy, hopped over his leg, and ran up a pillar of the banyan tree.

Rusty leant back against the broad trunk of the banyan, and listened to the lazy drone of the bees, the squeaking of the squirrels and the incessant bird talk.

He thought of Meena and of Kishen, and felt miserably happy; and then he remembered Somi and the chaat shop.

*

The chaat-walla, that god of the tikkees, handed Rusty a leaf bowl, and prepared aloo chhole: first sliced potatoes, then peas, then red and gold chilli powders, then a sprinkling of juices, then he shook it all up and down in the leaf bowl and, in a simplicity, the aloo chhole was ready.

Somi removed his slippers, crossed his legs, and looked a question.

'It's fine,' said Rusty.

'You are sure?'

There was concern in Somi's voice, and his eyes seemed to hesitate a little before smiling with the mouth.

'It's fine,' said Rusty. 'I'll soon get used to the room.'

There was a silence. Rusty concentrated on the aloo chhole, feeling guilty and ungrateful.

'Ranbir has gone,' said Somi.

'Oh, he didn't even say goodbye!'

'He has not gone for ever. And anyway, what would be the use of saying goodbye . . .'

He sounded depressed. He finished his aloo chhole and said,

'Rusty, best favourite friend, if you don't want this job I'll find you another.'

'But I like it, Somi, I want it, really I do. You are trying to do too much for me. Mrs Kapoor is wonderful, and Mr Kapoor is good fun, and Kishen is not so bad, you know ... Come on to the house and see the room. It's the kind of room in which you write poetry or create music.'

They walked home in the evening. The evening was full of sounds. Rusty noticed the sounds because he was happy, and a happy person notices things.

Carriages passed them on the road, creaking and rattling, wheels squeaking, hoofs resounding on the ground; and the whip cracks above the horse's ear, and the driver shouts, and round go the wheels, squeaking and creaking, and the hoofs go clippety-clippety, clip-clop-clop ...

A bicycle came swishing through the puddles, the wheels purring and humming smoothly, the bell tinkling ... In the bushes there was the chatter of sparrows and seven-sisters, but Rusty could not see them no matter how hard he looked.

And there were footsteps ...

Their own footsteps, quiet and thoughtful; and ahead of them an old man, with a dhoti round his legs and a black umbrella in his hand, walking at a clockwork pace. At each alternate step he tapped with his umbrella on the pavement; he wore noisy shoes, and his footsteps echoed off the pavement to the beat of the umbrella. Rusty and Somi quickened their own steps, passed him by, and let the endless tapping die on the wind.

They sat on the roof for an hour, watching the sun set; and Somi sang.

Somi had a beautiful voice, clear and mellow, matching the serenity of his face. And when he sang, his eyes wandered into the night, and he was lost to the world and to Rusty; for when he sang of the stars he was of the stars, and when he sang of a river he was a river. He communicated his mood to Rusty, as he could not have done in plain language; and, when the song ended, the silence returned and all the world fell asleep.

CHAPTER ELEVEN

❧

Rusty WATCHED THE DAWN blossom into light. At first everything was dark, then gradually objects began to take shape—the desk and chair, the walls of the room—and the darkness lifted like the raising of a veil, and over the tree-tops the sky was streaked with crimson. It was like this for some time, while everything became clearer and more distinguishable; and then, when nature was ready, the sun reached up over the trees and hills, and sent one tentative beam of warm light through the window. Along the wall crept the sun, across to the bed, and up the boy's bare legs, until it was caressing his entire body and whispering to him to get up, get up, it is time to get up ...

Rusty blinked. He sat up and rubbed his eyes and looked around. It was his first morning in the room, and perched on the window sill was a small brown and yellow bird, a maina, looking at him with its head cocked to one side. The maina was a common sight, but this one was unusual: it was bald: all the feathers had been knocked off its head in a series of fights.

Rusty wondered if he should get up and bathe, or wait for someone to arrive. But he didn't wait long. Something bumped him from under the bed.

He stiffened with apprehension. Something was moving beneath him, the mattress rose gently and fell. Could it be a jackal or a wolf that had stolen in through the open door during the night? Rusty trembled, but did not move ... It might be something even more dangerous, the house was close to the jungle ... or it might be a thief ... but what was there to steal?

Unable to bear the suspense, Rusty brought his fists down on the uneven lump in the quilt, and Kishen sprang out with a cry of pain and astonishment.

He sat on his bottom and cursed Rusty.

'Sorry,' said Rusty, 'but you frightened me.'

'I'm glad, because you hurt me, mister.'

'Your fault. What's the time?'

'Time to get up. I've brought you some milk, and you can have mine too. I hate it, it spoils the flavour of my chewing-gum.'

Kishen accompanied Rusty to the water-tank, where they met Somi. After they had bathed and filled their *sohrais* with drinking water, they went back to the room for the first lesson.

Kishen and Rusty sat cross-legged on the bed, facing each other. Rusty fingered his chin, and Kishen played with his toes.

'What do you want to learn today?' asked Rusty.

'How should I know? That's your problem, pardner.'

'As it's the first day, you can make a choice.'

'Let's play noughts and crosses.'

'Be serious. Tell me, bhaiya, what books have you read?'

Kishen turned his eyes up to the ceiling. 'I've read so many I can't remember the names.'

'Well, you can tell me what they were about.'

Kishen looked disconcerted. 'Oh, sure ... sure ... let me see now ... what about the one in which everyone went down a rabbit hole?'

'What about it?'

'Called *Treasure Island*.'

'Hell!' said Rusty.

'Which ones have you read?' asked Kishen, warming to the discussion.

'*Treasure Island* and the one about the rabbit hole, and you haven't read either. What do you want to be when you grow up, Kishen? A businessman, an officer, an engineer?'

'Don't want to be anything. What about you?'

'You're not supposed to be asking me. But if you want to know, I'm going to be a writer. I'll write books. You'll read them.'

'You'll be a great writer, Rusty, you'll be great ...'

'Maybe, who knows.'

'I know,' said Kishen, quite sincerely, 'you'll be a terrific writer. You'll be famous. You'll be a king.'

'Shut up ...'

*

The Kapoors liked Rusty. They didn't admire him, but they liked him. Kishen liked him for his company, Kapoor liked him for his flattering conversation, and Meena liked him because—well, because he liked her . . .

The Kapoors were glad to have him in their house.

Meena had been betrothed to Kapoor since childhood, before they knew each other, and despite the fact that there was a difference of nearly twenty years between their ages. Kapoor was a promising young man, intelligent and beginning to make money; and Meena, at thirteen, possessed the freshness and promise of spring. After they were married, they fell in love.

They toured Europe, and Kapoor returned a connoisseur of wine. Kishen was born, looking just like his father. Kapoor never stopped loving his wife, but his passion for her was never so great as when the warmth of old wine filled him with poetry. Meena had a noble nose and forehead ('Aristocratic,' said Kapoor, 'she has blue blood') and long raven-black hair ('Like seaweed,' said Kapoor, dizzy with possessive glory). She was tall, strong, perfectly formed, and she had grace and charm and a quick wit.

Kapoor lived in his beard and green dressing-gown, something of an outcast. The self-made man likes to boast of humble origins and initial poverty, and his rise from rags can be turned to effective publicity; the man who has lost much recalls past exploits and the good name of his family, and the failure at least publicizes these things. But Kapoor had gone full cycle: he could no longer harp on the rise from rags, because he was fast becoming ragged; and he had no background except the one which he himself created and destroyed; he had nothing but a dwindling bank balance, a wife and a son. And the wife was his best asset.

But on the evening of Rusty's second day in the room, no one would have guessed at the family's plight. Rusty sat with them in the front room, and Kapoor extolled the virtues of chewing-gum, much to Kishen's delight and Meena's disgust.

'Chewing-gum,' declared Kapoor, waving a finger in the air, 'is the secret of youth. Have you observed the Americans, how young they look, and the English, how haggard? It has nothing to do with responsibilities, it is chewing-gum. By chewing, you exercise your jaws and the muscles of your face. This improves your complexion and strengthens the tissues of your skin.'

'You're very clever, Daddy,' said Kishen.

'I'm a genius,' said Kapoor, 'I'm a genius.'

'The fool!' whispered Meena, so that only Rusty could hear.

Rusty said, 'I have an idea, let's form a club.'

'Good idea!' exclaimed Kishen. 'What do we call it?'

'Before we call it anything, we must decide what sort of club it should be. We must have rules, we must have a president, a secretary . . .'

'All right, all right,' interrupted Kishen, who was sprawling on the floor, 'you can be all those things if you like. But what I say is, the most important thing in a club is name. Without a good name what's the use of a club?'

'The Fools' Club,' suggested Meena.

'Inappropriate,' said Kapoor, 'inappropriate . . .'

'Everyone shut up,' ordered Kishen, prodding at his nose, 'I'm trying to think.'

They all shut up and tried to think.

This thinking was a very complicated process, and it soon became obvious that no one had been thinking of the club; for Rusty was looking at Meena thinking, and Meena was wondering if Kishen knew how to think, and Kishen was really thinking about the benefits of chewing-gum, and Kapoor was smelling the whisky bottles behind the screen and thinking of them.

At last Kapoor observed, 'My wife is a devil, a beautiful, beautiful devil!'

This seemed an interesting line of conversation, and Rusty was about to follow it up with a compliment of his own, when Kishen burst out brilliantly, 'I know! The Devil's Club? How's that?'

'Ah, ha!' exclaimed Kapoor, 'The Devil's Club, we've got it! I'm a genius.'

They got down to the business of planning the club's activities.

Kishen proposed carom and Meena seconded, and Rusty looked dismayed. Kapoor proposed literary and political discussions and Rusty, just to spite the others, seconded the proposal. Then they elected officers of the club. Meena was given the title of Our Lady and Patroness, Kapoor was elected President, Rusty the Secretary, and Kishen the Chief Whip. Somi, Ranbir and Suri, though absent, were accepted as Honorary Members.

'Carom and discussions are not enough,' complained Kishen, 'we must have adventures.'

'What kind?' asked Rusty.

'Climb mountains or something.'

'A picnic,' proposed Meena.

'A picnic!' seconded Kishen,'and Somi and the others can come too.'

'Let's drink to it,' said Kapoor, rising from his chair,'let's celebrate.'

'Good idea,' said Kishen, foiling his father's plan of action, 'we'll go to the chaat shop!'

As far as Meena was concerned, the chaat shop was the lesser of the two evils, so Kapoor was bundled into the old car and taken to the bazaar.

'To the chaat shop!' he cried, falling across the steering wheel. 'We will bring it home!'

The chaat shop was so tightly crowded that people were breathing each other's breath.

The chaat-walla was very pleased with Rusty for bringing in so many new customers—a whole family—and beamed on the party, rubbing his hands and greasing the frying-pan with enthusiasm.

'Everything!' ordered Kapoor. 'We will have something of everything.'

So the chaat-walla patted his cakes into shape and flipped them into the sizzling grease; and fashioned his gol-guppas over the fire, filling them with the juice of the devil.

Meena sat curled up on a chair, facing Rusty. The boy stared at her: she looked quaint, sitting in this unfamiliar posture. Her eyes encountered Rusty's stare, mocking it. In hot confusion, Rusty moved his eyes upward, up the wall, on to the ceiling, until they could go no further.

'What are you looking at?' asked Kishen.

Rusty brought his eyes to the ground, and pretended not to have heard. He turned to Kapoor and said, 'What about politics?'

The chaat-walla handed out four big banana leaves.

But Kapoor wouldn't eat. Instead, he cried, 'Take the chaat shop to the house. Put it in the car, we must have it! We must have it, we must have it!'

The chaat-walla, who was used to displays of drunkenness in one form or another, humoured Kapoor. 'It is all yours, lallaji, but take me with you too, or who will run the shop?'

'We will!' shouted Kishen, infected by his father's enthusiasm. 'Buy it, Daddy. Mummy can make the tikkees and I'll sell them and Rusty can do the accounts!'

Kapoor threw his banana leaf to the floor and wrapped his arms round Kishen. 'Yes, we will run it! Take it to the house!'

And, making a lunge at a bowl of chaat, fell to his knees.

Rusty helped Kapoor get up, then looked to Meena for guidance. She said nothing, but gave him a nod, and the boy found he understood the nod.

He said, 'It's a wonderful idea, Mr Kapoor, just put me in charge of everything. You and Meena go home and get a spare room ready for the supplies, and Kishen and I will make all the arrangements with the chaat-walla.'

Kapoor clung to Rusty, the spittle dribbling down his cheeks. 'Good boy, good boy ... We will make lots of money together, you and I ...' He turned to his wife and waved his arm grandiloquently, 'We will be rich again, Meena, what do you say?'

Meena, as usual, said nothing, but took Kapoor by the arm and bundled him out of the shop and into the car.

'Be quick with the chaat shop!' cried Kapoor.

'I will have it in the house in five minutes,' called Rusty.

'Get everything ready!'

He returned to Kishen, who was stuffing himself with chaat; his father's behaviour did not appear to have affected him, he was unconscious of its ridiculous aspect and felt no shame; he was unconscious too of the considerate manner of the chaat-walla, who felt sorry for the neglected child. The chaat-walla did not know that Kishen enjoyed being neglected.

Rusty said, 'Come, let's go . . .'

'What's the hurry, Rusty? Sit down and eat, there's plenty of dough tonight. At least give Mummy time to put the sleeping tablets in the whisky.'

So they sat and ate their fill, and listened to other people's gossip; then Kishen suggested that they explore the bazaar.

The oil lamps were lit, and the main road bright and crowded; but Kishen and Rusty went down an alleyway, where the smells were more complicated and the noise intermittent—two women spoke to each other from their windows on either side of the road, a baby cried monotonously, a cheap gramophone blared. Kishen and Rusty walked aimlessly through the maze of alleyways.

'Why are you white like Suri?' asked Kishen.

'Why is Suri white?'

'He is Kashmiri; they are fair.'

'Well, I am English . . .'

'English?' said Kishen disbelievingly. 'You? But you do not look like one.'

Rusty hesitated: he did not feel there was any point in raking up a past that was as much a mystery to him as it was to Kishen.

'I don't know,' he said. 'I never saw my parents. And I don't care what they were and I don't care what I am, and I'm not very interested . . .'

But he couldn't help wondering, and Kishen couldn't help wondering, so they walked on in silence, wondering . . . They reached the railway station, which was at the end of the bazaar; the gates were closed, but they peered through the railings at the goods wagons. A pleasure house did business near the station.

'If you want to have fun,' said Kishen, 'let's climb that roof. From the skylight you can see everything.'

'No fun in just watching,' said Rusty.

'Have you ever watched?'

'Of course,' lied Rusty, turning homewards; he walked with a distracted air.

'What are you thinking of?' asked Kishen.

'Nothing.'

'You must be in love.'

'That's right.'

'Who is it, eh?'

'If I told you,' said Rusty, 'you'd be jealous.'

'But I'm not in love with anybody. Come on, tell me, I'm your friend.'

'Would you be angry if I said I loved your mother?'

'Mummy!' exclaimed Kishen. 'But she's old! She's married. Hell, who would think of falling in love with Mummy? Don't joke, mister.'

'I'm sorry,' said Rusty.

They walked on in silence and crossed the maidan, leaving the bazaar behind. It was dark on the maidan, they could hardly see each other's faces; Kishen put his hand on Rusty's shoulder.

'If you love her,' he said, 'I'm not jealous. But it sounds funny . . .'

CHAPTER TWELVE

&

In his room, Rusty was a king. His domain was the sky and everything he could see. His subjects were the people who passed below, but they were his subjects only while they were below and he was on the roof; and he spied on them through the branches of the banyan tree. His close confidants were the inhabitants of the banyan tree; which, of course, included Kishen.

It was the day of the picnic, and Rusty had just finished bathing at the water-tank. He had become used to the people at the tank and had made friends with the ayahs and their charges. He had come to like their bangles and bracelets and ankle-bells. He liked to watch one of them at the tap, squatting on her haunches, scrubbing her feet, and making much music with the bells and bangles; she would roll her sari up to the knees to give her legs greater freedom, and crouch forward so that her jacket revealed a modest expanse of waist.

It was the day of the picnic, and Rusty had bathed, and now he sat on a disused chimney, drying himself in the sun.

Summer was coming. The litchis were almost ready to eat, the mangoes ripened under Kishen's greedy eye. In the afternoons the sleepy sunlight stole through the branches of the banyan tree, and made a patchwork of arched shadows on the walls of the house. The inhabitants of the trees knew that summer was coming; Somi's slippers knew it, and slapped lazily against his heels; and Kishen grumbled and became more untidy, and even Suri seemed to be taking a rest from his private investigations. Yes, summer was coming.

And it was the day of the picnic.

The car had been inspected, and the two bottles that Kapoor had hidden in the dickey had been found and removed; Kapoor was put into khaki drill trousers and a bush-shirt and pronounced fit to drive; a basket of food and a gramophone were in the dickey. Suri had a camera slung over his shoulders; Kishen was sporting a Gurkha hat; and Rusty had on a thick leather belt reinforced with steel knobs. Meena had dressed in a hurry, and looked the better for it. And for once, Somi had tied his turban to perfection.

'Everyone present?' said Meena. 'If so, get into the car.'

'I'm waiting for my dog,' said Suri, and he had hardly made the announcement when from around the corner came a yapping mongrel.

'He's called Prickly Heat,' said Suri. 'We'll put him in the back seat.'

'He'll go in the dickey,' said Kishen. 'I can see the lice from here.'

Prickly Heat wasn't any particular kind of dog, just a kind of dog; he hadn't even the stump of a tail. But he had sharp, pointed ears that wagged as well as any tail, and they were working furiously this morning.

Suri and the dog were both deposited in the dickey; Somi, Kishen and Rusty made themselves comfortable in the back seat, and Meena sat next to her husband in the front. The car belched and lurched forward, and stirred up great clouds of dust; then, accelerating, sped out of the compound and across the narrow wooden bridge that spanned the canal.

The sun rose over the forest, and a spiral of smoke from a panting train was caught by a slanting ray and spangled with gold. The air was fresh and exciting. It was ten miles to the river and the sulphur springs, ten miles of intermittent grumbling and gaiety, with Prickly Heat yapping in the dickey and Kapoor whistling at the wheel and Kishen letting fly from the window with a catapult.

Somi said, 'Rusty, your pimples will leave you if you bathe in the sulphur springs.'

'I would rather have pimples than pneumonia,' replied Rusty.

'But it's not cold,' and Kishen. 'I would bathe myself, but I don't feel very well.'

'Then you shouldn't have come,' said Meena from the front.

'I didn't want to disappoint you all,' said Kishen.

Before reaching the springs, the car had to cross one or two river-beds, usually dry at this time of the year. But the mountains had tricked the party, for there was a good deal of water to be seen, and the current was strong.

'It's not very deep,' said Kapoor, at the first river-bed, 'I think we can drive through easily.'

The car dipped forward, rolled down the bank, and entered the current with a great splash. In the dickey, Suri got a soaking.

'Got to go fast,' said Mr Kapoor, 'or we'll stick.'

He accelerated, and a great spray of water rose on both sides of the car. Kishen cried out for sheer joy, but at the back Suri was having a fit of hysterics.

'I think the dog's fallen out,' said Meena.

'Good,' said Somi.

'I think Suri's fallen out,' said Rusty.

'Good,' said Somi.

Suddenly the engines spluttered and choked, and the car came to a standstill.

'We are stuck,' said Kapoor.

'That,' said Meena bitingly, 'is obvious. Now I suppose you want us all to get out and push?'

'Yes, that's a good idea.'

'You're a genius.'

Kishen had his shoes off in a flash, and was leaping about in the water with great abandon. The water reached up to his knees and, as he hadn't been swept off his feet, the others followed his example.

Meena hitched up her sari to the thighs, and stepped gingerly into the current. Her legs, so seldom exposed, were very fair in contrast to her feet and arms, but they were strong and nimble, and she held herself erect. Rusty stumbled to her side, intending to aid her; but ended up clinging to her dress for support. Suri was not to be seen anywhere.

'Where is Suri?' said Meena.

'Here,' said a muffled voice from the floor of the dickey. 'I've got sick. I can't push.'

'All right,' said Meena. 'But you'll clean up the mess yourself.'

Somi and Kishen were looking for fish. Kapoor tootled the horn.

'Are you all going to push?' he said, 'or are we going to have the picnic in the middle of the river?'

Rusty was surprised at Kapoor's unusual display of common sense; when sober, Mr Kapoor did sometimes have moments of sanity.

Everyone put their weight against the car, and pushed with all their strength; and, as the car moved slowly forward, Rusty felt a thrill of health and pleasure run through his body. In front of him, Meena pushed silently, the muscles of her thighs trembling with the strain. They all pushed silently, with determination; the sweat ran down Somi's face and neck, and Kishen's jaws worked desperately on his chewing-gum.

But Kapoor sat in comfort behind the wheel, pressing and pulling knobs, and saying 'harder, push harder', and Suri began to be sick again. Prickly Heat was strangely quiet, and it was assumed that the dog was sick too.

With one last final heave, the car was moved up the opposite bank and on to the straight. Everyone groaned and flopped to the ground. Meena's hands were trembling.

'You shouldn't have pushed,' said Rusty.

'I enjoyed it,' she said, smiling at him. 'Help me to get up.'

He rose and, taking her hand, pulled her to her feet. They stood together, holding hands. Kapoor fiddled around with starters and chokes and things.

'It won't go,' he said. 'I'll have to look at the engine. We might as well have the picnic here.'

So out came the food and lemonade bottles and, miraculously enough, out came Suri and Prickly Heat, looking as fit as ever.

'Hey,' said Kishen, 'we thought you were sick. I suppose you were just making room for lunch.'

'Before he eats anything,' said Somi, 'he's going to get wet. Let's take him for a swim.'

Somi, Kishen and Rusty caught hold of Suri and dragged him along the riverbank to a spot downstream where the current was mild and the water warm and waist-high. They unrobed Suri, took off their own clothes, and ran down the sandy slope to the water's edge; feet splashed ankle-deep, calves thrust into the current, and then the ground suddenly disappeared beneath their feet.

Somi was a fine swimmer; his supple limbs cut through the water and, when he went under, he was almost as powerful; the chequered colours of his body could be seen first here and then there, twisting and turning, diving and disappearing for what seemed like several minutes, and then coming up under someone's feet.

Rusty and Kishen were amateurs. When they tried swimming underwater, their bottoms remained on the surface, having all the appearance of floating buoys. Suri couldn't swim at all but, though he was often out of his depth and frequently ducked, managed to avoid his death by drowning.

They heard Meena calling them for food, and scrambled up the bank, the dog yapping at their heels. They ate in the shade of a poinsettia tree, whose red long-fingered flowers dropped sensually to the running water; and when they had eaten, lay down to sleep or drowse the afternoon away.

When Rusty awoke, it was evening, and Kapoor was tinkering about with the car, muttering to himself, a little cross because he hadn't had a drink since the previous night. Somi and Kishen were back in the river, splashing away, and this time they had Prickly Heat for company. Suri wasn't in sight. Meena stood in a clearing at the edge of the forest.

Rusty went to Meena, but she wandered into the thicket. The boy followed. She must have expected him, for she showed no surprise at his appearance.

'Listen to the jungle,' she said.

'I can't hear anything.'

That's what I mean. Listen to nothing.'

They were surrounded by silence; a dark, pensive silence, heavy, scented with magnolia and jasmine.

It was shattered by a piercing shriek, a cry that rose on all sides, echoing against the vibrating air; and, instinctively, Rusty put his arm round Meena—whether to protect her or to protect himself, he did not really know—and held her tight.

'It is only a bird,' she said, 'of what are you afraid?'

But he was unable to release his hold, and she made no effort to free herself. She laughed into his face, and her eyes danced in the shadows. But he stifled her laugh with his lips.

It was a clumsy, awkward kiss, but fiercely passionate, and Meena responded, tightening the embrace, returning the fervour of the kiss. They stood together in the shadows, Rusty intoxicated with beauty and sweetness, Meena with freedom and the comfort of being loved.

A monkey chattered shrilly in a branch above them, and the spell was broken.

'Oh, Meena . . .'

'Shh . . . you spoil these things by saying them.'

'Oh, Meena . . .'

They kissed again, but the monkey set up such a racket that they feared it would bring Kapoor and the others to the spot. So they walked through the trees, holding hands.

They were barefooted, but they did not notice the thorns and brambles that pricked their feet; they walked through heavy foliage, nettles and long grass, until they came to a clearing and a stream.

Rusty was conscious of a wild urge, a desire to escape from the town and its people, and live in the forest with Meena, with no one but Meena . . .

As though conscious of his thoughts, she said, 'This is where we drink. In the trees we eat and sleep, and here we drink.'

She laughed, but Rusty had a dream in his heart. The pebbles on the bed of the stream were round and smooth, taking the flow of water without resistance. Only weed and rock could resist water: only weed or rock could resist life.

'It would be nice to stay in the jungle,' said Meena.

'Let us stay . . .'

'We will be found. We cannot escape—from—others . . .'

'The jungle is big.'

'Even the world is too small. Maybe there is more freedom in your little room than in all the jungle and all the world.'

Rusty pointed to the stream and whispered, 'Look!'

Meena looked, and at the same time a deer looked up. They looked at each other with startled, fascinated eyes, the deer and Meena. It was a spotted chital, a small animal with delicate, quivering limbs and muscles, and young green antlers.

Rusty and Meena did not move, nor did the deer; they might have gone on staring at each other all night if somewhere a twig hadn't snapped sharply.

At the snap of the twig, the deer jerked its head up with a

start, lifted one foot pensively, sniffed the air, then leapt the stream and, in a single bound, disappeared into the forest.

The spell was broken, the magic lost. Only the water ran on and life ran on.

'Let's go back,' said Meena.

They walked back through the dappled sunlight, swinging their clasped hands like two children who had only just discovered love.

Their hands parted as they reached the river-bed.

Miraculously enough, Kapoor had started the car, and was waving his arms and shouting to everyone to come home. Everyone was ready to start back except for Suri and Prickly Heat, who were nowhere to be seen. Nothing, thought Meena, would have been better than for Suri to disappear for ever, but unfortunately she had taken full responsibility for his well-being, and did not relish the thought of facing his strangely affectionate mother. So she asked Rusty to shout for him.

Rusty shouted, and Meena shouted, and Somi shouted, and then they all shouted together, only Suri didn't shout.

'He's up to his tricks,' said Kishen. 'We shouldn't have brought him. Let's pretend we're leaving, then he'll be scared.'

So Kapoor started the engine, and everyone got in, and it was only then that Suri came running from the forest, the dog at his heels, his shirt-tails flapping in the breeze, his hair wedged between his eyes and his spectacles.

'Hey, wait for us!' he cried. 'Do you want me to die?'

Kishen mumbled in the affirmative, and swore quietly.

'We thought you were in the dickey,' said Rusty.

Suri and Prickly Heat climbed into the dickey, and at the same time the car entered the river with a determined splashing and churning of wheels, to emerge the victor.

Everyone cheered, and Somi gave Kapoor such an enthusiastic slap on the back that the pleased recipient nearly caught his head in the steering-wheel.

It was dark now, and all that could be seen of the countryside was what the headlights showed. Rusty had hopes of seeing a panther or tiger, for this was their territory, but only a few goats blocked the road. However, for the benefit of Suri, Somi told a story of a party that had gone for an outing in a car and, on returning home, had found a panther in the dickey.

Kishen fell asleep just before they reached the outskirts of Dehra, his fuzzy head resting on Rusty's shoulder. Rusty felt protectively towards the boy, for a bond of genuine affection had grown between the two. Somi was Rusty's best friend, in the same way that Ranbir was a friend, and their friendship was on a high emotional plane. But Kishen was a brother more than a friend. He loved Rusty, but without knowing or thinking or saying it, and that is the love of a brother.

Somi began singing. Then the town came in sight, the bazaar lights twinkling defiance at the starry night.

CHAPTER THIRTEEN

RUSTY AND MR HARRISON met in front of the town's main grocery store, the 'wine and general merchant's'; it was part of the smart shopping centre, alien to the bazaar but far from the European community—and thus neutral ground for Rusty and Mr Harrison.

'Hullo, Mr Harrison,' said Rusty, confident of himself and deliberately omitting the customary 'sir'.

Mr Harrison tried to ignore the boy, but found him blocking the way to the car. Not wishing to lose his dignity, he decided to be pleasant.

'This is a surprise,' he said, 'I never thought I'd see you again.'

'I found a job,' said Rusty, taking the opportunity of showing his independence. 'I meant to come and see you, but didn't get the time.'

'You're always welcome. The missionary's wife often speaks of you, she'd be glad to see you. By the way, what's your job?'

Rusty hesitated; he did not know how his guardian would

take the truth—probably with a laugh or a sneer ('you're *teaching!*')—and decided to be mysterious about his activities.

'Baby-sitting,' he replied, with a disarming smile. 'Anyway, I'm not starving. And I've got many friends.'

Mr Harrison's face darkened, and the corners of his mouth twitched; but he remembered that times had changed, and that Rusty was older and also free, and that he wasn't in his own house; he controlled his temper.

'I can get you a job,' he said. 'On a tea estate. Or, if you like to go abroad, I have friends in Guiana . . .'

'I like baby-sitting,' said Rusty.

Mr Harrison smiled, got into the car, and lit a cigarette before starting the engine. 'Well, as I said, you're always welcome in the house.'

'Thanks,' said Rusty. 'Give my regards to the sweeper boy.'

The atmosphere was getting tense.

'Why don't you come and see him some time?' said Mr Harrison, as softly and as malevolently as he could.

It was just as well the engine had started.

'I will,' said Rusty.

'I kicked him out,' said Mr Harrison, putting his foot down on the accelerator and leaving Rusty in a cloud of dust.

But Rusty's rage turned to pleasure when the car almost collided with a stationary bullock-cart, and a uniformed policeman brought it to a halt. With the feeling that he had been the master of the situation, Rusty walked homewards.

The litchi trees were covered with their pink-skinned fruit, and the mangoes were almost ripe. The mango is a passionate fruit, its inner gold sensuous to the lips and tongue. The grass had not yet made up its mind to remain yellow or turn green, and would probably keep its dirty colour until the monsoon rains arrived.

Meena met Rusty under the banana trees.

'I am bored,' she said, 'so I am going to give you a haircut. Do you mind?'

'I will do anything to please you. But don't take it all off.'

'Don't you trust me?'

'I love you.'

Rusty was wrapped up in a sheet and placed on a chair. He looked up at Meena, and their eyes met, laughing, blue and brown.

Meena cut silently, and the fair hair fell quickly, softly, lightly to the ground. Rusty enjoyed the snip of the scissors, and the sensation of lightness; it was as though his mind was being given more room in which to explore.

Kishen came loafing around the corner of the house, still wearing his pyjamas, which were rolled up to the knees. When he saw what was going on, he burst into laughter.

'And what is so funny?' said Rusty.

'You!' spluttered Kishen. 'Where is your hair, your beautiful golden hair? Has Mummy made you become a monk? Or have you got ringworm? Or fleas? Look at the ground, all that beautiful hair!'

'Don't be funny, Kishen bhaiya,' said Meena, 'or you will get the same treatment.'

'Is it so bad?' asked Rusty anxiously.

'Don't you trust me?' said Meena.

'I love you.'

Meena glanced swiftly at Kishen to see if he had heard the last remark, but he was still laughing at Rusty's haircut and prodding his nose for all he was worth.

'Rusty, I have a favour to ask you,' said Meena. 'Mr Kapoor and I may be going to Delhi for a few weeks, as there is a chance of him getting a good job. We are not taking Kishen bhaiya, as he is only nuisance value, so will you look after him and keep him out of mischief? I will leave some money with you. About how much will you need for two weeks?'

'When are you going?' asked Rusty, already in the depths of despair.

'How much will you need?'

'Oh, fifty rupees . . . but when—'

'A hundred rupees!' interrupted Kishen. 'Oh boy, Rusty, we'll have fun!'

'Seventy-five,' said Meena, as though driving a bargain, 'and I'll send more after two weeks. But we should be back by then. There, Rusty, your haircut is complete.'

But Rusty wasn't interested in the result of the haircut; he felt like sulking; he wanted to have some say in Meena's plans, he felt he had a right to a little power.

That evening, in the front room, he didn't talk much. Nobody spoke. Kishen lay on the ground, stroking his stomach, his toes tracing imaginary patterns on the wall. Meena looked tired; wisps of hair had fallen across her face, and she did not bother to brush them back. She took Kishen's foot and gave it a pull.

'Go to bed,' she said.

'Not tired.'

'Go to bed, or you'll get a slap.'

Kishen laughed defiantly, but got up from the floor and ambled out of the room.

'And don't wake Daddy,' she said.

Kapoor had been put to bed early, as Meena wanted him to be fresh and sober for his journey to Delhi and his interviews there. But every now and then he would wake up and call out for something—something unnecessary, so that after a while no one paid any attention to his requests. He was like an irritable invalid, to be humoured and tolerated.

'Are you not feeling well, Meena?' asked Rusty. 'If you like, I'll also go.'

'I am only tired, don't go ...'

She went to the window and drew the curtains and put out the light. Only the table lamp burned. The lampshade was decorated with dragons and butterflies—it was a Chinese lampshade—and, as Rusty sat gazing at the light, the dragons began to move and the butterflies flutter. He couldn't see Meena, but felt her presence across the room.

She turned from the window; and silently, with hardly a rustle, slipped to the ground. Her back against the couch, her head resting against the cushion, she looked up at the ceiling. Neither of them spoke.

From the next room came sounds of Kishen preparing for the night, one or two thumps and a muttered imprecation. Kapoor snored quietly to himself, and the rest was silence.

Rusty's gaze left the revolving dragons and prancing butterflies to settle on Meena, who sat still and tired, her feet lifeless against the table legs, her slippers fallen to the ground. In the lamplight, her feet were like jade.

A moth began to fly round the lamp, and it went round and round and closer, till—with a sudden plop—it hit the lampshade and fell to the ground. But Rusty and Meena were still silent, their breathing the only conversation.

Chapter Fourteen

DURING THE DAY, FLIES circled the room with feverish buzzing, and at night the mosquitoes came singing in one's ears; summer days were hot and sticky, the nights breathless.

Rusty covered his body in citronella oil, which had been given him by Somi's mother; its smell, while pleasant to his own senses, was repugnant to mosquitoes.

When Rusty rubbed the oil on his limbs he noticed the change in his physique. He had lost his puppy fat, and there was more muscle to his body; his complexion was a healthier colour, and his pimples had almost disappeared. Nearly everyone had advised him about his pimples: drink dahi, said Somi's mother, don't eat fat; eat carrots, said Somi; plenty of fruit, mangoes! said Kishen; not at all, oranges; see a doctor, said Meena; have a whisky, said Kapoor: but the pimples disappeared without any of these remedies, and Rusty put it down to his falling in love.

The bougainvillaea creeper had advanced further into the room, and was now in flower; and watching Rusty oil himself, was the bald maina bird; it had been in so many fights that the feathers on its head never got a chance to grow.

Suri entered the room without warning and, wiping his spectacles on the bedsheet, said, 'I have written an essay, Mister Rusty, for which I am going to be marked in school. Correct it, if you please.'

'Let me finish with this oil ... It would be cheating, you know.'

'No, it won't. It has to be corrected some time, so you will save the master some trouble. Anyway, I'm leaving this rotten school soon. I'm going to Mussoorie.'

'To the same place as Ranbir? He'll be glad to see you.'

Suri handed Rusty the copy-book. On the cover was a pencil sketch of a rather over-developed nude.

'Don't tell me this is your school book!' exclaimed Rusty.

'No, only rough work.'

'You drew the picture?'

'Of course, don't you like it?'

'Did you copy it, or imagine it, or did someone pose for you?'

Suri winked. 'Someone posed.'

'You're a liar. And a pig.'

'Oh, look who's talking! You're not such a saint yourself, Mister Rusty.'

'Just what do you mean,' said Rusty, getting between Suri and the door.

'I mean, how is Mrs Kapoor, eh?'

'She is fine.'

'You get on well with her, eh?'

'We get on fine.'

'Like at the picnic?'

Suri rubbed his hands together, and smiled beatifically. Rusty was momentarily alarmed.

'What do you mean, the picnic?'

'What did you do together, Mister Rusty, you and Mrs Kapoor? What happened in the bushes?'

Rusty leant against the wall, and returned Suri's smile, and said, 'I'll tell you what we did, my friend. There's nothing to hide between friends, is there? Well, Mrs Kapoor and I spent all our time making love. We did nothing but love each other. All the time. And Mr Kapoor only a hundred yards away, and you in the next bush . . . Now what else do you want to know?'

Suri's smile was fixed. 'What if I tell Mr Kapoor?'

'You won't tell him,' said Rusty.

'Why not?'

'Because you are the last person he'll believe. And you'll probably get a kick in the pants for the trouble.'

Suri's smile had gone.

'Cheer up,' said Rusty. 'What about the essay, do you want me to correct it?'

*

That afternoon the old car stood beneath the banana trees with an impatient driver tooting on the horn. The dickey and bumpers were piled high with tin trunks and bedding-rolls, as though the Kapoors were going away for a lifetime. Meena wasn't going to let Kapoor drive her all the way to Delhi, and had taken on a professional instead.

Kapoor sat on the steps of the house, wearing his green dressing-gown, and making a throaty noise similar to that of the motor-horn.

'The devil!' he exclaimed, gesticulating towards Meena, who was bustling about indoors.'The devil of a wife is taking me to Delhi! Ha! The car will never get there.'

'Oh yes, it will,' said Meena, thrusting her head out of the window,'and it will get there with you in it,whether or not you shave and dress. So you might as well take a seat from now.'

Rusty went into the house, and found Meena locking rooms. She was looking a little tired and irritable.

'You're going sooner than I expected,' said Rusty. 'Has Kishen got the money?'

'No, you must keep it. I'll give it to you in five-rupee notes, wait a minute . . . He'll have to sleep with you, I'm locking the house . . .'

She opened a drawer and, taking out an envelope, gave it to Rusty.

'The money,' she said. Rusty picked up a small suitcase and followed Meena outside to the car. He waited until she was seated before handing her the case and, when he did, their hands touched. She laced her fingers with his, and gave him a quick smile, and squeezed his fingers.

From the front seat Kapoor beckoned Rusty. He grasped the boy's hand, and slipped a key into it.

'My friend,' he whispered, 'these are the keys of the back door. In the kitchen you will find six bottles of whisky. Keep them safe, until our return.'

Rusty shook Kapoor's hand, the hand of the man he laughed at, but whom he could not help loving as well.

In the confusion Kishen had gone almost unnoticed, but he was there all the time, and now he suffered a light kiss from his mother and a heavy one from his father.

The car belched and, after narrowly missing a banana tree, rattled down the gravel path, bounced over a ditch, and disappeared in a cloud of dust.

Kishen and Rusty were flapping their handkerchiefs for all they were worth. Kishen was not a bit sorry that his parents had gone away, but Rusty felt like crying. He was conscious now of a sense of responsibility, which was a thing he did not like having, and of a sense of loss. But the depression was only momentary.

'Hey!' said Kishen. 'Do you see what I see?'

'I can see a lot of things that you can see, so what do you mean?'

'The clothes! Mummy's washing, it is all on the rose bushes!'

Meena had left without collecting her washing which, as always, had been left to dry on the rose bushes. Mr Kapoor's underwear spread itself over an entire bush, and another tree was decorated with bodices and blouses of all colours.

Rusty said, 'Perhaps she means them to dry by the time she comes back.'

He began to laugh with Kishen, so it was a good thing, Meena's forgetfulness; it softened the pain of parting.

'What if we hadn't noticed?' chuckled Kishen.

'They would have been stolen.'

'Then we must reward ourselves. What about the chaat shop, bhai?'

At the risk of making himself unpopular, Rusty faced Kishen and, with a determination, said, 'No chaat shop. We have got seventy-five rupees to last a month, and I am not going to write for more once this finishes. We are having our meals with Somi. So, bhai, no chaat shop!'

'You are a swine, Rusty.'

'And the same to you.'

In this endearing mood they collected the clothes from the rose bushes, and marched upstairs to the room on the roof.

*

There was only one bed, and Kishen was a selfish sleeper; twice during the night Rusty found himself on the floor. Eventually he sat in the chair, with his feet on the table, and stared out of the window at the black night. Even if he had been comfortable, he would not have slept; he felt terribly lovesick. He wanted to write a poem, but it was too dark to write; he wanted to write a letter, but she hadn't been away a day; he wanted to run away with Meena, into the hills, into the forests, where no one could find them, and he wanted to be with her for ever and never grow old ... neither of them must ever grow old ...

Chapter Fifteen

In the morning there was a note from Suri. Rusty wondered how Suri had managed to leave it on the doorstep without being seen.

It went:

> Tomorrow I'm going up to Mussoorie. This is to request the
> pleasure of Misters Rusty and Kishen to my good-bye party,
> five o'clock sharp this same evening.

As soon as it became known that Suri was leaving, everyone
began to love him. And everyone brought him presents, just so
he wouldn't change his mind and stay.

Kishen bought him a pair of cheap binoculars so that he could
look at the girls more closely, and the guests sat down at a table
and Suri entertained them in grand style; and they tolerated
everything he said and were particularly friendly and gave him
three cheers, hooray, hooray, hooray, they were so glad he was
going.

They drank lemonade and ate cream cakes (specially obtained
from the smart restaurant amongst the smart shops) and Kishen
said, 'We are so sorry you are leaving, Suri,' and they had more
cream cakes and lemonade, and Kishen said, 'You are like a
brother to us, Suri dear'; and when the cream cakes had all been
finished, Kishen fell on Suri's neck and kissed him.

It was all very moving, those cream cakes and lemonade and
Suri going away.

Kishen made himself sick, and Rusty had to help him back to
the room. Kishen lay prostrate on the bed, whilst Rusty sat in
front of the window, gazing blankly into the branches of the
banyan tree.

Presently he said, 'It's drizzling. I think there'll be a storm, I've
never seen the sky so black.'

As though to confirm this observation, there was a flash of
lightning in the sky. Rusty's eyes lit up with excitement; he liked
storms, sometimes they were an expression of his innermost feelings.

'Shut the window,' said Kishen.

'If I shut the window, I will kill the flowers on the creeper.'

Kishen snorted, 'You're a poet, that's what you are!'

'One day I'll write poems.'

'Why not today?'

'Too much is happening today.'

'I don't think so. Nothing ever happens in Dehra. The place is dead. Why don't you start writing now? You're a great writer, I told you so before.'

'I know.'

'One day ... one day you'll be a king ... but only in your dreams ... Meanwhile, shut the window!'

But Rusty liked the window open, he liked the rain flecking his face, and he liked to watch it pattering on the leaves of the banyan tree.

'They must have reached Delhi now,' he said, half to himself.

'Daddy's drunk,' said Kishen.

'There's nothing for him to drink.'

'Oh, he'll find something. You know, one day he drank up all the hair-oil in the house. Hey, didn't he give you the keys of the back door? Let's drink one of the bottles ourselves ...'

Rusty didn't reply. The tense sky shuddered. The blanket of black cloud groaned aloud and the air, which had been still and sultry, trembled with electricity. Then the thunder gave a great clap, and all at once the hailstones came clattering down on the corrugated iron roof.

'What a noise!' exclaimed Kishen. 'You'd think a lot of skeletons were having a fight on the roof!'

The hail-stones, as big as marbles, bounced in from the doorway, and on the roof they were forming a layer of white ice. Through the window Rusty could see one of the ayahs tearing down the gravel path, the pram bouncing madly over the stones, the end of her head-cloth flapping wildly.

'Will you shut the window!' screamed Kishen.

'Why are you so cruel, bhai?'

'I'm not cruel, I'm *sick*! Do you want me to get sick all over the place?'

As gently as he could, Rusty pushed the creeper out of the window and laid it against the outside wall. Then he closed the window. This shut out the view, because the window was made of plywood and had no glass panes.

'And the door,' moaned Kishen.

With the door closed, the room was plunged into darkness.

'What a room,' complained Kishen, 'not even a light. You'll have to live downstairs when they come back.'

'But I like it here.'

The storm continued all night; it made Kishen so nervous that, instead of pushing Rusty off the bed, he put his arms round him for protection.

*

The rain had stopped by morning, but the sky was still overcast and threatening. Rusty and Kishen lay in bed, too bored to bestir themselves. There was some dried fruit in a tin, and they ate the nuts continuously. They could hear the postman making his rounds below, and Rusty suddenly remembered that the postman wouldn't know the Kapoors had left. He leapt out of bed, opened the door, and ran to the edge of the roof.

'Hey postman!' he called. 'Anything for Mr and Mrs Kapoor?'

'Nothing,' said the postman, 'but there is something for you, shall I come up?'

But Rusty was already on his way down, certain that it was a letter from Meena.

It was a telegram. Rusty's fingers trembled as he tore it open, and he had read it before he reached the room. His face was white when he entered the room.

'What's wrong,' said Kishen, 'you look sick. Doesn't Mummy love you any more?'

Rusty sat down on the edge of the bed, his eyes staring emptily at the floor.

'You're to go to Hardwar,' he said at last, 'to stay with your aunty.'

'Well, you can tell Mummy I'm staying here.'

'It's from your aunty.'

'Why couldn't Mummy say so herself?'

'I don't want to tell you.'

'But you have to tell me!' cried Kishen, making an ineffectual grab at the telegram. 'You have to tell me, Rusty, you have to!'

There was panic in Kishen's voice, he was almost hysterical.

'All right,' said Rusty, and his own voice was strained and hollow. 'The car had an accident.'

'And something happened to Daddy?'

'No.'

There was a terrible silence. Kishen looked helplessly at Rusty, his eyes full of tears and bewilderment; and Rusty could stand the strain no longer, and threw his arms round Kishen, and wept for himself and for his friend.

'Oh, Mummy, Mummy,' cried Kishen. 'Oh, Mummy . . .'

Chapter Sixteen

It was late evening the same day, and the clouds had passed and the whole sky was sprinkled with stars. Rusty sat on the bed, looking out at the stars and waiting for Kishen.

Presently bare feet sounded on the stone floor, and Rusty could make out the sharp lines of Kishen's body against the faint moon in the doorway.

'Why do you creep in like a ghost?' whispered Rusty. 'So's not to wake you.'

'It's still early. Where have you been, I was looking for you.'

'Oh, just walking . . .'

Kishen sat down beside Rusty, facing the same way, the stars. The moonlight ran over their feet, but their faces were in darkness.

'Rusty,' said Kishen.

'Yes.'

'I don't want to go to Hardwar.'

'I know you don't, bhaiya. But you will not be allowed to stay here. You must go to your relatives. And Hardwar is a beautiful place, and people are kind . . .'

'I'll stay with you.'

'I can't look after you, Kishen, I haven't got any money, any work . . . you must stay with your aunt. I'll come to see you.'

'You'll never come.'

'I'll try.'

Every night the jackals could be heard howling in the nearby jungle, but tonight their cries sounded nearer, much nearer the house.

Kishen slept. He was exhausted; he had been walking all evening, crying his heart out. Rusty lay awake, his eyes were wide open, brimming with tears; he did not know if the tears were for himself or for Meena or for Kishen, but they were for someone.

Meena is dead, he told himself, Meena is dead; if there is a God, then God look after her; if God is Love, then my love will be with her; she loved me; I can see her so clearly, her face speckled with sun and shadow when we kissed in the forest, the black waterfall of hair, her tired eyes, her feet like jade in the lamplight, she loved me, she was mine . . .

Rusty was overcome by a feeling of impotence and futility, and of the unimportance of life. Every moment, he told himself, every moment someone is born and someone dies, you can count them one, two, three, a birth and a death for every moment . . . what is this one life in the whole pattern of life, what is this one death but a passing of time . . . And if I were to die now, suddenly and without cause, what would happen, would it matter . . . we live without knowing why or to what purpose.

The moon bathed the room in a soft, clear light. The howl of the jackals seemed to be coming from the field below, and Rusty thought, 'A jackal is like death, ugly and cowardly and mad . . .' He heard a faint sniff from the doorway, and lifted his head.

In the doorway, a dark silhouette against the moonlight, stood the lean, craving form of a jackal, its eyes glittering balefully.

Rusty wanted to scream. He wanted to throw everything in the room at the snivelling, cold-blooded beast, or throw himself out of the window instead. But he could do none of these things.

The jackal lifted its head to the sky and emitted a long, blood-curdling howl that ran like an electric current through Rusty's body. Kishen sprang up with a gasp and threw his arms round Rusty.

And then Rusty screamed.

It was half shout, half scream, and it began in the pit of his stomach, was caught by his lungs, and catapulted into the empty night. Everything around him seemed to be shaking, vibrating to the pitch of the scream.

The jackal fled. Kishen whimpered and sprang back from Rusty and dived beneath the bedclothes.

And as the scream and its echo died away, the night closed in again, with a heavy, petrifying stillness; and all that could be heard was Kishen sobbing under the blankets, terrified not so much by the jackal's howl as by Rusty's own terrible scream.

'Oh, Kishen bhai,' cried Rusty, putting his arms around the boy, 'don't cry, please don't cry. You are making me afraid of myself. Don't be afraid, Kishen. Don't make me afraid of myself . . .'

*

And in the morning their relationship was a little strained.

Kishen's aunt arrived. She had a tonga ready to take Kishen away. She gave Rusty a hundred rupees, which she said was from Mr Kapoor; Rusty didn't want to take it, but Kishen swore at him and forced him to accept it.

The tonga pony was restless, pawing the ground and champing at the bit, snorting a little. The driver got down from the carriage and held the reins whilst Kishen and his aunt climbed on to their seats.

Kishen made no effort to conceal his misery.

'I wish you would come, Rusty,' he said.

'I will come and see you one day, be sure of that.'

It was very seldom that Kishen expressed any great depth of feeling; he was always so absorbed with comforts of the flesh that he never had any profound thoughts; but he did have profound feelings, though they were seldom thought or spoken.

He grimaced and prodded his nose.

'Inside of me,' he said, 'I am all lonely . . .'

The driver cracked his whip, the horse snorted, the wheels creaked, and the tonga moved forward. The carriage bumped up in the ditch, and it looked as though everyone would be thrown out; but it bumped down again without falling apart, and Kishen and his aunt were still in their seats. The driver jingled his bell, and the tonga turned on to the main road that led to the station; the horse's hoofs clip-clopped, and the carriage-wheels squeaked and rattled.

Rusty waved. Kishen sat stiff and upright, clenching the ends of his shirt.

Rusty felt afraid for Kishen, who seemed to be sitting on his own, apart from his aunt, as though he disowned or did not know her: it seemed as though he was being borne away to some strange, friendless world, where no one would know or care for him; and, though Rusty knew Kishen to be wild and independent, he felt afraid for him.

The driver called to the horse, and the tonga went round the bend in the road and was lost to sight.

Rusty stood at the gate, staring down the empty road. He thought, 'I'll go back to my room and time will run on and things will happen but *this* will not happen again . . . there will still be sun and litchis, and there will be other friends, but there will be no Meena and no Kishen, for our lives have drifted apart . . . Kishen and I have been going down the river together, but I have been caught in the reeds and he has been swept onwards; and if I do catch up with him, it will not be the same, it might be sad . . . Kishen has gone, and part of my life has gone with him, and inside of me I am all lonely.'

Chapter Seventeen

It was a sticky, restless afternoon. The water-carrier passed below the room with his skin bag, spraying water on the dusty path. The toy-seller entered the compound, calling his wares in a high-pitched sing-song voice, and presently there was the chatter of children.

The toy-seller had a long bamboo pole, crossed by two or three shorter bamboos, from which hung all manner of toys—little celluloid drums, tin watches, tiny flutes and whistles, and multi-coloured rag dolls—and when these ran out, they were replaced by others from a large bag, a most mysterious and fascinating bag, one in which no one but the toy-seller was allowed to look. He was a popular person with rich and poor alike, for his toys never cost more than four annas and never lasted longer than a day.

Rusty liked the cheap toys, and was fond of decorating the room with them. He bought a two-anna flute and walked upstairs, blowing on it.

He removed his shirt and sandals and lay flat on the bed staring up at the ceiling. The lizards scuttled along the rafters, the bald maina hopped along the window ledge. He was about to fall asleep when Somi came into the room.

Somi looked listless.

'I feel sticky,' he said, 'I don't want to wear any clothes.'

He too pulled off his shirt and deposited it on the table, then stood before the mirror, studying his physique. Then he turned to Rusty.

'You don't look well,' he said, 'there are cobwebs in your hair.'

'I don't care.'

'You must have been very fond of Mrs Kapoor. She was very kind.'

'I loved her, didn't you know?'

'No. My own love is the only thing I know. Rusty, best

favourite friend, you cannot stay here in this room, you must come back to my house. Besides, this building will soon have new tenants.'

'I'll get out when they come, or when the landlord discovers I'm living here.'

Somi's usually bright face was somewhat morose, and there was a faint agitation showing in his eyes.

'I will go and get a cucumber to eat,' he said, 'then there is something to tell you.'

'I don't want a cucumber,' said Rusty, 'I want a coconut.'

'I want a cucumber.'

Rusty felt irritable. The room was hot, the bed was hot, his blood was hot. Impatiently, he said, 'Go and eat your cucumber, I don't want any . . .'

Somi looked at him with a pained surprise; then, without a word, picked up his shirt and marched out of the room. Rusty could hear the slap of his slippers on the stairs, and then the bicycle tyres on the gravel path.

'Hey, Somi!' shouted Rusty, leaping off the bed and running out on to the roof. 'Come back!'

But the bicycle jumped over the ditch, and Somi's shirt flapped, and there was nothing Rusty could do but return to bed. He was alarmed at his liverish ill-temper. He lay down again and stared at the ceiling, at the lizards chasing each other across the rafters. On the roof two crows were fighting, knocking each other's feathers out. Everyone was in a temper.

What's wrong? wondered Rusty. I spoke to Somi in fever, not in anger, but my words were angry. Now I am miserable, fed up. Oh, hell . . .

He closed his eyes and shut out everything.

He opened his eyes to laughter. Somi's face was close, laughing into Rusty's.

'Of what were you dreaming, Rusty, I have never seen you smile so sweetly!'

'Oh, I wasn't dreaming,' said Rusty, sitting up, and feeling better now that Somi had returned. 'I am sorry for being so grumpy, but I'm not feeling . . .'

'Quiet!' admonished Somi, putting his finger to the other's lips. 'See I have settled the matter. Here is a coconut for you, and here is a cucumber for me!'

They sat cross-legged on the bed, facing each other; Somi with his cucumber, and Rusty with his coconut. The coconut milk trickled down Rusty's chin and on to his chest, giving him a cool, pleasant sensation.

Rusty said, 'I am afraid for Kishen. I am sure he will give trouble to his relatives, and they are not like his parents. Mr Kapoor will have no say, without Meena.'

Somi was silent. The only sound was the munching of the cucumber and the coconut. He looked at Rusty, an uncertain smile on his lips but none in his eyes; and, in a forced conversational manner, said, 'I'm going to Amritsar for a few months. But I will be back in the spring. Rusty, you will be all right here . . .'

This news was so unexpected that for some time Rusty could not take it in. The thought had never occurred to him that one day Somi might leave Dehra, just as Ranbir and Suri and Kishen had done. He could not speak. A sickening heaviness clogged his heart and brain.

'Hey, Rusty!' laughed Somi. 'Don't look as though there is poison in the coconut!'

The poison lay in Somi's words. And the poison worked, running through Rusty's veins and beating against his heart and hammering on his brain. The poison worked, wounding him.

He said, 'Somi . . .' but could go no further.

'Finish the coconut!'

'Somi,' said Rusty again, 'if you are leaving Dehra, Somi, then I am leaving too.'

'Eat the coco . . . what did you say?'

'I am going too.'

'Are you mad?'

'Not at all.'

Serious now, and troubled, Somi put his hand on his friend's wrist; he shook his head, he could not understand.

'Why, Rusty? Where?'

'England.'

'But you haven't money, you silly fool!'

'I can get an assisted passage. The British government will pay.'

'You are a British subject?'

'I don't know . . .'

'*Toba*!' Somi slapped his thighs and looked upwards in despair. 'You are neither Indian subject nor British subject, and you think someone is going to pay for your passage! And how are you to get a passport?'

'How?' asked Rusty, anxious to find out.

'*Toba*! Have you a birth certificate?'

'Oh, no.'

'Then you are not born,' decreed Somi, with a certain amount of satisfaction. 'You are not alive! You do not happen to be in this world!'

He paused for breath, then waved his finger in the air.

'Rusty, you cannot go!' he said.

Rusty lay down despondently.

'I never really thought I would,' he said, 'I only said I would because I felt like it. Not because I am unhappy—I have never been happier elsewhere—but because I am restless as I have always been. I don't suppose I'll be anywhere for long . . .'

He spoke the truth. Rusty always spoke the truth. He defined truth as feeling, and when he said what he felt, he said truth. (Only he didn't always speak his feelings.) He never lied. You don't have to lie if you know how to withhold the truth.

'You belong here,' said Somi, trying to reconcile Rusty with circumstance. 'You will get lost in big cities, Rusty, you will break your heart. And when you come back—if you come back—I will be grown-up and you will be grown-up—I mean more than we are now—and we will be like strangers to each other . . . And besides, there are no chaat shops in England!'

'But I don't belong here, Somi. I don't belong anywhere. Even if I have papers, I don't belong. I'm a half-caste, I know it, and that is as good as not belonging anywhere.'

What am I saying, thought Rusty, why do I make my inheritance a justification for my present bitterness? No one has cast me out ... of my own free will I want to run away from India ... why do I blame inheritance?

'It can also mean that you belong everywhere,' said Somi. 'But you never told me. You are fair like a European.'

'I had not thought much about it.'

'Are you ashamed?'

'No. My guardian was. He kept it to himself, he only told me when I came home after playing Holi. I was happy then. So, when he told me, I was not ashamed, I was proud.'

'And now?'

'Now? Oh, I can't really believe it. Somehow I do not really feel mixed.'

'Then don't blame it for nothing.'

Rusty felt a little ashamed, and they were both silent awhile, then Somi shrugged and said: 'So you are going. You are running away from India.'

'No, not from India.'

'Then you are running away from your friends, from me!'

Rusty felt the irony of this remark, and allowed a tone of sarcasm into his voice.

'You, Master Somi, you are the one who is going away. I am still here. You are going to Amritsar. I only want to go. And I'm here alone; everyone has gone. So if I do eventually leave, the only person I'll be running away from will be myself!'

'Ah!' said Somi, nodding his head wisely. 'And by running away from yourself, you will be running away from me and from India! Now come on, let's go and have chaat.'

He pulled Rusty off the bed, and pushed him out of the room. Then, at the top of the steps, he leapt lightly on Rusty's back, kicked him with his heels, and shouted: 'Down the steps, my tuttoo, my pony! Fast down the steps!'

So Rusty carried him downstairs and dropped him on the grass. They laughed: but there was no great joy in their laughter, they laughed for the sake of friendship.

'Best favourite friend,' said Somi, throwing a handful of mud in Rusty's face.

CHAPTER EIGHTEEN

NOW EVERYONE HAD GONE from Dehra. Meena would never return; and it seemed unlikely that Kapoor could come back. Kishen's departure was final. Ranbir would be in Mussoorie until the winter months, and this was still summer and it would be even longer before Somi returned. Everyone Rusty knew well had left, and there remained no one he knew well enough to love or hate.

There were, of course, the people at the water-tank—the servants, the ayahs, the babies—but they were busy all day. And when Rusty left them, he had no one but himself and memory for company.

He wanted to forget Meena. If Kishen had been with him, it would have been possible; the two boys would have found comfort in their companionship. But alone, Rusty realized he was not the master of himself.

And Kapoor. For Kapoor, Meena had died perfect. He suspected her of no infidelity. And, in a way, she *had* died perfect; for she had found a secret freedom. Rusty knew he had judged Kapoor correctly when scorning Suri's threat of blackmail; he knew Kapoor wouldn't believe a single disparaging word about Meena.

And Rusty returned to his dreams, that wonderland of his, where he walked in perfection. He spoke to himself quite often, and sometimes he spoke to the lizards.

He was afraid of the lizards, afraid and at the same time fascinated. When they changed their colours, from brown to red to green, in keeping with their immediate surroundings, they fascinated him. But when they lost their grip on the ceiling and fell to the ground with a soft, wet, boneless smack, they repelled him. One night, he reasoned, one of them would most certainly fall on his face . . .

An idea he conceived one afternoon nearly sparked him into sudden and feverish activity. He thought of making a garden on the roof, beside his room.

The idea took his fancy to such an extent that he spent several hours planning the set-out of the flower-beds, and visualizing the completed picture, with marigolds, zinnias and cosmos blooming everywhere. But there were no tools to be had, mud and bricks would have to be carried upstairs, seeds would have to be obtained; and, who knows, thought Rusty, after all that trouble the roof might cave in, or the rains might spoil everything . . . and anyway, he was going away . . .

His thoughts turned inwards. Gradually, he returned to the same frame of mind that had made life with his guardian so empty and meaningless; he began to fret, to dream, to lose his grip on reality. The full life of the past few months had suddenly ended, and the present was lonely and depressing; the future became a distorted image, created out of his own brooding fancies.

One evening, sitting on the steps, he found himself fingering a key. It was the key Kapoor had asked him to keep, the key to the back door. Rusty remembered the whisky bottles—'let's drink them ourselves' Kishen had said—and Rusty thought, 'why not, why not . . . a few bottles can't do any harm . . .' and before he could have an argument with himself, the back door was open.

In his room that night he drank the whisky neat. It was the first time he had tasted alcohol, and he didn't find it pleasant; but he wasn't drinking for pleasure, he was drinking with the sole purpose of shutting himself off from the world, and forgetting.

He hadn't drunk much when he observed that the roof had a definite slant; it seemed to slide away from his door to the field below, like a chute. The banyan tree was suddenly swarming with bees. The lizards were turning all colours at once, like pieces of rainbow.

When he had drunk a little more, he began to talk; not to

himself any more, but to Meena, who was pressing his head and trying to force him down on the pillows. He struggled against Meena, but she was too powerful, and he began to cry.

Then he drank a little more. And now the floor began to wobble, and Rusty had a hard time keeping the table from toppling over. The walls of the room were caving in. He swallowed another mouthful of whisky, and held the wall up with his hands. He could deal with anything now. The bed was rocking, the chair was sliding about, the table was slipping, the walls were swaying, but Rusty had everything under control, he was everywhere at once, supporting the entire building with his bare hands.

And then he slipped, and everything came down on top of him, and it was black.

In the morning when he awoke, he threw the remaining bottles out of the window, and cursed himself for a fool, and went down to the water-tank to bathe.

*

Days passed, dry and dusty, every day the same. Regularly, Rusty filled his earthen *sohrai* at the water-tank, and soaked the reed mat that hung from the doorway. Sometimes, in the field, the children played cricket, but he couldn't summon up the energy to join them. From his room he could hear the sound of ball and bat, the shouting, the lone voice raised in shrill disagreement with some unfortunate umpire . . . or the thud of a football, or the clash of hockey sticks . . . but better than these sounds was the jingle of the bells and bangles on the feet of the ayahs, as they busied themselves at the water-tank.

Time passed, but Rusty did not know it was passing. It was like living in a house near a river, and the river was always running past the house, on and away; but to Rusty, living in the house, there was no passing of the river; the water ran on, the river remained.

He longed for something to happen.

CHAPTER NINETEEN

Dust. It blew up in great clouds, swirling down the road, clutching and clinging to everything it touched; burning, choking, stinging dust. Then thunder.

The wind dropped suddenly, there was a hushed expectancy in the air. And then, out of the dust, came big black rumbling clouds.

Something was happening.

At first there was a lonely drop of water on the window sill; then a patter on the roof. Rusty felt a thrill of anticipation, and a mounting of excitement. The rains had come to break the monotony of the summer months; the monsoon had arrived!

The sky shuddered, the clouds groaned, a fork of lightning struck across the sky, and then the sky itself exploded.

The rain poured down, drumming on the corrugated roof. Rusty's vision was reduced to about twenty yards; it was as though the room had been cut off from the rest of the world by an impenetrable wall of water.

The rains had arrived, and Rusty wanted to experience the full novelty of that first shower. He threw off his clothes, and ran naked on to the roof, and the wind sprang up and whipped the water across his body so that he writhed in ecstasy. The rain was more intoxicating than the alcohol, and it was with difficulty that he restrained himself from shouting and dancing in mad abandon. The force and freshness of the rain brought tremendous relief, washed away the stagnation that had been settling on him, poisoning mind and body.

The rain swept over the town, cleansing the sky and earth. The trees bent beneath the force of wind and water. The field was a bog, flowers flattened to the ground.

Rusty returned to the room, exhilarated, his body weeping. He was confronted by a flood. The water had come in through the door and the window and the skylight, and the floor was flooded ankle-deep. He took to his bed.

The bed took on the glamour of a deserted island in the middle of the ocean. He dried himself on the sheets, conscious of a warm, sensuous glow. Then he sat on his haunches and gazed out through the window.

The rain thickened, the tempo quickened. There was the banging of a door, the swelling of a gutter, the staccato splutter of the rain rhythmically persistent on the roof. The drainpipe coughed and choked, the curtain flew to its limit; the lean trees swayed, swayed, bowed with the burden of wind and weather. The road was a rushing torrent, the gravel path inundated with little rivers. The monsoon had arrived!

But the rain stopped as unexpectedly as it had begun.

Suddenly it slackened, dwindled to a shower, petered out. Stillness. The dripping of water from the drainpipe drilled into the drain. Frogs croaked, hopping around in the slush.

The sun came out with a vengeance. On leaves and petals, drops of water sparkled like silver and gold. A cat emerged from a dry corner of the building, blinking sleepily, unperturbed and unenthusiastic.

The children came running out of their houses.

'Barsaat, barsaat!' they shouted. 'The rains have come!'

The rains had come. And the roof became a general bathing-place. The children, the night-watchmen, the dogs, all trooped up the steps to sample the novelty of a freshwater shower on the roof.

The maidan became alive with footballs. The game was called monsoon football, it was played in slush, in mud that was ankle-deep; and the football was heavy and slippery and difficult to kick with bare feet. The bazaar youths played barefooted because, in the first place, boots were too cumbersome for monsoon football, and in the second place they couldn't be afforded.

But the rains brought Rusty only a momentary elation, just as the first shower had seemed fiercer and fresher than those which followed; for now it rained every day . . .

Nothing could be more depressing than the dampness, the mildew, and the sunless heat that wrapped itself round the steaming land. Had Somi or Kishen been with Rusty, he might have derived some pleasure from the elements; had Ranbir been with him, he might have found adventure; but alone, he found only boredom.

He spent an idle hour watching the slow dripping from the pipe outside the door: where do I belong, he wondered, what am I doing, what is going to happen to me . . .

He was determined to break away from the atmosphere of timelessness and resignation that surrounded him, and decided to leave Dehra.

'I must go,' he told himself. 'I do not want to rot like the mangoes at the end of the season, or burn out like the sun at the end of the day. I cannot live like the gardener, the cook and the water-carrier, doing the same task every day of my life. I am not interested in today, I want tomorrow. I cannot live in this same small room all my life, with a family of lizards, living in other people's homes and never having one of my own. I *have* to break away. I want to be either somebody or nobody. I don't want to be anybody.'

He decided to go to Delhi and see the High Commissioner for the United Kingdom, who was sure to give him an assisted passage to England; and he wrote to Somi, telling him of this plan. On his way he would have to pass through Hardwar, and there he would see Kishen; he had the aunt's address.

At night he slept brokenly, thinking and worrying about the future. He would listen to the vibrant song of the frog who wallowed in the drain at the bottom of the steps, and to the unearthly cry of the jackal, and questions would come to him, disturbing questions about loving and leaving and living and dying, questions that crowded out his sleep.

But on the night before he left Dehra, it was not the croaking of the frog or the cry of the jackal that kept him awake, or the persistent questioning; but a premonition of crisis and of an end to something.

CHAPTER TWENTY

THE POSTMAN BROUGHT A letter from Somi.

Dear Rusty, best favourite friend,

Do not ever travel in a third-class compartment. All the way to Amritsar I had to sleep standing up, the carriage was so crowded.

I shall be coming back to Dehra in the spring, in time to watch you play Holi with Ranbir. I know you feel like leaving India and running off to England, but wait until you see me again, all right? You are afraid to die without having done something.You are afraid to die, Rusty, but you have hardly begun to live.

I know you are not happy in Dehra, and you must be lonely. But wait a little, be patient, and the bad days will pass.We don't know why we live. It is no use trying to know. But we have to live, Rusty, because we really want to. And as long as we want to, we have got to find something to live for, and even die for it. Mother is keeping well and sends you her greetings. Tell me whatever you need.

Somi

Rusty folded the letter carefully, and put it in his shirt pocket; he meant to keep it for ever. He could not wait for Somi's return; but he knew that their friendship would last a lifetime, and that the beauty of it would always be with him. In and out of Rusty's life, his turban at an angle, Somi would go, his slippers slapping against his heels for ever ...

Rusty had no case or bedding-roll to pack, no belongings at all; only the clothes he wore, which were Somi's, and about fifty rupees, for which he had to thank Kishen. He had made no preparations for the journey; he would slip away without fuss or bother; insignificant, unnoticed ...

An hour before leaving for the station, he lay down to rest. He gazed up at the ceiling, where the lizards scuttled about: callous creatures, unconcerned with his departure: one human was just the same as any other. And the bald maina, hopping on and off the window sill, would continue to fight and lose more feathers; and the crows and the squirrels in the mango tree, they would be missed by Rusty, but they would not miss him. It was true, one human was no different to any other—except to a dog or a human ...

When Rusty left the room, there was activity at the water-tank; clothes were being beaten on the stone, and the ayah's trinkets were jingling away. Rusty couldn't bear to say goodbye to the people at the water-tank, so he didn't close his door, lest they suspect him of leaving. He descended the steps—twenty-two of them, he counted for the last time—and crossed the drain, and walked slowly down the gravel path until he was out of the compound.

He crossed the maidan, where a group of students were playing cricket, whilst another group wrestled; prams were wheeled in and out of the sporting youths; young girls gossiped away the morning. And Rusty remembered his first night on the maidan, when he had been frightened and wet and lonely; and now, though the maidan was crowded, he felt the same loneliness, the same isolation. In the bazaar, he walked with a heavy heart. From the chaat shop came the familiar smell of spices and the crackle of frying fat. And the children bumped him, and the cows blocked the road; and, though he knew they always did these things, it was only now that he noticed them. They all seemed to be holding him, pulling him back.

But he could not return; he was afraid of what lay ahead, he dreaded the unknown, but it was easier to walk forwards than backwards.

The toy-seller made his way through the crowd, children clustering round him, tearing at his pole. Rusty fingered a two-anna piece, and his eye picked out a little plume of red feathers, that seemed to have no useful purpose, and he was determined to buy it.

But before he could make the purchase, someone plucked at his shirt-sleeve.

'*Chotta sahib, chotta sahib*,' said the sweeper boy, Mr Harrison's servant.

Rusty could not mistake the shaved head and the sparkle of white teeth, and wanted to turn away; ignore the sweeper boy, who was linked up with a past that was distant and yet uncomfortably close. But the hand plucked at his sleeve, and Rusty felt ashamed, angry with himself for trying to ignore someone who had never harmed him and who couldn't have been friendlier. Rusty was a sahib no longer, no one was his servant; and he was not an Indian, he had no caste, he could not call another untouchable . . .

'You are not at work?' asked Rusty.

'No work.' The sweeper boy smiled, a flash of white in the darkness of his face.

'What of Mr Harrison, the sahib?'

'Gone.'

'Gone,' said Rusty, and was surprised at not being surprised. 'Where has he gone?'

'Don't know, but he gone for good. Before he go, I get sack. I drop the bathroom-water on veranda, and the sahib, he hit me on the head with his hand, *put*! . . . I say, Sahib you are cruel, and he say cruelty to animals, no? Then he tell me I get sack, he leaving anyway. I lose two days pay.'

Rusty was filled with both relief and uncertainty, and for the same reason; now there could never be a return, whether he wanted to or not, he could never go back to his old home.

'What about the others?' asked Rusty.

'They still there. Missionary's wife a fine lady, she give me five rupees before I go.'

'And you? You are working now?'

Again the sweeper boy flashed his smile. 'No work . . .'

Rusty didn't dare offer the boy any money, though it would probably have been accepted; in the sweeper boy he saw nobility, and he could not belittle nobility.

'I will try to get you work,' he said, forgetting that he was on his way to the station to buy a one-way ticket, and telling the sweeper boy where he lived.

Instinctively, the sweeper boy did not believe him; he nodded his head automatically, but his eyes signified disbelief; and when Rusty left him, he was still nodding, and to nobody in particular.

*

On the station platform the coolies pushed and struggled, shouted incomprehensibly, lifted heavy trunks with apparent ease. Merchants cried their wares, trundling barrows up and down the platform: soda-water, oranges, betel-nut, *halwai* sweets ... The files swarmed around the open stalls, clustered on glass-covered sweet boxes; the mongrel dogs, ownerless and unfed, roved the platform and railway lines, hunting for scraps of food and stealing at every opportunity.

Ignoring Somi's advice, Rusty bought a third-class ticket and found an empty compartment. The guard blew his whistle, but nobody took any notice. People continued about their business, certain that the train wouldn't start for another ten minutes: the Hardwar Mail never did start on time.

Rusty was the only person in the compartment until a fat lady, complaining volubly, oozed in through the door and spread herself across an entire bunk; her plan, it seemed, was to discourage other passengers from coming in. She had beady little eyes, set in a big moon face; and they looked at Rusty in curiosity, darting away whenever they met with his.

Others came in, in quick succession now, for the guard had blown his whistle a second time: a young woman with a baby, a soldier in uniform, a boy of about twelve ... they were all poor people; except for the fat lady, who travelled third class in order to save money.

The guard's whistle blew again, but the train still refused to start. Being the Hardwar Mail, this was but natural; no one ever expected the Hardwar Mail to start on time, for in all its history, it hadn't done so (not even during the time of the British), and for it to do so now would be a blow to tradition. Everyone was for tradition, and so the Hardwar Mail was not permitted to arrive and depart at the appointed hour; though it was feared that one day some young fool would change the appointed hours. And imagine what would happen if the train did leave on time—the entire railway system would be thrown into confusion for, needless to say, every other train took its time from the Hardwar Mail . . .

So the guard kept blowing his whistle, and the vendors put their heads in at the windows, selling oranges and newspapers and soda-water . . .

'Soda-water!' exclaimed the fat lady. 'Who wants soda-water! Why, our farmer here has with him a *sohrai* of pure cool water, and he will share it with us, will he not? Paan-walla! Call the man, quick, he is not even stopping at the window!'

The guard blew his whistle again.

And they were off.

The Hardwar Mail, true to tradition, pulled out of Dehra station half an hour late.

*

Perhaps it was because Rusty was leaving Dehra for ever that he took an unusual interest in everything he saw and heard. Things that would not normally have been noticed by him, now made vivid impressions on his mind: the gesticulations of the coolies as the train drew out of the station, a dog licking a banana skin, a naked child alone amongst a pile of bundles crying its heart out . . .

The platform, fruit-stalls, advertisement boards, all slipped away.

The train gathered speed, the carriages groaned and creaked and rocked crazily. But, as they left the town and the station behind, the wheels found their rhythm, beating time with the rails and singing a song.

It was a sad song, persistent and fatalistic.

Another life was finishing.

One morning, months ago, Rusty had heard a drum in the forest, a single drum-beat, *dhum-tap*; and in the stillness of the morning it had been a call, a message, an irresistible force. He had cut away from his roots: he had been replanted, had sprung to life, new life. But it was too quick a growth, rootless, and he had withered. And now he had run away again. No drum now; instead, the pulsating throb and tremor of the train rushing him away; away from India, from Somi, from the chaat shop and the bazaar; and he did not know why, except that he was lost and lonely and tired and old: nearly seventeen, but old ...

The little boy beside him knelt in front of the window, and counted the telegraph-posts as they flashed by; they seemed, after a while, to be hurtling past whilst the train stood stationary. Only the rocking of the carriage could be felt.

The train sang through the forests, and sometimes the child waved his hand excitedly and pointed out a deer, the sturdy sambar or delicate chital. Monkeys screamed from tree-tops, or loped beside the train, mothers with their young clinging to their breasts. The jungle was heavy, shutting off the sky, and it was like this for half an hour; then the train came into the open, and the sun struck through the carriage windows. They swung through cultivated land, maize and sugar-cane fields; past squat, mud-hut villages, and teams of bullocks ploughing up the soil; leaving behind only a trail of curling smoke.

Children ran out from the villages—brown, naked children—and waved to the train, crying words of greeting; and the little boy in the compartment waved back and shouted merrily, and then turned to look at his travelling companions, his eyes shining with pleasure.

The child began to chatter about this and that, and the others listened to him good-humouredly; the farmer with simplicity and a genuine interest, the fat lady with a tolerant smile, and the soldier with an air of condescension. The young woman and the baby were both asleep. Rusty felt sleepy himself, and was unable to listen to the small boy; vaguely, he thought of Kishen, and of how surprised and pleased Kishen would be to see him.

Presently he fell asleep.

*

When he awoke, the train was nearing Hardwar; he had slept for almost an hour, but to him it seemed like five minutes.

His throat was dry; and, though his shirt was soaked with perspiration, he shivered a little. His hands trembled, and he had to close his fists to stop the trembling.

At midday the train steamed into Hardwar station, and disgorged its passengers.

The fat lady, who was determined to be the first out of the compartment, jammed the doorway; but Rusty and the soldier outwitted her by climbing out of the window.

Rusty felt better once he was outside the station, but he knew he had a fever. The rocking of the train continued, and the song of the wheels and the rails kept beating in his head. He walked slowly away from the station, comforted by the thought that at Kishen's aunt's house there would be food and rest. At night, he would catch the Delhi train.

CHAPTER TWENTY-ONE

THE HOUSE WAS ON top of a hill, and from the road Rusty could see the river below, and the temples, and hundreds of people moving about on the long graceful steps that sloped down to the water: for the river was holy, and Hardwar sacred, a place of pilgrimage.

He knocked on the door, and presently there was the sound of bare feet on a stone floor. The door was opened by a lady, but she was a stranger to Rusty, and they looked at each other with puzzled, questioning eyes.

'Oh . . . namaste ji,' faltered Rusty. 'Does—does Mr Kapoor or his sister live here?'

The lady of the house did not answer immediately. She looked at the boy with a detached interest, trying to guess at his business and intentions. She was dressed simply and well, she had a look of refinement, and Rusty felt sure that her examination of him was no more than natural curiosity.

'Who are you, please?' she asked.

'I am a friend from Dehra. I am leaving India and I want to see Mr Kapoor and his son before I go. Are they here?'

'Only Mr Kapoor is here,' she said.'You can come in.'

Rusty wondered where Kishen and his aunt could be, but he did not want to ask this strange lady; he felt ill at ease in her presence; the house seemed to be hers. Coming straight into the front room from bright sunshine, his eyes took a little time to get used to the dark; but after a moment or two he made out the form of Mr Kapoor, sitting in a cushioned armchair.

'Hullo, Mister Rusty,' said Kapoor. 'It is nice to see you.'

There was a glass of whisky on the table, but Kapoor was not drunk; he was shaved and dressed, and looked a good deal younger than when Rusty had last seen him. But something else was missing. His jovial friendliness, his enthusiasm, had gone. This Kapoor was a different man to the Kapoor of the beard and green dressing-gown.

'Hullo, Mister Kapoor,' said Rusty. 'How are you?'

'I am fine, just fine. Sit down, please. Will you have a drink?'

'No thanks. I came to see you and Kishen before leaving for England. I wanted to see you again, you were very kind to me . . .'

'That's all right, quite all right. I'm very glad to see you, but I'm afraid Kishen isn't here. By the way, the lady who just met you at the door, I haven't introduced you yet—this is my wife, Mister Rusty . . . I—I married again shortly after Meena's death.'

Rusty looked at the new Mrs Kapoor in considerable bewilderment, and greeted her quietly. It was not unusual for a man to marry again soon after his wife's death, and he knew it, but his heart was breaking with a fierce anger. He was revolted by the rapidity of it all; hardly a month had passed, and here was Kapoor with another wife. Rusty remembered that it was for this man Kapoor—this weakling, this drunkard, this self-opinionated, selfish drunkard—that Meena had given her life, all of it, devotedly and unselfishly she had remained by his side when she could have left, when there was no more fight in him and no more love in him and no more pride in him; and, had she left then, she would be alive, and he—*he* would be dead ...

Rusty was not interested in the new Mrs Kapoor. For Kapoor, he had only contempt.

'Mister Rusty is a good friend of the family,' Kapoor was saying. 'In Dehra he was a great help to Kishen.'

'How did Meena die?' asked Rusty, determined to hurt Kapoor—if Kapoor could be hurt ...

'I thought you knew. We had an accident. Let us not talk of it, Mister Rusty ...'

'The driver was driving, of course?'

Kapoor did not answer immediately, but raised his glass and sipped from it.

'Of course,' he said.

'How did it all happen?'

'Please, Mister Rusty, I do not want to describe it. We were going too fast, and the car left the road and hit a tree. I can't describe it, Mister Rusty.'

'No, of course not,' said Rusty. 'Anyway, I am glad nothing happened to you. It is also good that you have mastered your natural grief, and started a new life. I am afraid I am not as strong as you. Meena was wonderful, and I still can't believe she is dead.'

'We have to carry on ....'

'Of course. How is Kishen, I would like to see him.'

'He is in Lucknow with his aunt,' said Kapoor. 'He wished to stay with her.'

Mrs Kapoor had been quiet till now.

'Tell him the truth,' she said. 'There is nothing to hide.'

'You tell him then.'

'What do you mean?'

'He ran away from us. As soon as his aunt left, he ran away. We tried to make him come back, but it was useless, so now we don't try. But he is in Hardwar. We are always hearing about him. They say he is the most cunning thief on both sides of the river.'

'Where can I find him?'

'I don't know. He is wanted by the police. He robs for others, and they pay him. It is easier for a young boy to steal than it is for a man, and as he is quite a genius at it, his services are in demand. And I am sure he would not hesitate to rob us too . . .'

'But you must know where I can find him,' persisted Rusty. 'You must have some idea.'

'He has been seen along the river and in the bazaar. I don't know where he lives. In a tree, perhaps, or in a temple, or in a brothel. He is somewhere in Hardwar, but exactly where I do not know . . . no one knows. He speaks to no one and runs from everyone. What can you want with him?'

'He is my friend,' said Rusty.

'He will rob you too.'

'The money I have is what he gave me.'

He rose to leave; he was tired, but he did not want to stay much longer in this alien house.

'You are tired,' said Mrs Kapoor, 'will you rest, and have your meal with us?'

'No,' said Rusty, 'there isn't time.'

Chapter Twenty-two

❦

ALL HOPE LEFT RUSTY as he staggered down the hill, weak and exhausted. He could not think clearly; he knew he hadn't eaten since morning, and cursed himself for not accepting Mrs Kapoor's hospitality.

He was hungry, he was thirsty; he was tormented by thoughts of what might have happened to Kishen, of what might happen . . .

He stumbled down the long steps that led to the water. The sun was strong, striking up from the stone and shimmering against the great white temple that overlooked the river. He crossed the courtyard and came to the water's edge.

Lying on his belly on the riverbank, he drank of the holy waters. Then he pulled off his shirt and sandals, and slipped into the water. There were men and women on all sides, praying with their faces to the sun. Great fish swam round them, unafraid and unmolested, safe in the sacred waters of the Ganges.

When he had bathed and refreshed himself, Rusty climbed back on to the stone bank. His sandals and shirt had disappeared.

No one was near except a beggar leaning on a stick, a young man massaging his body with oils, and a cow examining an empty, discarded basket; and, of the three, the cow was the most likely suspect; it had probably eaten the sandals.

But Rusty no longer cared what happened to his things. His money was in the leather purse attached to his belt; and, as long as he had the belt, he had both money and pyjamas.

He rolled the wet pyjamas up to his thighs; then, staring ahead with unseeing eyes, ignoring the bowls that were thrust before him by the beggars, he walked the length of the courtyard that ran parallel to the rising steps.

Children were shouting at each other, priests chanting their prayers; vendors, with baskets on their heads—baskets of fruit and chaat—gave harsh cries; and the cows pushed their way around at will. Steps descended from all parts of the hill; broad, clean steps from the temple, and narrow, winding steps from the bazaars; and a maze of alleyways zigzagged about the hill, through the bazaar, round the temples, along the river, and were lost amongst themselves and found again and lost . . .

Kishen, barefooted and ragged and thin, but with the same supreme confidence in himself, leant against the wall of an alleyway, and watched Rusty's progress along the riverbank.

He wanted to shout to Rusty, to go to him, to embrace him, but he could not do these things. He did not understand the reason for his friend's presence, he could not reveal himself for fear of a trap. He was sure it was Rusty he watched, for who else was there with the same coloured hair and skin who would walk half-naked in Hardwar. It was Rusty, but why ... was he in trouble, was he sick? Why, why ...

Rusty saw Kishen in the alleyway. He was too weak to shout. He stood in the sun, and looked up the steps at Kishen standing in the alleyway.

Kishen did not know whether to run to Rusty, or run away. He too stood still, at the entrance of the alley.

'Hullo, Rusty,' he called.

And Rusty began to walk up the steps, slowly and painfully, his feet burning, his head reeling, his heart thundering with conflicting emotions.

'Are you alone?' called Kishen. 'Don't come if you are not alone.'

Rusty advanced up the steps, until he was in the alleyway facing Kishen. Despite the haze before his eyes, he noticed Kishen's wild condition; the bones protruded from the boy's skin, his hair was knotted and straggly, his eyes danced, searching the steps for others.

'Why are you here, Rusty?'

'To see you ...'

'Why?'

'I am going away.'

'How can you go anywhere? You look sick enough to die.'

'I came to see you, anyway.'

'Why?'

Rusty sat down on a step; his wrists hung loose on his knees, and his head drooped forward.

'I'm hungry,' he said.

Kishen walked into the open, and approached a fruit-vendor. He came back with two large watermelons.

'You have money?' asked Rusty.

'No. Just credit. I bring them profits, they give me credit.'

He sat down beside Rusty, produced a small but wicked-looking knife from the folds of his shirt, and proceeded to slice the melons in half.

'You can't go away,' he said.

'I can't go back.'

'Why not?'

'No money, no job, no friends.'

They put their teeth into the watermelon, and ate at terrific speed. Rusty felt much refreshed; he put his weakness and fever down to an empty stomach.

'I'll be no good as a bandit,' said Rusty. 'I can be recognized at sight, I can't go around robbing people, I don't think it's very nice anyway.'

'I don't rob poor people,' objected Kishen, prodding his nose. 'I only rob those who've got something to be robbed. And I don't do it for myself, that's why I'm never caught. People pay me to do their dirty work. Like that, they are safe because they are somewhere else when everything happens, and I am safe because I don't have what I rob, and haven't got a reason for taking it anyway . . . so it is quite safe. But don't worry, bhai, we will not do it in Dehra, we are too well-known there. Besides, I am tired of running from the police.'

'Then what will we do?'

'Oh we will find someone for you to give English lessons. Not one, but many. And I will start a chaat shop.'

'When do we go?' said Rusty; and England and fame and riches were all forgotten, and would soon be dreams again.

'Tomorrow morning, early,' said Kishen. 'There is a boat crossing the river. We must cross the river, on this side I am known, and there are many people who would not like me to leave. If we went by train, I would be caught at the station, for sure. On the other side no one knows me, there is only jungle.'

Rusty was amazed at how competent and practical Kishen had become; Kishen's mind had developed far quicker than his body, and he was a funny cross between an experienced adventurer and a ragged urchin. A month ago he had clung to Rusty for protection; now Rusty looked to Kishen for guidance.

I wonder, thought Rusty, will they notice my absence in Dehra? After all, I have only been away a day, though it seems an age ... The room on the roof will still be vacant when I return, no one but me could be crazy enough to live in such a room ... I will go back to the room as though nothing had happened, and no one will notice that anything has.

*

The afternoon ripened into evening.

As the sun sank, the temple changed from white to gold, from gold to orange, from orange to pink, and from pink to crimson, and all these colours were in turn reflected in the surrounding waters.

The noise subsided gradually, the night came on.

Kishen and Rusty slept in the open, on the temple steps. It was a warm night, the air was close and heavy. In the shadows lay small bundles of humanity, the roofless and the homeless, sleeping only to pass the time of night. Rusty slept in spasms, waking frequently with a nagging pain in his stomach; poor stomach, it couldn't stand the unfamiliar strain of emptiness.

CHAPTER TWENTY-THREE

BEFORE THE STEPS AND the riverbank came to life, Kishen and Rusty climbed into the ferry-boat. It would be crossing the river all day, carrying pilgrims from temple to temple, charging nothing. And though it was very early, and this the first crossing, a free passage across the river made for a crowded boat.

The people who climbed in were even more diverse than those Rusty had met on the train: women and children, bearded old men and wrinkled women, strong young peasants—not the prosperous or mercantile class, but the poor—who had come miles, mostly on foot, to bathe in the sacred waters of the Ganges, Ganga-Mai to Hindus.

On shore, the steps began to come to life. The previous day's cries and prayers and rites were resumed with the same monotonous devotion, at the same pitch, in the same spirit of timelessness; and the steps sounded to the tread of many feet, sandalled, slippered and bare.

The boat floated low in the water, it was so heavy, and the oarsmen had to strain upstream in order to avoid being swept down by the current. Their muscles shone and rippled under the grey iron of their weather-beaten skins. The blades of the oars cut through the water, in and out; and between grunts, the oarsmen shouted the time of the stroke.

Kishen and Rusty sat crushed together in the middle of the boat. There was no likelihood of their being separated now, but they held hands.

The people in the boat began to sing.

It was a low hum at first, but someone broke in with a song, and the voice—a young voice, clear and pure—reminded Rusty of Somi; and he comforted himself with the thought that Somi would be back in Dehra in the spring.

They sang in time to the stroke of the oars, in and out, and the grunts and shouts of the oarsmen throbbed their way into the song, becoming part of it.

An old woman, who had white hair and a face lined with deepruts, said, 'It is beautiful to hear the children sing.'

'Then you too should sing,' said Rusty.

She smiled at him, a sweet, toothless smile.

'What are you my son, are you one of us? I have never, on this river, seen blue eyes and golden hair.'

'I am nothing,' said Rusty.'I am everything.'

He stated it bluntly, proudly.

'Where is your home, then?'

'I have no home,' he said, and felt proud of that too.

'And who is the boy with you?' asked the old woman, a genuine busybody. 'What is he to you?'

Rusty did not answer; he was asking himself the same question: what was Kishen to him? He was sure of one thing, they were both refugees—refugees from the world . . . They were each other's shelter, each other's refuge, each other's help. Kishen was a jungli, divorced from the rest of mankind, and Rusty was the only one who understood him—because Rusty too was divorced from mankind. And theirs was a tie that would hold, because they were the only people who knew each other and loved each other.

Because of this tie, Rusty had to go back. And it was with relief that he went back. His return was justified.

He let his hand trail over the side of the boat: he wanted to remember the touch of the water as it moved past them, down and away: it would come to the ocean, the ocean that was life.

He could not run away. He could not escape the life he had made, the ocean into which he had floundered the night he left his guardian's house. He had to return to the room; *his* room; he had to go back.

The song died away as the boat came ashore. They disembarked, walking over the smooth pebbles; and the forest rose from the edge of the river, and beckoned them.

Rusty remembered the forest on the day of the picnic, when he had kissed Meena and held her hands, and he remembered the magic of the forest and the magic of Meena.

'One day,' he said, 'we must live in the jungle.'

'One day,' said Kishen, and he laughed. 'But now we walk back. We walk back to the roomon the roof! It is our room, we have to go back!'

They had to go back: to bathe at the water-tank and listen to the morning gossip, to sit in the fruit trees and eat in the chaat shop and perhaps make a garden on the roof; to eat and sleep; to work; to live; to die.

Kishen laughed.

'One day you'll be great, Rusty. A writer or an actor or a prime minister or something. Maybe a poet! Why not a poet, Rusty?'

Rusty smiled. He knew he was smiling, because he was smiling at himself.

'Yes,' he said,'why not a poet?'

So they began to walk.

Ahead of them lay forest and silence—and what was left of time . . .

VAGRANTS IN THE VALLEY

The Homeless

❦

On the road to Dehra a boy played on a flute as he drove his flock of sheep down the road. He was barefooted and his clothes were old. A faded red shawl was thrown across his shoulders. It was December and the sun was up, pouring into the banyan tree at the side of the road, where two boys were sitting on the great tree's gnarled, protruding roots.

The flute-player passed the banyan tree and glanced at the boys, but did not stop playing. Presently he was only a speck on the dusty road, and the flute music was thin and distant, subdued by the tinkle of sheep-bells.

The boys left the shelter of the banyan tree and began walking in the direction of the distant hills.

The road stretched ahead, lonely and endless, towards the low ranges of the Siwalik hills. The dust was in their clothes and in their eyes and in their mouths. The sun rose higher in the sky; and, as they walked, the sweat trickled down their armpits, and down their legs.

The older boy, Rusty, was seventeen. He walked with his hands in the pockets of his thin cotton trousers, and he gazed at the ground. His fair hair was matted with dust, and his cheeks and arms were scorched red by the fierce sun. His eyes were blue and thoughtful.

'We will be in Raiwala soon,' he said. 'Would you like to rest, bhaiya?'

Kishen shrugged his thin shoulders. 'We'll rest when we get to Raiwala. If I sit down now, I'll never be able to get up. I suppose we have walked about ten miles this morning.'

117

He was a slim boy, almost as tall as Rusty though he was two years younger. He had dark, rebellious eyes, and bushy eyebrows and thick black hair. His dusty white pyjamas were rolled up above his ankles, and he wore loose Peshawari chappals. An unbuttoned khaki shirt hung outside his pyjamas.

Like Rusty, he was without a home. Rusty had run away from an indifferent guardian a little over a year ago. Kishen had run away from a drunken father. He possessed distant relatives, but he preferred the risks and pleasures of vagrancy to the security of living with people he did not know. He had been with Rusty for a year, and his home was by his friend's side. He was Punjabi; Rusty was Anglo-Indian.

'From Raiwala we'll take the train,' said Rusty. 'It will cost us about five rupees.'

'Never mind,' said Kishen. 'We've done enough walking. And we've still got twelve rupees. Is there anything in our old rooms in Dehra that we can sell?'

'Let me see ... The table, the bed and the chair are not mine. There's an old tiger-skin, a bit eaten by rats, which no one will buy. There are one or two shirts and trousers.'

'Which we will need. These are all torn.'

'And some of my books ...'

'Which no one will buy.'

'I would not sell them. Well, those were the only things I got out of my guardian's house, before I ran away.'

'Somi!' interrupted Kishen. 'Somi will be in Dehra—he'll help us! He got you a job once, he can do it again.'

Rusty was silent, remembering his friend Somi, who had won him with a smile, and altered the course of his life. Somi, with his turban at an angle, a song on his lips ...

Kishen had left Dehra in a hurry and had been taken to Hardwar, a town on the banks of the sacred Ganges, by his aunt, and Rusty had followed him and his aunt. Only priests, beggars and shopkeepers could make a living in Hardwar, and the boys were soon back on the road to Dehra.

Now a cool breeze came across the plain, blowing down from

the hills. In the fields there was a gentle swaying movement as the wind stirred the wheat. Then the breeze hit the road, and the dust began to swirl and eddy about the footpath. The boys moved into the middle of the road, holding their hands to their eyes, and stumbling forward. Out of the dust behind them came the rumbling of bullock-cart wheels.

'Ho, there, out of my way!' shouted the driver of the cart. The bullocks snorted and came lumbering through the dust. The boys moved to the side of the road.

'Are you going to Raiwala?' called Rusty. 'Can you take us with you?'

'Climb up!' said the man, and the boys ran through the dust, and clambered on to the back of the moving cart.

The cart lurched and rattled and bumped, and they had to cling to its sides to avoid falling off. It smelt of dry grass and cow-dung cakes. The driver had a red cloth tied around his head, and wore a tight vest, and a dhoti around his waist. His feet and legs were bare, scorched black by the burning sun over the plains. He was smoking a bidi and shouting to his bullocks, cursing them at times, but sometimes speaking to them in endearing terms. He seemed to have forgotten the presence of the boys at the back, had dismissed them from his mind the moment they had climbed up. Rusty and Kishen were too busy clinging to the lopsided cart to bother about making conversation with the driver.

'I'd rather walk,' complained Kishen. 'Rusty, who suggested that we get into this silly old contraption? I am full of bumps and bruises already.'

'Beggars can't be choosers,' said Rusty.

'Please, we are not beggars—not yet, anyway ... And if we were, we'd be much better off financially, I can assure you! As far as the rest of the world is concerned, you are still the son of an English sahib, and I am still the distant relative of a distant maharaja.'

'A prince,' said Rusty derisively, 'and riding in a bullock-cart!'

'Well, not every prince can boast of the experience.'

A little later the bullock-cart rumbled across a canal and became involved in the traffic of Raiwala, a busy little market town. The boys jumped off and walked beside the cart.

'Should we give him something?' asked Rusty. 'We ought to offer him some money.'

'How can we?' said Kishen. 'Why didn't you think of that before we jumped on?'

'All right, we'll just thank him. Thank you, bhaiji!' he called, as the cart moved off. 'Thank you, bhaiji!' shouted Kishen.

But either the driver did not hear or did not bother to look around; he continued smoking his bidi and talking to his animals; and to all appearances had not even noticed that the boys had got down. He drove his bullock-cart away, leaving Rusty and Kishen standing on the road.

'I'm hungry,' said Kishen. 'We haven't eaten since last night.'

'Then we must eat,' said Rusty. 'Come on, bhaiya, we will eat.'

They walked through the narrow Raiwala bazaar, looking in at the tea and sweet shops, until they found a place that looked dirty enough to be cheap. A servant-boy brought them chappatis and dal and Kishen ordered an ounce of butter; this was melted and poured over the dal. The meal cost them a rupee, and for this amount they could eat as much as they liked. The butter was an extra, and cost six annas. They were left with a little over ten rupees.

When they came out, the sun was low in the sky and the day was cooler.

'We can't walk tonight,' said Rusty. 'We'll have to sleep at the railway station. Maybe we can get on the train without a ticket.'

'And if we are caught, we'll spend a month in jail. Free board and lodging.'

'And then the social workers will get you, or they'll put you in a remand home and teach you to make mattresses.'

'I think it's better to buy tickets,' said Kishen.

'I know what we'll do,' said Rusty. 'We won't get the train till past midnight, so let's not buy tickets. We'll get to Harrawala early in the morning. Then it's only about eight miles by road to Dehra.'

Kishen agreed, and they found their way to the railway station, where they made themselves comfortable in a first class waiting-room.

'We don't have tickets,' said Kishen.

'But *we* are first class, aren't we?'

Kishen settled down in an armchair and covered his face with a handkerchief. 'Wake me when the train comes in,' he said drowsily.

Rusty went into the bathroom. He put his head under a tap and allowed cold water to play over his neck. He washed his face, drying it with a handkerchief, before returning to the waiting-room.

A man entered, setting out his belongings on the big table in the centre of the room. Rusty judged him to be in his thirties. The man was white, but he was too restless to be a European. He looked virile, but tired; he had a lean, sallow face, and pouches under the eyes. Rusty sat down on the edge of Kishen's armchair.

'Going to Delhi?' asked the stranger. His accent, though not very pronounced, was American.

'No, the other way,' replied Rusty. 'We live in Dehra.'

'I've often been there,' said the man. 'I've been trying to popularize a new steel plough in northern India, but without much success. Are you a student?'

'Not now. I finished with school two years ago.'

'And your friend?' He inclined his head towards the sleeping boy.

'He's with me,' said Rusty vaguely. 'We're travelling together.'

'Buddies.'

'Yes.'

The American took a flask from his bag and looked inquiringly at Rusty. 'Will you join me in a drink while we're waiting? There's almost an hour left for my train to arrive.'

'Well, I don't drink,' said Rusty, hesitating.

'A small one won't harm you. Just to keep me company.'

He took two small glasses from his bag, wiped them with a clean white handkerchief, and set them down on the table. Then he poured some dark brown stuff from his flask.

'Brandy,' said Rusty, sniffing.

'So you recognize it. Yes, it's brandy.'

Rusty reached across the table and took the glass.

'Here's luck!' said the stranger.

'Thank you,' said Rusty, and gulped down a mouthful of neat liquor. He coughed and the tears came to his eyes. He put his head between his hands, but he was feeling better.

'You've come a long way,' said the American looking at the boy's clothes.

'On foot,' said Rusty. 'From Hardwar. Since morning.'

Rusty emptied his glass and set it down. The friendly stranger poured out more brandy. This is the way they do things in America, thought Rusty. When you meet a stranger, offer him a drink. He must go there one day.

'What made you walk?' asked the stranger again.

'Tomorrow we'll walk some more,' said Rusty.

'But why?'

'Because we have the time. We have all the time in the world.'

'How come?'

'Because we have no money. You can't have both time and money.'

'Oh, I agree. You are quite a philosopher. But what happened?' asked the American, looking at the sleeping boy. 'What is he to you?'

'He's with me,' said Rusty, ignoring the question. He was beginning to feel sleepy. The friendly stranger seemed to be getting further and further away and his voice came from a great distance.

'Tell me what happened.'

'I'll tell you,' said Rusty, leaning unsteadily across the table to see the other better, and speaking slowly. 'I ran away from home, nearly a year ago. I had a guardian, an Englishman—my parents died when I was very small—and I lived in his house, in his own community, and it was a world of our own and I never went outside it. Then one day in the rain I met Somi. I became his friend and he took me to his home, and to the bazaar, and he showed me India and the world and life itself. My guardian beat me when I came back from the bazaar, and he beat me when I played Holi and came home drenched in colour. I returned the beating, though, and ran away.'

Rusty paused in order to finish the drink and to see if the man was interested.

'Go on,' said the stranger.

'Somi was my good friend, he did a lot for me. He found a boy—Kishen over there—who needed English lessons, and his family took a liking to me and gave me a place to stay. She spent time with me often—I mean the boy's mother—Kishen's mother—and she was sweet and kind to me. She was beautiful. There will never be a woman as beautiful . . .'

He lapsed into silence for about a minute, gazed into the glass as though he sought something there other than brandy, and continued: 'But then they went away. Somi went away, everyone went away. What could I do, but go away too? What could I do, when Kishen's mother died, but go away? And if it wasn't for Kishen, I would never have come back. I tell you that straight, sir—I would never have come back. I wouldn't be here now, talking to you, if it wasn't for Kishen.

'But I didn't know Kishen was alone. He had run away from his father, who was too drunk to care, and he had been living on his wits for weeks—he is good at that. But when I found him, I had to come back, we both had to come back. We have only got each other, you see.'

'I follow you a little,' said the stranger, and he filled Rusty's glass again. 'What are you going to do in Dehra, both of you? Do you have jobs to go to? I guess not. Well, if ever you find yourself in Delhi, look me up. Here's my card.'

A bell clanged on the station platform, and the stranger looked at his watch and said it was almost time for his train to arrive. He wiped the glasses with his handkerchief and returned them to his bag, then went outside and stood on the platform, waiting for the Delhi train.

Rusty leant against the waiting-room door, staring across the railway tracks. He heard the shriek of the whistle as the front light of an engine played over the rails. The train came in slowly, the hissing engine sending out waves of steam. At the same time the carriage doors opened and people started pouring out.

There was a jam on the platform, while men, women and children pushed and struggled, and it was several minutes before anyone could get in or out of the carriage doors. The American had been swallowed up by the crowd. Bundles of belongings were passed through windows, over the heads of bystanders. Several young men climbed in at the windows, heads first, assisted by pushes from behind. Rusty assumed that there was another religious fair at Hardwar, for the rush was even greater than usual.

When the train had gone, a calm descended on the platform. A few people waiting for the morning train to Dehra still slept near their bundles. Vendors selling soda-water, lemons and curds, cups of tea, pushed their barrows down the platform, still calling their wares in desultory, sleepy voices. A baby cried, and the mother took the child to her bosom, but the baby kept on crying.

Rusty returned to the waiting-room. Kishen was still sound asleep in the armchair.

Rusty went to the light switch and turned it off, but the light from the platform streamed in through the gauze-covered doors. He did not think anyone would be coming in again that night. He sat down beside Kishen.

'Kishen, Kishen,' he whispered, touching the boy's shoulder.

Kishen stirred. 'What is it?' he mumbled drowsily. 'Why is it dark?'

'I put the light off,' said Rusty. 'You can sleep now.'

'I *was* sleeping,' said Kishen. 'But thank you all the same.'

THE FOREST ROAD

AT DOIWALA NEXT MORNING they had to leave the train. An inspector came round checking tickets, and Rusty and Kishen slipped out of the carriage from the side facing the jungle.

Doiwala stood just outside the Siwalik range, and already the field were giving way to jungle. But there were maize-fields stretching away from the bottom of the railway banking, and the boys went in amongst the corn and waited in the field until the train had left. Kishen broke three or four corn-cobs from their stalks, stuffing them into his pockets.

'We might not get anything else to eat,' he said. 'Rusty, have you got matches so that we can light a fire and roast the corn?'

'We'll get some at the station.'

At Doiwala station they bought a box of matches, but they did not roast the corn until they had walked two miles up the road, into the jungle. Kishen collected dry twigs, and when they sat down at the side of the road he made a small fire. Kishen turned the corn-cobs over the fire until they were roasted a dark brown, burnt black in places. They dug their teeth into them, eating with relish.

'I wish we had some salt,' said Kishen.

'That would only make us thirsty, and we have no water. I hope we find a spring soon.'

'How far is Dehra now?' asked Kishen.

'About twelve miles, I think. It's funny how some miles seem longer than others. It depends on what you are thinking about, I suppose. What *you* are thinking and what I am thinking. If our thoughts agree, the miles are not so long. We get on better when we are thinking together than when we are talking together!'

'All right then, stop talking.'

When they had finished eating they threw away the corn-cobs and began walking. They walked in silence; they had grown used to speaking only when they stopped to rest.

Rusty was thinking: I don't know how, but when we get to Dehra I've got to make a living for both of us. Kishen is too young to look after himself. He'll only get into trouble. I would not like to leave him alone even for a little while. Maybe I can get an English tuition. Or if I can write a story, a really good story, and sell it to a magazine, perhaps an American magazine ...

And Kishen was thinking: We will get money somehow. There are many ways of getting money. I don't mind anything as long as I am not alone.

Suddenly they heard the sound of rushing water. The road emerged from the jungle of sal trees and ended beside a river. There was a swift stream in the middle of the river-bed, coursing down towards the Ganges. A bridge had crossed this once, but it had been swept away during heavy monsoon rains, and the road ended at the riverbank.

They walked over sand and sharp rocks until they reached the water's edge, and they stood looking at the frothy water as it swirled below them.

'It's not deep,' said Kishen. 'I don't think it's above the waist anywhere.'

'It's not deep, but it's swift,' said Rusty. 'And the stones are slippery.'

'Shall we go back?'

'No, let's carry on—if it's too fast, we can turn back.'

They removed their shoes, tying them together by the laces, and hanging them about their necks, then holding hands for security, they stepped into the water.

The stones were slippery underfoot, and the boys stumbled, hindering rather than helping each other. When they were half-way across, the water was up to their waists. They stopped in midstream, unwilling to go further for fear they would be swept off their feet.

'I can hardly stand,' said Kishen. 'It will be difficult to swim against the current.'

'It won't get deeper now,' said Rusty hopefully.

Just then, Kishen slipped and went over backwards into the

water, bringing Rusty down on top of him. Kishen began kicking and threshing about, but eventually—by gripping on to Rusty's right foot—came spluttering out of the water.

When they found they were not being swept away by the current they stopped struggling and cautiously dragged themselves across to the opposite bank. They came out of the water about thirty yards downstream.

The sun beat down on them, as they lay exhausted on the warm sand. Kishen sucked at a cut in his hand, spitting the blood into the stream with a contemptuous gesture.

After some time they were walking again, though Kishen kept on bringing up mouthfuls of water.

'I'm getting hungry now,' he said, when he had emptied himself of water.

'We'll be in Dehra soon,' said Rusty. 'And then never mind the money, we'll eat like pigs.'

'Gourmets!' put in Kishen. 'I suppose there are still eight or ten miles left. Now I'm not even thinking. Are you?'

'I was thinking we should visit that river again one day, when we have plenty of food and nothing to worry about.'

'You won't get me coming here again,' said Kishen.

They shuffled along the forest path, tired and hungry, but quite cheerful. Then they rounded a bend and found themselves face to face with a tiger.

Well, not quite face to face. The tiger was about fifteen yards away from them, occupying the centre of the path. He was as surprised to see the boys as the boys were to see him. He lifted his head, and his tail swished from side to side, but he made no move towards them. The boys stood absolutely still in the middle of the path. They were too astonished to do anything else, which was just as well, because, had they run or shouted or shown fear, the tiger might well have been provoked into attacking them. And, after a moment's hesitation, he crossed the path and disappeared into the forest without so much as a growl.

Still the boys did not move, but they found their voices.

'You didn't tell me there were tigers here,' said Kishen in a hoarse whisper.

'I didn't think about it,' said Rusty.

'Shall we go forwards or backwards?'

'Do you want to cross the stream again? Anyway, the tiger didn't seem to worry about us. Let's go on.'

And they walked on through the forest without seeing the tiger again, though they saw several splendid peacocks and a band of monkeys. It was not until they had left the forest behind and were on an open road with fields and villages on either side that they relaxed and showed their relief by bursting into laughter.

'I think we frightened that tiger more than it frightened us,' said Kishen. 'Why, it didn't even roar!'

'And a good thing it didn't, otherwise we might not have been here.'

They laughed at themselves, and when they laughed they were happy.

Rusty felt more at ease with Kishen than he did with anyone else—probably because Kishen had been one of his first friends, because they had grown swiftly together from childhood into adolescence. Rusty had never been at ease with anyone until he had met Somi and Kishen. His mother had died when he was very young, and his father had not lived much longer. His mother was a shadowy figure, and though he remembered her, she seemed, in his mind, to have less substance than his father. He had hated his guardian, who had looked after him when his father died.

Those early years had been very English, and the only Indians he had known were the servants. When he was five, very proud, he had informed the cook that England was ten times as large as India, and the cook had believed him.

As he grew older, the forbidden India—the real India of bazaars and temples and sprawling villages—was discovered in bits and pieces; it was only when Rusty made Indian friends for the first time that he discovered it completely. His guardian had not liked his friends or his visits to the bazaars, and they had quarrelled, and Rusty had run away, living for a year with Kishen's family.

At first everything had been different; physically different—wearing Indian clothes, eating Indian food, bathing Indian fashion—and then different in another, more subtle way, which had him thinking differently too. For though he was old enough to have already absorbed certain Western values, he was young enough and flexible enough to be able to adapt himself to his new and unfamiliar environment, and to absorb something of Indian values. He was not conscious of any division of loyalties in himself, but rather of a double inheritance.

For one year he had led an almost idyllic life; he had loved, almost worshipped, Kishen's mother, Meena—loved her with all the mute and helpless fervour of a sixteen-year-old—and she had loved him too, but only as a woman loves a homeless child. Then Meena was killed in a car accident, and Kishen's father returned to his whisky bottle and took another wife. Rusty had been on his way to Delhi, to try and leave India, when he had met Kishen in Hardwar.

And together they were returning to Dehra which was their home.

*

The danger they had shared helped to revive their drooping spirits, and they grew light-hearted as they walked into the fertile valley that lay between the Siwaliks and the Himalayan foothills. Spreading over the valley were wheat and maize and sugar-cane fields, tea-gardens and orchards of guava, litchi and mango.

There was a small village on the outskirts of Dehra, and the village lamps were lit when the boys, dusty and dishevelled, walked through with dragging feet. Now that their journey was almost over, they became more aware of their weariness and their aches, and the town which had been their home seemed suddenly strange and heartless, as though it did not recognize them any more.

A Place to Sleep

❦

WHEN THEY GOT TO the Tandoori Fish Shop, Kishen and Rusty were too hungry and tired to think of going any further, so they sat down and ordered a meal. The fish came hot, surrounded by salad and lemon, and when they had finished it, they ate again, fish and salad and lemon, and drank glasses of hot, spiced tea.

'The best thing in life is food,' said Kishen. 'There is nothing to equal it.'

'I agree,' said Rusty. 'Bhaiya, you are absolutely right.'

Afterwards, they walked through the noisy, crowded bazaar, which they knew so well; past the Clock Tower, up the steps of their old room. They were ready to flop down on the string cot and sleep for a week. But when they reached the top of the steps they found the door locked. It was not their lock, but a heavy, unfamiliar padlock, and its presence was ominous.

'Let's smash it!' said Kishen.

'That's no use,' said Rusty. 'The landlord doesn't want us to have the room. He's shut us out at the first opportunity. Well, let's go and see his agent. Perhaps he'll let us have the room back. Anyway, our things are inside.'

Rusty stood at the top of the steps, looking thoughtfully at the grounds—the gravel path, the litchi and mango trees, the grass badminton court, now overgrown with weeds—and half-expected to hear Kishen's mother calling to him from below, calling to him to come and play, while the father, in his green dressing-gown, sat on the steps clutching a bottle. They had gone now, and would never come back. Rusty was not sure that he wanted to stay in the old room.

'Would you like to wait here while I get the key?' he asked.

'No,' said Kishen. 'I'd be afraid to wait here alone.'

'Why?'

'Because,' he looked to Rusty for understanding, 'because this was our house once, and my mother and father lived here, and

I'm afraid of the house when they are no longer in it. I'll come with you. I'd like to break the *munshi*'s neck, anyway.'

The *munshi* met them at the door of his house. He was a slow, bent and elderly man, dressed in a black coat and white dhoti; a pair of vintage spectacles balanced precariously on his nose. He was in the service of the *seth*, who owned a great deal of property in town; and his duties included the collection of rents, eviction of tenants—this had become increasingly difficult—and seeing to the repair and maintenance of the *seth*'s property.

'Your room has been rented out,' explained the *munshi*.

'What do you mean, mister?' said Kishen, bristling.

'Why has it been rented when we haven't given it up?' asked Rusty.

'You were never a tenant,' said the *munshi*, with a shrug that almost unsettled his spectacles. 'Mr Kapoor let you use one of the rooms. Now he has vacated the house. When you went away, I thought you had gone permanently.' The *munshi* made a helpless gesture with his hands, and anticipated the imminent fall of his spectacles by taking them off and wiping them on his shirt.

Finally he said: '*Sethji* ordered me to let the room immediately.'

'But how could I have gone permanently,' argued Rusty, 'when my things are still in the room?'

The *munshi* scratched his head. 'There were not many things, I thought you had no need for them. I thought you were going to England. You can have your things tomorrow. They are in the storeroom, and the key is with the *seth*. But I cannot let you have the room again.'

Uncertain as to what he should do next, Rusty continued to stand in the light thrown from the *munshi*'s front room. Kishen stepped forward.

'Give us another room, then,' he said belligerently.

'I cannot do that now,' said the *munshi*. 'It is too late. You will have to come tomorrow, and even then I cannot promise you anything. All our rooms are full. Just now I cannot help you. There must be some place where you can stay ...'

'We'll find a place,' said Rusty, tired of the whole business. 'Come on, bhaiya. There's always the railway platform.'

Kishen hesitated, scowling at the *munshi*, before following Rusty out of the gate.

'What now?' he grumbled. 'Where do we go now?'

They stood uncertainly in the middle of the road.

'Let's sit down somewhere,' suggested Rusty. 'Then we can think of something. We can't come to a decision simply by standing stupidly on the road.'

'We'll sit in the tea-shop,' said Kishen. 'We've had enough tea, but let's go there anyway.'

They found the tea-shop at the end of the bazaar, a make-shift wooden affair built over a gully. There were only two tables in the shop, and most of the customers sat outside on a bench, where they could listen to the shopkeeper, a popular storyteller.

Sitting on the ground in front of the shop was a thick-set youth with his head shaved, wearing rags. He was dumb—they called him the Goonga—and the customers often made sport of him, abusing him good-naturedly, and clouting him over the head from time to time. The Goonga did not mind this; he made faces at the others, and chuckled derisively at their remarks. He could say only one word, 'Goo' and he said it often. This kept the customers in fits of laughter.

'Goo!' he said, when he saw Kishen and Rusty enter the shop. He pointed at the boys, chuckled, and said 'Goo!' again. Everyone laughed. Someone got up from the bench and, with the flat of this hand, whacked the Goonga over his naked head. The Goonga sprang at the man, making queer, gurgling noises. Someone tripped him and sent him sprawling on the ground, and there was more laughter.

Rusty and Kishen sat at an inside table. Everyone, except the Goonga, was drinking tea.

'Give the Goonga a glass of tea,' said Kishen to the shopkeeper.

The shopkeeper grinned and made the tea. The Goonga looked at Kishen and Rusty and said, 'Goo!'

'Now how much money is left?' asked Kishen, getting down to business.

'About nine rupees,' said Rusty. 'If we are careful, it will last us a few days.'

'More than a week,' said Kishen. 'We can get enough food for a rupee a day, as long as we don't start eating chicken. But you should find some work in a day or two.'

'Don't be too optimistic about that.'

'Well, it's no use worrying as yet.'

There was an interesting story being told by the shopkeeper, about a jinn who used his abnormally long reach to steal sweets, and the boys forgot about their 'conference' until the story was finished.

'Now it's someone else's turn,' said the shopkeeper.

'The fair boy will tell us one,' said a voice, and everyone turned to look at Rusty.

The person who had made the request was one of the boys who served tea to the customers. He could not have been more than twelve years old, but he had a worldly look about him, in spite of the dimples in his cheeks and the mischievous glint in his eyes. His fair complexion and high cheekbones showed that he came from the hills, from one of the border districts.

'I don't know any stories,' said Rusty.

'That isn't possible,' said the shopkeeper. 'Everyone knows at least one story, even if it is his own.'

'Yes, tell us,' said the hill boy.

'You find us a room for the night,' said Kishen, always ready to bargain in true Punjabi fashion, 'and he'll tell you a story.'

'I don't know of any place,' said the shopkeeper, 'but you are welcome to sleep in my shop. You won't sleep much, because there are people coming and going all night, especially the truck drivers.'

'Don't worry,' said the hill boy. 'I know of many places where you can stay. Now tell us the story.'

So Rusty embarked on a ghost story which held his audience enthralled.

'All right, now tell us,' said Rusty, after his story was over, 'where are we going to sleep tonight? You can't get a hotel room for less than two rupees.'

'It's not too cold,' said Kishen. 'We can sleep on the maidan. There's shelter there.'

Rusty gave a sigh of resignation, and thought: A year ago when I ran away I slept on the maidan, and again I am going to sleep on the maidan. That's called 'Progress'.

He said, 'The last time I slept on the maidan, it rained. I woke up in a pool of mud.'

'But it won't rain today,' said Kishen cheerfully. 'There isn't a cloud in the sky.'

They looked out at the night sky. The moon was almost at the full, robbing the stars of their glory.

*

They left the shop and began walking towards the open grassland of the maidan. The bazaar was almost empty now, the shops closed, lights showing only from upper windows. Rusty became conscious of the sound of soft footfalls behind him, and looking over his shoulder, saw that they were being followed by the Goonga.

'Goo,' said the Goonga, on being noticed.

'Damn!' said Kishen. 'Why did we have to give him tea? He probably thinks we are rich and won't let us out of sight again.'

'He can do no harm,' said Rusty, though he quickened his step. 'He'll change his mind about us when he finds we're sleeping on the maidan.'

'Goo,' said the Goonga from behind, quickening his step.

They turned abruptly down an alleyway, trying to shake the Goonga off, but he padded after them, chuckling ghoulishly to himself. They cut back to the main road, but he was behind them at the Clock Tower.

At the edge of the maidan Rusty turned and said: 'Go away, Goonga. We've got no money, no food, no clothes. We are no better off than you. Go away!'

'Yes, buzz off!' said Kishen, a master of Indo-Anglian slang.

But the youth said, 'Goo!' and took a step forward, and his

shaved head glistened in the moonlight. Rusty shrugged, and led Kishen on to the maidan. The Goonga stood at the edge, shaking his head and chuckling. His dry black skin showed through his rags, and his feet were covered with mud. He watched the boys as they walked across the grass, watched them until they lay down; and then he shrugged his shoulders, and said, 'Goo', and went away.

THE OLD CHURCH

❦

'LET'S LEAVE OUR THINGS with the *munshi*,' said Rusty, yawning and stretching his limbs. 'It's no use collecting them until we have somewhere to stay. But I *would* like to change my clothes.'

It had been cold on the maidan until the sun threw its first pink glow over the hills. On the grass lay yesterday's remnants— a damp newspaper, a broken toy, a kite hanging helpessly from the branches of a tree. The boys were sitting on the dew-sodden grass, waiting for the sun to seep through to their skin and drive the chill from their bones. They had not slept much, and their eyes were ringed and heavy. Rusty's hair looked like a small, untidy stack of hay. Kishen's legs were swollen with mosquito bites.

'Why is it that you haven't been bitten as much as I have?' complained Kishen.

'No doubt you taste better,' said Rusty. 'We had better split up now, I suppose.'

'But why?'

'We will get more done that way. You go to the *munshi* and see if you can persuade him to let us have another room. But don't pay anything in advance! Meanwhile, I'll call at the schools to see if I can get any English tuitions.'

'All right, Rusty. Where do we meet?'

'At the Clock Tower. At about twelve o'clock.'

'Then we can eat,' said Kishen with enthusiasm.

Rusty smiled. He had not smiled so brightly for a long time; and seeing the smile on Rusty's face, Kishen felt sure everything would come out all right.

'Eating is something we always agree upon,' said Rusty.

They washed their faces at the public tap at the edge of the maidan, where the wrestlers were usually to be found. The wrestlers had not assembled that morning, and the pit was empty, otherwise Rusty might have encountered a friend of his, called Hathi, who often came there to wrestle and use the weights. Scrubbing his back and shoulders at the tap, he realized that he needed a haircut and, worse still, a shave.

'I will have to get a shave,' he said ruefully. 'You're lucky to have only a little fluff on your cheeks so far. I have to shave at least once a week, do you know that?'

'How extravagant!' exclaimed Kishen. 'Can't you grow a beard? A shave will cost four annas.'

'Nobody will give me a tuition if they see this growth on my face.'

'Oh, all right,' grumbled Kishen, stroking the faint beginning of a moustache. 'You take four annas and have your shave, but I will keep the rest of the money with me in case I have to give the *munshi* something. It will be all right to let him have a rupee or two in advance, if he can give us a room.'

He left Rusty at the tap and went straight to the *munshi*'s house, but he had no luck there. The *munshi* asked for an advance of fifteen rupees before he would rent them a room. He was polite but firm: he was only the *seth*'s servant, he insisted, and he had to carry out orders. Kishen made a few insulting remarks about the *seth* before leaving.

Disgruntled, but far from depressed (it was not in his nature to be easily depressed), Kishen sauntered off into the alleyways behind the bazaar. There were two hours ahead of him before he could meet Rusty; he was not sure what he should do with himself.

In a courtyard off one of the alleyways, three young men

squatted in the sun, playing cards. Kishen watched them for a while, until one of the players beckoned to him, inviting him to join in the game.

Kishen was with the card-players till twelve o'clock.

*

Rusty went to the barber's shop and had his shave for four annas. And the barber, who was a special friend of his, and took great pleasure in running his fingers through Rusty's fair hair, gave him a head massage into the bargain.

It was a wonderful massage and included not only the head, but Rusty's eyes, neck and forehead. The barber was a dark, glistening man, with broad shoulders and a chest like a drum; he wore a fine white Lucknow shirt, through which you could see his hard body. His strong fingers drummed and stroked and pressed; and with the palms and sides of his hands he thumped and patted Rusty's forehead. Rusty felt the blood rush to his temples; and when the massage was finished, he was hardly conscious of having a head, and walked into the street with a peculiar, elated, headless feeling.

He made a somewhat fruitless round of the three principal schools. At each of them he was told that if anything in his line turned up, they would certainly let him know; but they did not ask him where he could be found if he was wanted. The last school asked him to call again in a day or two.

On the outskirts of the town Rusty found the old church of St Paul's, which had been abandoned for over a year, due to meagre parish resources and a negligible attendance. The Catholics of Dehra had been able to afford the upkeep of their church and convent, but nobody outside Dehra had bothered about St Paul's, and eventually the padre had locked the building and gone away. Rusty regretted this, not because he had been fond of church-going—he had always disliked large gatherings of people—but because it was old, with historic and personal associations, and he hated to see old things, old people, suffer lonely deaths.

The plaster was crumbling, the paint peeling off the walls, moss growing in every crack. Wild creepers grew over the stained-glass windows. The garden, so well-kept once, was now a jungle of weeds and irrepressible marigolds.

Rusty leaned on the gate and gazed at the church. There had been a time when he hated visiting this place, for it had meant the uncomfortable presence of his guardian, the gossip of middle-aged women, the boredom of an insipid sermon; but now, seeing the neglected church, he felt sorry for it—not only for the people who had been there, but for the place itself, and for those who were buried in the graves that kept each other silent company in the grounds. People he had known lay there, and some of them were people his father had known.

He opened the creaking wooden gate and walked up the overgrown path. The front door was locked. He walked round, trying the side doors, finding them all closed. There was no lock on the vestry door, though it seemed to be bolted from within. Two panes of glass were set in the top of the door. Standing on his toes, Rusty reached up to them, pressing his fingers against the panes to test the thickness of the glass. He stood back from the door, took his handkerchief from his pocket and wrapped it round his hand. Standing on his toes again, he pushed his fist through one of the panes.

There was a tinkle of falling glass. Rusty groped around and found the bolt. Then he stepped back and kicked at the door.

The door opened. The handkerchief had fallen from his hand and one of his knuckles was bleeding. He picked up the handkerchief and wrapped it round the cut; then he stepped into the vestry.

The place was almost empty. A cupboard-door hung open on one hinge and a few old cassocks lay on a shelf in a dusty pile. An untidy heap of prayer books and hymnals was stacked in a packing-case, and a mouse sat on top of a half-eaten hymnal, watching the intruder.

Rusty went through the vestry, into the church hall, where it was lighter. Sunlight poured through a stained-glass window, throwing patches of mellow orange and gold on the pews and on the frayed red carpet that ran down the aisle. The windows were full of cobwebs. As Rusty walked down the aisle, he broke through cordons of cobwebs, sending the frightened spiders scurrying away across the pews.

He left the church by the vestry door, closing it behind him, and, removing the splintered glass from the window, he threw the pieces into the bushes.

*

Kishen could always find plenty to do in the bazaar, apart from gambling with cards. The bazaar was a mile long, stretching from the station to the Clock Tower; little alleys led off the main road, winding towards the stench of the fish market or the wet freshness of the vegetable market.

Another alley led to the junk, or *kabari*, market which was always interesting. Here you could get anything from valuable antiques and rare books to old footballs, shoes, haversacks, tins and bottles. Most of the *kabaris* were Muslims, who had been either too old or too poor to leave Dehra after the Partition of the country. They made up only a small part of the town's very mixed population, which included sturdy little Gurkhas from Nepal, easy-going smiling Garhwalis from the hills, and bustling Punjabi Hindus and Sikhs.

The Punjabis had brought activity and noise to this once-sleepy little town, and small shops and hotels had mushroomed up on all the roads. Skilled tailors and carpenters and businessmen who had lost nearly everything in their flight across the border when the country was divided, had set to work again, to make new livings and new fortunes. Only a Punjabi can make and lose a fortune with both speed and daring, and Kishen (who was Punjabi) could do it too, in his own small way.

He met Rusty at the Clock Tower, and together they went to the chaat shop to have a cheap meal of spiced fruits and vegetables. Kishen had been again to the *munshi*, to get into the storeroom, and now carried a bundle of clothes; he had done this to please Rusty, as the matter of the card-game would be difficult to explain.

'The *munshi* wouldn't give me a room without an advance of fifteen rupees,' he said. 'But I got some clothes, anyway.'

'It doesn't matter about the room. I've found a place to stay.'

'Oh good! What is it like?'

'Wait till you see it. I had no luck at the schools, though there may be something for me in a day or two. How much money did you say was left?'

'Eight rupees,' said Kishen, looking guilty, and stuffing his mouth with potatoes to hide his confusion.

'I thought it was nine rupees,' said Rusty.

'It was nine,' said Kishen. 'But I lost one rupee. I was sure I could win, but those fellows had a trick I didn't know!'

'I see,' said Rusty resignedly. 'From now on I'll keep everything.'

Without any shame Kishen put the notes and coins on the table. Rusty separated the money into two piles, put the notes in his pocket, and pushed six annas across the table to Kishen.

Kishen grinned. 'So you are letting me keep something, after all?'

'That's to pay for the chaat,' said Rusty, and Kishen's grin turned into a grimace.

*

They walked to the church, Kishen grumbling a little, Rusty feeling very cheerful. Sometimes it would be the other way round. They were seldom cheerful together; and they never grumbled together, which was fortunate.

'I want a bath,' said Kishen unreasonably. 'How far is this place where you've got a room?'

'I didn't say anything about a room, and there's no place for a bath. But there's a stream not far away, in the jungle behind the road.'

Kishen looked puzzled and scratched his fuzzy head, but he did not say anything, reserving judgement till later.

'Hey, where are you going, Rusty?' he said, when Rusty turned in at the church gate.

'To the church,' said Rusty.

'What for—to pray?' asked Kishen anxiously. 'I never knew you were religious.'

'I'm not. But we're going to live in the place.'

Kishen slapped his forehead in astonishment, then burst into laughter. 'The places we stay at!' he exclaimed. 'Railway stations. Maidan. And now cathedrals!'

'It's not a cathedral, it's a church.'

'What's the difference? It's the same religion. A mosque can be different from a temple, but how is a cathedral different from a church?'

Rusty did not try to explain, but led Kishen in through the vestry door. Kishen crept cautiously into the quiet church, looking nervously at the dark, spidery corners, at the high windows, the bare altar, the gloom above the rafters.

'I can't stay here,' he said. 'There must be a ghost in the place.' He ran his fingers over the top of a pew, leaving tracks in the thick dust.

'We can sleep on the benches or on the carpet,' said Rusty. 'And we can cover ourselves with those old cassocks.'

'Why are they called cassocks?'

'I haven't the slightest idea.'

'Then don't lecture me about cathedrals. If someone finds out we are staying here, there will be trouble.'

'Nobody will find out. Nobody comes here any more. The place is not looked after, as you can see. Those who used to come have all gone away. Only I am left, and I never came here willingly.'

'Up till now,' said Kishen. 'Let some air in.'

Rusty climbed on a bench and opened one of the high windows. Fresh air rushed in, smelling sweet, driving away the mustiness of the closed hall.

'Now let's go to the stream,' said Rusty.

They left the church by the vestry door, passed through the unkempt garden and went into the jungle. A narrow path led through the sal trees, and they followed it for about a quarter of a mile. The path had not been used for a long time, and they had to push their way through thorny bushes and brambles. Then they heard the sound of rushing water.

They had to slide down a rock face into a small ravine, and there they found the stream running over a bed of shingle. Removing their shoes and rolling up their trousers, they crossed the stream. Water trickled down from the hillside, from amongst ferns and grasses and wild flowers; and the hills, rising steeply on either side, kept the ravine in shadow. The rocks were smooth, almost soft, and some of them were grey and some yellow. A small waterfall fell across them, forming a deep, round pool of apple-green water.

They removed their clothes and jumped into the pool. Kishen went too far out, felt the ground slipping away from beneath his feet, and came splashing back into the shallows.

'I didn't know it was so deep', he said.

Soon they had forgotten the problem of making money, had forgotten the rigours of their journey. They swam and romped about in the cold mountain water. Kishen gathered the clothes together and washed them in the stream, beating them out on the smooth rocks, and spreading them on the grass to dry. When they had bathed, they lay down on the grass, under a warm afternoon sun, talking spasmodically and occasionally falling into a light sleep.

'I am going to write to Somi,' said Rusty, 'but I don't know his address.'

'Isn't his mother still here?' said Kishen.

Rusty sat up suddenly. 'I never thought of her. Somi said he was the only one leaving Dehra. She must be here.'

'Then let us go and see her,' said Kishen. 'She might be able to help us.'

'We'll go now,' said Rusty.

They waited until their clothes were dry, and then they dressed and went back along the forest path. The sun was setting when Rusty and Kishen arrived at Somi's house, which was about a mile from the church, in the direction of the station. It was an old yellow bungalow, almost lost amongst litchi and guava trees, and as Rusty passed beneath the trees he remembered a day when Somi, a golden boy singing in the sun, had sat on the limb of a guava tree, had fallen lightly on Rusty's shoulders, ruffling his hair and shouting, 'Run, my pony, my best favourite friend!'

He missed Somi's welcoming laughter as he walked up the veranda steps, but he found Somi's mother busy in the kitchen, while the baby sister crawled about on the floor. Rusty took the child in his arms and lifted her high above his head; and the little girl screamed with delight as he tossed her in the air. Somi's mother, grey-haired, smiling, and dressed in a simple white sari, put her hands to her cheeks.

'Master Rusty!' she exclaimed. 'And Kishen bhaiya! Where have you been all these weeks?'

'Travelling,' said Rusty. 'We have been doing a world tour.'

'On foot,' added Kishen.

They sat in cane chairs on the veranda, and Rusty gave Somi's mother an account of their journey, deliberately omitting to mention that they were without work or money. But she had sensed their predicament.

'Are you having any trouble about your room?' she asked.

'We left it,' said Rusty. 'We are staying in a bigger place now.'

'Yes, much bigger,' said Kishen.

'What about that book you were going to write—is it published?'

'No, I'm still writing it,' said Rusty.

'How much have you done?'

'Oh, not much as yet. These things take a long time.'

'And what is it about?'

'Oh, everything I suppose,' said Rusty, feeling guilty and changing the subject, for his novel had not progressed beyond the second chapter. 'I'm starting another tuition soon. If you know of any people who want their children to learn English, please pass them on to me.'

'Of course I will. Somi would not forgive me if I did not do as you asked. But why don't you stay here? There is plenty of room.'

'Oh, we are quite comfortable in our place,' said Rusty.

'Oh, yes, very comfortable,' said Kishen glaring at him.

Somi's mother made them stay for dinner, and they did not take much persuading, for the aroma of rich Punjabi food had been coming to them from the kitchen. They were prepared to sleep in churches and waiting-rooms all their lives, provided there was always good food to be had—rich, fleshy food, for they scorned most vegetables . . .

Somi's mother gave them a feast of tandoori bread and buffalo's butter, meat cooked with spinach, vegetables with cheese, a sour pickle of turnip and lemon, and jug of *lassi*. They did full justice to the meal, and Somi's mother watched them with satisfaction—the satisfaction of a mother and a good cook.

'Do you need any money?' she asked, when they had finished.

'Oh, no,' said Rusty, 'we have plenty of that.'

Kishen kicked him under the table.

'Enough for a week, anyway,' said Rusty.

After the meal, he took Somi's Amritsar address, with the intention of writing to him the next day. He also stuffed his pockets with pencils and writing-paper. When they were about to leave, Somi's mother thrust a ten-rupee note into Rusty's hand, and he blushed, unable to refuse the money.

Once on the road, he said: 'We didn't come to borrow money, bhaiya.'

'But you can pay it back in a few days. What's the use of having friends if you can't go to them for help?'

'I would have gone when there was nothing left. Until there is nothing left, I don't want to trouble anyone.'

They walked back to the church, buying two large candles on the way. Rusty lit one candle at the church gate, and led the way down the dark, disued path.

New Encounters

'IT's CREEPY,' SAID KISHEN, keeping close to Rusty. 'It's so quiet here. I think we should go back and stay at Somi's house. There must be something wrong with sleeping in a church.'

'It is no more wrong than sleeping in a tree.'

When they were inside, Rusty placed the burning candle on the altar steps. A bat swooped down from the rafters and Kishen ducked under a pew. 'I would rather sleep in the maidan,' he said.

'It's better here,' said Rusty. He came back from the vestry with a bundle of cassocks, which he dumped on the floor. 'I'll do some writing,' he said, sitting down near the candle and producing pencil and paper from his pocket.

Kishen sat down on a bench and removed his shoes, rubbing his feet and playing with his toes. When he had got used to the bats diving overhead, he stood up and undressed. Long and bony in his vest and underpants, he sat down on the pile of cassocks; and with his elbows resting on his knees, and his chin cupped in the palms of his hands, he watched Rusty write.

He knew better than to interrupt when Rusty was writing or reading, particularly so when he was reading. Once Rusty was absorbed in a book, only something disastrous would get him away from it. He had been a bookworm ever since he had learnt to read, but the final commitment had been made at the age of twelve.

At this ripe and impressionable age he had been taken, by his guardian and several other sportsmen, on a shikar expedition into the Terai jungles near Dehra. The prospect of a week in the jungle, as camp-follower to several egotistic adults with guns, filled Rusty with dismay. He knew that many long weary hours would be spent tramping behind tall, professional-looking huntsmen, who spoke in terms of bagging this tiger or that wild elephant, when all they ever got, if they were lucky, was a hare or a partridge. Tigers and excitement, it seemed, came only to Jim Corbett. Rusty had been on several shikar trips and had always been overtaken by ennui.

That particular expedition had been different, but not because the hunters had been more than usually successful. At the end of the week all they had shot were two miserable, underweight wild fowl. But Rusty had contrived, on the second day, to be left behind in the forest rest house; and there he discovered a shelf of books half-hidden in a corner of the old bungalow.

Who had left them there? A literary forest officer? Some memsahib who had been bored with her husband's campfire boasting? Or someone who, pained at the prospect of slaughtering wild animals, insured himself against boredom by bringing his library along. But why leave it behind? For fellow sufferers, perhaps. Or possibly the poor fellow had gone into the jungle one day, as a sort of gesture to his more bloodthirsty companions, and been trampled by an elephant, or gored by a wild boar, or (more likely) accidentally shot by one of the shikaris—and his sorrowing friends had taken his remains away, but left his books behind.

Anyway, there they were—a shelf of some thirty volumes. The shelf was catholic in its contents—and Rusty had soaked up Dickens, Wodehouse, M.R. James, George Eliot, Maugham and Barrie, while the big-game hunters, instead of feasting on roast pig or venison, opened their tins of corned meat.

*

In the early hours of the morning a mouse nibbled at Kishen's toes and the boy woke with a yelp and shook Rusty.

'I've been bitten,' said Kishen urgently. Rusty surfaced from the cassocks. 'I've been bitten by a church mouse.'

'At least it isn't a cathedral rat,' said Rusty. 'I've had one crawling over me all night.' He shook out the cassocks, and, with a squeak, a mouse leapt from the clothes and made a dash for safety.

Kishen put out his hand and touched Rusty's shoulder. The warmth of his friend's body reassured him, and he drew nearer and went to sleep with his arm round Rusty.

They rose before the sun was up, and went straight to the pool. It was a cold morning. They gasped and cried out from the shock of the ice-cold mountain water. Rusty was brown on his arms and legs, where the sun had burnt him, and the rest of his body was pink from the slap of the water. Kishen had long loose limbs, and he threshed the water vigorously, but with little skill. They both tried diving off a rock, but landed on their bellies every time.

As they swam about, the sun came striking through the sal trees, making emeralds of the dewdrops, and pouring through the clear water till it touched the yellow sand. Rusty felt the sun touch his skin, felt it sink deep into his blood and bones and marrow, and, exulting in it, he hurled himself at Kishen. They tumbled over in the water, going down with a wild kicking of legs, and came spluttering to the surface, gasping and shouting. Then they lay on the rocks till they were dry.

When they left the pool, they walked to the maidan.

Every morning a group of young men wrestled at one end of the maidan, in a pit of soft, newly-dug earth. Hathi was one of the wreslers. He was like a young bull, with a magnificent chest, and great broad thighs. His light brown hair and eyes were in startling contrast to the rest of his dark body.

Hathi relied more on strength than skill, and with a sweep of his broad hand he could level an opponent to the ground. Rusty had met him when he used to watch the wrestling with Somi and Kishen, and Hathi had always greeted them with a wide smile, inviting them to wrestle.

Kishen and Rusty found him at the tap, washing the mud and oil from his body, pummelling himself with resounding slaps. When he looked up and saw Rusty, he gave a shout of recognition, left the tap running, and gave Rusty an exuberant wet hug, transferring a fair amount of mud and oil on to his friend's already soiled shirt.

'My friend! Where have you been all these weeks? I thought
you had forgotten me. And Kishen bhaiya, how are you?'

Kishen received the bear-hug with a grumble: 'I've already
had my bath, Hathi.'

But Hathi continued talking, while he put on his shirt and
pyjamas. 'You are just in time to see me, as I am going away in
a day or two,' he said.

'Where are you going?' asked Rusty.

'To my village in the hills. I have land there, you know—I am
going back to took after it. Come and have tea with me—come!
I wanted to make both of you wrestlers, but you disappeared,
and now it is too late.'

He took them to the tea-shop near the Clock Tower, where he
mixed each of them a glass of hot milk, honey and beaten egg.
The morning bath had refreshed them and they were feeling
quite energeric.

'How do you get to your village?' asked Rusty. 'Is there a
motor road?'

'No. The road ends at Lansdowne. From there one has to walk
about thirty miles. It is a steep road, and you have to cross two
mountains, but it can be done in a day if you start out early
enough. Why don't you come with me?' he asked suddenly.
'There you will be able to write many stories. That is what you
want to do, isn't it? There will be no noise or worry.'

'I can't come just now,' said Rusty. 'Maybe later, but not now.'

'You come too, Kishen,' pressed Hathi. 'Why not?'

'Kishen would be bored by mountains,' said Rusty.

'How do you know?' said Kishen, looking annoyed.

'Well, if you want to come later,' said Hathi, 'you have only to
take the bus to Lansdowne, and then take the north-east road for
the village of Manjari. You can come whenever you like. I will be
living alone.'

'If we come,' said Rusty, 'we should be of some use to you
there.'

'I will make farmers of you!' exclaimed Hathi, slapping himself
on the thigh.

'Kishen is too lazy.'

'And Rusty too clumsy.'

'Well, maybe we will come,' said Rusty. 'But first I must see if I can get some sort of work here. I'm going to one of the schools again today. What will you do, Kishen?'

Kishen shrugged. 'I'll wait for you in the bazaar.'

'Stay with me,' said Hathi. 'I have nothing to do except recover money from various people. If I don't get it now, I will never get it.'

*

While Hathi was engaged at the Sindhi Sweet Shop, arguing with a man about a certain amount of money, Kishen wandered off on his own, lounging about in front of the shops. He was standing in front of a cloth shop when he saw an old family friend, Mrs Bhushan, with her vixenish, fifteen-year-old daughter, Aruna, an old playmate of his. They were in the shop, haggling with the shopkeeper over the price of a sari. Mrs Bhushan was in the habit of going from shop to shop, like a bee sampling honey; she would have bales of cloth unfurled for inspection, but she seldom bought anything. Aruna was a dark, thin girl. She had pretty green eyes, and a mischievous smile, and she was not as innocent as she looked. Kishen would have liked to speak to her, but he did not relish the prospect of meeting Mrs Bhushan, who would make things awkward for him, so he turned his back on the shop and looked around for Hathi. He was about to walk away when he felt a heavy hand descend on his shoulder, and, turning, found himself looking into the large, disagreeable eyes of Mrs Bhushan.

Mrs Bhushan was an imposing women of some thirty-five years and she walked with a heavy determination that kept people, and even bulls, out of her way. Her dogs, her husband, and her servants were all afraid of her and submitted to her dictates without a murmur. A masculine woman, she bullied men and children, and lavished most of her affection on dogs.

Her cocker spaniels slept on her bed, and her husband slept in the drawing-room.

'Kishen!' exclaimed Mrs Bhushan, pouncing upon the poor boy. 'What are you doing here?' And at the same time Aruna saw him, and her green eyes brightened, and she cried, 'Kishen! What are you doing here? We thought you were in Hardwar!'

Kishen was confused. To have Mrs Bhushan towering over him was like experiencing an eclipse of the sun. Moreover, he did not know how to explain his presence in Dehra. He contented himself with grinning sheepishly at Aruna.

'Where have you been, boy?' demanded Mrs Bhushan, getting business-like. 'Your clothes are all torn and you're a bundle of bones!'

'Oh, I've been on a walking-tour,' said Kishen unconvincingly.

'A walking-tour! Alone?'

'No, with a friend . . .'

'You're too young to be wandering about like a vagrant. What do you think relatives are for? Now get into the car and come home with us.'

Kishen had not noticed the pre-war Hillman that stood beneath the tamarind tree. It had once belonged to a British magistrate, who had sold it cheap when he went away after Indian Independence. Mrs Bhushan, in her aggressive way, had done her best to shorten the car's life, but it had lasted into the middle of the 1950s.

'What about my friend?' asked Kishen unhappily.

'You can see him later, can't you? Come on, Aruna, get in. there's something fishy about this walking-tour business, and I mean to get to the bottom of it!' And she trod on the accelerator with such ferocity that a lame beggar, who had been dawdling in the middle of the road, suddenly regained the use of both legs and sprang nimbly on to the pavement.

*

When they arrived at Mrs Bhushan's smart white bungalow, Kishen was placed in an armchair and subjected to Mrs Bhushan's own brand of third degree, which consisted of snaps and snarls and snorts of disapproval. The cocker spaniels, disapproving of Kishen's ragged condition, snapped at his long-suffering legs, which had, so far, endured blisters, mosquito bites, and the nibbling of mice.

Before long, Kishen had told them the whole story of his journey from Hardwar with Rusty. Aruna listened to every word, full of admiration for the two boys, but Mrs Bhushan voiced her disapproval in strong terms.

'Well, this is the end of your wanderings, young man,' she said. 'You're staying right here in this house. I won't have you wandering about the country with a lot of loafers.'

Mrs Bhushan, who was given to exaggeration, had visualized Rusty not as one person, but as several, an entire gang of tramps.

'Who would you rather stay with?' she demanded. 'Your father or me?'

'With you,' said Kishen hurriedly, certain that he had no choice.

'Then go and have a bath, while I get some clean clothes ready for you.'

Kishen spent half an hour under a hot shower, luxuriating in its warmth, while steam filled the room and his skin began to glow. It was weeks since he had used soap, and he lathered himself from head to foot, and watched the effect in the bathroom mirror. The water sent the soap scurrying down his legs, across the floor and down the drain and into the garden. He dried himself briskly and, hating the sight of his dusty old clothes, wrapped the towel around his waist and walked barefoot into the drawing-room.

Mrs Bhushan was searching for a pair of her husband's pyjamas to fit Kishen, and Aruna was alone in the room, reclining on the carpet. She pulled Kishen down beside her, and held his hand.

'I wish I had been with you,' she said.

'Have you ever slept with a rat?' said Kishen. 'Because I did last night.'

'What about your friend Rusty? I can ask Mummy to let him stay with us for some time.'

'He won't come.'

'Why not?'

'He just won't come.'

'Is he too proud?'

'No, but you are proud. That's why he won't come.'

Aruna tossed the hair away from her face. 'Then let him stay where he is.'

'But I must go and tell him what has happened. He'll be waiting for me at the Clock Tower.'

'Not today, you won't,' said Mrs Bhushan, marching back into the room with a pink pyjama over her shoulder. 'You can see him tomorrow, when we will drive you over in the car. I'm sure he can look after himself all right. If he had any sense, he'd have taken you home when he found you. The fellow must be an absolute rogue!'

And so, for the rest of the day, Kishen was held prisoner in Mrs Bhushan's comfortable drawing-room where Aruna kept him company, feeding him with chicken curry and soft juicy papayas.

*

The school to which Rusty had been (the visit proved fruitless) stood near the dry river-bed of the Rispana, and on the other side of the river-bed lay mustard fields and tea-gardens. As he had more than an hour left before meeting Kishen, he crossed the sandy river-bed and wandered through the fields. A peacock ran along the path with swift, ungainly strides.

A small canal passed through the tea-gardens, and Rusty followed the canal, counting the horny grey lizards that darted in and out of the stones. He picked a tea leaf from a bush and, holding it to his nose, found the smell sweet and pleasant. When he had walked about a mile, he came to a small clearing. There was a house in the clearing, surrounded by banana and poinsettia trees, the poinsettia leaves hanging down like long red tongues of fire. Bougainvillaea and other creepers covered the front of the house.

Sitting in a cane chair on the veranda was an Englishman. At least, Rusty assumed that the gentleman he saw was an Englishman. He may have been a German or an American or a Russian, but the only Europeans Rusty had known were Englishmen, and he immediately took the white-haired gentleman in the cane chair to be English—and he happened to be right.

The gentleman was elderly, red-faced, dressed in a tweed coat and flannel shorts and thick woollen stockings. Sola-topees had gone out of fashion, otherwise he might have been wearing one. An unlit pipe was held between his teeth, and on his knees lay a copy of the *Times Literary Supplement*.

It was over a year since Rusty had seen an Englishman. The last one had been his guardian, and he had hated his guardian. But the old man in the chair seemed, somehow, bluff and amiable. Rusty advanced cautiously up the veranda steps, then waited for the old man to look up from his paper.

The old man did not look up, but he said, 'Yes, come in, boy. Pull up a chair and sit down.'

'I hope I'm not disturbing you,' said Rusty.

'You are, but it doesn't matter. Don't be so self-effacing.' The old man looked up at Rusty, and his grey eyes softened a little, but he did not smile; it was too much trouble to remove the pipe from his mouth.

Rusty pulled up a chair and sat down awkwardly, twiddling his thumbs. The old man looked him up and down, said, 'Have a drink, I expect you're old enough,' and producing another glass from beneath the table, poured out two fingers of Solan whisky into Rusty's glass. He poured three fingers into his own glass. Then, from under the table, he produced two soda-water bottles and an opener. The bottle-tops flew out of the veranda with loud pops, and the golden liquid rose fuzzily to the top of the glass.

'Cheers,' said the old man, tossing down most of his drink. 'Pettigrew is the name,' said the old man. 'They used to call me Petty, though, down in Bangalore.'

'I'm pleased to meet you, Mr Pettigrew,' said Rusty politely. 'Is this your house?'

'Yes, the house is mine,' said Mr Pettigrew, knocking out his pipe on the table. 'It's about all that is still mine; the house and my library. These garden were mine, once, but I only have a share in them now. It's third-grade tea, anyway. Only used for mixing.'

'Isn't there anyone to look after you?' asked Rusty, noticing the emptiness of the house.

'Look after me!' exclaimed Pettigrew indignantly. 'Whatever for? Do you think I'm a blooming invalid! I'm seventy, my boy, and I can ride a horse better than you can sit a bicycle!'

'I'm sure you can,' said Rusty hastily. 'And you don't look a year older than sixty. But I suppose you have a servant.'

'Well, I always thought I had one. But where the blighter is half the time, I'd like to know. Running after some wretched woman, I suppose.' A look of reminiscence passed over his face. 'I can remember the time when I did much the same thing. That was in the Kullu valley. There were two things Kullu used to be famous for—apples and pretty women!' He spluttered with laughter, and his face became very red. Rusty was afraid the old man's big blue veins were going to burst.

'Did you ever marry anyone?' he asked.

'Marry!' exclaimed Pettigrew. 'Are you off your head, young fellow? What do you think a chap like me would want to marry for? Only invalids get married, so that they can have someone to look after them in their old age. No man's likely to be with one woman in his life.'

He stopped then, and looked at Rusty in a peculiar defiant way, and Rusty gathered that the old man was not really as cynical as he sounded.

'You're Harrison's boy, aren't you?' he asked suddenly.

'He was my guardian,' said Rusty. 'How did you know?'

'Never mind; I know. You ran off on your own a year ago, didn't you? Well, I don't blame you. Never could stand Harrison myself. Awful old bounder. Never bought a man a drink if he could help it. Guzzled other people's though. Don't blame you for running away. But what made you do it?'

'He was mean and he thrashed me and didn't allow me to make Indian friends. I was fed up. I wanted to live my own life.'

'Naturally. You're a man now. Your father was a fine man, too.'

'Did you know him?'

'Of course I knew him. He managed this estate for me once. I wanted to see you before, but Harrison never gave me the opportunity.'

'It was just chance that brought me this way.'

'I know. That's how everything happens.'

'Tell me about my father,' said Rusty. 'I was too small, when he died, to remember much of him now.'

'Well, he was a good friend of mine, and we saw quite a lot of each other. He was interested in birds and insects and wild flowers—in fact, anything that had to do with natural history. Both of us were great readers and collectors of books, and that was what brought us together. But what I've been wanting to tell you was this. When he died, he had been living with an aunt of yours in the hills—near some village in Garhwal. Well, I may be wrong, but I think that if there was anything of value that your father may have wanted you to have, he'd have left it in the keeping of this aunt of yours. He trusted her—he trusted her a great deal more than he trusted Harrison, your legal guardian.'

'What was her name?' asked Rusty.

'I don't remember. I never saw her myself. But I do know she lived in the hills, where she had some land of her own.'

'Do you think I should look for her?' asked Rusty, surprised at his growing interest and enthusiasm.

'It might be a good idea,' said Mr Pettigrew. 'She must be about forty, now. I think she lived in a small house on the banks of the river, about forty miles from Lansdowne. You'll have to walk much of the way from Lansdowne.'

'I'm used to walking. I have a Garhwali friend; perhaps he can help me.' Rusty was thinking of Hathi. He rose to go, anxious to tell Kishen and Hathi about this new development.

'Don't be in a hurry,' said Mr Pettigrew. 'Have you got any money?'

'A little.'

'Well, if you need any help, remember I'm here. I was your father's friend, you know.'

'Thank you, Mr Pettigrew. I'll see you again before I leave.'

After Rusty had gone, Mr Pettigrew refilled his pipe but did not bother to light it. Idly, he turned the pages of his paper, and when his servant came rushing up the path he forgot to reprimand the boy for being late. He was thinking of Rusty, and of how wonderful it was to be young, and regretting that he was now too old to climb mountains and look for lost friends.

'Damn!' he said in disgust, and threw the empty soda bottle into the bushes.

PROSPECT OF A JOURNEY

RUSTY WAITED AT THE Clock Tower for almost an hour, until it was nearly one o'clock. He had been feeling slightly impatient, not because he was anxious about Kishen, but because he wanted to tell him about Mr Pettigrew and the aunt in the hills. He presumed Kishen was loafing somewhere in the bazaar, or spending money at the Sindhi Sweet Shop. This did not worry him, as he had kept most of the money; but one never knew what indiscretions Kishen might indulge in.

Rusty leant against the wall of the Clock Tower, watching the peddlers move lazily about the road, calling their wares in desultory, afternoon voices; the toy-seller, waiting for the schools to close for the day and spill their children out into the streets; the fruit-vendor, with his basket of papayas, oranges, bananas and Kashmiri apples, which he continually sprinkled with water to make them look fresh; a cobbler drowsing in the shade of the tamarind tree, occasionally fanning himself with a strip of uncut leather. Rusty saw them all, without being very conscious of their existence, for his thoughts were far away, visualizing a strange person in the mountains.

A tall Sikh boy, with a tray hanging by a string from his shoulders, approached Rusty. He wore a bright red turban, broad white pyjamas, and black Peshawari chappals which had been left unbuckled. He had long hands and feet, and if he was slim it was because he was still growing and had not had time to fill out. Though he was tall, he was upright, and his light brown eyes were friendly and direct. In the tray hanging from his neck lay an assortment of goods—combs, buttons, key-rings, reels of thread, bottles of cheap perfume, soaps and hair oils. He stopped near Rusty, but did not ask the boy if there was anything he wanted to buy. He stopped only to look at Rusty.

Rusty, feeling the other's gaze upon him, came out of his dreams, and looked at the Sikh. They stared at each other for a minute, with mutual interest; it was the first time they had set eyes on each other, but there was a compelling expression in the stranger's eyes, a haunting, half-sad, half-happy quality, that held Rusty's attention, appealing to some odd quirk in his nature. The atmosphere was charged with this quality of sympathy.

A crow flapped down between them, and the significance of the moment vanished, and the bond of sympathy was broken.

Rusty turned away, and the Sikh boy wandered on down the road.

*

After waiting for another ten minutes, Rusty left the Clock Tower and began walking in the direction of the church, thinking that perhaps Kishen had gone there instead. He had not walked far when he found the Sikh boy sitting in the shade of a mango tree, with his tray beside him and a book in his hands. Rusty paused to take a look at the book. It was Goldsmith's *The Traveller*. That was enough to make Rusty talk.

'Do you like the book?' he asked.

The Sikh looked up with a smile. 'It is in my Intermediate course. My exams begin next month. But I read other books, too,' he added.

'But when do you go to school?' asked Rusty, looking at the tray, which was obviously the boy's means of livelihood.

'In the evenings there are classes. During the day I sell this rubbish. I make enough to eat and to pay for my tuition. My name is Devinder.'

'My name is Rusty.'

Rusy leant against the trunk of the mango tree. 'What about your parents?' he asked. In India, when strangers meet, they must know each other's personal history before they can be friends: Rusty was well versed with the formalities.

'They are dead,' said Devinder. He spoke bluntly. 'They were killed during Partition, in 1947, when we had to leave the Punjab. I was looked after in the refugee camp. But I prefer to be on my own, like this. I am happier this way.'

'And where do you stay?'

'Anywhere,' said Devinder, closing the book and standing up. 'In somebody's kitchen or veranda, or in the maidan. During the summer months it doesn't matter where I sleep, and in the winter people are kind and find some place for me.'

'You can sleep with us,' said Rusty compulsively. 'But I live in a church. I've been there since yesterday. It isn't very comfortable, but it's big.'

'Are you a refugee too?' asked Devinder with a smile.

'Well, I'm a displaced person all right.'

They began walking down the road. They walked at a slow, easy pace, stopping now and then to sit on a wall or lean against a gate. They were not in a hurry to get anywhere. They had everywhere to go, and they could take their own time going there, and there was no one to hurry them on. Kishen would always have one foot in Rusty's world, and the other foot in a world of middle-class homes. Devinder had both his feet planted in the greater world, the open world, the world that is both lonely and free. He had been in it even longer than Rusty.

Rusty told Devinder about himself and about Kishen, and when he found that Kishen was not waiting at the church he really began to worry, but there was nothing he could do except wait for him. Devinder left his tray in the church, and went with Rusty to the pool. They bathed and lay in the sun, and they were at the pool for about an hour.

The Goonga must have been following Rusty again, for he was sitting on the vestry steps when they returned to the church. 'Goo,' he said chuckling at his own cunning.

'Now I suppose he'll stay here too,' said Rusty.

*

In the company of Aruna, Kishen managed to forget Rusty for a few hours. They played carom and listened to the radio. Kishen took her hand and, examining her palm, predicted misery; his predictions were made at length, for he enjoyed holding Aruna's hand. Forgetting—or pretending to forget—that they were almost grown-up people, they began wrestling on the white Afghan carpet until Mrs Bhushan, who had been visiting the neighbours to tell them about Kishen, came home and lifted them off the carpet by the scruffs of their necks.

Aruna had to do her school homework, so she got Kishen to help her with arithmetic. They carried a bench and table out under a sweet-smelling pomelo tree.

As Kishen leant over Aruna, explaining sums which he did not understand, he became acutely conscious of the scent of her hair and the proximity of her right ear, and the sum gradually lost its urgency. The right ear, with its soft creamy lobe, was excruciatingly near. Kishen was tempted to bite it.

'You have a nice ear, Aruna,' he said.

Aruna smiled at the sum.

*

But at night, lying in bed, he began to think of Rusty sitting alone in the empty church, waiting for him. It was an intolerable vision.

He was sleeping in a separate room. Mrs Bhushan and Aruna

slept together in the big bedroom. (Mr Bhushan was in Delhi, enjoying a week's freedom.) Kishen had only to open his window and slip out into the garden.

He crept quietly out of bed and slipped off Mr Bhushan's pink pyjamas. Soft moonlight came in from the window, playing on his naked legs. He hunted about the room until he found his old pyjamas and then, taking his chappals in his hands, he went slowly to the bedroom door. Opening it slowly, he peered into the other room.

Mrs Bhushan lay flat on her back, her bosom heaving as though it were in the throes of a minor earthquake, her breath making strange, whistling sounds. There was no likelihood of her waking up. But Aruna was wide awake. She sat up in bed, staring at Kishen.

Kishen put a finger to his lips and approached the bed.

'I'm going to see Rusty,' he whispered. 'I will come back before morning.'

His fingers found hers and squeezed them, then he left the room, climbing out of the window, and running down the path to the gate. He kept running until he reached the church.

He was about to enter the vestry when he was almost startled out of his wits by a wild, frightening figure that suddenly loomed up before him.

'Goo!' said the Goonga.

'Oh, it's you!' gasped Kishen. 'I might have known it.'

He was even more taken aback to find Rusty sitting on the ground with Devinder, reading from *The Traveller*. The Sikh boy had removed his turban, and his long hair fell over his shoulders, giving him a wild, rather dangerous look.

Rusty looked up from the book as Kishen's shadow fell across the page.

'Where have you been, bhaiya?' he asked. 'You did not tell me you would be so late.'

'I was kidnapped,' said Kishen, sitting down on a bench and looking suspiciously at Devinder.

'He is our new member,' exclaimed Rusty lightly. 'He will be staying here too, from now on.'

Kishen gave Devinder a hostile nod. He was inclined to be possessive in his friendships, and resented anyone else being too close to Rusty.

'Is the Goonga staying here too?' he asked.

'He followed me again. We can use him as a chowkidar. But tell me, what happened to you?'

'I met Mrs Bhushan, an old friend of my mother's. I bluffed her that I was on a walking-tour, but she didn't believe me. I had to go home with her, and it was only when she went to sleep that I managed to get away. But she will be sure to arrive here in the morning. What should I do then?'

'You never trouble to make up your own mind, do you bhaiya?'

'I don't want to live with relatives.'

'But we can't wander about aimlessly for ever.'

'We have stopped wandering now,' said Kishen.

'You have. I think I must go away again. There is a relative of mine living in the hills. Perhaps she can help me.'

'I am definitely going with you!' exclaimed Kishen.

'And if I do not find her, what happens? We will both be stuck on a mountain without anything. If you stay here, you might be able to help me later.'

'Well, when are you going?' asked Kishen impatiently.

'As soon as I collect some money.'

'I will try to get some from Mrs Bhushan, she has plenty, but she is a miser. Will he go with you?' said Kishen, looking at Devinder.

'I cannot go,' said Devinder. 'I have my examinations in a month.'

Kishen kicked off his shoes and made himself comfortable on a pew. Rusty began aloud from *The Traveller*, and everyone listened—Kishen, with his feet stuck upon a pew-support; Devinder, with his chin resting on his knees and his eyes on Rusty; and the Goonga (not understanding a word) grinning in the candlelight.

*

Next morning the three boys went down to the pool to bathe. The smell of the neem trees, the sound of the water, the touch of the breeze, intoxicated them, filled them with a zest for living. They ran over the wild wood-sorrel, over the dew-drenched grass, down to the water.

The Goonga, who on principle refused to bathe, sat on top of the rocks and looked on with detached amusement at the others swimming in the pool and wrestling in the shallow water.

Devinder could stand in the deepest part of the pool and still have his head above water. To keep his long hair out of the way, he tied it in a knot, like a bun, on top of his head. His hair was almost auburn in colour, his skin was a burnished gold. He slipped about in the water like a long glistening fish.

Kishen began making balls from loose mud, which he threw at Devinder and Rusty. A mud fight developed. It was like playing snowballs, but more messy. At the height of the battle, the Goonga suddenly appeared on a buffalo.

They took turns mounting the buffalo, but only the Goonga managed to make it move. When Kishen or Rusty sat on it, kicking and shouting, the buffalo refused to budge; at the most, it would roll over on its side in the slush, taking the boys down as well. But it did not matter how muddy they got, because they had only to dive into the pool to be clean again.

They were a long time at the pool. When they returned to the church they found the Hillman parked at the gate, with an impatient and irate Mrs Bhushan sitting at the wheel. She was in a mood to be belligerent, but seeing Kishen accompanied not only by Rusty but by two other dangerous-looking youths, her worst fears were confirmed: Kishen was in the hands of cut-throats, and discretion would be the better part of valour.

'Kishen, my son,' she pleaded, 'we have been worrying about you very much. You should not have left without telling us! Aruna is very unhappy.'

Kishen stood sulkily near his friends.

'You had better go, Kishen,' said Rusty. 'You will be of more help to me if you stay with Mrs Bhushan.'

'But when will I see you?'

'As soon as I come back from the hills.'

Once Kishen was in the car, Rusty confronted Mrs Bhushan and said, 'He won't leave you now. But if he is not happy with you, we will come and take him away.'

'We are his *friends*,' said Mrs Bhushan.

'No, you are like a relative. *We* are his friends.'

Kishen said, 'If you don't come back soon, Rusty, I will start looking for you.' He scowled affectionately at Rusty, and waved to Devinder and the Goonga as the car took him away.

'He might run back again tonight,' said Devinder.

'He will get used to Mrs Bhushan's house,' said Rusty. 'Soon he will be liking it. He will not forget us, but he will remember us only when he is alone. We are only something that happened to him once upon a time. But we have changed him a little. Now he knows there are others in the world besides himself.'

'I could not understand him,' said Devinder. 'But still I liked him.'

'I understood him,' said Rusty, 'and *still* I liked him.'

The Lafunga

'If you have nothing to do,' said Devinder, 'will you come with me on my rounds?'

'First we will see Hathi. If he has not left yet, I can accompany him to Lansdowne.'

Rusty set out with Devinder in the direction of the bazaar. As it was early morning, the shops were just beginning to open. Vegetable vendors were busy freshening their stock with liberal sprinklings of water, calling their prices and their wares; children dawdled in the road on their way to school, playing hopscotch or marbles. Girls going to college chattered in groups like gay, noisy parrots. Men cycled to work, and bullock-carts came in from the villages, laden with produce. The dust, which had taken all night to settle, rose again like a mist.

Rusty and Devinder stopped at the tea-shop to eat thickly buttered buns and drink strong, sweet tea. Then they looked for Hathi's room, and found it above a cloth shop, lying empty, with its doors open. The string bed leant against the wall. On shelves and window ledges, in corners and on the floor, lay little coloured toys made of clay—elephants and bulls, horses and peacocks, and images of Krishna and Ganesha; a blue Krishna, with a flute to his lips, a jolly Ganesha with a delightful little trunk. Most of the toys were rough and unfinished, more charming than the completed pieces. Most of the finished products would now be on sale in the bazaar.

It came as a surprise to Rusty to discover that Hathi, the big wrestler, made toys for a living. He had not imagined there would be delicacy and skill in his friend's huge hands. The pleasantness of the discovery offset his disappointment at finding Hathi had gone.

'He has left already,' said Rusty. 'Never mind. I know he will welcome me, even if I arrive unexpectedly.'

He left the bazaar with Devinder, making for the residential part of the town. As he would be leaving Dehra soon, there was no point in his visiting the school again; later, though, he would see Mr Pettigrew.

When they reached the Clock Tower, someone whistled to them from across the street, and a tall young man came striding towards them.

He looked taller than Devinder, mainly because of his long legs. He wore a loose-fitting bush-shirt that hung open in front. His face was long and pale, but he had quick, devilish eyes, and he smiled disarmingly.

'Here comes Sudheer the Lafunga,' whispered Devinder. 'Lafunga means loafer. He probably wants some money. He is the most charming and the most dangerous person in town.' Aloud, he said, 'Sudheer, when are you going to return the twenty rupees you owe me?'

'Don't talk that way, Devinder,' said the Lafunga, looking offended. 'Don't hurt my feelings. You know your money is safer with me than it is in the bank. It will even bring you dividends, mark my words. I have a plan that will come off in a few days, and then you will get back double your money. Please tell me, who is your friend?'

'We stay together,' said Devinder, introducing Rusty. 'And he is bankrupt too, so don't get any ideas.'

'Please don't believe what he says of me,' said the Lafunga with a captivating smile that showed his strong teeth. 'Really I am not very harmful.'

'Well, completely harmless people are usually dull,' said Rusty.

'How I agree with you! I think we have a lot in common.'

'No, he hasn't got anything,' put in Devinder.

'Well then, he must start from the beginning. It is the best way to make a fortune. You will come and see me, won't you, mister Rusty? We could make a terrific combination, I am sure. You are the kind of person people trust! They take only one look at me and then feel their pockets to see if anything is missing!'

Rusty instinctively put his hand to his own pocket, and all three of them laughed.

'Well, I must go,' said Sudheer the Lafunga, now certain that Devinder was not likely to produce any funds. 'I have a small matter to attend to. It may bring me a fee of twenty or thirty rupees.'

'Go,' said Devinder. 'Strike while the iron is hot.'

'Not I,' said the Lafunga, grinning and moving off. 'I make the iron hot by striking.'

*

'Sudheer is not too bad,' said Devinder, as they walked away from the Clock Tower. 'He is a crook, of course—*Shree 420*—but he would not harm people like us. As he is quite well educated, he manages to gain the confidence of some well-to-do people, and acts on their behalf in matters that are not always respectable.

But he spends what he makes, and is too generous to be successful.'

They had reached a quiet, tree-lined road, and walked in the shade of neem, mango, jamun and eucalyptus trees. Clumps of tall bamboo grew between the trees. Nowhere, but in Dehra, had Rusty seen so many kinds of trees. Trees that had no names. Tall, straight trees, and broad, shady trees. Trees that slept or brooded in the afternoon stillness. And trees that shimmered and moved and whispered even when the winds were asleep.

Some marigolds grew wild on the footpath, and Devinder picked two of them, giving one to Rusty.

'There is a girl who lives at the bottom of the road,' he said. 'She is a pretty girl. Come with me and see her.'

They walked to the house at the end of the road and, while Rusty stood at the gate, Devinder went up the path. Devinder stood at the bottom of the veranda steps, a little to one side, where he could be seen from a window, and whistled softly.

Presently a girl came out on the veranda. When she saw Devinder she smiled. She had a round, fresh face, and long black hair, and she was not wearing any shoes.

Devinder gave her the marigold. She took it in her hand and, not knowing what to say, ran indoors.

That morning Devinder and Rusty walked about four miles. Devinder's customers ranged from decadent maharanis and the wives of government officials to gardeners and sweeper women. Though his merchandise was cheap, the well-to-do were more finicky about a price than the poor. And there were a few who bought things from Devinder because they knew his circumstances and liked what he was doing.

A small girl with flapping pigtails came skipping down the road. She stopped to stare at Rusty, as though he were something quite out of the ordinary, but not unpleasant.

Rusty took the other marigold from his pocket, and gave it to the girl. It was a long time since he had been able to make anyone a gift.

*

After some time they parted, Devinder going back to the town, while Rusty crossed the river-bed. He walked through the tea-gardens until he found Mr Pettigrew's bungalow.

The old man was not on the veranda, but a young servant salaamed Rusty and asked him to sit down. Apparently Mr Pettigrew was having his bath.

'Does he always bathe in the afternoon?' asked Rusty.

'Yes, the sahib likes his water to be put in the sun to get warm. He does not like cold baths or hot baths. The afternoon sun gives his water the right temperature.'

Rusty walked into the drawing-room and nearly fell over a small table. The room was full of furniture and pictures and bric-à-brac. Tiger-heads, stuffed and mounted, snarled down at him from the walls. On the carpet lay several cheetal skins, a bit worn at the sides. There were several shelves filled with books bound in morocco or calf. Photographs adorned the walls—one of a much younger Mr Pettigrew standing over a supine leopard, another of Mr Pettigrew perched on top of an elephant, with his rifle resting on his knees ... Remembering his own experiences, Rusty wondered how such an active shikari ever found time for reading. While he was gazing at the photographs, Pettigrew himself came in, a large bathrobe wrapped round his thin frame, his grizzly chest looking very raw and red from the scrubbing he had just given it.

'Ah, there you are!' he said. 'The bearer told me you were here. Glad to see you again. Sit down and have a drink.'

Mr Pettigrew found the whisky and poured out two stiff drinks. Then, still in his bathrobe and slippers, he made himself comfortable in an armchair. Rusty said something complimentary about one of the mounted tiger-heads.

'Bagged it in Assam,' he said. 'Back in 1928, that was. I spent three nights on a machan before I got a shot at it.'

'You have a lot of books,' observed Rusty.

'A good collection, mostly flora and fauna. Some of them are extremely rare. By the way, ' he said, looking around at the wall, 'did you ever see a picture of your father?'

'Have you got one?' asked Rusty. 'I've only a faint memory of what he looked like.'

'He's in that group photograph over there,' said Mr Pettigrew, pointing to a picture on the wall.

Rusty went over to the picture and saw three men dressed in white shirts and flannels, holding tennis rackets, and looking very self-conscious.

'He's in the middle,' and Pettigrew. 'I'm on his right.'

Rusty saw a young man with fair hair and a fresh face. He was the only player who was smiling. Mr Pettigrew, sporting a fierce moustache, looked as though he was about to tackle a tiger with his racket. The third person was bald and uninteresting.

'Of course, he's very young in that photo,' said Pettigrew. 'It was taken long before you were ever thought of—before your father married.'

Rusty did not reply. He was trying to imagine his father in action on a tennis court, and wondered if he was a better player than Pettigrew.

'Who was the best player among you?' he asked.

'Ah, well, we were both pretty good, you know. Except for poor old Wilkie on the left. He got in the picture by mistake.'

'Did my father talk much?' asked Rusty.

'Well, we all talked a lot, you know, especially after a few drinks. He talked as much as any of us. He could sing, when he wanted to. His rendering of the "Kashmiri Song" was always popular at parties, but it wasn't often he sang, because he didn't like parties . . . Do you remember it? "Pale hands I loved beside the Shalimar . . ."'

Pettigrew began singing in a cracked, wavering voice, and Rusty was forced to take his eyes off the photograph. Half-way through the melody, Pettigrew forgot the words, so he took another gulp of whisky and began singing "The Rose of Tralee". The sight of the old man singing love songs in his bathrobe, with a glass of whisky in his hand, made Rusty smile.

'Well,' said Pettigrew, breaking off in the middle of the song, 'I don't sing as well as I used to. Never mind. Now tell me, boy, when are you going to Garhwal?'

'Tomorrow, perhaps.'

'Have you any money?'

'Enough to travel with. I have a friend in the hills, with whom I can stay for some time.'

'And what about money?'

'I have enough.'

'Well, I'm lending you twenty rupees,' he said, thrusting an envelope into the boy's hands. 'Come and see me when you return, even if you don't find what you're looking for.'

'I'll do that, Mr Pettigrew.'

The old man looked at the boy for some time, as though summing him up.

'You don't really have to find out much about your father,' he said. 'You're just like him, you know.'

*

Returning to the bazaar, Devinder found Sudheer at a paan shop, his lips red with betel juice. Devinder went straight to the point.

'Sudheer,' he said, 'you owe me twenty rupees. I need it, not for myself, but for Rusty, who has to leave Dehra very urgently. You must get me the money by tonight.'

The Lafunga scratched his head.

'It will be difficult,' he said, 'but perhaps it can be managed. He really needs the money? It is not just a trick to get your own money back?'

'He is going to the hills. There may be money for him there, if he finds the person he is looking for.'

'Well, that's different,' said the Lafunga, brightening up. 'That makes Rusty an investment. Meet me at the Clock Tower at six o'clock, and I will have the money for you. I am glad to find you making useful friends for a change.'

He stuffed another roll of paan into his mouth, and taking leave of Devinder with a bright red smile, strolled leisurely down the bazaar road.

As far a appearances went, he had little to do but loll around in the afternoon sunshine, frequenting tea-shops, and gambling with cards in small back rooms. All this he did very well—but it did not make him a living.

To say that he lived on his wits would be an exaggeration. He lived a great deal on other people's wits. There was the *seth* for instance, Rusty's former landlord, who owned much property and dabbled in many shady transactions, and who was often represented by the Lafunga in affairs of an unsavoury nature.

Sudheer came originally from the Frontier, where little value was placed on human life; and while still a boy, he had wandered, a homeless refugee, over the border into India. A smuggler adopted him, taught him something of the trade, and introduced him to some of the best hands in the profession; but in a border-foray with the police, Sudheer's foster-father was shot dead, and the youth was once again on his own. By this time he was old enough to look after himself. With the help of his foster-father's connections, he soon attained the service and confidence of the *seth*.

Sudheer was no petty criminal. He practised crime as a fine art, and believed that thieves, and even murderers, had to have certain principles. If he stole, then he stole from a rich man, who could afford to be robbed, or from a greedy man, who deserved to be robbed. And if he did not rob poor men, it was not because of any altruistic motive—it was because poor men were not worth robbing.

He was good to those friends, like Devinder, who were good to him. Perhaps his most valuable friends, as sources of both money and information, were the dancing-girls who followed their profession in an almost inaccessible little road in the heart of the bazaar. His best friends were Hastini and Mrinalini. He borrowed money from them very freely, and seldom paid back more than half of it.

Hastini could twang the sitar, and dance—with a rather heavy tread—among various other accomplishments.

Mrinalini, a much smaller woman, had grown up in the

profession. She was looked after by her mother, a former entertainer, who kept most of the money that Mrinalini made.

Sudheer woke Hastini in the middle of her afternoon siesta by tickling her under the chin with a feather.

'And who were you with last night, little brother?' she asked running her fingers through his thick brown hair. 'You are smelling of some horrible perfume.'

'You know I do not spend my nights with anyone,' said Sudheer. 'The perfume is from yesterday.'

'Someone new?'

'No, my butterfly. I have known her for a week.'

'Too long a time,' said Hastini petulantly. 'A dangerously long time. How much have you spent on her?'

'Nothing so far. But that is not why I came to see you. Have you got twenty rupees?'

'Villain!' cried Hastini. 'Why do you always borrow from me when you want to entertain some stupid young thing? Are you so heartless?'

'My little lotus flower!' protested Sudheer, pinching her rosy cheeks. 'I am not borrowing for any such reason. A friend of mine has to leave Dehra urgently, and I must get the money for his train fare. I owe it to him.'

'Since when did you have a friend?'

'Never mind that. I have one. And I come to you for help because I love you more than any one. Would you prefer that I borrow the money from Mrinalini?'

'You dare not,' said Hastini. 'I will kill you if you do.'

Between Hastini, of the broad hips, and Mrinalini, who was small and slender, there existed a healthy rivalry for the affections of Sudheer. Perhaps it was the great difference in their proportions that animated the rivalry. Mrinalini envied the luxuriousness of Hastini's soft body, while Hastini envied Mrinalini's delicacy, poise, slenderness of foot, and graceful walk. Mrinalini was the colour of milk and honey; she had the daintiness of a deer, while Hastini possessed the elegance of an elephant.

Sudheer could appreciate both these qualities.

He stood up, looking young even for his twenty-two years, and smiled a crooked smile. He might have looked effeminate had it not been for his hands—they were big, long-fingered, strong hands.

'Where is the money?' he asked.

'You are so impatient! Sit down, sit down. I have it here beneath the mattress.'

Sudheer's hand made its way beneath the mattress and probed about in search of the money.

'Ah, here it is! You have a fortune stacked away here. Yes, ten rupees, fifteen, twenty—and one for luck . . . now give me a kiss!'

*

About an hour later Sudheer was in the street again, whistling cheerfully to himself. He walked with a long, loping stride, his shirt hanging open. Warm sunshine filled one side of the narrow street, and crept up the walls of shops and houses.

Sudheer passed a fruit stand, where the owner was busy talking to a customer, and helped himself to a choice red Kashmiri apple. He continued on his way down the bazaar road, munching the apple.

The bazaar continued for a mile, from the Clock Tower to the railway station, and Sudheer could hear the whistle of a train. He turned off at a little alley, throwing his half-eaten apple to a stray dog. Then he climbed a flight of stairs—wooden stairs that were loose and rickety, liable to collapse at any moment . . .

Mrinalini's half-deaf mother was squatting on the kitchen floor, making a fire in an earthen brazier. Sudheer poked his head round the door and shouted: 'Good morning, Mother, I hope you are making me some tea. You look fine today!' And then, in a lower tone, so that she could not hear: 'You look like a dried-up mango.'

'So it's you again,' grumbled the old woman. 'What do you want now?'

'Your most respectable daughter is what I want,' said Sudheer.

'What is that?' She cupped her hand to her ear and leaned forward.

'Where's Mrinalini?' shouted Sudheer.

'Don't shout like that! She is not here.'

'That's all I wanted to know,' said Sudheer, and he walked through the kitchen, through the living-room, and on to the veranda balcony, where he found Mrinalini sitting in the sun, combing out her long silken hair.

'Let me do it for you,' said Sudheer, and he took the comb from her hand and ran it through the silky black hair. 'For one so little, so much hair. You could conceal yourself in it, and not be seen, except for your dainty little feet.'

'What are you after, Sudheer? You are so full of compliments this morning. And watch out for Mother—if she sees you combing my hair, she will have a fit!'

'And I hope it kills her.'

'Sudheer!'

'Don't be so sentimental about your mother. You are her little gold mine, and she treats you as such—soon I will be having to fill in application forms before I can see you! It is time you kept your earnings for yourself.'

'So that it will be easier for you to help yourself?'

'Well, it would be more convenient. By the way, I have come to you for twenty rupees.'

Mrinalini laughed delightedly, and took the comb from Sudheer. 'What were you saying about my little feet?' she asked slyly.

'I said they were the feet of a princess, and I would be very happy to kiss them.'

'Kiss them, then.'

She held one delicate golden foot in the air, and Sudheer took it in his hands (which were as large as her feet) and kissed her ankle.

'That will be twenty rupees,' he said.

She pushed him away with her foot. 'But, Sudheer, I gave you fifteen rupees only three days ago. What have you done with it?'

'I haven't the slightest idea. I only know that I must have more. It is most urgent, you can be sure of that. But if you cannot help me, I must try elsewhere.'

'Do that, Sudheer. And may I ask, whom do you propose to try?'

'Well, I was thinking of Hastini.'

'*Who?*'

'You know, Hastini, the girl with this wonderful figure . . .'

'I should think I do! Sudheer, if you so much as dare to take a rupee from her, I'll never speak to you again!'

'Well then, what shall I do?'

Mrinalini beat the arms of the chair with her little fists, and cursed Sudheer under her breath. Then she got up and went into the kitchen. A great deal of shouting went on in the kitchen before Mrinalini came back with flushed cheeks and fifteen rupees.

'You don't know the trouble I had getting it,' she said.'Now don't come asking for more until at least a week has passed.'

'After a week, I will be able to supply you with funds. I am engaged tonight on a mission of some importance. In a few days I will place golden bangles on your golden feet.'

'What mission?' asked Mrinalini, looking at him with an anxious frown. 'If it is anything to do with the *seth*, please leave it alone. You know what happened to Satish Dayal. He was smuggling opium for the *seth*, and now he is sitting in jail, while the *seth* continues as always.'

'Don't worry about me. I can deal with the *seth*.'

'Then be off! I have to entertain a foreign delegation this evening. You can come tomorrow morning if you are free.'

'I may come. Meanwhile, goodbye!'

He walked backwards into the living-room, pivoted into the kitchen and, bending over the old woman, kissed her on the forehead.

'You dried-up old mango,' he said. And went away, whistling.

To the Hills

❧

In the church, on the night of his departure, Rusty felt the sadness of one leaving a familiar home and familiar faces. Up till now he had been with friends, people who had given him help and comradeship; but now he would be on his own, without Kishen or Devinder. That was the way it had always turned out.

He gave his spare clothes to the Goonga, because he did not feel like carrying them with him. He left his books with Devinder.

'Stay here, Devinder,' he said. 'Stay here until I come back. I want to find you in Dehra.'

A breeze from the open window made the candles flutter, and the shadows on the walls leapt and gesticulated; but Devinder stood still, the candle-light playing softly on his face.

'I'm always here, Rusty,' he said.

*

The northern-bound train was not crowded, because in December few people went to the hills. Rusty had no difficulty in finding an empty compartment.

It was a small compartment with only two lower berths. Lying down on one of them, he stared out of the far window, at the lights across the railway tracks. He fell asleep, and woke only when the train jerked into motion.

Looking out of the window, he saw the station platform slipping away, while the shouts of the coolies and vendors grew fainter, until they were lost in the sound of the wheels and the rocking of the carriage. The town lights twinkled, grew distant, were swallowed up by the trees. The engine went panting through the jungle, its red sparks floating towards the stars.

There were four small stations between Dehra and Hardwar, and the train stopped for five or ten minutes at each station. At Doiwala he was woken from a light sleep by a tap at the window. It was dark outside, and he could not make out the face that was pressed against the glass. When he opened the door, a familiar, long-legged youth stepped into the carriage, swiftly shutting the door behind him. Before sitting down, he dropped all the shutters on the side facing the platform.

'We meet again,' said the youth, sitting down opposite Rusty, as the train began to move. 'Don't you remember me? I'm Sudheer. I met you at the Clock Tower with Devinder.'

Rusty did not know that the money Devinder had given him had come through Sudheer, but it did not take him long to recognize the Lafunga.

'Of course, I remember you,' he said. 'When I saw you just now, appearing suddenly out of the dark, I had the feeling you were someone I had seen seldom but knew quite well. But what are you doing on this train?'

'I'm going to Hardwar,' said Sudheer, a smile playing about the corners of his mouth. 'On business. Don't ask me for details.'

'Why didn't you get on the train at Dehra?'

'Because I have to use strategy, my friend.' He kicked off his shoes, and put his feet on the opposite bunk. 'And where are you going now?'

'I'm going to the hills, to see a friend.' Rusty was not sure if he should confide his plans to Sudheer, but if Devinder could trust him, why not?

'And when you come back? I suppose you will come back.'

'I'm not sure what I'll do. I want to give myself a chance to be a writer, because I may succeed. It is the only kind of work I really want to do—if you can call it work.'

'Yes, it is work. Real work is what you want to do. It is only when you work for yourself that you really work. I use my eyes and fingers and my wits. I have no morals and no scruples . . .'

'But you have principles, I think.'

'I don't know about that.'

'You have feelings?'

'Yes, but I pay no attention to them.'

'I cannot do that.'

'You are too noble! Why don't you join me? I can guarantee money, excitement, friendship—my friendship, anyway . . .'

Sudheer leant forward and took Rusty's hand. There was earnestness in his maner, and also a challenge.

'Come on. Be with me. The day I met you, I wanted you to be with me. I'm a crook, and I don't have any real friends. I don't ask you to be a crook. I ask you to be my friend.'

'I will be your friend,' said Rusty, taking a sudden liking to Sudheer; he almost said, 'I will be a crook, too,' but thought better of it.

'Why not get down at Hardwar?'

'Why not come with me to Lansdowne?'

'I have work in Hardwar.'

'And I in the hills.'

'That is why friends are so difficult to keep.' Sudheer smiled and leant back in the seat. 'All right, then. We will join up later. I will meet you in the hills. Wait for me, remember me, don't put me out of your mind.'

*

When the train drew into Hardwar, Sudheer got up and stood near the door.

'I have to go quickly,' he said. 'I will see you again.'

As the engine slowed down, and the station lights became brighter, Sudheer opened the carriage door and jumped down to the railway banking.

Alarmed, Rusty ran to the open door and shouted, 'Are you all right, Sudheer?'

'Just worry about yourself!' called Sudheer, his voice growing faint and distant. 'Good luck!'

He was hidden from view by a signal box, and then the train drew into the brightly-lit, crowded station, and pilgrims began climbing into the compartments.

Two policemen came down the platform, looking in at carriage windows and asking questions. They stopped at Rusty's window, and asked him if he had had a companion during the journey, and gave him an unmistakable description of Sudheer.

'He got off the train long ago,' lied Rusty. 'At Doiwala, I think. Why, what do you want him for?'

'He has stolen one thousand rupees from a *seth* in Dehra,' said the policemen. 'If you see him again, please pull the alarm cord.'

*

Two days later, Rusty was in Hathi's house, sitting on a string cot out in the courtyard. There was snow on the tiled roof and in the fields, but the sun was quite warm. The mountains stretched away, disappearing into sky and cloud. Rusty felt he belonged there, to the hills and the pine and deodar forests, and the clear mountain streams.

There were about thirty families in the village. There were not many men about, and the few that could be found were either old or inactive. Most young men joined the army or took jobs in the plains, for the village economy was poor. The women remained behind to do the work. They fetched water, kept the houses clean, cooked meals, and would soon be ploughing the fields. The old men just sat around and smoked hookahs and gossiped the morning away.

It had been a long, lonely walk from the bus terminus at Lansdowne to Hathi's village. Rusty had walked fast, because there had been no one to talk to, and no food to be had on the way. But he had met a farmer, coming from the opposite direction, and had shared the man's meal. All the farmer had were some onions and a few chappatis; but Rusty was hungry and he enjoyed the meal. When he had finished, he said goodbye, and they went their different ways.

At first he walked along a smooth slippery carpet of pine-needles; then the pine trees gave way to oak and rhododendron. It was cool and shady; but after Rusty had done about fifteen miles, the forest ended, the hills became bare and rocky, and the earth, the colour of copper. He was thirsty, but there was nothing to drink. His tongue felt thick and furry and he could barely move his lips. All he could do was walk on mechanically, hardly conscious of his surroundings or even of walking.

When the sun went down, a cool breeze came whispering across the dry grass. And then, as he climbed higher, the grass grew greener, there were trees, water burst from the hillsides in small springs, and birds swooped across the path—bright green parrots, tree-pies, and paradise flycatchers. He was walking beside a river, above the turbulent water rushing down a narrow gorge. It was a steep climb to Hathi's village; and as it grew dark, he had to pick his way carefully along the narrow path.

As he approached Hathi's house, on the outskirts of the village, he was knocked down by a huge Tibetan mastiff. He got up, and Hathi came out of the house and ran to greet Rusty and knocked him over again. Then he was in the house, drinking hot milk. And later he lay on a sofa quilt, and a star was winking at him from the skylight.

The house was solid, built of yellow granite, and it had a black-tiled roof. There was an orange tree in the courtyard, and though there were no oranges on it at that time of the year, the young leaves smelt sweet. When Rusty looked around, he saw mountains, blue and white-capped, with dark clouds drifting down the valleys. Pale blue woodsmoke climbed the hill from the houses below, and people drifted about in the warm winter sunshine.

When Rusty and Hathi walked in the hills they sometimes went barefoot. Once they walked a few miles upstream, and found a waterfall dashing itself down on to smooth rocks fifty feet below. Here the forest was dark and damp, and at night bears and leopards roamed the hillsides. When the leopards were hungry, they did not hesitate to enter villages and carry off stray dogs.

Once Rusty heard the hunting-cry of a leopard on the prowl. It was evening, and he was close to the village, when he heard the harsh, saw-like cry, something between a grunt and a cough. Then the leopard appeared to his right, slinking through the trees, crouching low, a swift black shadow ...

There was only one shop in the village, and that was also the post office; it sold soap and shoes and the barest necessities. When Rusty passed it, he was hailed by the shopkeeper, who was brandishing a postcard. Rusty was surprised that there should be a letter for him.

He was even more surprised when he discovered that the card was from Sudheer, the Lafunga.

It said: 'Join me at Lansdowne. I have news of your aunt. We will travel together. I have money for both of us, as I consider you a good investment.'

RUM AND CURRY

SUDHEER AND RUSTY LEFT Lansdowne early one morning, and by the time they reached the oak and deodar forests of Kotli they were shivering with the cold.

'I am not used to this sort of travel,' complained Sudheer. 'If this is a wild goose chase, I will curse you, Rusty. At least we should have mules to sit on.'

'We are sure to find a village soon,' said Rusty. 'We can spend a night there. As for it being a wild goose chase, it was you who told me that my aunt lived somewhere here. If she is not in this direction, it is all your fault, Lafunga.'

There was little light in the Kotli forest, for the tall, crowded deodars and oaks kept out the moonlight. The road was damp and covered with snails.

They were relieved to find a few small huts clustered together in an open clearing. A light showed from only one of the houses. Rusty rapped on the hard oak door, and called out: 'Is anyone there? We want a place to spend the night.'

'Who is it?' asked a nervous, irritable voice.

'Travellers,' said Sudheer. 'Tired, hungry and poor.'

'This is not a *dharamsala*,' grumbled the man inside. 'This is no place for pilgrims.'

'We are not pilgrims,' said Sudheer, trying a different approach. 'We are road inspectors, servants of the government—so open up, my friend!'

They heard much ill-natured muttering before the door opened, revealing an old and dirty man, who had stubble on his chin, warts on his feet, and grease on his old clothes.

'Where do you come from?' he asked suspiciously.

'Lansdowne,' said Rusty. 'We have walked twenty miles since morning. Can we sleep in your house?'

'How do I know you are not thieves?' asked the old man, who did not look very honest himself.

'If we were thieves,' said Sudheer impatiently, 'we would not stand here, talking to you. We would have cut your throat and thrown you to the vultures, and carried off your beautiful daughter.'

'I have no daughter here.'

'What a pity! Never mind. My friend and I will sleep in your house tonight. We are not going to sleep in the forest.'

Sudheer strode into the lighted room, but backed out almost immediately, holding his fingers to his nose.

'What dead animal are you keeping here?' he cried.

'They are sheepskins, for curing,' said the old man. 'What is wrong?'

'Nothing, nothing,' said Sudheer, not wishing to hurt their host's feelings so soon; but in an aside to Rusty, he whispered, 'There is such a stink, I doubt if we will wake up in the morning.'

They stumbled into the room, and Rusty dumped his bundle on the ground. The room was bare, except for dilapidated sheep and deer skins hanging on the walls. There was a small fire in a corner of the room. Sudheer and Rusty got as close to it as they could, stamping their feet and chafing their hands. The old man sat down on his haunches and glared suspiciously at the intruders. Sudheer looked at him, and then at Rusty, and shrugged eloquently.

'May we know your name?' asked Rusty.

'It is Ram Singh,' said the old man grudgingly.

'Well, Ram Singh, my host,' said Sudheer solicitiously, 'have you had your meal as yet?'

'I take it in the morning,' said Ram Singh.

'And in the evening?' Sudheer's voice held a note of hope.

'It is not necessary to eat more than once a day.'

'For a rusty old fellow like you, perhaps,' said Sudheer, 'but we have got blood in our veins. Is there nothing here to eat? Surely you have some bread, some vegetables?'

'I have nothing,' said the old man.

'Well, we will have to wait till morning,' said Sudheer. 'Rusty, take out the blanket and the bottle of rum.'

Rusty took the blanket from their bag, and a flask of rum slipped out from the folds. Ram Singh showed unmistakable signs of coming to life.

'Is that medicine you have?' asked the old man. 'I have been suffering from headaches for the last month.'

'Well, this will give you a worse headache,' said Sudheer, gulping down a mouthful of rum and licking his lips. 'Besides, for people who eat only once a day, it is dangerous stuff.'

'We could get something to eat,' said the old man eagerly.

'You said you had nothing,' said Rusty, taking the bottle from Sudheer and putting it to his lips.

'There are some pumpkins on the roof,' said the old man. 'And I have a few potatoes and some spices. Shall I make a curry?'

And an hour later, warmed by rum and curry, they sat round the fire in a most convivial fashion. Rusty and Sudheer had gathered their only blanket about their shoulders, and Ram Singh had covered himself in sheepskins. He had been asking them questions about life in the cities—a life that was utterly foreign to him.

'You are men of the world,' said Ram Singh. 'You have been in most of the cities of India, you have known all kinds of men and women. I have never travelled beyond Lansdowne, nor have I seen the trains and ships which I hear so much about. I am seventy and I have not seen these things, though I have sons who have been away many years, and one who has even been out of

India with his regiment. I would like to ask your advice. It is lonely living alone, and though I have had three wives, they are all dead.'

'If you have had three wives,' said Sudheer, 'you are a man of the world!'

He had his back to the wall, his feet stuck out towards the fire. Rusty was half-asleep, his head resting on Sudheer's shoulder.

'My daughters are all married,' continued Ram Singh. 'I would like to get married again, but tell me, how should I go about it?'

Sudheer laughed out loud. The old man in his youth must have been as crafty a devil as the Lafunga himself.

'Well, you would have to pay for her, of course,' said Sudheer.

'Tell me of a suitable woman. She should be young, of course. Her nose—what kind of nose should she have?'

'A flat nose,' said Sudheer, without the ghost of a smile. 'The nostrils should not be turned up.'

'Ah! And the shape of her body?'

'Not too manly. She should not be crooked. Do not expect too much, old man!'

'Her head?' aked the old man eagerly. 'What should her head be like?'

Sudheer gave this a moment's consideration. 'The head should not be bald,' he said.

Ram Singh nodded his approval; his opinion of Sudheer was going up by leaps and bounds.

'And her colour, should it be white?'

'No, not very white.'

'Black?'

'Not too black. But she would have to be evil-smelling, otherwise she would not stay with you.'

*

A bear kept them awake during the early part of the night. It clambered up on the roof and made a meal of the old man's store of pumpkins.

'Can it get in?' asked Rusty.

'It comes every night,' said Ram Singh. 'But it is a vegetarian and eats only the pumpkins.'

There was a thud as a pumpkin rolled off the roof and landed on the ground. Then the bear climbed down from the roof and shambled off into the forest.

The fire was glowing feebly, but Sudheer and Rusty were warm beneath their blanket and, being very tired, were soon asleep, despite the efforts of an army of bugs to keep them awake. But at about midnight they were woken by a loud cry and, starting up, found the lantern lit, and the old man throwing a fit.

Ram Singh was leaping about the room, waving his arms, going into contortions, and bringing up gurgling sounds from the back of his throat.

'What is the matter?' shouted Rusty, from under the blanket. 'Have you gone mad?'

For reply, the old man gurgled and shrieked, and continued his frenzied dance.

'A demon!' he shouted. 'A demon has entered me!'

Sudheer leapt to his feet. He had heard of the superstitions of some hill-people, of their belief in spirits, but he had never expected to witness such a performance.

'It's the medicine you gave me!' cried Ram Singh. 'The medicine was evil, it is all your doing!' And he continued dancing about the room.

'Should I throw the medicine away?' asked Sudheer.

'No, don't do that!' shouted Ram Singh, appearing normal for a moment. 'Throw yourself on the ground!'

Sudheer threw himself on the ground.

'On your back!' gasped the old man.

Sudheer turned over on to his back. Rusty had lifted a corner of the blanket, and was watching, fascinated.

'Raise your left foot,' said the old man. 'Take it in your mouth. That will charm the demon away.'

'I will not put my foot in my mouth,' said Sudheer, getting to his feet, having lost faith in the genuineness of the old man's fit. 'I don't think there is any demon in you. It is probably your curry. Have something more to drink, and you will be all right.'

He produced the all but empty flask of rum, made the old man open his mouth, and poured the rest of the spirit down his throat.

Ram Singh choked, shook his head violently, and grinned at Sudheer. 'The demon has gone now,' he said.

'I am glad to know it,' said Sudheer. 'But you have emptied the bottle. Now let us try to sleep again.'

The cold had come in through the blanket, and Rusty found sleep difficult. Instead, he began to think of the purpose of his journey, and wondered if it would not have been wiser to stay in Dehra. Outside, the air was still; the wind had stopped whistling through the pines. Only a jackal howled in the distance. The old man was tossing and turning on his sheepskins.

'Ram Singh,' whispered Rusty. 'Are you awake?'

Ram Singh groaned softly.

'Tell me,' said Rusty. 'Have you heard of a woman living alone in these parts?'

'There are many old women here.'

'No, I mean a well-to-do woman. She must be about forty. At one time she was married to a white sahib.'

'Ah, I have heard of such a woman . . . She was beautiful when she was young, they tell me.'

Rusty was silent. He was afraid to ask any further questions; afraid to know too much; afraid of finding out too soon that there was nothing for him and nowhere to go.

'Ram Singh,' he whispered. 'Where does this woman live?'

'She had her house on the road to Rishikesh . . .'

'And the woman, where is she? Is she dead?'

'I do not know, I have not heard of her recently,' said Ram Singh. 'Why do you ask of her? Are you related to the sahib?'

'No,' said Rusty. 'I have heard of her, that's all.'

Silence. The old man grumbled to himself, muttering quietly, and then began to snore. The jackal was silent, the wind was up again; the moon was lost in the clouds. Rusty felt Sudheer's hand slip into his own, and press his fingers. He was surprised to find him awake.

'Forget it,' whispered Sudheer. 'Forget the dead, forget the past. Trouble your heart no longer. I have enough for both of us, so let us live on it till it is finished, and let us be happy. Rusty, my friend, let us be happy . . .'

Rusty did not reply, but he held the Lafunga's hand and returned the pressure of his fingers to let him know that he was listening.

'This is only the beginning,' said Sudheer. 'The world is waiting for us.'

*

Rusty woke first, scratching and rubbing his legs. Looking up at the skylight, he saw the first glimmer of dawn. He slipped on his clothes and torn socks and, without waking Sudheer or the old man, unlatched the door and stepped outside.

Before him lay a world of white.

It had snowed in the early hours of the morning, while they had been sleeping. The snow lay thick on the ground carpeting the hillside. There was not a breath of wind; the pine trees stood blanched and still, and a deep silence hung over the forest and the hills.

Rusty did not immediately wake up the others. He wanted this all to himself—the snow and the silence and the coming of the sun . . .

Towards the horizon, the sky was red; and then the sun came over the hills and struck the snow; and Rusty ran to the top of the hill and stood in the dazzling sunlight, shading his eyes from the glare, taking in the range of mountains and the valley and the stream that cut its way through the snow like a dark trickle of oil. He ran down the hill and into the house.

'Wake up!' he shouted, shaking Sudheer. 'Get up, and come outside!'

'Why—have you found your treasure?' complained Sudheer sleepily. 'Or has the old man had another fit?'

'More than that—it has snowed!'

'Then I shall definitely not come outside,' said Sudheer. And turning over, he went to sleep again.

Lady with a Hookah

Rusty glimpsed the house as they came through the trees, and he knew at once that it was the place they had been looking for. It had obviously been built by an Englishman, with its wide veranda and sloping corrugated roof, like the house in Dehra where he had lived with his guardian. It stood in the knoll of a hill, surrounded by an orchard of apple and plum trees.

'This must be the place,' said Sudheer. 'Shall we just walk in?'

'Well, the gate is open,' said Rusty.

They had barely entered the gate when a huge black Tibetan mastiff appeared on the front veranda. It did not bark, but a low growl rumbled in its throat, and this was a more dangerous portent. The dog bounded down the steps and made for the gate, and Sudheer and Rusty scrambled back up the hillside, showing no signs of their weariness. The dog remained at the gate, growling as before.

A servant-boy appeared on the veranda and called out, 'Who is it? What do you want?'

'We wish to see the lady who lives here,' replied Sudheer.

'She is resting,' said the boy. 'She cannot see anyone now.'

'We have come all the way from Dehra,' said Sudheer. 'My friend is a relative of hers. Tell her that, and she will see him.'

'She isn't going to believe that,' Rusty whispered fiercely.

The boy, with a doubtful glance at both of them, went indoors, and was gone for some five minutes. When he reappeared on the veranda, he called the dog inside and chained it to the railing.

Then he beckoned to Rusty and Sudheer to follow him. They went in cautiously at the gate.

He was a fair, lynx-eyed boy, and he stared appraisingly at them for a few moments, before saying, 'She is at the back. Come with me.'

They went round the house, along a paved path, and on to another veranda which looked out on the mountains. Rusty looked first at the view, and took his eyes away from the hills only when Sudheer tugged at his sleeve; then he looked into the veranda, but he could see nothing at first because of a difference in light. Only when he stepped into the shade was he able to make out someone—a woman reclining, barefooted and wearing a white sari, on a string cot. An elaborate hookah was set before her, and its long, pliable stem rose well above the level of the bed, so that she could manoeuvre it with comfort.

She looked surprisingly young. Rusty had expected to find an older woman. His aunt did not look over thirty-five; she was, in fact, forty. Having met an aged contemporary of his father's in Mr Pettigrew, he had expected his aunt to be an old woman; but now he remembered that she had been the wife of his father's younger brother. She came from a village in the higher ranges; and this accounted for her good colour, her long black hair—and her hookah. She looked physically strong, and her face, though lacking femininity, was strikingly handsome.

'Please sit down,' she said; and Sudheer and Rusty, finding that chairs had materialized from behind while they stood staring at the lady, sank into them. The boy pattered away into the interior of the house.

'You have come a long way to see me,' she said. 'It must be important.' And she looked from Rusty to Sudheer, and back to Rusty, curious to know which of them concerned her. Her eyes rested on Rusty, on his eyes, and she said,' You are *angrez*, aren't you?'

'Partly,' he said. 'I came to see you, because—because you knew my father—and I was told—I was told you would see me ...' Rusty did not quite know what he should say, or how to say it.

'Your father?' she said encouraging him, and he noticed a flicker of interest in her eyes. 'Who is your father?'

'He died when I was very young,' said Rusty. And when he told her his father's name, she thrust the hookah aside and leaned forward to look closely at the boy. 'You *are* his son, then . . .'

Rusty nodded.

'Yes, you are his son. You have his eyes and nose and forehead. I would have known it without your telling me if it had not been so dark in here.' With an agility that was another surprise to Rusty, she sprang off the cot, and pulled aside the curtains that covered one side of the veranda. Sunlight streamed in, bringing out the richness of her colouring.

'So you are only a boy,' she said smiling at him indulgently. 'You must be sixteen—seventeen—I remember you only as a child, being taken up and down the Mall, in Mussoorie. Fourteen, fifteen years ago . . .' She put her hands to her cheeks, as though she would feel the lines of advancing age; but her cheeks were still smooth, her youth was still with her. It came of living in the hills; of not having had children, perhaps; of having just enough of everything and not too much.

'I came to you because you knew my father well.'

They were sitting again, and Sudheer's long legs stretched across the width of the veranda. Rusty sat beside his aunt's cot.

'I wish there was something of your father's which I could give you,' she said. 'He did not leave much money. I would have offered to look after you, but I was told you had a guardian, one of your father's relatives. You must have been in good hands. Later, after my husband's death, I tried to get news of you; but I lived far from any town and was out of touch with what was happening elsewhere. I am alone now. But I don't mind. Your uncle left me this house and the land around it. I have my dog.' She stroked the huge mastiff who sat devotedly beside her. 'And I have the boy. He is a good boy and looks after me well. You are welcome to stay with us, Rusty.'

'No, I did not come for that,' said Rusty. 'You are very generous, but I do not want to be a burden on anyone.'

'You will be no burden. And if you are, it doesn't matter.' She shook her head sadly. 'How was he to know? He was well and strong one day, dying the next. But let us not depress ourselves. Come, tell me about your tall friend, and what you propose to do, and where you are going from here. It is late, and you must take your meal with us and stay the night. You will need an entire day if you are going to Rishikesh. I have rooms and beds sufficient for several large families.'

*

They sat together in the twilight, and Rusty told his aunt about his quarrel with his guardian, of his friendship with Kishen and Devinder and Sudheer the Lafunga. When it was dark, his aunt drew a shawl around her shoulders and took them indoors; and Bisnu, the boy, brought them food on brass *thalis*, from which they ate sitting on the ground. Afterwards, they remained talking for about an hour, and the Lafunga expressed his admiration for a woman who could live alone in the hills without giving way to loneliness or despair. Rusty tried smoking the hookah, but it gave him a splitting headache, and when eventually he went to bed he could not sleep. Sudheer set up a rhythmic snoring, each snore gaining in tone and vibrancy, reminding Rusty of the brain-fever bird he often heard in Dehra.

He left his bed and walked out on the veranda. The moon showed through the trees, and he walked down the garden path where fallen apples lay rotting in the moonlight. When he turned at the gate to walk back towards the house, he saw someone standing in the veranda. Could it be a ghost? No, it was his aunt in her white sari, watching him.

'What is wrong, Rusty?' she asked, as he approached. 'Why are you wandering about at this time? I thought you were a ghost—and I was frightened, because I haven't seen one in years.'

'I've never seen one at all,' said Rusty. 'What are ghosts really like?'

'Oh, they are usually the spirits of immoral women, and they have their feet facing backwards. They are called *churels*. There are other kinds, too. But why are you out here?'

'I have a headache. I couldn't sleep.'

'All right. Come and talk to me.' And taking Rusty by the hand, she led him into her large moonlit room, and made him lie down. Then she took his head in her hands, and with her strong cool fingers pressed his forehead and massaged his temples; and she began telling him a story, but her fingers were more persuasive than her tongue, and Rusty fell asleep before the tale could be finished.

Next morning, while Sudheer slept late, she took Rusty round the house and grounds.

'I have some of your books,' she said, when they came indoors. 'You are probably too old for some of them now, but your father asked me to keep them for you. Especially *Alice in Wonderland*. He was particular about that one, I don't know why.'

She brought the books out, and the sight of their covers brought back the whole world of his childhood—lazy afternoons in the shade of a jackfruit tree, a book in his hand, while squirrels and magpies chattered in the branches above. The book-shelf in his grandfather's study; the books had not been touched for years when Rusty first discovered them. *Alice* had been there, and *Treasure Island*, and *Mister Midshipman Easy*—they had been Rusty's grandfather's, then his father's and finally his own. He had read them by the time he was eight; but he had been in boarding-school when his father died, and he did not see the books again after going to live in his guardian's house.

Now, after ten years, they had turned up once more, in the possession of this strange aunt who lived alone in the mountains.

He decided to take the books, because they had once been part of his life. They were the only link between him and his father— they were his only legacy.

'Must you go back to Dehra?' asked his aunt.

'I promised my friends I would return. Later, I will decide what I should do and where I should go. During these last few months I have been a vagrant. And I used to dream of becoming a writer!'

'You can write here,' she said. 'And you can be a farmer, too.'

'Oh no, I will just be a nuisance. And anyway, I must stand on my own feet. I'm too old to be looked after by others.'

'You are old enough to look after me,' she said putting her hand on his. 'Let us be burdens on each other. I am lonely, sometimes. I know you have friends, but they cannot care for you if you are sick or in trouble. You have no parents. I have no children. It is as simple as that.'

She looked up as a shadow fell across the doorway. Sudheer was standing there in his pyjamas, grinning sheepishly at them.

'I'm hungry,' he said. 'Aunty, will you feed us before we reluctantly leave your house?'

THE ROAD TO RISHIKESH

SUDHEER AND RUSTY SET out on foot for Rishikesh, that small town straddling the banks of the Ganges where the great river emerges from the hills to stretch itself across the wide plains of northern India. In this town of saints and mendicants and pilgrims, Sudheer proposed to set up headquarters. Dehra was no longer safe, with the police and the *seth* still looking for him. He had already spent a considerable sum from the money he had appropriated; and he hoped that in Rishikesh, where all manner of men congregated, there would be scope for lucrative projects. And from Rishikesh, Rusty could take a bus to Dehra whenever he felt like returning. He had no immediate plan in mind, but was content to be on the road again with the Lafunga, as he had been with Kishen. He knew that he would soon tire of this aimless wandering, and wondered if he should return to his aunt. But for the time being he was content to wander; and with the Lafunga beside him, he felt carefree and reckless, ready for almost anything.

At noon, they arrived at a small village on the Rishikesh road. From here a bus went twice daily to Rishikesh, and they were just in time to catch the last one.

Though there was no snow, there had been rain. The road was full of slush and heaps of rubble that had fallen from the hillside. The bus carried very few passengers. Sacks of flour and potatoes took up most of the space.

The driver—unshaven, smoking a bidi—did not inspire confidence. Throughout the journey he kept up a heated political discussion with a passenger seated directly behind him. With one hand on the steering-wheel, he used the other hand to make his point, gesticulating, and shouting in order to be heard above the rattle of the bus.

Nevertheless, Sudheer and Rusty enjoyed the ride. Rusty laughed whenever Sudheer's head hit the roof, and Sudheer sought comfort from the other passengers' discomfiture.

A stalwart, good-looking young farmer sitting opposite Sudheer, said, 'I would feel safer if this was a government bus. Then, if we were killed, there would be some compensation for our families—or for us, if we were not dead!'

'Yes, let us be cheerful about these things,' said Sudheer. 'Take our driver, for instance. Do you think he is troubled at the thought of being reborn as a snake tomorrow? Not he!'

'Why should he be a snake?' asked the farmer. 'Why not a rat?'

'Well, he could be a rat,' said Sudheer. 'He's a political person, as you can see.'

They gazed out of the window, down a sheer two-hundred-foot cliff that fell to a boulder-strewn stream. The road was so narrow that they could not see the edge. Trees stood out perpendicularly from the cliff-face. A waterfall came gushing down from the hillside and sprayed the top of the bus, splashing in at the windows. The wheels of the bus turned up stones and sent them rolling downhill; they mounted the rubble of a landslip and went churning through a stretch of muddy water.

The driver was so immersed in his discussion that when he saw a boulder right in the middle of the road he did not have time to apply the brakes. It must be said to his credit that he did not take the bus over the cliff; instead, he rammed it into the hillside, and there it stuck. Being quite used to accidents of this nature, the driver sighed, re-lit his bidi, and returned to his argument.

As there were only eight miles left for Rishikesh, the passengers decided to walk.

Sudheer once more got into conversation with the farmer, whose name he now knew to be Ganpat. Most of the produce in the bus was Ganpat's; no doubt the bus would take an extra day to arrive in Rishikesh, and that would give him an excuse for prolonging his stay in town and enjoying himself out of sight of his family.

'Is there any place in Rishikesh where we can spend the night?' asked Sudheer.

'There are many *dharamsalas* for pilgrims,' said Ganpat.

Finding some purpose to their enforced trek, they set out with even longer and more vigorous strides. Ganpat had a fine sun-darkened body, a strong neck set on broad shoulders, and a heavy, almost military, moustache. He wore his dhoti well; his strong ankles and broad feet were burnished by the sun, hardened by years of walking barefoot through the fields.

Soon he and the Lafunga had discovered something in common—they were both connoisseurs of beautiful women.

'I like them tall and straight,' said Ganpat, twirling his moustache. 'They must not be too fussy, and not too talkative. How does one please them?'

'Have you heard of the great sage Vatsayana? He had three wives. One he pleased with secret confidences, the other with secret respect, and the third with secret flattery.'

'You are a strange fellow,' said Ganpat.

*

Rusty had hurried on ahead of the others. Feeling fresh and exhilarated, he had an urge to reach the river before anything else. He wanted to be waiting for Sudheer at Rishikesh; and he wanted to be alone for a while.

A thickly forested mountain hid the river, but Rusty knew it was there and where it was and what it looked like. He had heard, from Hathi, of the fish in its waters, of its rocks and currents, and it only remained for him to touch the water and know it personally.

The path dropped steeply into a valley, then rose and went round a big mountain. Rusty passed a woodcutter and asked him how far it was to the river. The woodcutter was a short stocky man, with a creased and weathered face.

'Seven miles,' he said, fairly accurately. 'Why do you want to know?'

'I am going to Rishikesh,' said Rusty.

'Alone?'

'The others are following, but I cannot wait for them. You will meet them on the way. When you see the Lafunga, the tall one, tell him I will be waiting at the river.'

'I will tell him,' said the woodcutter, and took his leave.

The path descended steeply, and Rusty had to run a little. It was a dizzy, winding path; he slipped once or twice. The hillside was covered with lush green ferns, and, in the trees, unseen birds sang loudly. Soon he was in the valley, and the path straightened out. A girl was coming from the opposite direction. She held a long, curved knife, with which she had been cutting grass and fodder. There were rings in her nose and ears, and her arms were covered with heavy bangles. She smiled innocently at Rusty—no girl in the plains had ever done that; the bangles made music when she moved her hands—it was as though her hands spoke a language of their own.

'How far is it to the river?' asked Rusty.

The girls had probably never been near the river, or she may have been thinking of another one, for she replied, 'Twenty miles,' without any hesitation.

Rusty laughed and ran down the path. A parrot screeched suddenly, flew low over his head, a flash of blue and green. It took the course of the path, and Rusty followed its dipping flight, running until the path rose and the bird disappeared in the trees. He loved these hills, which offered him their freedom, their own individual strength, allowing the boy to be himself, Rusty. Yes, he would want to come back to them . . .

A trickle of water came out of the hillside, and Rusty stopped to drink. The water was cold and sharp and very refreshing. He had walked alone for nearly an hour. Presently he saw another boy ahead of him, driving a few goats down the path.

'How far is the river?' asked Rusty, when he had caught up with the boy.

The village boy said, 'Oh, not far, just round the next hill and then straight down.'

Rusty, feeling hungry, produced some dry bread from his pocket and, breaking it in two, offered one half to the boy. They sat on the hillside and ate in silence. When they had finished, they walked on together and began talking; and talking, Rusty did not notice the smarting of his feet or the distance he had covered. But after some time his companion had to diverge along another path, and Rusty was once more on his own.

He missed the village boy; he looked up and down the path, but could see no one, no sign of Sudheer, and the river was not in sight either. He began to feel discouraged; he felt tired and isolated. But he walked on, along the dusty, stony path; past terraced fields and huts, until there were no more fields, only forest and sun and silence.

The silence was impressive and a little frightening; different from the silence of a room or an empty street. There was not much movement either, except for the bending of grass beneath his feet, and the circling of a hawk high above the pine trees.

And then, as he rounded a sharp bend, the silence broke into sound.

The sound of the river.

Far down in the valley, the river stretched and opened into broad, beautiful motion, and Rusty gasped and began to run. He slipped and stumbled, but still he ran. Then he was ankle-deep in the cold mountain water.

And the water was blue and white and wonderful.

End of a Journey

IT WAS THE FESTIVAL of the Full Moon. The temples at Rishikesh lay bathed in a soft clear light. The broad, slow-moving Ganges caught the moonlight and held it, to become a river of liquid silver. Along the shore, devotees floated little lights downstream. The wicks were placed in earthen vessels, where they burned for a few minutes, a red-gold glow. Rusty lay on the sand and watched them float by, one by one, until they went out or were caught amongst rocks and shingle.

Sudheer and Ganpat had gone into the town to seek amusement, but Rusty preferred to stay by the river, at a little distance from the embankment where hundreds of pilgrims had gathered.

Had it been summer, he could have slept on the sand, but it was cold, and his blanket was no protection against the icy wind that blew down from the mountains. He went into a lighted *dharamsala*, and settled down in a corner of the crowded room. Rolling himself into his blanket, he closed his eyes, listening to the desultory talk of pilgrims sheltering in the building.

The full moon does strange things to some people. In the hills, it is inclined to touch off a little madness; and its effect on those who are already a little mad—like Sudheer—is to make them madder.

When the moon is at the full, some converse with spirits, others lose all their inhibitions and dance in frenzied abandon; some love more ardently, and a few kill more readily. 'Do not sleep in the light of a full moon,' warn the pundits, 'it will bewitch you, and turn you to beautiful but evil thoughts.'

The moon made Sudheer the Lafunga a little drunk. But the moon not being enough, he consumed a bottle of country-made liquor with Ganpat. The drink had confused Ganpat and affected his judgement—was he dreaming, or did he really see Sudheer hopping about in the middle of the street, slapping himself on the buttocks?

'Sudheer,' he said, steadying himself. 'Are you dancing in the road, or am I drunk?'

'You are drunk,' said Sudheer. 'But it is true that I am dancing in the road.'

'Why do you do it?' asked Ganpat.

'Because I feel happy,' said Sudheer.

'Then I must try it,' said Ganpat. And he, too, began hopping about on the road, and slapping himself on the buttocks.

*

Rishikesh comes to life at an early hour. The priests, sanyasis and their disciples rise at three, as soon as there is a little light in the sky, and begin their ablutions and meditation. From about five o'clock, pilgrims start coming down to the river to bathe. Along the bathing-steps walk saffron-robed sadhus and wandering mendicants, whilst the older and senior men sit on small edifices beneath shady trees, where they receive money and gifts from pilgrims, and dispense blessings in return.

Rusty had bathed early, leaving Sudheer and Ganpat asleep in the *dharamsala*. These two revellers had come in at two o'clock in the morning, disturbing others in the shelter. They did not get up until the sun had risen. Then Ganpat crossed the river in a ferry boat, in order to visit the temples on the other side, there to propitiate the gods with offerings of his own. Sudheer made his way outside to try and acquire a suitable disguise, as he had to visit Dehra for a few days. Dressed as he was, he world soon be spotted by the *seth*'s informers. Later, he met Rusty at the bus-stand.

'I will be back tomorrow,' said Sudheer. 'I do not take you with me, because in Dehra my company would be dangerous for you.'

'Why must you be going to Dehra, then?' asked Rusty.

'Well, there are one or two people who owe me money,' he said. 'And though, as you know, we have plenty to go on with, these people are not loved by me, so why should they keep my money? And another thing. There are two beautiful women in Dehra—one is Hastini and the other Mrinalini—and I must return the money I borrowed from them.'

'And why did you borrow money from them?' asked Rusty.

'Because I owed a debt to Devinder,' said Sudheer, with a wide smile. 'And he wanted the money for you! Isn't life complicated?'

When the bus moved off in a cloud of dust, Rusty turned away. He sauntered through the bazaar, going from one sweet shop to another, assessing the quality of their different wares. Eventually he bought eight annas worth of hot, fresh, golden jalebis and, carrying them in a large plate made of banana leaves, went down to the river.

At the river-side grew a banyan tree, and Rusty sat in its shade and ate his sweets. The tree was full of birds—parrots and bulbuls and rosy pastors—feeding on the ripe red figs of the banyan. Rusty enjoyed leaning back against the trunk of the tree, listening to the chatter of the birds, studying their plumage.

When the sweets were finished, he rose and wandered along the banks of the river. On a stretch of sand two boys were wrestling. They were on their knees, arms interlocked, pressing forward like mad bulls, each striving to throw the other. The taller boy had the advantage at first; the smaller boy, who was dark and pock-marked, appeared to be yielding; but then there was a sudden flurry of arms and legs, and the small boy sat victorious across his opponent's chest.

When they saw Rusty watching them, the boys asked him if he would like to wrestle. But Rusty declined the invitation. He had eaten too many jalebis and felt sick.

He walked until the sickness had passed and he was hungry again (the trek to Rishikesh had increased his already healthy appetite), and returning to the bazaar, he feasted on puris and a well-spiced vegetable curry.

Well-stuffed with puris, he returned to the banyan tree, and slept right through the afternoon.

*

At midnight, in Dehra, Sudheer was paying a clandestine visit to Mrinalini. Knowing that he would have to stay away for some time, he wished to see her just once again, in order to make her a gift and a promise of his fidelity.

It took him a few seconds to climb the treacherous flight of stairs that led to Mrinalini's rooms. Every time he climbed those stairs, they swayed and plunged about more heavily.

Mrinalini was preparing herself for a visitor; she sat in front of a cracked, discoloured mirror which distorted her fine features into hideous dimensions. Whenever she looked into the distorting mirror, and saw the bloated face, the crooked eyes, the smear of paint, she thought: One day I will look like that; one day, not long from now, I will be as ugly as that reflection ... And when she looked in the mirror again, it was always the reflection of her mother that she saw.

By contrast, Sudheer's reflection, when it appeared beside her in the mirror, reminded her of a horse—a horse with a rather long and silly face. And seeing it there, she laughed.

'What are you laughing at?' said Sudheer.

'At you, of course! You look so stupid in the mirror!'

'I did not know that,' said Sudheer, his vanity a little hurt. 'Hastini does not think so.'

'Hastini is a fool. She liked you because she thinks you are handsome. I like you because you have a face like a horse.'

'Well, your horse is going to be away from Dehra for some time. I hope you will not miss him.'

'You are always coming and going, but never staying.'

'That's life.'

'Doesn't it make you lonely?'

Mrinalini had stood up from the mirror, and now she went over to the bed, where she made herself comfortable against a pillow.

'When I am lonely, I do something,' said Sudheer, standing over her, looking very tall. 'I go out and do something foolish or dangerous. When I am not doing things, I am lonely. But I was not made for loneliness.'

'I am lonely sometimes.'

'You! With your mother? She never leaves you alone. And you have visitors nearly every day, and many new faces.'

'Yes. The more people I see, the lonelier I get. You must have some companion, someone to talk to and quarrel with, if you are not to be lonely. You can find such a companion. But who can I find? My mother is old and deaf and heartless.'

'One day I will come and take you away from here. I have some money now, Mrinalini. As soon as I have started a business in another town, I will call you there. Meanwhile, why not stay with Hastini?'

'I hate her.'

'You do not know her yet. When you know her, you will love her!'

'You love her.'

'I love her because she is so comfortable. I love you because you are so sweet. Can I help it if I love you both?'

'You are strange,' said Mrinalini with one of her rare smiles. 'Go now. Someone will be coming.'

'Then keep this for me,' said Sudheer.

He took a thin gold ring from his finger, and slipped it on to the third finger of Mrinalini's right hand.

'Keep it for me till I return,' he said. 'And if I do not return, then keep it for ever. Sell it only if you are in need. All right?'

Mrinalini stared at the ring for some time, turning it about on her finger, so that the light fell on it in different places. She slipped it off her finger and hid it in her blouse.

'If I keep it on my hand, my mother will be sure to take it.'

Sudheer said, 'If only you would allow me, I'd finish off your mother for you.'

'Don't talk like that! She has not long to live . . .'

'She is doing her best to outlive all of us. I would not be violent, I promise you. I would not even touch her. I would simply frighten her to death. I could pounce on her from a dark alley, or let off a firecracker . . .'

'Sudheer!' cried Mrinalini. 'How can you be so cruel?'

'It would be a kindness.'

'Go now! Stay away from Dehra as long as you can.'

*

It was a wonderful morning in Rishikesh. There was a hint of spring in the air. Birds flashed across the water, and monkeys chased each other over the rooftops. Rusty lay on a stretch of sand, drinking in the crisp morning air, letting the sun sink into his body.

He had risen early, and had gone down to the river to bathe. Even before the *pujaris* had risen, he had run into the river, gasping with the shock of the cold water, threshing and embracing it, until the sluggishness left his body, and he felt clean and fresh and happy.

The touch of the water brought memories of his own secret pool that lay in the forest behind the church. Perhaps Devinder would be there now; perhaps Kishen, too, had joined him for the morning dip; and the Goonga would be sitting on a buffalo.

Rusty sat on the sand, nostalgically thinking of his friends; but there was another pull now, from the house in the hills; and he was certain that his future did not lie in Dehra. He decided he would leave Rishikesh immediately as soon as the Lafunga returned. After all, Sudheer was experienced in the ways of the world, and was never lacking in friends. Devinder and Kishen were of Rusty's age. He could understand and love them; and they could join him later. He could only love the Lafunga; he could not understand him.

Rusty lay on the white sand until the voices of distant bathers reached him, and the sun came hurrying over the hills. Slipping on his shirt and trousers, he went to the bazaar, where he found a little tea-shop; and there he drank a glass of hot, sweet, milky tea, and ate six eggs, to the amazement of the shopkeeper.

When he had finished eating, he strolled down to the bus-stand to see if Sudheer had returned. The second bus from Dehra had arrived, but Sudheer was not to be seen anywhere. Rusty was about to go back when, turning, he found himself looking into the eyes of a distinguished-looking young sadhu, who had three vermilion stripes across his forehead, an orange robe wound about his thighs and shoulders, and an extremely unsaintly grin on his face. The disguise might have deceived Rusty, but not the grin.

'So now you have become a sadhu,' said Rusty. 'And for whose benefit is this?'

'It was for some business in Dehra,' said Sudheer. 'I did not wish to be seen by the *seth* or his servants. Let us find a quiet place where we can talk. And let us get some fruit, I am hungry.'

Rusty bought six apples from a stall, and took Sudheer to the banyan tree. They sat on the ground, talking and munching apples.

'Did you see your friends?' asked Rusty.

'Yes, I went to them first. The bus had made me tired and angry, and there is no one like Hastini for soothing and refreshing one. Then I went to Mrinalini and asked her to come to Rishikesh, but she is still waiting for her mother to die. In life, people do nothing but wait for other people to die.'

Sudheer was already making new plans. 'Do I look all right?' he asked.

'You look as handsome as ever.'

'I know that. But do I look like a sadhu?'

'Yes, a very handsome sadhu.'

'All the better. Come, let us go.'

'Where do we go?' asked Rusty.

'To look for disciples, of course. A sadhu, such as I, must have disciples, and they should be rich disciples. There must be many fat, rich men in the world, who are unhappy about their consciences. Come, we will be their consciences! We will be respectable, Rusty. There is more money to be made that way. Yes, we will be respectable—what an adventure that will be!'

They began walking towards the bazaar.

'Wait!' said Rusty. 'I cannot come with you, Sudheer!'

Sudheer came to an abrupt halt. He turned and faced Rusty, a puzzled and disturbed expression on his face.

'What do you mean, you cannot come with me?'

'I must return to Dehra. I may come this way again, if I want to live with my aunt.'

'But why? You have just left her. You came to the hills for money, didn't you? And she didn't have any money.'

'I wanted to see her, too. I wanted to know what she was like. It isn't just a matter of money.'

'Well, you saw her. And there is no future for you with her, or in Dehra. What's the use of returning?'

'I don't know, Sudheer. What's the use of anything, for that matter? What would be the use of staying with you? I want to give some direction to my life. I want to work, I want to be free, I want to be able to write. I can't wander about the hills and plains with you for ever.'

'Why not? There is nothing to stop you, if you like to wander. India has always been the home of wanderers.'

'I might join you again, if I fail at everything else.'

Sudheer looked sullen and downcast.

'You do not realize . . .' he began; but stopped, groping for the right words; he had seldom been at a loss of words. 'I have got used to you, that is all,' he said.

'And I have got used to you, Sudheer. I don't think anyone else has ever done that.'

'That's why I don't want to lose you. But I cannot stop you from going.'

'I shall come to see you, I will, really . . .'

Sudheer brightened up a little. 'Do you promise? Or do you say that just to please me?'

'Both.'

Sudheer was his old self again, smiling, and digging his fingers into Rusty's arms. 'I'll be waiting for you,' he said. 'Whenever you want to look for treasure, come to me! Whenever you are looking for fun, come to me!'

Then he was silent again, and a shadow passed across his face. Did he, after all, know the meaning of loneliness? Perhaps Mrinalini had been right when she had said, 'You must have some companion, someone to talk to and quarrel with, if you are not to be lonely . . .'

'Let us part now,' said Sudheer. 'Let us not prolong it. You go down the street, to the bus-stand, and I'll go the other way.'

He held out his hand to Rusty. 'Your hand is not enough,' he said, and he put his arms round Rusty, and embraced him.

People stopped to stare; not because two youths were demonstrating their affection for each other—that was common enough—but because a sadhu in a saffron robe was behaving out of character.

When Sudheer realized this, he grinned at the passers-by; and they, embarrassed by his grin, and made nervous by his height, hurried on down the street.

Sudheer turned and walked away.

Rusty watched him for some time. The Lafunga stood out distinctly from the crowd of people in the bazaar, tall and handsome in his flowing robe.

First and Last Impressions

BECAUSE HE HAD TOLD no one of his return, there was no one to meet Rusty at Dehra station when he stepped down from a third class compartment. But on his way through the bazaar he met one of the tea-shop boys, who told him that Devinder might be found near the Clock Tower. And so he went to the Clock Tower, but he could not find his friend. Another familiar, a shoeshine boy, said he had last seen Devinder near the Courts, where business was brisk that day.

Rusty, feeling tired and dirty after his journey, decided he would look for Devinder later, and made his way to the church compound where he left his bag. Then he went through the jungle to the pool.

The Goonga was already there, bathing in the shallows,

gesticulating and shouting incomprehensibles at a band of langur monkeys who were watching him from the sal trees. When the Goonga saw Rusty, he chortled with delight, and rushed out of the water to give his friend and protector a hug.

'And how are you?' asked Rusty.

'Goo,' said the Goonga.

He was evidently very well. Devinder had been feeding him, and he no longer had need to prowl around tea-shops and receive kicks and insults in exchange for a glass of tea or a stale bun.

Rusty took off his clothes and leapt into the cold, sweet, delicious water of the pool. He floated languidly on the water, gazing up through the branches of an overhanging sal, through a pattern of broad tree leaves, into a blind-blue sky. The Goonga sat on a rock and grinned at the monkeys, making encouraging sounds. Looking from the Goonga to the monkeys and back to the hairy, long-armed youth, Rusty wondered how anyone could doubt Darwin's theories.

'And quite obviously, I belong to the same species,' he thought, joining the Goonga on the rock and making noises of his own. 'Oh, to be a langur, without a care in the world. Acorns and green leaves to feed on, lots of friends, and no romantic complications. But no books either. I suppose being human has its advantages. Not that it would make any difference to the Goonga.'

He was soon dry. He lay on his tummy, flat against the warm smooth rock surface. He wanted to sink deep into that beautiful rock.

'Goo,' said the Goonga, as though he approved.

Then the sun was in the pool and the pool was in the sky and the rock had swallowed Rusty up, and when he woke he thought the Goonga was still beside him; but when he raised his head and looked, he saw that Devinder sat there—Devinder looking cool and clean in a white shirt and pyjamas, his tray lying on the ground a little way off.

'How long have you been here?' asked Rusty.

'I just came. It is good to see you. I was afraid you had left for good.'

'I'm hungry,' said Rusty.

'I'm glad you haven't lost your appetite. I have brought you something to eat.' He produced a paper bag filled with hot bazaar food, and a couple of oranges.

While Rusty ate, he told Devinder of his journey. Devinder was disappointed.

'So there was nothing for you, except a few books. I know money isn't everything, but it's time you had some of it, Rusty. How long can you carry on like this? You can't sell combs and buttons like me. You wouldn't know how to; you're a dreamer, a kind of poet, and you can't live on dreams. You don't have rich friends and relatives, like Kishen, to provide intervals of luxury. You're not like Sudheer, able to live on your wits. There's only this aunt of yours in the hills—and you can't spend the rest of your life lost in the mountains like a hermit. It will take you years to become a successful writer. Look at Goldsmith— borrowing money all the time! And you haven't even started yet.'

'I know, Devinder. You don't have to tell me. Tomorrow I'll go and see Mr Pettigrew. Perhaps he can help me in some way— perhaps he can find me a job.'

They were silent, gazing disconsolately into the pool.

'Have you seen Kishen?' asked Rusty.

'Once in the bazaar. He was with that girl, his cousin. They were on bicycles. I think they were going to the cinema. Kishen seemed happy enough. He stopped and spoke to me and asked me when you would be back. They will soon be sending him back to school. That's good, isn't it? He'll never be able to manage without a proper education. Degrees and things.'

'Well, Sudheer has managed well enough without one. You might call him self-educated. And Kishen is worldly enough. Also he's a Punjabi. No one is likely to get the better of him. All the same, you're right. A couple of degrees behind your name could make all the difference, even if you can't put them down in the right order!'

Already the dream was fading. That's life, thought Rusty; you can't run away from it and survive. You can't be a vagrant for ever. You're getting nowhere, so you've got to stop somewhere. Kishen has stopped; he's thrown in his lot with the settled incomes; he had to. Even Mowgli left the wolf-pack to return to his own people. And India was changing. This great formless mass was taking some sort of shape at last. He had to stop now, and find a place for himself, or go forward to disaster.

'I'll see him tomorrow,' said Rusty. 'I'll see Kishen and say goodbye.'

*

Rusty decided he would leave his books with Mr Pettigrew instead of in the church vestry, a transient abode; so he put them in his bag and, after tea with Devinder near the Clock Tower, set out for the tea-gardens.

He crossed the dry river-bed and the yellow mustard fields which stretched away to the foothills, and found Mr Pettigrew sitting on his veranda as though he had not moved from his cane chair since Rusty had last visited him. Pettigrew gazed out across the flat tea bushes. He seemed to look through Rusty, and at first the boy thought he had not been recognized. Perhaps the old man had forgotten him!

'Good morning,' said Rusty. 'I'm back.'

'The poinsettia leaves have turned red,' said Pettigrew. 'Another winter is passing.'

'Yes.'

'Full sixty hot summers have besieged my brow. I'm growing old so *slowly*. I wish there could be some action to make the process more interesting. Not that I feel very active, but I'd like to have something happening around me. A jolly old riot would be just the thing. You know what I mean, of course?'

'I think so,' said Rusty.

It was loneliness again. In a week Rusty had found two lonely people—his aunt, and this elderly gentleman, moving slowly through the autumn of their lives. It was beginning to affect him. He looked at Mr Pettigrew and wondered if he would be like that one day—alone, not very strong, living in the past, with a bottle of whisky to sustain him through the still, lonely evenings. Rusty had friends—but so had Pettigrew, in his youth. Rusty had books to read, and books to write—but Pettigrew had books, too; did they make much difference? Weren't there any permanent flesh and blood companions to be found outside the conventions of marriage and business?

Pettigrew seemed suddenly to realize that Rusty was standing beside him. A spark of interest showed in his eyes. It flickered and grew into comprehension.

'Drinking in the mornings, that's my trouble. You've returned very soon. Sit down, my boy, sit down. Tell me—did you find the lady? Did she know you? Was it any good?'

Rusty sat down on a step, for there was no chair on the veranda apart from Mr Pettigrew's.

'Yes, she knew me. She was very kind and wanted to help me. But she had nothing of mine, except some old books which my father had left with her.'

'Books! Is that all? You've brought them with you, I see.'

'I thought perhaps you'd keep them for me until I'm properly settled somewhere.'

Mr Pettigrew took the books from Rusty and thumbed through them.

'Stevenson, Ballantyne, Marryat, and some early P.G. Wodehouse. I expect you've read them. And here's *Alice in Wonderland*. "How doth the little crocodile ..." Tenniel's drawings. It's a first edition, methinks! It couldn't be—or *could* it?'

Mr Pettigrew fell silent. He studied the title page and the back of the title-leaf with growing interest and solicitude and then with something approaching reverence; for he knew something about books and printing and the value of the first edition. And a first edition of *Alice* would be a rare find.

'It could be, at that,' said Pettigrew, almost to himself, and Rusty was bewildered by the transformation on the old man's face. Ennui had given place to enthusiasm.

'Could be what, sir?'

'A first edition.'

'It was once my grandfather's book. His name is on the fly-leaf.'

'It *must* be a first. No wonder your father treasured it.'

'Is being a first edition very important?'

'Yes, from the book-collector's point of view. In England, on the Continent, and in America, there are people who collect rare works of literature—manuscripts, and the first editions of books that have since become famous. The value of a book depends on its literary worth, its scarcity, and its condition.'

'Well, *Alice* is a famous book. And this is a good copy. Is a first edition of it rare?'

'It certainly is. There are only two or three known copies.'

'And do you think this is one?'

'Well, I'm not an expert, but I do know something about books. This is the first printing. And it's in good condition, except for a few stains on the fly-leaf.'

'Let's rub them off.'

'No, don't touch a thing—don't tamper with its condition. I'll write to a bookseller friend of mine in London for his advice. I think this should be worth a good sum of money to you—several hundred pounds.'

'Hundreds!' exclaimed Rusty disbelievingly.

'Five or six hundred, may be more. Your father must have known the book was valuable amd meant you to have it one day. Perhaps this was his legacy.'

Rusty was silent, taking in the import of what Mr Pettigrew had told him. He had never had much money in his life. A few hundred pounds would take him anywhere he wanted to go. It was also, he knew, quite easy to go through a sum of money, no matter how large the amount.

Pettigrew was glancing through the other books. 'None of these are first, except the Wodehouse novels, and you'll have to wait some time with those. But *Alice* is the real thing. My friend will arrange its sale.'

'It would be nice to keep it,' said Rusty.

Mr Pettigrew looked up in surprise. 'In other circumstances, my boy, I'd say keep it. Become a book-collector yourself. But when you're down on your beam-ends, you can't afford to be sentimental. Now leave this business in my hands, and let me advance you some money. Furthermore, this calls for a celebration!'

He poured himself a stiff whisky and offered Rusty a drink.

'I don't mind if I do,' said Rusty, bestowing his rare smile on the old man.

Later, after lunching with Mr Pettigrew, Rusty sat out on the veranda with the old man and discussed his future.

'I think you should go to England,' said Mr Pettigrew.

'I've thought of that before,' said Rusty, 'but I've always felt that India is my home.'

'But can you make a living here? After all, even Indians go abroad at the first opportunity. And you want to be a writer. You can't become one overnight, certainly not in India. It will take years of hard work, and even then—even if you're good—you may not make the reputation that means all the difference between failure and success. In the meantime, you've got to make a living at something. And what can you do in India? Let's face it, my boy, you've only just finished school. There are graduates who can't get jobs. Only last week a young man with a degree in the Arts came to me and asked my help in getting him a job as a petty clerk in the tea-estate manager's office. A clerk! Is that why he went to college—to become a clerk?'

Rusty did not argue the point. He knew that it was only people with certain skills who stood a chance. It was an age of specialization. And he did not have any skills, apart from some skill with words.

'You can always come back,' said Mr Pettigrew. 'If you are successful, you'll be free to go wherever you please. And if you aren't successful, well then, you can make a go of something else—if not in England, then in some other English-speaking country, America or Australia or Canada or the Cook Islands!'

'Why didn't you leave India, Mr Pettigrew?'

'For reasons similar to yours. Because I'd lived many years in India and had grown to love the country. But unlike you, I'm at the fag-end of my life. And it's easier to fade away in the hot sun than in the cold winds of Blighty.'

He looked out rather wistfully at his garden, at the tall marigolds and bright clumps of petunia and the splurge of bougainvillaea against the wall.

'My journeyings are over,' he said. 'And yours have just begun.'

*

It was dark when Rusty slipped over a wall and moved silently round the porch of Mrs Bhushan's house. There was a light showing in the front room and Rusty crept up to the window and looked in, pressing his face against the glass. He felt the music in the room even before he heard it. It came vibrating through the glass with a pulsating rhythm. Kishen and Aruna, both barefooted, were gyrating on the floor in a frenzy of hip-shivering movement. Their faces were blank. They did not sing. All expression was confined to their plunging torsos.

Rusty decided it was not a propitious moment for calling on his old friend. And this was confirmed a few minutes later by the throaty blare of a horn and the glare of a car's headlights. Mrs Bhushan's Hillman was turning in at the gate. The music came to a sudden stop. Rusty dodged behind a rose-bush, stung his hands on nettle, and remained hidden until Mrs Bhushan had alighted from her car. He was moving cautiously through the shrubbery when one of the dogs started barking. Others took up the chorus.

Rusty was soon clambering over the wall, with two or three cockers snapping at his feet and trousers. He ran down the road until he found the entrance to a dark lane, down which he disappeared.

He slowed to a walk as he approached the crowded bazaar area. He was annoyed and a little depressed at not having been able to see Kishen, but he had to admit that Kishen appeared to be quite happy in Mrs Bhushan's house. Aruna had made all the difference, for Kishen was beginning to grow up.

Perhaps, thought Rusty, I'd better not see him at all.

Start of a Journey

Events moved swiftly—as they usually do, once a specific plan is set in motion—and within a few weeks Rusty was in possession of a passport, a rail ticket to Bombay, his boat ticket, an income tax clearance certificate (this had been the most difficult to obtain, in spite of the fact that he had no income), a smallpox vaccination certificate, various other bits and pieces of paper, and about fifty rupees in cash advanced by Mr Pettigrew. The money for *Alice* would not be realized for several months, and could be drawn upon in London.

He was late for his train. The tonga he had hired turned out to be the most ancient of Dehra's dwindling fleet of pony-drawn carriages. The pony was old, slow and dyspeptic. It stopped every now and then to pass quantities of wind. The tonga-driver turned out to be a bhang-addict who had not quite woken up from his last excursion into dreamland. The carriage itself was a thing of shreds and patches. It lay at an angle, and rolled from side to side. This motion seemed designed to suit the condition of the driver, who dozed off every now and then.

'If it hadn't been for your luggage,' said Devinder, 'we would have done better to walk.'

At their feet was a new suitcase and a spacious hold-all given to Rusty by Mr Pettigrew. Devinder, Rusty and the tonga-driver were the only occupants of the carriage.

'Please hurry,' begged Rusty of the tonga-driver. 'I'll miss the train.'

'Miss the train?' mumbled the tonga-driver, coming out of his coma. 'No one ever misses the train—not when *I* take them to the station!'

'Why, does the train wait for you to arrive?' asked Devinder.

'Oh, no,' said the driver. 'But it waits.'

'Well, it should have left at seven,' said Rusty. 'And it's five past seven now. Even if it leaves on time, which means ten minutes late, we won't catch it at this speed.'

'You will be there in ten minutes, sahib.' And the man called out an endearment to his pony.

Neither Rusty nor Devinder could make out what the tonga-driver said, but it did wonders to the pony. The beast came to life as though it had been injected with a new wonder hormone. Rusty and Devinder were jerked upright in their seats. The pony kicked up its hind legs and plunged forward, and cyclists and pedestrians scattered for safety. They raced through the town, followed by oaths and abuse from a vegetable-seller whose merchandise had been spilled on the road. Only at the station entrance did the pony slow down and then, as suddenly and unaccountably as it had come to life, it returned to its former dispirited plod.

Paying off the man, Rusty and Devinder grabbed hold of the luggage and tumbled on to the railway platform. Here they barged into Kishen who, having heard of Rusty's departure (from the barber, who had got it from an egg-vendor, who had got it from Devinder), had come to see him off.

'You didn't tell me anything,' said Kishen with an injured look. 'You seem to have forgotten me altogether.'

'I hadn't forgotten you, bhaiya. I did come to see you once— but I couldn't bring myself to say goodbye. It seems so final, saying goodbye. I wanted to slip away quietly, that's all.'

'How selfish you are!' said Kishen.

A last-minute quarrel with Kishen was the last thing Rusty wanted.

'We must hurry,' said Devinder urgently. 'The train is about to leave.'

The guard was blowing his whistle, and there was a final scramble among the passengers. If sardines could take a look at the situation in a third class railway compartment, they would not have anything to complain about. It is a perfect example of the individual being swallowed up by the mass, of a large number of identities merging into one corporate whole. Your leg, you discover, is not yours but your neighbour's; the growth of hair on your shoulder is someone's beard; and the cold wind whistling down your neck is his asthmatic breath, a baby materializes in your lap and is reclaimed only after it has wet your trousers; and the corner of a seat which you had happily thought was your own green spot on this earth is suddenly usurped by a huge Sikh with a sword dangling at his side. Rusty knew from experience in third class compartments that if he did not get into one of them immediately, his way would be permanently barred.

'There's no room anywhere,' said Kishen cheerfully. 'You'd better go tomorrow.'

'The boat sails in three days,' said Rusty.

'Then come on, let's squeeze you in somewhere.'

Managing the luggage themselves, and ignoring the protests of the station coolies, they hurried down the length of the platform looking for a compartment less crowded than most. They discovered an open door and a space within, and bundled Rusty and his worldly goods into it.

'It's empty!' said Rusty in delight. 'There's no one in it.'

'Of course not,' said Kishen. 'It's a first class compartment.'

But the train was already in motion and there was no time to get out.

'You can shift into another compartment after Hardwar,' said Kishen. 'The train won't be so crowded, then.'

Rusty closed the door and stuck his head out of the window. Perhaps this mad, confusing departure was the best thing that could have happened. It was impossible to say goodbye in dignified solemnity. And Rusty would have hated a solemn, tearful departure. Devinder and Kishen had time only to look relieved—relieved at having been able to get Rusty into the train. They would not realize, till later, that he was going forever out of their lives.

He waved to them from the window, and they waved back, smiling and wishing him luck. They were not dismayed at his departure. Rather, they were pleased that Rusty's life had taken a new direction; they were impressed by his good fortune, and they took it for granted that he would come back some day, with money and honours. Such is the optimism of youth.

Rusty waved until his friends were lost in the milling throng on the platform, until the station lights were a distant glow. And then the train was thundering through the swift-falling darkness of India. He looked in the glass of the window and saw his own face dimly reflected. And he wondered if he would ever come back.

There was someone else's reflection in the glass, and he realized that he was not alone in the compartment. Someone had just come out of the washroom and was staring at Rusty in some surprise. A familiar face, a foreigner. The man Rusty had met at the Raiwala waiting-room, when he had been travelling with Kishen to Dehra in different circumstances.

'We meet again,' said the American. 'Remember me?'

'Yes,' said Rusty. 'We seem to share a fondness for trains.'

'Well, I have to make this journey every week.'

'How is your work?'

'Much the same. I'm trying, but with little success, to convince farmers that a steel plough will pay greater dividends than a wooden plough.'

'And they aren't convinced?'

'Oh, they're quite prepared to be convinced. Trouble is, they find it cheaper and easier to repair a wooden plough. You see how complicated everything is? It's a question of parts. For want of a bolt, the plough was lost, for want of a plough the crop was lost, for want of a crop . . . And where are *you* going, friend? I see you're alone this time.'

'Yes, I'm going away. I'm leaving India.'

'Where are you going? England?'

Rusty nodded. He looked out of the window in time to see a shooting-star skid across the heavens and vanish. A bad omen; but he was defiant of omens.

'I'm going to England,' he said. 'I'm going to Europe and America and Japan and Timbuctoo. I'm going everywhere, and no one can stop me!'

DELHI IS NOT FAR

Chapter One

❧

My balcony is my window on the world. I prefer it to my room.

The room has just one window, a square hole in the wall crossed by three iron bars. The view from it is a restricted one. If I crane my neck sideways, and put my nose to the bars, I can see the extremities of the building. If I stand on tiptoe and lean forward, I can see part of the narrow courtyard below where children—the children of all classes of people—play together. (When they are older, they will become conscious of the barriers of class and caste.)

Across the courtyard, on a level with my room, are three separate windows, belonging to three separate rooms, each window barred in the same unimaginative way. During the day it is difficult to look into these rooms. The harsh, cruel sunlight fills the courtyard, making the windows patches of darkness.

My room is small. I have paced about in it so often that I know its exact measurements. My foot, from heel to toe, is eleven inches. That makes the room just over twelve feet in length; when I measure the last foot, my toes turn up against the wall. In breadth, the room is exactly seven feet.

The plaster has been peeling off the walls, and there are many greasy stains and patches which are difficult to hide. I cover the worst stains with pictures cut from magazines, but as there is no symmetry about the stains there is none about the pictures. My personal effects are few, and none of them precious.

On a shelf in the wall are a pile of paperbacks, in English, Hindi and Urdu; among them my two Urdu thrillers, *Khoon*

(Blood) and *Jasoos* (Detective). They did not take long to write. Some passages were my own, some free translations from English authors. Having been brought up in a Hindu home in a Muslim city—and in an English school—I was fairly proficient in three languages. The books have sold quite well—for my publisher . . .

My publisher, who operates from a Meerut by-lane, paid me two hundred rupees for each book; a flat and final payment, no royalties. I could not get better terms from any other publisher. It is a good country for publishers but not for writers. To quote Byron: 'Now Barabbas was a publisher . . .'

'If you want to make money, Arun,' he confided in me when he handed me my last cheque, 'publish your own books. Not detective stories. They have a limited market. Haven't you realized that India is fuller than ever of young people trying to pass exams? It is a desperate matter, this race for academic qualifications. Half the entrants fall by the wayside. The other half are even more unfortunate. They pass their exams and then they fall by the wayside. The point is, millions are sitting for exams, for MA, BSc, PhD . . . They all want to get these degrees the easy way, without reading too many books or attending more than half a dozen lectures—and that's where a smart person like you comes in! Why should they wade through five volumes of political history when they can get a dozen model answer papers? They are seldom wrong, the guess papers. All you have to do is make friends with someone on the University Board, write your papers, print them cheaply—never mind a few printing errors—and flood the market. They'll sell like hot cakes,' he concluded, using an English expression.

I told him I would think about his proposal, but I never really liked the idea. I preferred spilling the blood of fictitious prostitutes to spoon-feeding the brains of misguided students.

Besides, it would have been very boring.

A friend who shall be nameless offered to teach me the art of pickpocketing. But I had to give up after a few clumsy attempts on his pocket. To pick someone's pocket successfully is an art. My friend practised his craft at various railway stations and made a good living from it. I knew I could not. I would have to stick to writing cheap thrillers.

CHAPTER TWO

❧

THE STRING OF MY charpai needs tightening. The dip in the middle of the bed is so pronounced that invariably I wake up in the morning with a backache. But I am hopeless at tightening charpai strings and will have to wait until one of the boys from the tea-shop pays me a visit.

Under the charpai is my tin trunk. Its contents range from old, rejected manuscripts to photographs, clothes, newspaper cuttings and all that goes with the floating existence of an itinerant bachelor.

I do not live entirely alone. Sometimes a beggar, if he is not diseased, spends the night on the balcony; during cold or rainy weather the boys from the tea-shop, who normally sleep on the pavement, crowd into my room. But apart from them, there are the lizards on the walls—friends, these—and a large rat who gets in and out of the window and carries away manuscripts and clothing; definitely an enemy.

*

June nights are the most uncomfortable of all. Mosquitoes emerge from all the ditches and gullies and ponds, and take over control of Pipalnagar. Bugs, finding it uncomfortable inside the woodwork of the charpai, scramble out at night and find their way under my sheet. I wrap myself up in the sheet like a corpse, but the mosquitoes bite through the thin material, and the bugs get in at the tears and holes.

The lizards wander listlessly over the walls, impatient for the monsoon rains, when they will be able to feast off thousands of insects.

Everyone is waiting for the cool, quenching relief of the monsoon. But two months from now, when roofs have fallen in, the road is flooded, and the drinking water contaminated, we will be cursing the monsoon and praying for its speedy retreat.

To wake in the morning in summer is not difficult, as sleep is fitful, uneasy, crowded with dreams and fantasies. I know it is five o'clock when I hear the first bus coming out of the shed. If I am to defecate in private, I must be up and away into the fields beyond the railway tracks. The public lavatory near the station hasn't been cleaned for over a week.

Afterwards I return to the balcony and, slipping out of my vest and pyjamas, rub down my body with mustard oil. If the boy from the tea-shop is awake, I get him to massage me, while I lie flat on my back or on my belly, dreaming of things less mundane than life in Pipalnagar.

I dream of Delhi, only two hundred miles away, where so much is happening: Five Year Plans (so the papers say), and plans for big dams, airports, new industries, and a grand new city coming up in Chandigarh. I see all this in the newsreels at our local cinema, along with pictures of a smiling Mr Nehru laying foundation stones for his 'new temples of India'. And pictures of him playing with his grandchildren, waving to adoring crowds, or walking in his rose garden. Oh, for a rose garden in Pipalnagar. It might inspire me to write my own *Gulistan*!

*

As the passengers alight from the first bus of the day into Pipalnagar, I sit in the barber shop and talk to Deep Chand while he lathers my face with soap. The knife moves cleanly across my cheeks and throat, and Deep Chand's breath, smelling of cloves and cardamoms—he is a perpetual eater of paan—plays on my face. In the next chair the sweetmeat-seller is having the hair shaved from under his great flabby armpits; he is looked after by Deep Chand's younger brother, Ramu, who is deputed to attend to the less popular customers. Ramu flashes a smile at me when

I enter the shop; we have had a couple of nocturnal excursions together.

Deep Chand is a short, thick-set man, very compact, dark and smooth-skinned from his waist upwards. Below his waist, from his hips to his ankles, he is a mass of soft black hair. An extremely virile man, he is very attractive to women.

Deep Chand and Ramu know all there is to know about me— in fact, all there is to know about Pipalnagar.

'When are you going to get married, brother?' Deep Chand asked me recently.

'Oh, after five or ten years,' I replied.

'You are twenty-five now,' he said. 'This is the time to marry. Once you are thirty, it will not be so easy to find a wife. In Pipalnagar, when you are thirty you are old.'

'I feel too old already,' I said. 'Don't talk to me of marriage, but give a massage. My brain is not functioning well these days. In my latest book I have killed three people in one chapter, and still it is dull.'

'Well, finish it soon,' said Deep Chand, beginning the ritual of the head-massage. 'Then you can clear your debts. When you have paid your debts you will leave Pipalnagar, won't you?'

I could not answer because he had started thumping my skull with his hard, communicative fingers, tugging at the roots of my hair, and squeezing my temples with the palms of his hands. No one gave a better massage than Deep Chand. Had his income been greater, he could have shifted his trade to another locality and made a decent living. Here, in our Mohalla, his principal customers were shopkeepers, truck drivers, labourers from the railway station. He charged only two rupees for a hair-cut; in other places it was three rupees.

While Deep Chand ran his fingers through my hair, exerting a gentle pressure on my temples, I made a mental inventory of all the people who owed me money and to whom I was in debt.

The amounts I had loaned out—to various bazaar acquaintances—were small compared to the amounts I owed others. There was my landlord, Seth Govind Ram, who was in fact the landlord of half Pipalnagar and the proprietor of the dancing-girls—they did everything but dance—who lived in a dormitory near the bus stop; I owed him six months' rent. Sixty rupees.

He does not bother me just now, but in six months' time he will be after my blood, and I will have to pay up somehow.

Seth Govind Ram possesses a bank, a paunch and, allegedly, a mistress. The bank and the paunch are both conspicuous landmarks in Pipalnagar. Few people have seen his mistress. She is kept hidden away in an enormous Rajput-style house outside the city, and continues to be a challenge to my imagination.

Seth Govind Ram is a prominent member of the municipality. Publicly, he is a staunch supporter of the ruling party; privately, he supports all parties with occasional contributions towards their funds. He owns, as I have said, most of the buildings in the Pipalnagar Mohalla; and though he is always promising to pull them down and build new ones, he finds it more profitable to leave them as they are.

Perhaps some day I really will settle my debts with Seth Govind Ram. Aziz believes that I will. Aziz visits me occasionally for a loan of two or three rupees, which he returns in kind, whenever I visit his junk shop. He is a Muslim boy of eighteen. He lives in a small room behind the junk shop.

The shop has mud walls and a tin roof. The walls are always in danger of being washed away during the monsoon, and the roof of sailing away during a dust-storm. The rain comes in, anyway, and the floor is awash most of the time; bound copies of old English magazines gather mildew, and the pots and pans and spare parts grow rusty. Aziz, at eighteen, is beginning to collect dust and age and disease.

But he is an optimistic soul, even though there is nothing for him to be optimistic about, and he is always asking me when I intend keeping my vow of going to Delhi to make my fortune. He does not doubt that I will. I am to keep an eye out for a favourable shop-site near Chandni Chowk where he can open a more up-to-date junk shop. He is saving towards this end; but what he saves trickles away in paying for his wife's upkeep at the Pipalnagar Home, where he was forced to send her after his family pronounced her insane. Pipalnagar has many candidates for the Home, but it's a place of last resort; no one ever comes back.

CHAPTER THREE

MY EFFORTS AT MAKING a fortune were many and varied. I had, for three days, kept a vegetable stall; invested in an imaginary tea-shop; and even tried my hand as a palmist. This last venture was a failure, not because I was a poor palmist—I had intuition enough to be able to guess what a man or woman would be happy to know—but because prospective customers were few in Pipalnagar. My friends and neighbours had grown far too cynical of the future to expect any bonuses.

'When a child is born,' asserted Deep Chand, 'his fists are clenched. They have been clenched for so long that little creases form on his palms. That is the only meaning in our lines. What have they to do with our future?'

I agreed with Deep Chand, but I thought fortune-telling might be an easy way of making money. Others did it, from saffron-robed sadhus to BAs and BComs, and did it fairly successfully, so that I felt I should try it too. It did not take me long to read a book on the subject, and to hang a board from my balcony, announcing my profession. That I did not succeed was probably due to the fact that I was too well-known in Pipalnagar. Half the Mohalla thought it was a joke; the other half, quite understandably, didn't believe in my genuineness.

The vegetable stall was more exciting. Down the road, near the clock tower, a widow kept a grocery store. She sold rice, spices, pulses, almost everything except meat and vegetables. The widow did not think vegetables were worth the risk of an initial investment, but she was determined to try them out, and persuaded me to put up the money.

I found it difficult to refuse. She was a strong woman, ample-bosomed, known to fight in public with any man who tried to get the better of her. She was a persuasive saleswoman, too, and soon had me conjuring up visions of a vegetable stall of my own full of succulent fruits and fresh green vegetables.

Full it was, from beginning to end. I didn't sell a single cabbage or cauliflower or salad leaf. Before the vegetables went bad, I gave them away to Deep Chand, Pitamber, and other friends. The widow had insisted that I charge ten paise per kilo more than others charged, a disastrous thing to do in Pipalnagar, where the question of preferring quality to quantity did not arise. She said that for the extra ten paise customers would get cleaner and greener vegetables. She was wrong. Customers wanted them cleaner and greener and cheaper.

Still, it had been exciting on the first morning, getting up at five (I hadn't done this for years) and walking down to the vegetable market near the railway station, haggling with the wholesalers, piling the vegetables into baskets, and leading the coolie back to the bazaar with a proprietorial air.

The railway station, half a mile from the bus stop, had always attracted me. As a boy I had been fascinated by trains (as I suppose most boys are), and waved to the passengers as the trains flew through the fields, and was always delighted when one of them waved back to me. I had wondered about the people in the carriages—where they were going, and why . . . Trains had meant romance, escape into another world. Until the Nawabgunj crash that took my parents' lives. That set me adrift, but it was the end of romance.

'What you should do,' advised Deep Chand, while he lathered my face with soap—(there were several reasons why I did not shave myself; laziness, the desire to gossip, the fact that Deep Chand used his razor as an artist uses a brush . . .)—'What you should do, is marry a wealthy woman. It would solve all your problems. She would be only too happy to possess a young man of sexual accomplishments. You could then do your writing at leisure, with slaves to fan you and press your legs.'

'Not a bad idea,' I said, 'but where does one find such a woman? I expect Seth Govind Ram has a wife in addition to a mistress, but I have never seen her; and the Seth doesn't look as though he is going to die.'

'She doesn't have to be a widow. Find a young woman who is married to a fat and important millionaire. She will support you.' Deep Chand was a married man himself, with several children. I had never bothered to count them.

His children, and others, give one the impression that in Pipalnagar children outnumber adults five to one. This is really the case, I suppose. The census tells us that one in four of our population is in the age-group of five to fifteen years. They swarm over the narrow streets, appearing to belong to one vast family—a race of pot-bellied little men, half-naked, dusty, quarrelling and laughing and crying and having so little in common with the race of adults who have brought them into the world.

On either side of my room there are families, each with about a dozen members—each family living in a room a little bigger than mine, which is used for cooking, eating, sleeping and loving. The men work in the sugar factory and bring home about fifty rupees a month. The older children attend the Pipalnagar High School, and come home only for their food. The younger ones are in and out all day, their pockets full of stones and marbles and small coins.

Tagore wrote: 'Every child comes with the message that God is not yet discouraged of man.'

At noon, when the shadows shift and cross the road, a band of children rush down the empty, silent street, shouting and waving their satchels. They have been at their desks from early morning, and now, despite the hot sun, they will have their fling while their elders sleep on string charpais beneath leafy neem trees.

On the soft sand near the river-bed boys wrestle or play leapfrog. At alley-corners, where tall buildings shade narrow passages, the favourite game is gulli-danda. Elsewhere, in open spaces, it is kabaddi, a game for both children and young men. It is a village game, and calls for good control of the breath and much agility and strength.

Pitamber, a young wrestler who migrated here from a nearby village only recently, excels at kabbadi. He knows all the holds, and is particularly adept at capturing an opponent. He took me to his village once. All the boys there were long-limbed and sun-browned, erect and at the same time relaxed. There is a sense of vitality and confidence in Pitamber's village, which I have not seen in Pipalnagar.

In Pipalnagar there is not exactly despair, but resignation, an indifference to both living and dying. The town is almost truly reflected in the Pipalnagar Home, where in an open courtyard surrounded by mud walls a score of mental patients wander about, listless and bored. A man jabbers excitedly, but most of the inmates are quiet, sad and resentful.

Such sights depress me sometimes. The world seems crowded with unfinished lives.

'I wonder why God ever bothered to make men, when he had the whole wide beautiful world to himself,' I said to Suraj one summer night. 'Why did he find it necessary to share it with others?'

'Perhaps he felt lonely,' said Suraj.

CHAPTER FOUR

I DO NOT KNOW if Suraj ever wished that our first meeting had been different. He never talked about it.

I was walking through the fields beyond the railway tracks, when I saw someone lying on the footpath, his head and body hidden by the ripening wheat. The wheat was shaking where he lay, and as I came nearer I saw that one of his legs kept twitching convulsively.

Thinking that perhaps it was a case of robbery with violence, I prepared to run; but then, cursing myself for being a shallow coward, I approached the agitated person.

He was a youth of about eighteen, and he appeared to be in the throes of a violent fit.

His face was white, except where a little blood had trickled from his mouth. His leg kept twitching, and his hands moved restlessly, helplessly amongst the wheat.

I spoke to him: 'What is wrong?' I asked, but he was obviously unconscious and could not answer. So I ran down the path to the well, and dipping the end of my shirt in a shallow trough of water, soaked it well, and ran back to the boy.

By that time he seemed to have recovered from the fit. The twitching had ceased, and though he still breathed heavily, his face was calm and his hands still. I wiped the blood from his mouth, and he opened his eyes and stared at me without any immediate comprehension.

'You have bitten your tongue.' I said. 'There's no hurry. I'll stay here with you.'

We rested where we were for some minutes without saying anything. He was no longer agitated. Resting his chin on his knees, he passed his hands around his drawn-up legs.

'I am all right now,' he said.

'What happened?'

'It was nothing, it often happens. I don't know why. I cannot stop it.'

'Have you seen a doctor?'

'I went to the hospital when it first began. They gave me some pills. I had to take them every day. But they made me so tired and sleepy that I couldn't do any work. So I stopped taking them. I get the attack about once a week, but I am useless if I take those pills.'

He got to his feet, smiling as he dusted his clothes.

He was a thin boy, long-limbed and bony. There was a little fluff on his cheeks and the promise of a moustache. His pyjamas were short for him, accentuating the awkwardness of his long, bony feet. He had beauty, though; his eyes held secrets, his mouth hesitant smiles.

He told me that he was a student at the Pipalnagar College, and that his terminal examination would be held in August. Apparently his whole life hinged on the result of the coming examination. If he passed, there was the prospect of a scholarship, and eventually a place for himself in the world. If he failed, there was only the prospect of Pipalnagar, and a living eked out by selling combs and buttons and little vials of perfume.

I noticed the tray of merchandise lying on the ground. It usually hung at his waist, the straps going round his neck. All day he walked about Pipalnagar, covering ten to fifteen miles a day, selling odds and ends to people at their houses. He made about two rupees a day, which gave him enough for his food; and he ate irregularly, at little tea-shops, at the stalls near the bus stops, or on the roadside under shady jamun and mango trees. When the jamuns were ripe, he would sit in a tree, sucking the sour fruit till his lips were stained purple with their juice. There was always the fear that he would get a fit while sitting in a tree, and fall off; but the temptation to eat jamuns was too great for him, and he took the risk.

'Where do you stay?' I asked. 'I will walk back with you to your home.'

'I don't stay anywhere in particular. Sometimes in a dharamsala, sometimes in the Gurudwara, sometimes on the Maidan. In the summer months I like to sleep on the Maidan, on the grass.'

'Then I'll walk with you to the Maidan,' I said.

There was nothing extraordinary about his being a refugee and an orphan. During the communal holocaust of 1947 thousands of homes had been destroyed, women and children killed. What was extraordinary was his sensitivity—or should I say sensibility—a rare quality in a Punjabi youth who had been brought up in the Frontier Provinces during one of the most cruel periods in the country's history. It was not his conversation that impressed me—though his attitude to life was one of hope, while in Pipalnagar people were too resigned even to be desperate—but the gentle persuasiveness of his voice, eyes, and also of his hands, long-fingered, gliding hands, and his smile which flickered with amusement and sometimes irony.

CHAPTER FIVE

ONE MORNING, WHEN I opened the door of my room, I found Suraj asleep at the top of the steps. His tray lay a short distance away. I shook him gently, and he woke up immediately, blinking in the bright sunlight.

'Why didn't you come in,' I said. 'Why didn't you tell me?'

'It was late,' he said. 'I didn't want to disturb you.'

'Someone could have stolen your things while you slept.'

'So far no one has stolen from me.'

I made him promise to sleep in my room that night, and he came in at ten, curled up on the floor and slept fitfully, while I lay awake worrying if he was comfortable enough.

He came several nights, and left early in the morning, before I could offer him anything to eat. We would talk into the early hours of the morning. Neither of us slept much.

I liked Suraj's company. He dispelled some of my own loneliness, and I found myself looking forward to the sound of his footsteps on the stairs. He liked my company because I was full of stories, even though some of them were salacious; and because I encouraged his ambitions and gave him confidence.

I forget what it was I said that offended him and hurt his feelings—something unintentional, and, of course, silly: one of those things that you cannot remember afterwards but which seem terribly important at the time. I had probably been giving him too much advice, showing off my knowledge of the world and women, and joking about his becoming a prime minister one day: because the next night he didn't come to my room.

I waited till eleven o'clock for the sound of his footsteps, and then when he didn't come, I left the room and went in search of him. I couldn't bear the thought of an angry and unhappy Suraj sleeping alone on the Maidan. What if he should have another fit? I told myself that he had been through scores of fits without my being around to help him, but already I was beginning to feel protective towards him.

The shops had closed and lights showed only in upper windows. There were many sleeping on the sidewalk, and I peered into the faces of each, but I did not find Suraj. Eventually I found him on the Maidan, asleep on a bench.

'Suraj,' I said, and he awoke and sat up.

'What is it?'

'I've been looking for you for the last two hours. Come on home.'

'Why don't you spend the night here?' he said. 'This is my home.'

I felt angry at first, but then I felt ashamed of my anger.

I said, 'Thank you for your kind offer, my friend, it will be a privilege to be your guest,' and sat down on the bench beside him.

We were silent for some time, while a big yellow moon played hide and seek with the clouds. Then it began to drizzle.

'It's raining,' I said. 'Why didn't you make a roof over your house? Now let us go back to mine.'

I thought he might still refuse to return with me, but he got up, smiling; perhaps it was my own sudden humility, or perhaps it was the rain . . . I think it was my own humility, because it made him feel he had wronged me. He did not feel for himself that way, and so it was not the rain.

*

In the afternoon Pipalnagar is empty. The temperature has touched 106°F! To walk barefoot on the scorching pavement is possible only for the beggars and labourers whose feet have developed several layers of hard protective skin. And even they lie stretched out in the shade given by shops and walls, their open sores festering in the hot sun.

Suraj will be asleep in the shade of a pipal or banyan tree, a book lying open beside him, his tray a few feet away. Sometimes the crows are fascinated by his many coloured combs, and come down from the trees to inspect them.

At this hour of the day I lie naked on the stone floor of my room, because the floor is the coolest place of all; and as I am too listless to work or sleep, I study my navel, the hair on my belly, the languid aspect of my genitals, and the hair on my legs and thighs. I study my toes, and with the dust that has accumulated on my feet, I trace patterns on the walls and disturb the flaking plaster which in itself has formed a score of patterns—birds and snakes and elephants ... With a little imagination I can conjure up the entire world of the *Panchatantra* ...

Of all the joys of the senses, I think it is the sense of touch I relish most—contact of the cool floor on a hot day. That is why I lie naked in my room, so that all my flesh is in touch with the cool stones.

The touch of the earth—soft earth, stony earth, grass, mud. Sometimes the road is so hot that it scorches the most hardened feet; sometimes it is cold and hard and cruel. Grass is good, especially dew-drenched grass; then the feet are stained with juices, and the sap seems to pass into the body. Wet earth is soft and sensuous, and when the mud cakes on one's feet it is interesting to bathe at a tap and watch the muddy water run away, like a young stream eager to reach elsewhere.

*

There are days and there are nights, and then there are other days and other nights, and all the days and nights in Pipalnagar are the same.

A few things reassure me ... The desire to love and be loved. The beauty and ugliness of the human body, the intricacy of its design. Sometimes I make love as a sort of exploration of all that is physical; and sometimes falling in love becomes an exploration of the mind. Love takes me to distant, happier places.

Chapter Six

&

IT IS DIFFICULT TO fall asleep some nights. Apart from the mosquitoes and the oppressive atmosphere, there are the loudspeakers blaring all over Pipalnagar—at cinemas, marriages and religious gatherings. There is a continuous variety of fare—religious music and film music. I do not care much for either, and yet I am compelled to listen, both repelled and fascinated by the sounds that permeate the midnight air.

Strangely enough, it does not trouble Suraj. He is immune to noise. Once he is asleep, it would take a bomb to disturb him. At the first blare of the loudspeaker, he pulls a pillow or towel over his head, and falls asleep. He has been in Pipalnagar longer than I, and has grown accustomed to living against a background of noise. And yet he is a silent person, silent in his movements and in his moods; and I, who love silence so much—I am clumsy and garrulous.

Suraj does not know if his parents are dead or alive. He lost them, literally, when he was seven.

His father had been a cultivator, a dark unfathomable man, who spoke little, thought perhaps even less, and was vaguely aware that he possessed a son—a weak boy, who resembled his mother to a disconcerting degree in that he not only looked like her but was given to introspection and dawdling at the riverbank when he should have been at work in the fields.

The boy's mother was a subdued, silent woman—frail and consumptive. Her husband did not expect that she would live long. Perhaps the separation from her son put an end to her interest in life—or perhaps it has urged her to live on somewhere, in the hope that she will find him again.

Suraj lost his parents at Amritsar railway station, where trains coming over the border disgorged themselves of thousands of refugees—or pulled into the station half-empty, drenched with blood and piled with corpses.

Suraj and his parents were lucky to escape the massacre. Had they been able to travel on an earlier train (they had tried desperately to get into one) they might easily have been killed; but circumstances favoured them then, only to trick them later.

Suraj was clinging to his mother's sari, while she kept close to her husband, who was elbowing his way through the frightened, bewildered throng of refugees. Looking over his shoulder at a woman sobbing on the ground, Suraj collided with a burly Sikh and lost his grip on his mother's sari.

The Sikh had a long, curved sword at his waist, and Suraj stared up at him in terror and fascination, at his long hair, which had fallen loose, and his wild black beard, and the blood-stains on his white shirt. The Sikh pushed him out of the way, and when Suraj looked round for his mother she was not to be seen.

He could hear her calling to him, 'Suraj, where are you, Suraj?' and he tried to force his way through the crowd, in the direction of her voice, but he was carried the other way.

CHAPTER SEVEN

At a certain age a boy is like young wheat, growing, healthy, on the verge of manhood. His eyes are alive, his mind quick, his gestures confident. You cannot mistake him.

This is the most fascinating age, when a boy becomes a man— it is interesting both physically and mentally: the growth of the boy's hair, the toning of the muscles, the consciousness of growing and changing and maturing—never again will there be so much change and development in so short a period of time. The body exudes virility, is full of currents and counter-currents.

For a girl, puberty is a frightening age when alarming things begin to happen to her body; for a boy it is an age of self-assertion, of a growing confidence in himself and in his attitude to the world. His physical changes are a source of happiness and pride.

In Suraj, I see all of this. I do not envy him; I am happy for him, and with him.

*

There were no inhibitions in my friendship with Suraj. We spoke of bodies as we spoke of minds, and discussed the problems of one as we would discuss those of the other, for they are really the same problems.

He was beautiful, with the beauty of the short-lived, a transient, sad beauty. It made me sad sometimes even to look at his pale slim limbs. It hurt me to look into his eyes. There was death in his eyes.

He told me that he was afraid of women, that he constantly felt the urge to possess a woman, but that when confronted with one he might just as well have been a eunuch.

I told him that not every woman was made for every man, and that I would bring him a girl with whom he would be happy.

This was Kamla, a very friendly person from the house run by Seth Govind Ram. She was very small, and rather delicate, but more skilled in love-making than any of her colleagues. She was patient, and particularly fond of the young and inexperienced. She was only twenty-three, but had been four years in the profession.

*

Kamla's hands and feet are beautiful. That in itself is satisfying. A beautiful face leaves me cold if the hands and feet are ugly. Perhaps this is some sort of phobia with me.

Kamla first met me when I came up the stairs shortly after I had moved into the room above the bus stop. She was sitting on the steps, eating a melon; and when she saw me, she smiled and held out a slice.

'Will you eat melon, bhai sahib?' she asked, and her voice was so appealing and her eyes so mischievous that I couldn't help taking the melon from her hands.

'Sit down,' she said, patting the step. I had never come across a girl so openly friendly and direct. As I sat down, I discovered the secret of her smile; it lay in the little scar on her right check; when she smiled, the scar turned into a dimple.

'Don't you do any work?' she asked.

'I write stories and things,' I said.

'Is that work?'

'Well, I live by it.'

'Show me,' she demanded.

I brought her a magazine and began turning the pages for her. She could read a little, if the words were simple enough. But she didn't get as far as my story, because her attention was arrested by a picture of a girl with an urchin hair-cut.

'It is a girl?' she asked; and, when I assured her it was: 'But her hair, how is it like that?'

'That's the latest fashion,' I protested. 'Thousands of women keep hair like that. At least they did a year ago,' I added, looking at the date on the magazine.

'Is it easy to make?'

'Yes, you just take a pair of scissors and cut away until it looks untidy enough.'

'I like it. You give it to me. I'll go and get scissors.'

'No, no!' I said. 'You can't do that, your family will be most upset.'

She stamped her bare foot on the step. 'I have no family, silly man! I have a husband who is happy only if I can make myself attractive to others. He is skinny and smells of garlic, and he has given my father five acres of land for the favour of having a wife half his age. But it is Seth Govind Ram who really owns me; my husband is only his servant.'

'Why are you telling me all this?'

'Why shouldn't I tell you?' she said, and gave me a dark, defiant look. 'You like me, do you not?'

'Of course I like you,' I hastened to assure her.

*

I think I hate families. I am jealous of them. Their sense of security, of interdependence, infuriates me. To every family I am an outsider, because I have no family. A man without a family is a social outcast. He has no credentials. A man's credentials are his father and his father's property. His mother is another quantity; it is her family—her father—that matter.

So I am glad that I do not belong to a family, and at the same time sad, because in our country if you do not belong to a family you are a piece of driftwood. And so two pieces of driftwood come together, and finding themselves caught in the same current, move along with it until they are trapped in a counter-current, and dispersed.

And that is the way it is with me. I must cling to someone as long as circumstances will permit it.

*

Having no family of our own, it was odd and even touching that Kamla should have adopted us both as her brothers during the Raksha Bandhan festival.

It was a change to have Kamla visiting us early in the morning instead of late at night; and we were surprised, and rather disconcerted, to be treated as her brothers.

She tied the silver tinsel round our wrists, and I said, 'Kamla, we are proud to be your brothers, and we would like to make you some gift, but at the moment there is no money with us.'

'I want your protection, not your money,' said Kamla. 'I want to feel that I am not alone in the world.'

So that made three of us. But we could hardly call ourselves a family.

*

Kamla visited us about once a week, when she found time to spare from her professional duties.

I think she preferred Suraj to me. He was gentle and he was beautiful, and I think she felt, as I did, that he would not live very long. She wanted to give him as much of herself as she could in so short a time.

Suraj was always a bit embarrassed with her around. At first I thought it was because of my presence in the room; but when I offered to leave, he protested. He told me that he would have been completely helpless if I was not present all the time.

CHAPTER EIGHT

SURAJ AND I WERE sitting in the tea-shop one night. Most of the customers were outside on a bench, where they could listen to the shopkeeper, a popular story-teller. Sitting on the ground in front of the shop was a thick-set youth, with a shaved head. He was dumb—they called him Goonga—and the customers often made sport of him, abusing him and clouting him over the head from time to time. The Goonga didn't mind this; he made faces at the others, and chuckled derisively at their remarks. He could say only one word, 'Goo,' and he said it often. This kept the customers in fits of laughter.

'Goo,' he said, when he saw Suraj enter the shop with me. He pointed at us, chuckled, and said, 'Goo.'

Everyone laughed. Someone got up from the bench and, with the flat of his hand, whacked the Goonga over his bald head. The Goonga sprang at the man making queer noises in his throat, and then someone tripped him and sent him sprawling on the ground. There was more laughter.

We were sitting at an inside table, and everyone was drinking tea, except the Goonga.

'Give the Goonga a glass of tea,' I told the shopkeeper. The shopkeeper grinned but complied with the order. The Goonga looked at me and said, 'Goo.'

When we left the shop, the full moon floated above us, robbing the stars of their glory. We walked in the direction of the Maidan, towards my room. The bazaar was almost empty, the shops closed. I became conscious of the sound of soft footfalls behind me and, looking over my shoulder, found that we were being followed by the Goonga.

'Goo,' he said, on being noticed.

'Why did you have to give him tea?' said Suraj. 'Now he probably thinks we are rich, and won't let us out of sight again.'

'He can do no harm,' I said, though I quickened my step. 'We'll pretend we're going to sleep on the Maidan, then he'll change his mind about us.'

'Goo,' said the Goonga from behind, and quickened his step as well.

We turned abruptly down an alley-way, trying to shake him off; but he padded after us, chuckling ghoulishly to himself. We cut back to the main road, but he was behind us at the clock tower. At the edge of the Maidan I turned and said:

'Go away, Goonga. We've got very little, and can't do anything for you. Go away.'

But the youth said 'Goo' and took a step forward, and his shaved head glistened in the moonlight. I shrugged, and led Suraj on to the Maidan. The Goonga stood at the edge of the Maidan, shaking his head and chuckling to himself. His body showed through his rags, and his feet were covered with mud. He watched us as we walked across the grass, watched us until we sat down on a bench; then he shrugged his shoulders and said 'Goo' and went away.

*

The beggars on the whole are a thriving community, and it came as no surprise to me when the municipality decided to place a tax on begging.

I know that some beggars earned, on an average, more than a chaprasi or a clerk; I knew for certain that the one-legged man, who had been hobbling about town on crutches long before I come to Pipalnagar, sent money orders home every month. Begging had become a profession, and so perhaps the municipality felt justified in taxing it, and besides, the municipal coffers needed replenishing.

Shaggy old Ganpat Ram, who was bent double and couldn't straighten up, didn't like it at all, and told me so. 'If I had known this was going to happen,' he mumbled, 'I would have chosen some other line of work.'

Ganpat Ram was an aristocrat among beggars. I had heard that he had once been a man of property, with several houses and a European wife; when his wife packed up and returned to Europe, together with all their savings, Ganpat had a nervous breakdown from which he never recovered. His health became steadily worse until he had to hobble about with a stick. He never made a direct request for money, but greeted you politely, commented on the weather or the price of things, and stood significantly beside you.

I suspected his story to be half true because whenever he approached a well-dressed person, he used impeccable English. He had a white beard and twinkling eyes, and was not the sort of beggar who invokes the names of the gods and calls on the mercy of the passer-by. Ganpat would rely more on a good joke. Some said he was a spy or a policeman in disguise, but so devoted to his work that he would probably remain a beggar for another five years.

I don't know how blind the blind man was, because he always recognized me in the street, even when he was alone. He would invoke blessings on my head, or curses, as the occasion demanded. I didn't like the blind man, because he made too much capital out of his affliction; there were opportunities for him to work with other blind people, but he found begging more profitable. The boy who sometimes led him around town didn't beg from me, but would ask, 'Have you got an anna on you?' as though he were merely borrowing the money, or needed it only for a minute or two. He was quite friendly, and even came up to my room, to see how I was getting on. He was very solicitous about my welfare. If he saw me from a hundred yards down the street, he would run all the way up to inquire about my health, and borrow an anna. He had a crafty, healthy face, and wore a long, dirty cloak draped over his shoulders, and very little else. He didn't care about the tax on begging, that was the blind man's problem.

In fact, the tax didn't affect the boys at all; with them, begging was a pastime and not a profession. They had big watery eyes, and it was difficult to resist their appeal.

'I haven't any small change,' I would say defensively.

'I'll change your note,' offers the boy.

'It's not a note; it's a fifty paise coin.'

'What do you want to change that for? Give me the coin and I won't trouble you for the rest of the week.'

'That's very kind of you.' But even if I gave him the two annas, he would accost me again at the first opportunity and wheedle something more from my pocket. There was a time when beggars asked for one or two pice; but these days, what with the rise in the cost of living, they never ask for anything less than an anna.

Friday is Leper Day. There is a leper colony a little way out of town, on the banks of a muddy, mosquito-ridden ditch, the other side of the railway station. The lepers come into Pipalnagar once a week to beg, and wander through the town in small groups, making for wealthy-looking individuals who give them something if only to avoid being followed down the road. (Of course the danger of contagion is very real, but if the municipal authorities do not let the lepers beg, they will have to support them, and that would prove expensive).

Some of the leper girls have good faces, but their hands are withered stumps, or their arms and legs are eaten away: the older ones have lost their ears and noses, and the men shuffle about with one or two limbs missing. Most of the sufferers belong to the hill areas, where it is still widely believed that leprosy is punishment for sins committed in a former life; the victim is ostracized and often driven out by his family; he goes into the towns and, in order to get work, makes a secret of his affliction; it is only when it can no longer be concealed that he goes for treatment, and then it is too late. The few who get into the hospitals are soldiers and policemen, who are looked after by the State, and a few others whose families have not disclaimed responsibility for them.

But the tax didn't affect the lepers either. It was aimed at the professionals, those who had made a business of begging over the past few years. It was rumoured that one beggar, after spending the day on the pavement calling for alms, would have a taxi drawn up beside him in the evening, and would be driven off to his residence outside town. And when, some months back, news got around that the Pipalnagar Bank was ready to crash, one beggar, who had never been seen to stand on his own two feet, leapt from the pavement and sprinted for the Bank. The professionals are usually crippled or maimed in one way or another—many of them have maimed themselves, others have gone through rigorous training schools in their youth, where they are versed in the fine art of begging. A few cases are genuine, and those are not so loud in their demands for charity, with the result that they don't make much. There are some who sing for their money, and I do not class these as beggars unless they sing badly.

Well, when the municipality decided to place a tax on begging, you should have seen the beggars get together; anyone would have thought they had a union. About a hundred of them took a procession down the main road to the municipal offices, shouting slogans and even waving banners to express the injustice felt by the beggar fraternity over this high-handed action of the authorities. They came on sticks and in carts, a dirty, ragged bunch, one or two of them stark naked; and they stood for two hours outside the municipal offices, to the embarrassment of the working staff and anyone who tried to enter the building.

Eventually somebody came out and told them it was all a rumour, and that no such tax had been contemplated; it would be far too impractical, for one thing. The beggars could all go home and hoard their earnings without any fear of official interference.

So the beggars returned jubilant, feeling they had won a moral victory, conscious of the power of group action. They went out of their way to develop their union, and now there is a fully fledged Beggars' Union. Different districts are allotted to different beggars, and woe betide the trespasser. It is even rumoured that they intend staging demonstrations outside the houses of those who refuse to be charitable!

But my own personal beggars, old Ganpat Ram and the boys, don't take advantage of their growing power; they treat me with due respect and affection; they do not consider me just another member of the public, who has to be blackmailed into charity, but look upon me as a friend who can be counted upon to make them a small loan from time to time, without expecting any immediate return.

CHAPTER NINE

'SHOULD I GO TO Delhi, Suraj?'

'Why not? You are always talking about it. You should go.'

'I would like you to come with me. Perhaps they can make you better there, even cure you of your fits.'

'Not now. After my examinations.'

'Then I will wait . . .'

'Go now, if there is a chance of making a living in Delhi.'

'There is nothing definite. But I know the chance will not come until I leave this place and make my chances. There are one or two editors who have asked me to look them up. They could give me some work. And if I find an honest publisher I might be encouraged to write an honest book.'

'Write the book, even if you don't find a publisher.'

'I will try.'

We decided to save a little money, from his small earnings and from my occasional erratic payments which came by money order. I would need money for my trip to Delhi; sometimes there were medicines to be paid for; and we had no warm clothes for the cold weather. We managed to put away twenty rupees one week, but withdrew it the next, as Pitamber needed a loan for repairs on his cycle-rickshaw. He returned the money in three instalments and it disappeared in meeting various small bills.

Pitamber and Deep Chand and Ramu and Aziz all had plans for visiting Delhi. Only Kamla could not foresee such a move for herself. She was a woman and she had no man.

Deep Chand dreamt of his barber shop. Pitamber planned to own a scooter-rickshaw, which would involve no physical exertion and bring in more money. Ramu had a hundred-and-one different dreams, all of which featured beautiful women. He was a sweet boy, with little intelligence but much good nature.

Once, when he had his arm gashed by a knife in a street fight, he came to me for treatment. The hospital would have had to report the matter to the police. I washed his wound, poured benzedrine over it to stop the bleeding, and bandaged his arm rather crudely. He was very grateful and rewarded me with the story of his life. It was a chronicle of disappointed females, all of whom had been seduced by Ramu in fantastic circumstances and had been discarded by him after he had slept with each but once. Ramu boasted that he did not go twice to the same woman.

All this was good-natured lying, as it was well-known that a girl-teaser like Ramu had never seen anything more than a well-shaped ankle; but apparently Ramu believed in many of his own adventures, which in his own mind had acquired a legendary aspect.

I did not ask him how he got his arm cut, because I know he

would have given me a fantastic explanation involving his honour and a lady's dishonour. Later I discovered that an irate brother had stabbed him for spreading discreditable rumours about his sister.

Ramu slept in my room that night. It was the sweet sleep of childhood. Suraj read his books, and Kamla came and went, while Ramu dreamt—he told us about it in the morning—of a woman with three breasts.

Chapter Ten

'Look, Ganpat,' I said one day, 'I've heard a lot of stories about you, and I don't know which is true. How did you get your crooked back?'

'That's a very long story,' he said, flattered by my interest in him. 'And I don't know if you will believe it. Besides, it is not to anyone that I would speak freely.'

He had served his purpose in whetting my appetite. I said, 'I'll give you four annas if you tell me your story. How about that?'

He stroked his beard, considering my offer. 'All right,' he said, squatting down on his haunches in the sunshine, while I pulled myself up on a low wall. 'But it happened more than twenty years ago, and you cannot expect me to remember very clearly.'

In those days (said Ganpat) I was quite a young man, and had just been married. I owned several acres of land and, though we were not rich, we were not very poor. When I took my produce to the market, five miles away, I harnessed the bullocks and drove down the dusty village road. I would return home at night.

Every night, I passed a pipal tree, and it was said this tree was haunted. I had never met the ghost and did not believe in him, but his name, I was told, was Bippin, and long ago he had been hanged on the pipal tree by a band of dacoits. Ever since, his ghost had lived in the tree, and was in the habit of pouncing upon any person who resembled a dacoit, and beating him severely. I suppose I must have looked dishonest, for one night Bippin decided to pounce on me. He leapt out of the tree and stood in the middle of the road, blocking the way.

'You, there!' he shouted. 'Get off your cart. I am going to kill you!'

I was, of course, taken aback, but saw no reason why I should obey.

'I have no intention of being killed,' I said. 'Get on the cart yourself!'

'Spoken like a man!' cried Bippin, and he jumped up on the cart beside me. 'But tell me one good reason why I should not kill you?'

'I am not a dacoit,' I replied.

'But you look one. That is the same thing.'

'You would be sorry for it later, if you killed me. I am a poor man, with a wife to support.'

'You have no reason for being poor,' said Bippin, angrily.

'Well, make me rich if you can.'

'So you think I don't have the power to make you rich? Do you defy me to make you rich?'

'Yes,' I said, 'I defy you to make me rich.'

'Then drive on!' cried Bippin. 'I am coming home with you.' I drove the bullock-cart on to the village, with Bippin sitting beside me.

'I have so arranged it,' he said, 'that no one but you will be able to see me. And another thing. I must sleep beside you every night, and no one must know of it. If you tell anyone about me, I'll kill you immediately!'

'Don't worry,' I said. 'I won't tell anyone.'

'Good. I look forward to living with you. It was getting lonely in that pipal tree.'

So Bippin came to live with me, and he slept beside me every night, and we got on very well together. He was as good as his word, and money began to pour in from every conceivable and inconceivable source, until I was in a position to buy more land and cattle. Nobody knew of our association, though of course my friends and relatives wondered where all the money was coming from. At the same time, my wife was rather upset at my refusing to sleep with her at night. I could not very well keep her in the same bed as a ghost, and Bippin was most particular about sleeping beside me. At first, I had told my wife I wasn't well, that I would sleep on the veranda. Then I told her that there was someone after our cows, and I would have to keep an eye on them at night: Bippin and I slept in the barn.

My wife would often spy on me at night, suspecting infidelity, but she always found me lying alone with the cows. Unable to understand my strange behaviour, she mentioned it to her family. They came to me, demanding an explanation.

At the same time, my own relatives were insisting that I tell them the source of my increasing income. Uncles and aunts and distant cousins all descended on me one day, wanting to know where the money was coming from.

'Do you want me to die?' I said, losing patience with them. 'If I tell you the cause of my wealth, I will surely die.'

But they laughed, taking this for a half-hearted excuse; they suspected I was trying to keep everything for myself. My wife's relatives insisted that I had found another woman. Eventually, I grew so exhausted with their demands that I blurted out the truth.

They didn't believe the truth either (who does?), but it gave them something to think and talk about, and they went away for the time being.

But that night, Bippin didn't come to sleep beside me. I was all alone with the cows. And he didn't come the following night. I had been afraid he would kill me while I slept, but it appeared that he had gone his way and left me to my own devices. I was certain that my good fortune had come to an end, and so I went back to sleeping with my wife.

The next time I was driving back to the village from the market, Bippin leapt out of the pipal tree.

'False friend!' he cried, halting the bullocks. 'I gave you everything you wanted, and still you betrayed me!'

'I'm sorry,' I said. 'You can kill me, if you like.'

'No, I cannot kill you,' he said. 'We have been friends for too long. But I will punish you all the same.'

Picking up a stout stick, he struck me three times across the back, until I was bent up double.

'After that,' Ganpat concluded, 'I could never straighten up again and, for over twenty years, I have been a crooked man. My wife left me and went back to her family, and I could no longer work in the fields. I left my village and wandered from one city to another, begging for a living. That is how I came to Pipalnagar, where I decided to remain. People here seem to be more generous than they are in other towns, perhaps because they haven't got so much.'

He looked up at me with a smile, waiting for me to produce the four annas.

'You can't expect me to believe that story,' I said. 'But it was a good invention, so here is your money.'

'No, no!' said Ganpat, backing away and affecting indignation. 'If you don't believe me, keep the money. I would not lie to you for a mere four annas!'

He permitted me to force the coin into his hand, and then went hobbling away, having first wished me a pleasant afternoon.

CHAPTER ELEVEN

PITAMBER IS A YOUNG lion. A shaggy mane of black hair tumbles down the nape of his neck; his body, though, is naked and hairless, burnt a rich chocolate by the summer sun. His only garment is a pair of knickers. When he pedals his cycle-rickshaw through the streets of Pipalnagar, the muscles of his calves and thighs stand out like lumps of grey iron. He has carried in his rickshaw fat baniyas and their fat wives, and this has given him powerful legs, a strong back and hollow cheeks. His thighs are magnificent, solid muscle, not an ounce of surplus flesh. They look as though they have been carved out of teak.

His face, though, is gaunt and hollow, his eyes set deep in their sockets: but there is a burning intensity about his eyes, and sometimes I wonder if he, too, is tubercular, like many in Pipalnagar. You cannot tell just by looking at a person if he is sick. Sometimes the weak will last for years, while the strong will suddenly collapse and die.

Pitamber has a wife and three children in his village five miles from Pipalnagar. They have a few acres of land on which they grow maize and sugarcane. One day he made me sit in his rickshaw, and we cycled out of the town, along the road to Delhi; then we had to get down and push the rickshaw over a rutted cart-track, until we reached his village.

This visit to Pitamber's village had provided me with an escape route from Pipalnagar. Some weeks later I persuaded Suraj to put aside his tray and his books, and hiring a cycle from a stand near the bus stop (on credit), I seated Suraj in front of me on the cross-bar, and rode out of Pipalnagar.

It was then that I made the amazing discovery that by exerting my legs a little, I could get out of Pipalnagar, and that, except for the cycle-hire, it did not involve any expense or great sacrifice.

It was a hot, sunny morning, and I was perspiring by the time we had gone two miles; but a fresh wind sprang up suddenly, and I could smell rain in the air, though there were no clouds to be seen.

When Suraj began to feel cramped on the saddle-bar, we got down, and walked along the side of the road.

'Let us not go to the village,' said Suraj. 'Let us go where there are no people at all. I am tired of people.'

We pushed the cycle off the road, and took a path through a paddy-field, and then a field of young maize, and in the distance we saw a tree, a crooked tree, growing beside a well.

I do not know the name of that tree. I had never seen one of its kind before. It had a crooked trunk, and crooked branches, and it was clothed in thick, broad crooked leaves, like the leaves on which food is served in the bazaars. In the trunk of the tree was a hole, and when I set my cycle down with a crash, two green parrots flew out of the hole, and went dipping and swerving across the fields.

There was grass around the well, cropped short by grazing cattle, so we sat in the shade of the crooked tree, and Suraj untied the red cloth in which he had brought our food.

We ate our rotis and spiced vegetables, and meanwhile the parrots returned to the tree.

'Let us come here every week,' said Suraj, stretching himself out on the grass and resting his head against my shoulder.

It was a drowsy day, the air humid, and soon Suraj fell asleep. I, too, stretched myself out on the grass, and closed my eyes— but I did not sleep; I was aware instead of a score of different sensations.

I heard a cricket singing in the crooked tree; the cooing of pigeons which dwelt in the walls of the old well; the quiet breathing of Suraj; a rustling in the leaves of the tree; the distant hum of an aeroplane.

I smelt the grass, and the old bricks round the well and the promise of rain.

I felt Suraj's fingers touching my arm, and the sun creeping over my cheek.

I opened my eyes, and I saw the clouds on the horizon, and Suraj still asleep, his arm thrown across his eyes to keep away the glare.

Being thirsty, I went to the well, and putting my shoulders to it, turned the wheel, walking around the well four times, while cool clean water gushed out over the stones and along the channel to the fields.

I drank from one of the trays and the water was sweet with age.

Suraj was sitting up, looking at the sky.

'It is going to rain,' he said. When he had taken his fill of water we pushed the cycle back to the main road and began cycling homewards, but we were still two miles out of Pipalnagar when it began to rain.

A lashing wind swept the rain across our faces, but we exulted in it, and sang at the tops of our voices until we reached the bus stop.

I left the cycle at the hire-shop. Suraj and I ran up the rickety, swaying steps to my room.

Soon there were puddles on the floor, where we had left our soaking clothes, and Suraj was sitting on the bed, a sheet wrapped round his chest.

He became feverish that evening, and I pulled out an old blanket, and covered him with it. I massaged his scalp with mustard oil, and he fell asleep while I did this.

It was dark by then, and the rain had stopped, and the bazaar was lighting up. I curled up at the foot of the bed, and slept for a little while; but at midnight I was woken by the moon shining full in my face; a full moon, shedding its light exclusively on Pipalnagar and peeping and prying into every room, washing the empty streets, silvering the corrugated tin roof.

People are restless tonight, with the moon shining through their windows. Suraj turns restlessly in his sleep. Kamla, having sent away a drunken customer, will be bathing herself, as she always does before she finally sleeps ... Deep Chand is tossing on his cot, dreaming of electric razors and a plush hair-cutting saloon in the capital, with the Prime Minister as his client. And Seth Govind Ram, unable to sleep because of the accusing moonlight, paces his veranda, worrying about his rent, counting up his assets, and wondering if he should stand for election to the Legislative Assembly.

In the temple the moonlight rests gently on the generous Ganesh, and in the fields Krishna is playing his flute and Radha is singing ... 'I follow you, devoted ... How can you deceive me, so tortured by love's fever as I am ...'

Chapter Twelve

In June, the lizards hang listlessly on the walls, scanning their horizon in vain. Insects seldom show up—either the heat has killed them, or they are sleeping and breeding in cracks in the plaster. The lizards wait—and wait . . .

All Pipalnagar is waiting for its release from the oppressive heat of June.

One day clouds loom up on the horizon, growing rapidly into enormous towers. A faint breeze springs up. Soon it is a wind, which brings with it the first raindrops. This is the moment everyone is waiting for. People run out of their chawls and houses to take in the fresh breeze and the scent of those first raindrops on the parched, dusty earth.

Underground, in their cracks and holes, the insects are moving. Termites and white ants, which have been sleeping through the hot season, emerge from their lairs. They have work ahead of them.

Now, on the second or third night of the monsoon, comes the great yearly flight of the insects into the cool brief freedom of the night. Out of every crack, from under the roots of trees, huge winged ants emerge, at first fluttering about heavily, on this the first and last flight of their lives. At night there is only one direction in which they can fly—towards the light; towards the electric bulbs and smoky kerosene lamps that illuminate Pipalnagar.

The street lamp opposite the bus stop, beneath my room, attracts a massive quivering swarm of clumsy termites, which give the impression of one thick, slowly revolving body.

The first frog has arrived and comes hopping on to the balcony to pause beneath the electric bulb. All he has to do is gobble, as the insects fall about him.

This is the hour of the lizards. Now there are rewards for those days of patient waiting. Plying their sticky pink tongues, they devour the insects as fast as they come. For hours they cram their stomachs, knowing that such a feast will not be theirs again for another year.

How wasteful nature is ... Through the whole hot season the insect world prepares for this flight out of darkness into light, and not one of them survives its freedom.

*

As most of my writing is done at night and much of my sleeping by day, it often happens that at about midnight I put down my pen and go out for a walk. In Pipalnagar this is a pleasant time for a walk, provided you are not taken for a burglar. There is the smell of jasmine in the air, the moonlight shining on sandy stretches of wasteland, and a silence broken only by the hideous bellow of the chowkidar.

This is the person who, employed by the residents of our Mohalla, keeps guard over us at night, and walks the roads calling like a jackal: 'Khabardar!' (Beware) for the benefit of prospective evil-doers. Apart from keeping half the population awake, he is successful in warning thieves of his presence.

The other night, in the course of a midnight stroll I encountered our chowkidar near a dark corner, and wished him a good evening. He leapt into the air like a startled rabbit, and immediately shouted 'Khabardar!' as though this were some magic word that would bring me down on my knees begging for mercy.

'It's quite all right,' I assured him. 'I'm only one of your clients.'

The chowkidar laughed nervously and said he was glad to hear it; he hoped I didn't mind his shouting 'Khabardar' at me, but these were grim times and robbers were on the increase.

I said yes, there were probably quite a few of them at work this very night. Had he ever tried creeping up on them quietly? He might catch a few that way.

But why should he catch them, the chowkidar wanted to

know. It was his business to frighten them away. He could do that better by roaring defiantly on the roads than by accosting them on someone's premises—violence must be avoided, if he could help it.

'Besides,' he said, 'the people who live here like me to shout at night. It makes them feel safe, knowing that I am on guard. And if I didn't shout "Khabardar" every few minutes they would think I had fallen asleep, and I would be dismissed.'

This was a logical argument. I asked him what he would do if, by accident, he encountered a gang of thieves. He said he would keep shouting 'Khabardar' until the people came out of their houses to help him. I said I doubted very much if they would come out of their houses, but wished him luck all the same, and continued with my walk.

Every five minutes or so I heard his cry, followed by a 'Khabardar' which grew fainter until the chowkidar had reached the far side of the Mohalla. I thought it would be a good idea to give him a helping hand from my side, so I cupped my hands to my mouth and shouted, 'Khabardar, Khabardar!'

It worked like magic.

Three dark figures scrambled over a neighbouring wall and fled down the empty road. I shouted 'Khabardar' a second time, and they ran faster. Imagine the thieves' confusion when they were met by more 'Khabardars' in front, coming from the chowkidar, and realized that there were now two chowkidars operating in the Mohalla.

*

On those nights when sleep was elusive we left the room and walked for miles around Pipalnagar. It was generally about midnight that we became restless. The walls of the room would give out all the heat they had absorbed during the day, and to lie awake sweating in the dark only gave rise to morbid and depressing thoughts.

In our singlets and pyjamas Suraj and I would walk barefooted through the empty Mohalla, over the cooling brick pavements, until we were out of the bazaar and crossing the Maidan, our feet sinking into the springy dew-fresh grass. The Maidan was broad and spacious, and the star-swept sky seemed to meet each end of the plain.

Then out of the town, through lantana scrub, till we came to the dry river-bed, where we walked amongst rocks and boulders, sitting down occasionally, while great quiet lizards watched us from between the stones.

Across the river-bed fields of maize stretched away for a few miles, until there came a dry region, where thorns and a few bent trees grew, the earth splitting up in jagged cracks like a jigsaw puzzle; and where water had been, the skin was peeling off the earth in great flat pancakes. Dotting the landscape were old abandoned brick kilns, and it was said that thieves met there at nights, in the trenches around the kilns; but we never saw any.

When it rained heavily the hollows filled up with water. Suraj and I came to one of these places to bathe and swim. There was an island in the middle of one of the hollows, and on this small mound stood the ruins of a hut, where a night-watchman once lived and looked after the bricks at night.

We swam out to the island, which was only a few yards away. There was a grassy patch in front of the hut, and here we lay and sunned ourselves in the early morning, until it became too hot. We would oil and massage each other's bodies, and wrestle on the grass.

Though I was heavier than Suraj, and my chest was as sound as a new drum, he had a lot of power in his long arms and legs and often pinioned me about the waist with his bony knees or fastened me with his strong fingers.

Once while we wrestled on the new monsoon grass, I felt his body go tense, as I strained to press his back to the ground. He stiffened, his thigh jerked against me, and his legs began to twitch. I knew that he had a fit coming on, but I was unable to extricate myself from his arms, which gripped me more tightly as the fit took possession of him. Instead of struggling, I lay still, and tried desperately to absorb some of his anguish; by embracing him, I felt my own body might draw some of the agitation to itself; it was only a strange fancy, but I felt that it made a difference, that by consciously sharing his unconscious condition I was alleviating it. At other times, I have known this same feeling. When Kamla was burning with a fever, I had thought that by taking her in my arms I could draw the fever from her, absorb the heat of her body, transfer to hers the coolness of my own.

Now I pressed against Suraj, and whispered soothingly and lovingly into his ear, though I knew he had no idea what I could be saying; and then when I noticed his mouth working, I thrust my hand in sideways to prevent him from biting his tongue.

But so violent was the convulsion that his teeth bit into the flesh of my palm and ground against my knuckles. I gasped with pain and tried to jerk my hand away, but it was impossible to loosen the grip of his teeth. So I closed my eyes and counted one, two, three, four, five, six, seven—until I felt his body relax again and his jaws give way slowly.

My hand had blood on it, and was trembling: I bound it in a handkerchief, before Suraj came to himself.

We walked back to the town without talking much. He looked depressed and hopeless, though I knew he would be buoyant again before long. I kept my hand concealed beneath my singlet, and he was too dejected to notice this. It was only at night, when he returned from his classes, that he noticed it was bandaged, and then I told him I had slipped on the road, cutting my hand on some broken glass.

CHAPTER THIRTEEN

Rain upon Pipalnagar: and until the rain stops, Pipalnagar is fresh and clean and alive. The children run out of their houses, glorying in their nakedness. They are innocent and unashamed. Older children, by no means innocent, but by all means unashamed, romp through the town, inviting the shocked disapproval of their elders and, presumably, betters.

Before we are ten, we are naked and free and unafraid; after ten, we must cloak our manhood, for we are no longer certain that we are men.

The gutters choke, and the Mohalla becomes a mountain stream, coursing merrily down towards the bus stop. And it is at the bus stop that pandemonium breaks loose; for newly-arrived passengers panic at sight of the sea of mud and rain water that surrounds them on all sides, and about a hundred tongas and cycle-rickshaws try all at once to take care of a score of passengers. Result: only half the passengers find a conveyance, while the other half find themselves knee-deep in Pipalnagar mire.

Pitamber has, of course, succeeded in acquiring as his passenger the most attractive and frightened young woman in the bus, and proceeds to show off his skill and daring by taking her home by the most devious and uncomfortable route, and when she gets her feet covered with mud, wipes them with the seedy red cloth that he ties about his neck.

The rain swirls over the trees and roofs of the town, and the parched earth soaks it up, exuding a fragrance that comes only once in a year, the fragrance of quenched earth, the most exhilarating of all smells.

And in my room, too, I am battling against the elements, for the door will not shut against the breeze, and the rain is sweeping in through the opening and soaking my cot.

When eventually I succeed in barricading the floor, I find the roof leaking, and the water trickling down the walls, obliterating the dusty designs I have made on the plaster with my foot. I place a tin here and a mug there, and then, satisfied that everything is under control, sit on my cot and watch the roof-tops through my window.

But there is a loud banging on the door. It flies open with the pressure, and there is Suraj, standing on the threshold, shaking himself like a wet dog. Coming in, he strips off all his clothes, and then he dries himself with a torn threadbare towel, and sits shivering on the bed while I make frantic efforts to close the door again.

'You are cold, Suraj, I will make you some tea.'

He nods, forgetting to smile for once, and I know his mind is elsewhere, in one of a thousand places and all of them dreams.

When I have got the fire going, and placed the kettle on the red hot coals, I sit down beside Suraj and put my arm around his bony shoulders and dream a little with him.

'One day I will write a book,' I tell him. 'Not a murder story, but a real book, about real people. Perhaps it will be about you and me and Pipalnagar. And then we will break away from Pipalnagar, fly away like eagles, and our troubles will be over and fresh new troubles will begin. I do not mind difficulties, as long as they are new difficulties.'

'First I must pass my exams,' said Suraj. 'Without a certificate one can do nothing, go nowhere.'

'Who taught you such nonsense? While you are preparing for your exams, I will be writing my book. That's it! I will start tonight. It is an auspicious night, the first night of the monsoon. Let us start tonight.'

And by the time we had drunk our tea it was evening and growing dark. The light did not come on; a tree must have fallen across the wires. So I lit a candle and placed it on the window sill (the rain and wind had ceased), and while the candle spluttered in the steady stillness, Suraj opened his books and with one hand on a book, and the other playing with his toes— this helped him to read—he began his studies.

I took the ink down from the shelf, and finding the bottle empty, added a little rain-water to it from one of the mugs. I sat down beside Suraj and began to write; but the pen was no good, and made blotches all over and I didn't really know what to write about, though I was full of writing just then.

So I began to look at Suraj instead; at his eyes, hidden in the shadows, his hands in the candle light; and felt his breathing and the slight movement of his lips as he read shortly to himself.

*

A gust of wind came through the window, and the candle went out.

I swore softly in Punjabi.

'Never mind,' said Suraj, 'I was tired of reading.'

'But I was writing.'

'Your book?'

'No, a letter . . .'

'I have never known you to write letters, except to publishers asking them for money. To whom were you writing?'

'To you,' I said. 'And I will send you the letter one day, perhaps when we are no longer together.'

'I will wait for it, then. I will not read it now.'

CHAPTER FOURTEEN

AT TEN O'CLOCK ON a wet night Pipalnagar had its first earthquake in thirty years. It lasted exactly five seconds. A low, ominous rumble was followed by a few quick shudders, and the water surahi jumped off the window ledge and crashed on the floor.

By the time Suraj and I had tumbled out of the room, the shock was over; but panic prevailed, and the entire population of the Mohalla was out in the street. One old man of seventy leapt from a first floor balcony and broke his neck; a large crowd had gathered round his body. Several women had fainted. On the other hand, many were shrieking and running about. Only a few days back astrologers had predicted the end of the world, and everyone was convinced that this was only the first of a series of earthquakes.

At temples and other places of worship prayer meetings were

held. People moved about the street, pointing out the cracks that had appeared in their houses. Some of these cracks had, of course, been there for years, and were only now being discovered.

At midnight, men and women were still about; and, as though to justify their prudence, another, milder tremor made itself felt. The roof of an old house, weakened by many heavy monsoons, was encouraged to give way, and fell with a suitably awe-inspiring crash. Fortunately no one was beneath it. Everyone was soaking wet by now, as the rain had come down harder, but no one dared venture indoors, especially after a roof had fallen in.

Worse still, the electricity failed and the entire Mohalla plunged into darkness. People huddled together, fearing the worst, while the rain came down incessantly.

'More people will die of pneumonia than earthquake,' observed Suraj. 'Let's go for a walk, it is better than standing about doing nothing.'

We rolled up our pyjamas and went splashing through the puddles. On the outskirts of the town we met Pitamber dancing in the middle of the road. He was very merry, and quite drunk.

'Why are you dancing in the road?' I asked.

'Because I am happy, that's why,' said Pitamber.

'And what makes you so happy, my friend?'

'Because I am dancing in the road,' he replied.

We began walking home again. The rain had stopped. There was a break in the clouds and a pale moon appeared. The neem trees gave out a strong, sweet smell.

There were no more tremors that night. When we got back to the Mohalla, the sky was lighter, and people were beginning to move into their houses again.

*

We lay on our island, in the shade of a thorn bush, watching a pair of sarus cranes on the opposite bank prancing and capering around each other; tall, stork-like birds, with naked red heads and long red legs.

'We might be saruses in some future life,' I said.

'I hope so,' said Suraj. 'Even if it means being born on a lower level. I would like to be a beautiful white bird. I am tired of being a man, but I do not want to leave the world altogether. It is very lovely, sometimes.'

'I would like to be a sacred bird,' I said. 'I don't wish to be shot at.'

'Aren't saruses sacred? Look how they enjoy themselves.'

'They are making love. That is their principal occupation apart from feeding themselves. And they are so devoted to each other that if one bird is killed the other will haunt the scene for weeks, calling distractedly. They have even been known to pine away and die of grief. That's why they are held in such affection by people in villages.'

'So many birds are sacred.'

We saw a blue jay swoop down from a tree—a flash of blue—and carry off a grasshopper.

'Both the blue jay and Lord Siva are called Nilkanth. Siva has a blue throat, like the blue jay, because out of compassion for the human race he swallowed a deadly poison which was meant to destroy the world. He kept the poison in his throat and would not let it go any further.'

'Are squirrels sacred?' asked Suraj, curiously watching one fumbling with a piece of bread which we had thrown away.

'Krishna loved them. He would take them in his arms and stroke them with his long, gentle fingers. That is why they have four dark lines down their backs from head to tail. Krishna was very dark-skinned, and the lines are the marks of his fingers.'

'We should be gentle to animals . . . Why do we kill so many of them?'

'It is not so important that we do not kill them—it is important that we respect them. We must acknowledge their right to live on this earth. Everywhere, birds and animals are finding it more difficult to survive, because we are destroying their homes. They have to keep moving as the trees and the green grass keep disappearing.'

*

Flowers in Pipalnagar—do they exist?

I have known flowers in poetry, and as a child I knew a garden in Lucknow where there were fields of flowers, and another garden where only roses grew. In the fields round Pipalnagar I have seen dandelions that evaporate when you breathe on them, and sometimes a yellow buttercup nestling among thistles. But in our Mohalla, there are no flowers except one. This is a marigold growing out of a crack in my balcony.

I have removed the plaster from the base of the plant, and filled in a little earth which I water every morning. The plant is healthy, and sometimes it produces a little orange marigold, which I pluck and give away before it dies.

Sometimes Suraj keeps the flower in his tray, among the combs and scent bottles and buttons that he sells. Sometimes he offers the flower to a passing child—to a girl who runs away; or it might be a boy who tears the flower to shreds. Some children keep it; others give flowers to Suraj when he passes their houses.

Suraj has a flute which he plays whenever he is tired of going from house to house.

He will sit beneath a shady banyan or pipal, put his tray aside, and take out his flute. The haunting little notes travel down the road in the afternoon stillness, and children come to sit beside him and listen to the flute music. They are very quiet when he plays, because there is a little sadness about his music, and children especially can sense that sadness.

Suraj has made flutes out of pieces of bamboo; but he never sells them, he gives them away to the children he likes. He will sell anything, but not his flutes.

Sometimes Suraj plays his flutes at night, when I am lying awake on the cot, unable to sleep; and even when I fall asleep, the flute is playing in my dreams. Sometimes he brings it with him to the crooked tree, and plays it for the benefit of the birds; but the parrots only make harsh noises and fly away.

Once, when Suraj was playing his flute to a group of children, he had a fit. The flute fell from his hands, and he began to roll about in the dust on the roadside. The children were frightened and ran away.

But they did not stay away for long. The next time they heard the flute play, they came to listen as usual.

CHAPTER FIFTEEN

As SURAJ AND I walked over a hill near the limestone quarries, past the shacks of the Bihari labourers, we met a funeral procession on its way to the cremation ground. Suraj placed his hand on my arm and asked me to wait until the procession had passed. At the same time a cyclist dismounted and stood at the side of the road. Others hurried on, without glancing at the little procession.

'I was taught to respect the dead in this way,' said Suraj. 'Even if you do not respect a man in life, you should respect him in death. The body is unimportant, but we should honour it out of respect for the man's mind.'

'It is a good custom,' I said.

'It must be difficult to live on after one you have loved has died.'

'But you do,' I said, reminded of my mother. 'And if a love is strong, I cannot see its end ... It cannot end in death, I feel ... Even physically, you would exist for me somehow.'

*

He was asleep when I returned late at night from a card-game in which I had lost fifty rupees. I was a little drunk, and when I tripped near the doorway, he woke up; and though he did not open his eyes, I felt he was looking at me.

I felt very guilty and ashamed, because he had been ill that day, and I had forgotten it. Now there was no point in saying I was sorry. Drunkenness is really a vice, because it degrades a man, and humiliates him.

Prostitution is degrading, but a prostitute can still keep her dignity; thieving is degrading according to the character of the theft; begging is degrading but it is not as undignified as drunkenness. In all our vices we are aware of our degradation; but in drunkenness we lose our pride, our heads, and, above all, our natural dignity. We become so obviously and helplessly 'human', that we lose our glorious animal identity.

I sat down at the side of the bed, and bending over Suraj, whispered, 'I got drunk and lost fifty rupees, what am I to do about it?'

He smiled, but still he didn't open his eyes, and I kicked off my sandals and pulled off my shirt and lay down across the foot of the bed. He was still burning with fever, I could feel it radiating through the sheet.

We were silent for a long time, and I didn't know if he was awake or asleep; so I pressed his foot and said, 'I'm sorry,' but he was asleep now, and did not hear me.

*

Moonlight.

Pipalnagar looks clean in the moonlight, and my thoughts are different from my daytime thoughts.

The streets are empty, and the moon probes the alley-ways, and there is a silver dustbin, and even the slush and the puddles near the bus stop shimmer and glisten.

Kisses in the moonlight. Hungry kisses. The shudder of bodies clinging to each other on the moonswept floor.

A drunken quarrel in the street. Voices rise and fall. The chowkidar waits for the trouble to pass, and then patrols the street once more, banging the lathi on the pavement.

Kamla asleep. She sleeps like an angel. I go downstairs and walk in the moonlight. I meet Suraj coming home, his books under his arm; he has been studying late with Aziz, who keeps a junk shop near the station. Their exams are only a month off. I am confident that Suraj will be successful; I am only afraid that he will work himself to a standstill; with his weak chest and the uncertainty of his fits, he should not walk all day and read all night.

When I wake in the early hours of the morning and Kamla stirs beside me in her sleep (her hair so laden with perfume that my own sleep has been fitful and disturbed), Suraj is still squatting on the floor, reading by the light of the kerosene lamp.

And even when he has finished reading he does not sleep, but asks me to walk with him before the sun rises, and, as women were not made to get up before the sun, we leave Kamla stretched out on the cot, relaxed and languid; small breasts and a boy's waist; her hair tumbling about the pillow; her mouth slightly apart, her lips still swollen and bruised with kisses.

Chapter Sixteen

It was Lord Krishna's birthday, and the rain came down as heavily as it must have done the day Krishna was born in Brindaban. Krishna is the best beloved of all the gods. Young mothers laugh and weep as they read or hear about the pranks of his childhood; young men pray to be as tall and strong as Krishna was when he killed Kamsa's elephant and Kamsa's wrestlers; young girls dream of a lover as daring as Krishna to carry them off like Rukmani in a war chariot; grown up men envy the wisdom and statesmanship with which he managed the affairs of his kingdom.

The rain came suddenly and took everyone by surprise. In a few seconds, people were drenched to the skin, and within ten minutes the Mohalla was completely flooded. The temple tank overflowed, the railway lines disappeared, and the old wall near the bus stop shivered and fell silently, the noise of the collapse drowned by the rain.

Those whose beard had not yet appeared enjoyed themselves

immensely. Children shrieked with excitement, and five naked young men with a dancing bear cavorted in the middle of the vegetable market.

Wading knee-deep down the road, I saw roadside vendors salvaging what they could. Plastic toys, cabbages and utensils floated away and were seized upon by urchins. The water had risen to the level of the shop-fronts, and the floors were awash. Aziz was afloat in his junk shop. Deep Chand, Ramu and a customer were using buckets to bail the water out of their premises. Pitamber churned through the stream in his cycle-rickshaw, offering free lifts to the women in the bazaar with their saris held high above their knees.

The rain stopped as suddenly as it had begun. The sun came out. The water began to find an outlet, flooding other low-lying areas, and a paper-boat came sailing between my legs.

*

'When did you last go out of Pipalnagar?' I asked Suraj. 'I mean far out, to another part of the country?'

'Not since I came here,' he said. 'I have never had the funds. And you?'

'I don't remember. I have been stagnating in Pipalnagar for five years without a break. I would like to see the hills again. Once, when I was a child, my parents took me to the hills. I remember them vividly—pine trees, the wind at night, men carrying loads of wood up the steep mountain paths—yes, I would like to see the hills again ...'

'I have never seen them,' said Suraj.

'How strange! I don't think that a man can be complete until he has lived in the hills. Of course we are never complete, but there is something about a mountain that adds a new dimension to life. The change in air and altitude makes one think and feel and act differently. Suraj, we must go to the hills! This is the time to go. Let's get away from this insufferable heat, from these drains and smells and noises—even if it is only for a few days ...'

'But my exams are only a few weeks off.'

'Good. The change will help. Bring your books along. You will study much better there. You will feel better. I can guarantee that you will not have a single fit all the time we are away!'

I was carried away in a flood of enthusiasm. I waved my arms about and described the splendour of the sun rising—or setting—behind Nanda Devi, and talked about the book I could write if I stayed a few weeks in the hills.

'But what about money?' interrupted Suraj, breaking in on my oration. 'How do we go there?'

'Money?' I said contemptuously. 'Money?' I said again, more respectfully. And then doubtfully, 'Money.'

'Yes, money,' I muttered to myself, and sat down on the string cot, suddenly deflated and discouraged.

Suraj burst into laughter.

'What are you laughing about?' I hissed.

'I can't help it,' he said, holding his sides with mirth. 'It's your face. One minute it was broad with smiles, now it is long and mournful, like the face of a horse.'

'We'll get money!' I shouted, springing up again. 'How much do we need—two hundred, five hundred—it's easy! My gold ring can be pawned. On our return we shall retrieve it. The book will see to that.'

I was never to see my ring again, but that did not matter. We managed to raise a hundred rupees, and with it we prepared ourselves feverishly for our journey, afraid that at the last moment something would prevent us from going.

We were to travel by train to the railway terminus, a night's journey, then take the bus. Though we hoped to be away for at least a week, our funds did not in fact last more than four days.

We locked our room, left the key with Kamla, and asked Deep Chand to keep an eye on both her and our things.

In the train that night Suraj had a mild fit. It helped reduce the numbers in our compartment. Some, thinking he suffered from a communicable disease, took themselves and their belongings elsewhere; others, used to living with illness, took no notice. But

Suraj was not to have any more fits until we returned to Pipalnagar.

We slept fitfully that night, continually shifting our positions on the hard bench of the third-class compartment; Suraj with his head against my shoulder, I with my feet on my bedding roll. Above us, a Sikh farmer slept vigorously, his healthy snores reverberating through the compartment. A woman with her brood of four or five children occupied the bunk opposite; they had knocked over their earthen surahi, smashing it and flooding the compartment. Two young men in the corner played cards and exchanged lewd jokes. No general companionship was at all evident, but whenever the train drew into a station everyone cooperated in trying to prevent people on the outside from entering the already crowded compartment; and if someone did manage to get in—usually by crawling through a window—he would fall in with the same policy of keeping others out.

We woke in the early hours of the morning and looked out of the window at the changing landscape. It was so long since I had seen trees—not trees singly or in clumps, but forests of trees, thick and dark and broody, commencing at the railway tracks and stretching away to the foothills. Trees full of birds and monkeys; and in the forest clearing we saw a deer, it's head raised, scenting the wind.

Chapter Seventeen

THERE WERE MANY SMALL hotels in the little town that straddled two or three hills; but Suraj and I went to a dharamsala where we were given a small room overlooking the valley. We did not spend much time there. There were too many hills and streams and trees inviting us on all sides; it seemed as though they had been waiting all those years for our arrival. Each tree has an individuality of its own—perhaps more individuality than a man—and if you look at a tree with a personal eye, it will give you something of itself, something deep and personal; its smell, its sap, its depth and wisdom.

So we mingled with the trees. We felt and understood the dignity of the pine, the weariness of the willow, the resignation of the oak. The blossoms had fallen from the plum and apricot trees, and the branches were bare, touched with the light green of new foliage. Pine needles made the ground soft and slippery, and we went sliding downhill on our bottoms.

Then we took paper and pencil and some mangoes, and went among some rocks, and there I wrote odd things that came into my head, about the hills and the sounds we heard.

The silence of the mountains was accentuated by the occasional sounds around us—a shepherd boy shouting to his mate, a girl singing to her cattle, the jingle of cow bells, a woman pounding clothes on a flat stone ... Then, when these sounds stopped, there were quieter, subtler sounds—the singing of crickets, whistling of anonymous birds, the wind soughing in the pine trees.

It was hot in the sun, until a cloud came over, and then it was suddenly cool, and our shirts flapped against us in the breeze.

The hills went striding away into the distance. The nearest hill was covered with oak and pine, the next was brown and naked and topped with a white temple, like a candle on a fruit-cake. The furthest hill was a misty blue.

Chapter Eighteen

THE 'SEASON' AS THEY called it, was just beginning in the hills. Those who had money came to the hill-station for a few weeks, to parade up and down the Mall in a variety of costumes ranging from formal dinner jackets to cowboy jeans. There were the Anglicized elite, models of English gentry, and there was the younger set, imitating western youth as depicted in films and glossy magazines. Suraj and I felt out of place walking down the Mall in kameez and pyjamas; we were foreigners on our own soil. Were these really Indians exhibiting themselves, or were they ghastly caricatures of the West?

The town itself had gone to seed. English houses and cottages, built by unimaginative Victorians to last perhaps fifty years, were now over a hundred years old, all in a state of immediate collapse. No one repaired them, no one tore them down. Some had been built to look like Swiss chateaux, others like *Arabian Nights* castles, most like homely English cottages—all were out of place, incongruous oddities desecrating a majestic mountain.

Though the Sahibs had gone long ago, coolie-drawn rickshaws still plied the steep roads, transporting portly Bombay and Delhi businessmen and their shrill, quarrelsome wives from one end of the hill-station to the other. It was as though a community of wealthy Indians had colonized an abandoned English colony, and had gone native, adopting English clothes and attitudes.

*

A lonely place on a steep slope, hidden by a thicket of oaks through which the sun filtered warmly. We lay on crisp dry oak leaves, while a cool breeze fanned our naked bodies.

I wondered at the frail beauty of Suraj's body, at the transient beauty of all flesh, the vehicle of our consciousness. I thought of Kamla's body—firm, supple, economical, in spite of the indignities to which it had been put; of the body of a child, soft and warm and throbbing with vigour; the bodies of pot-bellied glandular males; and bodies bent and deformed and eaten away ... The armours of our consciousness, every hair from the head to the genitals a live and beautiful thing ...

But let me not confine myself to the few years between this birth and this death—which is, after all, only the period I can remember well ... I believe in the death of flesh, but not in the end of living.

When, at the age of six, I saw my first mountain, it did not astonish me; it was something new and exhilarating, but all the same I felt I had known mountains before. Trees and flowers and rivers were not strange things. I had lived with them, too. In new places, new faces, we see the familiar. Even as children we are old in experience. We are not conscious of a beginning, only of an eternity.

Death must be an interval, a rest for a tired and misused body, which has to be destroyed before it can be renewed. But consciousness is a continuing thing. Our very thoughts have an existence of their own. Are we so unimaginative as to presume that life is confined to the shells that are our bodies? Science and religion have not even touched upon the mysteries of our existence.

In moments of rare intimacy, for instance, two people are of one mind and one body, speaking only in thoughts, brilliantly aware of each other.

I have felt this way about Suraj even when he is far away; his thoughts hover about me, as they do now.

He lies beside me with his eyes closed and his head turned away, but all the time we are talking, talking, talking . . .

*

To a temple on the spur of a hill. Scrambling down a slippery hillside, getting caught in thorny thickets, among sharp rocks; along a dry water-course, where we saw the skeleton of a jungle-cat, its long, sharp teeth still in perfect condition.

A footpath, winding round the hill to the temple; a forest of silver oaks shimmering in the breeze. Cool, sweet water bubbling out of the mountain side, the sweetest, most delicious water I have ever tasted, coming through rocks and ferns and green grasses.

Then up, up, up the steep mountain, where long-fingered cacti point to the sloping sky and pebbles go tumbling into the valley below. A giant langur, with a five-foot long tail, leaps from tree to jutting boulder, anxious lest we invade its domain among the unattended peach trees.

On top of the hill, a little mound of stones and a small cross. I wondered what lonely, romantic foreigner, so different from his countrymen, could have been buried here, where sky and mountain meet.

CHAPTER NINETEEN

THOUGH WE HAD LOST weight in the hills, through climbing and riding, the good clean air had sweetened our blood, and we felt like spartans on our return to Pipalnagar.

That Suraj was gaining in strength I knew from the way he pinned me down when we wrestled on the sand near the old brick-kilns. It was no longer necessary for me to yield a little to him. Though his fits still occurred from time to time as they would continue to do—the anxiety and the death had gone from his eyes.

Suraj passed his examinations. We never doubted that he would. Still, neither of us could sleep the night before the results appeared. We lay together in the dark and spoke of many things—of living and dying, and the reason for all striving—we asked each other the same questions that thousands have asked themselves—and like those thousands, we had no answers; we could not even comfort ourselves with religion, because God eluded us.

Only once had I felt the presence of God. I woke one morning, and finding Suraj asleep beside me, was overcome by a tremendous happiness, and kept saying, 'Thank you, God, thank you for giving me Suraj . . .'

The newspapers came with the first bus, at six in the morning. A small crowd of students had gathered at the bus stop, joking with each other and hiding their nervous excitement with a hearty show of indifference.

There were not many passengers on the first bus, and there was a mad grab for the newspapers as the bundle landed with a thud on the pavement. Within half an hour the newsboy had sold all his copies. It was the only day of the year when he had a really substantial sale.

Suraj did not go down to meet the bus, but I did. I was more nervous than he, I think. And I ran my eye down the long columns of roll numbers so fast that I missed his number the first time. I began again, in a panic, then found it at the top of the list, among the successful ones.

I looked up at Suraj who was standing on the balcony of my room, and he could tell from my face that he had passed, and he smiled down at me. I joined him on the balcony, and we looked down at the other boys comparing newspapers, some of them exultant, some resigned; a few still hopeful, still studying the columns of roll numbers—each number representing a year's concentration on dull, ill-written text books.

Those who had failed had nothing to be ashamed of. They had failed through sheer boredom.

*

I had been called to Delhi for an interview, and I needed a shirt. The few I possessed were either torn at the shoulders or frayed at the collars. I knew writers and artists were not expected to dress very well, but I felt I was not in a position to indulge in eccentricities. Why display my poverty to an editor, of all people.

Where was I to get a shirt? Suraj generally wore an old red-striped T-shirt; he washed it every second evening, and by morning it was dry and ready to wear again; but it was tight even for him. What I needed was something white, something respectable.

I went to Deep Chand. He had a collection of shirts. He was only too glad to lend me one. But they were all brightly coloured things—yellow and purple and pink. They would not impress an editor. No editor could possibly take a liking to an author who wore a pink shirt. They looked fine on Deep Chand when he was cutting people's hair.

Pitamber was also unproductive; he had only someone's pyjama coat to offer.

In desperation, I went to Kamla.

'A shirt?' she said. 'I'll soon get a shirt for you. Why didn't you ask me before? I'll have it ready for you in the morning.'

And not only did she produce a shirt next morning, but a pair of silver cuff-links as well.

'Whose are these?' I asked.

'One of my visitors', she replied with a shrug. 'He was about your size. As he was quite drunk when he went home, he did not realize that I had kept his shirt. He had removed it to show me his muscles, as I kept telling him he hadn't any to show. Not where it really mattered.'

I laughed so much that my belly ached (laughing on a half empty stomach is painful) and kissed the palms of Kamla's hands and told her she was wonderful.

*

Freedom.

The moment the bus was out of Pipalnagar, and the fields opened out on all sides, I knew I was free; that I had always been free; held back only by my own weakness, lacking the impulse and the imagination to break away from an existence that had become habitual for years.

And all I had to do was sit in a bus and go somewhere.

Only by leaving Pipalnagar could I help Suraj. Brooding in my room, I was no good to anyone.

I sat near the open window of the bus and let the cool breeze freshen my face. Herons and snipe waded among the lotus on flat green ponds; blue jays swooped around the telegraph poles; and children jumped naked into the canals that wound through the fields.

Because I was happy, it seemed that everyone else was happy—

the driver, the conductor, the passengers, the farmers in their fields, on their bullock-carts. When two women began quarrelling over a coat behind me, I intervened, and with tact and sweetness soothed their tempers. Then I took a child on my knee, and pointed out camels and buffaloes and vultures and pariah-dogs.

And six hours later the bus crossed the swollen river Yamuna, passed under the giant red walls of the fort built by Shahjahan, and entered the old city of Delhi.

Chapter Twenty

THE EDITOR OF THE Urdu weekly had written asking me if I would care to be his literary editor; he was familiar with some of my earlier work—poems and stories—and had heard that my circumstances and the quality of my work had deteriorated. Though he did not promise me a job, and did not offer to pay my fare to Delhi, or give me any idea of what my salary might be, there was the offer and there was the chance—an opportunity to escape, to enter the world of the living, to write, to read, to explore.

On my second night in Delhi I wrote to Suraj from the station waiting room, resting the pad on my knee as I sat alone with my suitcase in one corner of the crowded room. Women chattered amongst themselves, or slept silently, children wandered about on the platform outside, babies cried or searched for their mothers' breasts.

*

Dear Suraj:
    It is strange to be in a city again, after so many years of Pipalnagar. It is a little frightening, too. You suffer a loss of identity, as you feel your way through the indifferent crowds in

Chandni Chowk late in the evening; you are an alien amongst the Westernized who frequent the restaurants and shops at Connaught Place; a stranger amongst one's fellow refugees who have grown prosperous now and live in the flat treeless colonies that have mushroomed around the city. It is only when I am near an old tomb or in the garden of a long-forgotten king, that I become conscious of my identity again.

I wish you had accompanied me. That would have made this an exciting, not an intimidating experience!

Anyway, I shall see you in a day or two. I think I have the job. I saw my editor this morning. He is from Hyderabad. Just imagine the vastness of our country, that it should take almost half a lifetime for a north Indian to meet a south Indian for the first time in his life.

I don't think my editor is very fond of north Indians, judging from some of his remarks about Punjabi traders and taxi-drivers in Delhi; but he liked what he called my unconventionality (I don't know if he meant my work or myself). I said I thought he was the unconventional one. This always pleases, and he asked me what salary I would expect if he offered me a position on his staff. I said three hundred; he said he might not manage to get me so much, but if they offered me one-fifty, would I accept? I said I would think about it and let him know the next day.

Now I am cursing myself for not having accepted it there and then; but I did not want to appear too eager or desperate, and I must not give the impression that a job is indispensable to me. I told him that I had actually come to Delhi to do some research for a book I intended writing about the city. He asked me the title, and I thought quickly and said, 'Delhi Is Still Far' Nizamuddin's comment when told that Tughlaq Shah was marching to Delhi—and he was suitably impressed.

Thinking about it now, perhaps it would be a good idea to do a book about Delhi—its cities and kings, poets and musicians . . . I walked the streets all day, wandering through the bazaars, down the wide shady roads of the capital, resting under the jamun trees near Humayun's tomb, and thinking all the time of what you and I can do here; and while I wander about Delhi, you must be wandering around Pipalnagar, with that wonderful tray of yours . . .

*

Chandni Chowk has not changed in character even if its face has a different look. It is still the heart of Delhi, still throbbing with vitality—more so perhaps, with the advent of the enterprising Punjabi. The old buildings and landmarks are still there, the lanes and alleys are as tortuous and mysterious as ever. Travellers and cloth merchants and sweetmeats-sellers may have changed name and character, but their professions have not given place to new ones. And if on a Sunday the shops must close, they may spill out on the pavement and across the tramlines—toys, silks, cottons, glassware, china, basket-work, furniture, carpets, perfumes—it is as busy as on any market-day and the competition is louder and more fierce.

In front of the Town Hall the statue of Queen Victoria frowns upon the populace, as ugly as all statues, flecked with pigeon droppings. The pigeons, hundreds of them sit on the railings and the telegraph wires, their drowsy murmuring muted by the sounds of the street, the cries of vendors and tonga drivers and the rattle of the tram.

The tram is a museum-piece. I don't think it has been replaced since it was first installed over fifty years ago. It crawls along the crowded thoroughfare, clanging at an impatient five miles an hour, bursting at the seams with its load of people, while urchins hang on by their toes and eyebrows.

An ash-smeared ascetic sits at the side of the road, and cooks himself a meal; a juggler is causing a traffic jam; a man has a lotus tattooed on his forearm. From the balcony of the Sonehri the invader Nadir Shah watched the slaughter of Delhi's citizens. I walk down the Dariba, famed street of the Silversmiths, and find myself at the steps of the Jama Masjid, surrounded by bicycle shops, junk shops, fish shops, bird shops, and fat goats ready for slaughter. Cities and palaces have risen and fallen on the plains of Delhi, but Chandni Chowk is indestructible, the heart of both old and new.

*

All night long I hear the shunting and whistling of engines, and like a child I conjure up visions of places with sweet names like Kumbekonam, Krishnagiri, Mahabalipuram and Polonnarurawa; dreams of palm-fringed beaches and inland lagoons; of the echoing chambers of some deserted city, red sandstone and white marble; of temples in the sun, and elephants crossing wide slow-moving rivers ...

I have a sudden desire to travel. Right now I feel I could travel forever through my country; I don't think I will ever tire of it. Ours is a land of many people, many races; their diversity gives it colour and character. For all Indians to be alike would be as dull as for all sexes to be the same, or for all humans to be normal. In Delhi, too, there is a richness of race, though the Punjabi predominates—in shops, taxis, motor workshops and carpenters' sheds. But in the old city there are still many Muslims following traditional trades—bakers, butchers, painters, makers of toys and kites. South Indians have filled our offices; Rajasthanis move dexterously along the scaffolding of new buildings springing up everywhere; and in the surrounding countryside nomadic Gujjars still graze their cattle, while settled villagers find their lands selected for trails of new tubewells, pumps, fertilizers and ploughs.

*

The city wakes early. The hour before sunrise is the only time when it is possible to exercise. Once the sun is up, people must take refuge beneath fans or in the shade of jamun and neem trees. September in Delhi is sultry and humid, relieved only by an occasional monsoon downpour. In the old city there is always the danger of cholera; in the new capital, people fall ill from sitting too long in air-conditioned cinemas and restaurants.

At noon the streets are almost empty; but early in the morning everyone is about, young and old, shopkeeper and clerk, taxi driver and shoeshine boy, flooding the maidans and open spaces in their vests and underwear. Some sprint around the maidans; some walk briskly down the streets, swinging their arms like soldiers; young men wrestle, or play volley-ball or kabaddi; others squat on their haunches, some stand on their heads; some pray, facing the sun; some study books, mumbling to themselves, or make speeches to vast, invisible audiences; scrub their teeth with neem twigs, bathe at public taps, wash clothes, tie dhotis or turbans and go about their business.

The sun is up, clerks are asleep with their feet up at their desks, government employees drink innumerable cups of tea, and the machinery of bureaucracy and civilization runs on as smoothly as ever.

Soon I will be part of all this.

CHAPTER TWENTY-ONE

❧

SURAJ WAS ON THE platform when the Pipalnagar Express steamed into the station in the early hours of a warm late September morning. I wanted to shout to him from the carriage window, to tell him that everything was well, that the world was wonderful, and that I loved him and the world and everything in it.

But I couldn't say anything until we had left the station and I was drinking hot tea on the string-bed in our room.

'It is three hundred a month,' I said, 'but we should be able to manage on that, if we are careful. And now that you have done your matriculation, you will be able to join the Polytechnic. So we will both be busy. And when we are not working, we shall have all Delhi to explore. It will be better in the city. One should live either in a city or in a village. In a village, everyone knows you intimately. In a city, no one has the slightest interest in you. But in a town like Pipalnagar, everyone knows you, nobody loves you; when you die, you are forgotten; while you live, you are only a subject for malicious conversation. Poor Pipalnagar . . . Will you be sorry to leave the place, Suraj?'

'Yes, I will be sorry. This is where I have lived.'

'This is where I've existed. I only began to live when I realized I could leave the place.'

'When we went to the hills?'

'When I met you.'

'How did I change anything? I am still an additional burden.'

'You have made me aware of who and what I am.'

'I don't understand.'

'I don't want you to. That would spoil it.'

*

There was no rent to be paid before we left, as Seth Govind Ram's Munshi had taken it in advance, and there were five days to go before the end of the month; there was little chance of the balance being returned to us.

Deep Chand was happy to know that we were leaving. 'I shall follow you soon,' he said. 'There is money to be made in Delhi, cutting hair. Why, even girls are beginning to keep short hair. I shall keep a special saloon for ladies, which Ramu can attend. Women feel safe with him, he looks so pretty and innocent.'

Ramu winked at me in the mirror. I could not imagine anyone less innocent. Girls going to school and college still complained that he harassed them and threatened to remove their pigtails with his razor.

The snip of Deep Chand's scissors lulled me to sleep as I sat in his chair; his fingers beat a rhythmic tattoo on my scalp; his razor caressed by cheeks. It was my last shave, and Deep Chand did not charge me anything. I promised to write to him as soon as I had settled down in Delhi.

*

Kamla had gone home for a few days. Her village was about five miles from Pipalnagar in the opposite direction to Pitamber's, among the mustard and wheat fields that sloped down to the banks of the little water-course. I worked my way downstream until I came to the fields.

I waited behind some trees on the outskirts of the village until I saw her playing with a little boy; I whistled and stepped out of the trees, but when she saw me she motioned me back, and took the child into one of the small mud houses.

I waited amongst the sal trees until I heard footsteps a short distance away.

'Where are you?' I called, but received no answer. I walked in the direction of the footsteps, and found a small path going through the trees. After a short distance the path turned to meet a stream, and Kamla was waiting there.

'Why didn't you wait for me?' I asked.

'I wanted to see if you could follow me.'

'Well, I am good at it.' I said, sitting down beside her on the bank of the stream. The water was no more than ankle-deep, cool and clear. I took off my shoes, rolled up my trousers, and put my feet in the water. Kamla was barefooted, and so she had to tuck up her sari a little, before slipping her feet in.

With my feet I churned up the mud at the bottom of the stream. As the mud subsided, I saw her face reflected in the water; and looking up at her again, into her dark eyes, I wanted to care for her and protect her, I wanted to take her away from Pipalnagar; I wanted her to live like other people. Of course, I had forgotten all about my poor finances.

I kissed the tips of her fingers, then her neck. She ran her fingers through my hair. The rain began splatting down and Kamla said, 'Let us go.'

We set off. Soon the rain began pelting down. Kamla shook herself free and we dashed for cover. She was breathing heavily and I kissed her again. Kamla's hair came loose and streamed down her body. We had to hop over pools, and avoid the soft mud. And then I thought she was crying, but I wasn't sure, it might have been the raindrops on her cheeks, and her heavy breathing.

'Come with me,' I said. 'Come away from Pipalnagar.'

She smiled.

'Why can't you come?'

'Because you really do not want me to. For you, a woman would only be a liability. You are free like birds, you and Suraj, you can go where you like and do as you like. I cannot help you in any way. And what use is a woman to a man if she cannot help him? I have helped you to pass your time in Pipalnagar. That is something. I am part of this place. Neither Pipalnagar nor I can change. But you can, simply by going away.'

'Will you come later, once I have started making a living in Delhi?'

'I am married, it is as simple as that . . .'

'If it is that simple, you can come.'

'I have to think of my parents, you know. It would ruin them if I ran away.'

'Yes, but they do not care if they have broken your heart.'

She shrugged and looked away towards the village. 'I am not so unhappy. He is an old fool, my husband, and I get some fun out of teasing him. He will die one day, and so will the Seth, and then I will be free.'

'Will you?'

'Why not? And anyway, you can always come to see me, and nobody will be made unhappy by it.'

I felt sad and frustrated but I couldn't take my frustration out on anyone or anything.

'It was Suraj, not I, who stole your heart,' she said.

She touched my face softly and then abruptly ran towards her little hut. She waved once and then was gone.

CHAPTER TWENTY-TWO

❧

At six every morning the first bus arrives, and the passengers alight, looking sleepy and dishevelled, and rather depressed at the sight of our Mohalla. When they have gone their various ways, the bus is driven into the shed and the road is left clear for the arrival of the municipal van. The cows congregate at the dustbin, and the pavement dwellers come to life, stretching their dusty limbs on the hard stone steps. I carry the bucket up three steps to my room, and bathe for the last time on the open balcony. Our tin trunks are packed, and Suraj's tray is empty.

At Pitamber's village the buffaloes are wallowing in green ponds, while naked urchins sit astride them, scrubbing their backs, and a crow or water-bird perches on a glistening neck. The parrots are busy in the crooked tree, and a slim green snake basks in the sun on our island near the brick-kiln. In the hills, the mists have lifted and the distant mountains are covered with snow.

It is autumn, and the rains are over. The earth meets the sky in one broad sweep of the creator's brush.

*

A land of thrusting hills. Terraced hills, wood-covered and windswept. Mountains where the gods speak gently to the lonely heart. Hills of green and grey rock, misty at dawn, hazy at noon, molten at sunset; where fierce fresh torrents rush to the valleys below.

A quiet land of fields and ponds, shaded by ancient trees and ringed with palms, where sacred rivers are touched by temples; where temples are touched by the southern seas.

This is the real land, the land I should write about. My Mohalla is but a sickness, a wasting disease, and I should turn aside from it to sing instead of the splendours of tomorrow. But only yesterdays are splendid . . . There are other singers, sweeter than I, to sing of tomorrow. I can only sing of today, of Pipalnagar, where I have lived and loved.

Yesterday I was sad, and tomorrow I may be sad again, but today I know that I am happy. I want to live on and on, delighting like a pagan in all that is physical; and I know that this one lifetime, however long, cannot satisfy my heart.

A Flight of Pigeons

INTRODUCTION

I REMEMBER MY FATHER telling me the story of a girl who had a recurring dream in which she witnessed the massacre of the congregation in a small church in northern India. A couple of years later she found herself in an identical church in Shahjahanpur, where she was witness to the same horrifying scenes which had now become a reality.

My father was born in Shahjahanpur and had probably heard the tale from his soldier father who had been stationed there afterwards. Whether the girl in question was Ruth Labadoor (or possibly Lemaistre) or someone else, one cannot say at this point in time. But Ruth's story is true. She survived the killings and her subsequent ordeal, and lived to tell her story to more than one person; mention of it crops up time and again in old records and accounts of the 'Mutiny' of 1857.

In retelling the tale for today's reader I attempted to bring out the common humanity of most of the people involved—for in times of conflict and inter-religious or racial hatred, there are always a few (just a few) who are prepared to come to the aid of those unable to defend themselves.

I published this account as a novella about thirty years ago. I feel it still has some relevance today, when communal strife and religious intolerance threaten the lives and livelihood of innocent, law-abiding people. It was Pascal who wrote: 'Men never do evil so completely and cheerfully as when they do it from religious conviction.' Fortunately for civilization, there are exceptions.

March 2002   **Ruskin Bond**

PROLOGUE

᠁

THE REVOLT BROKE OUT at Meerut on the 10th of May, at the beginning of a very hot and oppressive summer. The sepoys shot down their English officers; there was rioting and looting in the city; the jail was broken open, and armed convicts descended on English families living in the city and cantonment, setting fire to houses and killing the inmates. Several mutinous regiments marched to Delhi, their principal rallying-point, where the peaceable, poetry-loving Emperor Bahadur Shah suddenly found himself the figurehead of the revolt.

The British Army, which had been cooling off in Shimla, began its long march to Delhi. But meanwhile, the conflict had spread to other cities. And on the 30th of May there was much excitement in the magistrate's office at Shahjahanpur, some 250 miles east of Delhi.

A bungalow in the cantonment, owned by the Redmans, an Anglo-Indian family, had been set on fire during the night. The Redmans had been able to escape, but most of their property was looted or destroyed. A familiar figure had been seen flitting around the grounds that night; and Javed Khan, a Rohilla Pathan, well known to everyone in the city, was arrested on suspicion of arson and brought before the magistrate.

Javed Khan was a person of some importance in the bazaars of Shahjahanpur. He had a reputation for agreeing to undertake any exploit of a dangerous nature, provided the rewards were high. He had been brought in by the authorities for a number of offences. But Javed knew the English law, and challenged the court to produce witnesses. None came forward to identify him as the man who had been seen running from the blazing bungalow. The case was adjourned until further evidence could be collected. When Javed left the courtroom, it was difficult to tell whether he was being escorted by the police or whether he was escorting them. Before leaving the room, he bowed contemptuously to Mr Ricketts, the magistrate, and said: 'My witnesses will be produced tomorrow, whether you will have them or not.'

*

The burning of the Redmans' bungalow failed to alert the small English community in Shahjahanpur to a sense of danger. Meerut was far away, and the *Mofussilite*, the local news sheet, carried very little news of the disturbances. The army officers made their rounds without noticing anything unusual, and the civilians went to their offices. In the evening they met in the usual fashion, to eat and drink and dance.

On the 30th of May it was Dr Bowling's turn as host. In his drawing-room, young Lieutenant Scott strummed a guitar, while Mrs Bowling sang a romantic ballad. Four army officers sat down to a game of whist, while Mrs Ricketts, Mr Jenkins, the Collector, and Captain James, discussed the weather over a bottle of Exshaw's whisky.

Only the Labadoors had any foreboding of trouble. They were not at the party.

Mr Labadoor was forty-two, his wife thirty-eight. Their daughter, Ruth, was a pretty girl, with raven black hair and dark, lustrous eyes. She had left Mrs Shield's school at Fatehgarh only a fortnight before, because her mother felt she would be safer at home.

Mrs Labadoor's father had been a French adventurer who had served in the Maratha army; her mother came from a well known Muslim family of Rampur. Her name was Mariam. She and her brothers had been brought up as Christians. At eighteen, she married Labadoor, a quiet, unassuming man, who was a clerk in the magistrate's office. He was the grandson of a merchant from Jersey (in the Channel Islands), and his original Jersey name was Labadu.

While most of the British wives in the cantonment thought it beneath their dignity to gossip with servants, Mariam Labadoor, who made few social calls, enjoyed these conversations of hers. Often they enlivened her day by reporting the juiciest scandals, on which they were always well-informed. But from what Mariam had heard recently, she was convinced that it was only a matter of hours before rioting broke out in the city. News of the events at Meerut had reached the bazaars and sepoy lines, and a fakir, who lived near the River Khannaut, was said to have predicted the end of the English East India Company's rule in the coming months. Mariam made her husband and daughter stay at home the evening of the Bowlings' party, and had even suggested that they avoid going to church the next day, Sunday: a surprising request from Mariam, a regular church-goer.

Ruth liked having her way, and insisted on going to church the next day; and her father promised to accompany her.

*

The sun rose in a cloudless, shimmering sky, and only those who had risen at dawn had been lucky enough to enjoy the cool breeze that had blown across the river for a brief spell. At seven o'clock the church bell began to toll, and people could be seen making their way towards the small, sturdily built cantonment church. Some, like Mr Labadoor, and his daughter, were on foot, wearing their Sunday clothes. Others came in carriages, or were borne aloft in *dolies* manned by sweating *dolie*-bearers.

St Mary's, the little church in Shahjahanpur, was situated on the southern boundary of the cantonment, near an ancient mango grove. There were three entrances: one to the south, facing a large compound known as Buller's; another to the west, below the steeple; and the vestry door opening to the north. A narrow staircase led up to the steeple. To the east there were open fields sloping down to the river, cultivated with melon; to the west, lay an open plain bounded by the city; while the parade ground stretched away to the north until it reached the barracks of the sepoys. The bungalows scattered about the side of the parade ground belonged to the regimental officers, Englishmen who had slept soundly, quite unaware of an atmosphere charged with violence.

I will let Ruth take up the story . . .

At the Church

&

FATHER AND I HAD just left the house when we saw several sepoys crossing the road, on their way to the river for their morning bath. They stared so fiercely at us that I pressed close to my father and whispered, 'Papa, how strange they look!' But their appearance did not strike him as unusual: the sepoys usually passed that way when going to the River Khannaut, and I suppose Father was used to meeting them on his way to office.

We entered the church from the south porch, and took our seats in the last pew to the right. A number of people had already arrived, but I did not particularly notice who they were. We had knelt down, and were in the middle of the Confession, when we heard a tumult outside and a lot of shouting, that seemed nearer every moment. Everyone in the church got up, and Father left our pew and went and stood at the door, where I joined him.

There were six or seven men on the porch. Their faces were covered up to their noses, and they wore tight loincloths as though they had prepared for a wrestling bout; but they held naked swords in their hands. As soon as they saw us, they sprang forward, and one of them made a cut at us. The sword missed us both and caught the side of the door where it buried itself in the wood. My father had his left hand against the door, and I rushed out from under it, and escaped into the church compound.

A second and third cut were made at my father by the others, both of which caught him on his right cheek. Father tried to seize the sword of one of his assailants, but he caught it high up on the blade, and so firmly, that he lost two fingers from his right hand.

These were the only cuts he received; but though he did not fall, he was bleeding profusely. All this time I had stood looking on from the porch, completely bewildered and dazed by what had happened. I remember asking my father what had happened to make him bleed so much.

'Take the handkerchief from my pocket and bandage my face,' he said.

When I had made a bandage from both our handkerchiefs and tied it about his head, he said he wished to go home. I took him by the hand and tried to lead him out of the porch; but we had gone only a few steps when he began to feel faint, and said, 'I can't walk, Ruth. Let us go back to the church.'

*

The armed men had made only one rush through the church, and had then gone off through the vestry door. After wounding my father, they had run up the centre of the aisle, slashing right and left. They had taken a cut at Lieutenant Scott, but his mother threw herself over him and received the blow on her ribs; her tight clothes saved her from a serious injury. Mr Ricketts, Mr Jenkins, the Collector, and Mr MacCullam, the Minister, ran out through the vestry.

The rest of the congregation had climbed up to the belfry, and on my father's urging me to do so, I joined them there. We saw Captain James riding up to the church, quite unaware of what was happening. We shouted him a warning, but as he looked up at us, one of the sepoys, who were scattered about on the parade ground, fired at him, and he fell from his horse. Now two other officers came running from the Mess, calling out to the sepoys: 'Oh! Children, what are you doing?' They tried to pacify their men, but no one listened to them. They had, however, been popular officers with the sepoys, who did not prevent them from joining us in the turret with their pistols in their hands.

Just then we saw a carriage coming at full speed towards the church. It was Dr Bowling's and it carried him, his wife and child, and the nanny. The carriage had to cross the parade ground, and they were halfway across when a bullet hit the doctor who was sitting on the coach box. He doubled up in his seat, but did not let go of the reins, and the carriage had almost reached the church, when a sepoy ran up and made a slash at Mrs Bowling, missing her by inches. When the carriage reached the church, some of the officers ran down to help Dr Bowling off the coach box. He struggled in their arms for a while, and was dead when they got him to the ground.

I had come down from the turret with the officers, and now ran to where my father lay. He was sitting against the wall, in a large pool of blood. He did not complain of any pain, but his lips were parched, and he kept his eyes open with an effort. He told me to go home, and to ask Mother to send someone with a cot or a *dolie*, to carry him back. So much had happened so quickly that I was completely dazed, and though Mrs Bowling and the other women were weeping, there wasn't a tear in my eye. There were two great wounds on my father's face, and I was reluctant to leave him, but to run home and fetch a *dolie* seemed to be the only way in which I could help him.

Leaving him against the stone wall of the church, I ran round to the vestry side and almost fell over Mr Ricketts, who was lying about twelve feet from the vestry door. He had been attacked by an expert and powerful swordsman, whose blow had cut through the trunk from the left shoulder separating the head and the right hand from the rest of the body. Sick with horror, I turned from the spot and began running home through Buller's compound.

Nobody met me on the way. No one challenged me or tried to intercept or molest me. The cantonment seemed empty and deserted; but just as I reached the end of Buller's compound, I saw our house in flames. I stopped at the gate, looking about for my mother, but could not see her anywhere. Granny, too, was missing, and the servants. Then I saw Lala Ramjimal walking down the road towards me.

'Don't worry, my child,' he said. 'Mother, Granny and the others are all safe. Come, I will take you to them.'

There was no question of doubting Lala Ramjimal's intentions. He had held me on his knee when I was a baby, and I had grown up under his eyes. He led me to a hut some thirty yards from our old home. It was a mud house, facing the road, and its door was closed. Lala knocked on the door, but received no answer; then he put his mouth to a chink and whispered, 'Missy-baba is with me, open the door.'

The door opened, and I rushed into my mother's arms.

'Thank God!' she cried. 'At least one is spared to me.'

'Papa is wounded at the church,' I said. 'Send someone to fetch him.'

Mother looked up at Lala and he could not resist the appeal in her eyes.

'I will go,' he said. 'Do not move from here until I return.'

'You don't know where he is,' I said. 'Let me come with you and help you.'

'No, you must not leave your mother now,' said Lala. 'If you are seen with me, we shall both be killed.'

He returned in the afternoon, after several hours. 'Sahib is dead,' he said, very simply. 'I arrived in time to see him die. He had lost so much blood that it was impossible for him to live. He could not speak and his eyes were becoming glazed, but he looked at me in such a way that I am sure he recognized me . . .'

LALA RAMJIMAL

LALA LEFT US IN the afternoon, promising to return when it grew dark, then he would take us to his own house. He ran a grave risk in doing so, but he had promised us his protection, and he was a man who, once he had decided on taking a certain course of action, could not be shaken from his purpose. He was not a Government servant and owed no loyalties to the British; nor had he conspired with the rebels, for his path never crossed theirs.

He had been content always to go about his business (he owned several *dolies* and carriages, which he hired out to Europeans who could not buy their own) in a quiet and efficient manner, and was held in some respect by those he came into contact with; his motives were always personal and if he helped us, it was not because we belonged to the ruling class—my father was probably the most junior officer in Shahjahanpur—but because he had known us for many years, and had grown fond of my mother, who had always treated him as a friend and equal.

I realized that I was now fatherless, and my mother, a widow; but we had no time to indulge in our private sorrow. Our own lives were in constant danger. From our hiding place we could hear the crackling of timber coming from our burning house. The road from the city to the cantonment was in an uproar, with people shouting on all sides. We heard the tramp of men passing up and down the road, just in front of our door; a moan or a sneeze would have betrayed us, and then we would have been at the mercy of the most ruffianly elements from the bazaar, whose swords flashed in the dazzling sunlight.

There were eight of us in the little room: Mother, Granny, myself; my cousin, Anet: my mother's half-brother, Pilloo, who was about my age, and his mother; our servants, Champa and Lado; as well as two of our black and white spaniels, who had followed close on Mother's heels when she fled from the house.

The mud hut in which we were sheltering was owned by Tirloki, a mason who had helped build our own house. He was well known to us. Weeks before the outbreak, when Mother used to gossip with her servants and others about the possibility of trouble in Shahjahanpur, Tirloki had been one of those who had offered his house for shelter should she ever be in need of it. And Mother, as a precaution, had accepted his offer, and taken the key from him.

Mother afterwards told me that as she sat on the veranda that morning, one of the gardener's sons had come running to her in great haste and had cried out: 'Mutiny broken out, Sahib and *Missy-baba* killed!' Hearing that we had both been killed, Mother's first impulse was to throw herself into the nearest well; but Granny caught hold of her, and begged her not to be rash, saying, 'And what will become of the rest of us if you do such a thing?' And so she had gone across the road, followed by the others and had entered Tirloki's house and chained the door from within.

*

We were shut up in the hut all day, expecting, at any moment, to be discovered and killed. We had no food at all, but we could not have eaten any had it been there. My father gone, our future appeared a perfect void, and we found it difficult to talk. A hot wind blew through the cracks in the door, and our throats were parched. Late in the afternoon, a *chatty* of cold water was let down to us from a tree outside a window at the rear of the hut. This was an act of compassion on the part of a man called Chinta, who had worked for us as a labourer when our bungalow was being built.

At about ten o'clock, Lala returned, accompanied by Dhani, our old bearer. He proposed to take us to his own house. Mother hesitated to come out into the open, but Lala assured her that the roads were quite clear now, and there was little fear of our being molested. At last, she agreed to go.

We formed two batches. Lala led the way with a drawn sword in one hand, his umbrella in the other. Mother and Anet and I followed, holding each other's hands. Mother had thrown over us a counterpane which she had been carrying with her when she left the house. We avoided the main road, making our way round the sweeper settlement, and reached Lala's house after a fifteen-minute walk. On our arrival there, Lala offered us a bed to sit upon, while he squatted down on the ground with his legs crossed.

Mother had thrown away her big bunch of keys as we left Tirloki's house. When I asked her why she had done so, she pointed to the smouldering ruins of our bungalow and said: 'Of what possible use could they be to us now?'

The bearer, Dhani, arrived with the second batch, consisting of dear Granny, Pilloo and his mother, and Champa and Lado, and the dogs. There were eight of us in Lala's small house; and, as far as I could tell, his own family was as large as ours.

We were offered food, but we could not eat. We lay down for the night—Mother, Granny and I on the bed, the rest on the ground. And in the darkness, with my face against my mother's bosom, I gave vent to my grief and wept bitterly. My mother wept, too, but silently, and I think she was still weeping when at last I fell asleep.

In Lala's House

Lala Ramjimal's family consisted of himself, his wife, mother, aunt and sister. It was a house of women, and our unexpected arrival hadn't changed that. It must indeed have been a test of Lala's strength and patience, with twelve near-hysterical females on his hands!

His family, of course, knew who we were, because Lala's mother and aunt used to come and draw water from our well, and offer bel leaves at the little shrine near our house. They were at first shy of us; and we, so immersed in our own predicament, herded together in a corner of the house, looked at each other's faces and wept. Lala's wife would come and serve us food in platters made of stitched leaves. We ate once in twenty-four hours, a little after noon, but we were satisfied with this one big meal.

The house was an ordinary mud building, consisting of four flat-roofed rooms, with a low veranda in the front, and a courtyard at the back. It was small and unpretentious, occupied by a family of small means.

Lala's wife was a young woman, short in stature, with a fair complexion. We didn't know her name, because it is not customary for a husband or wife to call the other by name; but her mother-in-law would address her as *dulhan*, or bride.

Ramjimal himself was a tall, lean man, with a long moustache. His speech was always very polite, like that of most Kayasthas but he had an air of determination about him that was rare in others.

On the second day of our arrival, I overheard his mother speaking to him: 'Lalaji, you have made a great mistake in bringing these *Angrezans* into our house. What will people say? As soon as the rebels hear of it, they will come and kill us.'

'I have done what is right,' replied Lala very quietly. 'I have not given shelter to *Angrezans*. I have given shelter to friends. Let people say or think as they please.'

He seldom went out of the house, and was usually to be seen seated before the front door, either smoking his small hookah, or playing chess with some friend who happened to drop by. After a few days, people began to suspect that there was somebody in the house about whom Lala was being very discreet, but they had no idea who these guests could be. He kept a close watch on his family, to prevent them from talking too much; and he saw that no one entered the house, keeping the front door chained at all times.

It is a wonder that we were able to live undiscovered for as long as we did, for there were always the dogs to draw attention to the house. They would not leave us, though we had nothing to offer them except the leftovers from our own meals. Lala's aunt told Mother that the third of our dogs, who had not followed us, had been seen going round and round the smoking ruins of our bungalow, and that on the day after the outbreak, he was found dead, sitting up—waiting for his master's return!

*

One day, Lala came in while we were seated on the floor talking about recent events. Anxiety for the morrow had taken the edge off our grief, and we were able to speak of what had happened without becoming hysterical.

Lala sat down on the ground with a foil in his hand—the weapon had become his inseparable companion, but I do not think he had yet had occasion to use it. It was not his own, but one that he had found on the floor of the looted and ransacked courthouse.

'Do you think we are safe in your house, Lala?' asked Mother. 'What is going on outside these days?'

'You are quite safe here,' said Lala, gesturing with the foil. 'No one comes into this house except over my dead body. It is true, though, that I am suspected of harbouring kafirs. More than one person has asked me why I keep such a close watch over my house. My reply is that as the outbreak has put me out of employment, what would they have me do except sit in front of my house and look after my women? Then they ask me why I have not been to the Nawab, like everyone else.'

'What Nawab, Lala?' asked Mother.

'After the sepoys entered the city, their leader, the Subedar-Major, set up Qadar Ali Khan as the Nawab, and proclaimed it throughout the city. Nizam Ali, a pensioner, was made Kotwal, and responsible posts were offered to Javed Khan and to Nizam Ali Khan, but the latter refused to accept office.'

'And the former?'

'He has taken no office yet, beause he and Azzu Khan have been too busy plundering the sahibs' houses. Javed Khan also instigated an attack on the treasurer. It was like this . . .'

'Javed Khan, as you know, is one of the biggest ruffians in the city. When the sepoys had returned to their lines after proclaiming the Nawab, Javed Khan paid a visit to their commander. On learning that the regiment was preparing to leave Shahjahanpur and join the Bareilly brigade, he persuaded the Subedar-Major, Ghansham Singh, to make a raid on the Rosa Rum Factory* before leaving. A detachment, under Subedar Zorawar Singh, accompanied Javed Khan, and they took the road which passes by Jhunna Lal the treasurer's house. There they halted, and

---

*The Rosa Rum Factory survives to this day.

demanded a contribution from Jhunna Lal. It so happened that he had only that morning received a sum of six thousand rupees from the Tehsildar of Jalalabad, and this the Subedar seized at once. As Jhunna Lal refused to part with any more, he was tied hand and foot and suspended from a tree by his legs. At the same time Javed Khan seized all his account books and threw them into a well, saying, "Since you won't give us what we need, there go your accounts! We won't leave you with the means of collecting money from others!"

'After the party had moved on, Jhunna Lal's servants took him down from the tree. He was half-dead with fright and from the rush of blood to his head. But when he came to himself, he got his servants to go down the well and fish up every account book!'

'And what about the Rosa Factory?' I asked.

'Javed Khan's party set fire to it, and no less than 70,000 gallons of rum, together with a large quantity of loaf sugar, were destroyed. The rest was carried away. Javed Khan's share of loaf sugar was an entire cartload!'

*

The next day when Lala came in and sat beside us—he used to spend at least an hour in our company every day—I asked him a question that had been on my mind much of the time, but the answer to which I was afraid of hearing: the whereabouts of my father's body.

'I wonder have told you before, *Missy-baba*,' he said, 'but I was afraid of upsetting you. The day after I brought you to my house I went again to the church, and there I found the body of your father, of the Collector-Sahib, and the doctor, exactly where I had seen them the day before. In spite of their exposure and the great heat they had not decomposed at all, and neither the vultures nor the jackals had touched them. Only their shoes had gone.

'As I turned to leave I saw two persons, Muslims, bringing in the body of Captain James, who had been shot at a little distance from the church. They laid it beside that of your father and Dr Bowling. They told me that they had decided to bury the mortal remains of those Christians who had been killed. I told them that they were taking a risk in doing so, as they might be accused by the Nawab's men of being in sympathy with the *Firangis*. They replied that they were aware of the risk, but that something had impelled them to undertake this task, and that they were willing to face the consequences.

'I was put to shame by their intentions, and, removing my long coat, began to help them carry the bodies to a pit they had dug outside the church. Here I saw, and was able to identify, the bodies of Mr MacCullam, the *Padri*-Sahib, and Mr Smith, the Assistant Collector. All six were buried side by side, and we drew parallel lines to mark each separate grave. We finished the work within an hour, and when I left the place I felt a satisfaction which I cannot describe . . .'

*

Later, when we had recovered from the emotions which Ramjimal's words had aroused in us, I asked him how Mr MacCullam, the chaplain, had met his death; for I remembered seeing him descending from his pulpit when the ruffians entered the church, and running through the vestry with Mr Ricketts's mother.

'I cannot tell you much,' said Lala. 'I only know that while the sepoys attacked Mr Ricketts, Mr MacCullam was able to reach the melon field and conceal himself under some creepers. But another gang found him there, and finished him off with their swords.'

'Poor Mr MacCullam!' sighed Mother. 'He was such a harmless little man. And what about Arthur Smith, Lala?' Mother was determined to find out what had happened to most of the people we had known.

'Assistant-Sahib was murdered in the city,' said Lala. 'He was in his bungalow, ill with fever, when the trouble broke out. His idea was to avoid the cantonment and make for the city, thinking it was only the sepoys who had mutinied. He went to the courts, but found them a shambles, and while he was standing in the street, a mob collected round him and began to push him about. Somebody prodded him with the hilt of his sword. Mr Smith lost his temper and, in spite of his fever, drew his revolver and shot at the man. But alas for Smith-Sahib, the cap snapped and the charge refused to explode. He levelled again at the man, but this time the bullet had no effect, merely striking the metal clasp of the man's belt and falling harmlessly to the ground. Mr Smith flung away his revolver in disgust, and now the man cut at him with his sword and brought him to his knees. Then the mob set upon him. Fate was against Smith-Sahib. The Company Bahadur's prestige had gone, for who ever heard of a revolver snapping, or a bullet being resisted by a belt?'

A CHANGE OF NAME

ACCORDING TO THE REPORTS we received from Lala Ramjimal, it seemed that by the middle of June every European of Shahjahanpur had been killed—if not in the city, then at Muhamdi, across the Khannaut, where many, including Mrs Bowling and her child, had fled. The only survivors were ourselves and (as we discovered later) the Redmans. And we had survived only because the outer world believed that we, too, had perished. This was made clear to us one day when a woman came to the door to sell fish.

Lala's wife remarked: 'You have come after such a long time. And you don't seem to have sold anything today?'

'Ah, Lalain!' said the woman. 'Who is there to buy from me? The *Firangis* are gone. There was a time when I used to be at the Labadoor house every day, and I never went away without making four or five annas. Not only did the memsahib buy from me, but sometimes she used to get me to cook the fish for her, for which she used to pay me an extra two annas.'

'And what has become of them?' asked Lalain.

'Why, the sahib and his daughter were killed in the church, while the memsahib went and threw herself in the river.'

'Are you sure of this?' asked Lalain.

'Of course!' said the woman. 'My husband, while fishing next morning, saw her body floating down the Khannaut!'

*

We had been in Lala Ramjimal's house for two weeks, and our clothes had become dirty and torn. There had been no time to bring any clothing with us, and there was no possibility of changing, unless we adopted Indian dress. And so Mother borrowed a couple of petticoats and light shawls from Lalain, and altered them to our measurements. We had to wash them in the courtyard whenever they became dirty, and stand around wrapped in sheets until they were half-dry.

Mother also considered it prudent to take Indian names. I was given the name of Khurshid, which is Persian for 'sun', and my cousin Anet, being short of stature, was called Nanni. Pilloo was named Ghulam Husain, and his mother automatically became known as Ghulam Husain's mother. Granny was, of course, Bari-bi. It was easier for us to take Mohammedan names, because we were fluent in Urdu, and because Granny did in fact come from a Muslim family of Rampur. We soon fell into the habits of Lala's household, and it would have been very difficult for anyone, who had known us before, to recognize us as the Labadoors.

Life in Lala's house was not without its touches of humour. There lived with us a woman named Ratna, wife to Imrat Lal, a relative of Lala's. He was a short, stout man. She was tall, and considered ugly. He had no children by her, and after some time, had become intimate with a low-caste woman who used to fill water for his family and was, like himself, short and stout. He had two sons by her, and though his longing for children was now satisfied, his peace of mind was soon disturbed by the wranglings of his two wives. He was an astrologer by profession; and, one day, after consulting the stars, he made up his mind to desert his family and seek his fortune elsewhere. His wives, left to themselves, now made up their differences and began to live together. The first wife earned a living as a seamstress, the second used to grind. Occasionally, there would be outbreaks of jealousy. The second wife would taunt the first for being barren, and the seamstress would reply, 'When you drew water, you had corns on your hands and feet. Now grinding has given you corns on your fingers. Where next are you going to get corns?'

Imrat Lal had, meanwhile, become a yogi and soothsayer and began to make a comfortable living in Hardwar. Having heard of his whereabouts, the second wife had a petition writer draw up a letter for her, which she asked me to read to her, as I knew Urdu. It went something like this:

'O thou who hast vanished like mustard oil which, when absorbed by the skin, leaves only its odour behind; thou with the rotund form dancing before my eyes, and the owl's eyes which were wont to stare at me vacantly; wilt thou still snap thy fingers at me when this letter is evidence of my unceasing thought of thee? Why did you call me your *lado*, your loved one, when you had no love for me? And why have you left me to the taunts of that stick of a woman whom you in your perversity used to call a precious stone, your Ratna? Who has proved untrue, you or I? Why have you sported thus with my feelings? Drown yourself in a handful of water, or return and make my hated rival an ornament for your neck, or wear her effigy nine times round your arm as a charm against my longings for you.'

But she received no reply to this letter. Probably when Imrat Lal read it, he consulted the stars again, and decided it was best to move further on into the hills, leaving his family to the care of his generous relative, Lala Ramjimal.

*

As the hot weather was now at its height everyone slept out in the courtyard, including Lala and the female members of his household. We had become one vast family. Everyone slept well, except Mother, who, though she rested during the day, stayed awake all night, watching over us. It was distressing to see her sit up night after night, determined not to fall asleep. Her forebodings of danger were as strong as before. Lala would fold his hands to her and say, 'Do sleep, Mariam. I am no Mathur if I shirk my duty.' But her only reply was to ask him for a knife that she could keep beside her. He gave her a rusty old knife, and she took great pains to clean it and sharpen its edges.

A day came when Mother threatened to use it.

It was ten o'clock and everyone had gone to bed, except Mother, who still sat at the foot of my cot. I was just dozing off when she remarked that she could smell jasmine flowers, which was strange, because there was no jasmine bush near the house. At the same time a clod of earth fell from the high wall, and looking up, we saw in the dark the figure of a man stretched across it. There was another man a little further along, concealed in the shadows of a neem tree that grew at the end of the yard. Mother drew her knife from beneath her pillow, and called out that she would pierce the heart of the first man who attempted to lay his hands on us. Impressed by her ferocity, which was like that of a tigress guarding her young, the intruders quietly disappeared into the night.

This incident led us to believe that we were still unsafe, and that our existence was known to others. A few days later something else happened that made us even more nervous.

Lado, one of the two servants who had followed us, had been permitted by Lala to occupy a corner of the house. She had a daughter married to a local sword-cleaner, who had been going about looking for Lado ever since the outbreak. Hearing the rumour that there were *Firangis* hiding in Lala's house, he appeared at the front door on the 23rd of June, and spoke to Lala.

'I am told that my mother-in-law is here,' he said. 'I have

inquired everywhere and people tell me that she was seen to come only as far as this. So, Lalaji, you had better let me take her away, or I shall bring trouble upon you.'

Lala denied any knowledge of Lado's whereabouts, but the man was persistent, and asked to be allowed to search the house.

'You will do no such thing,' said Ramjimal. 'Go your way, insolent fellow. How dare you propose to enter my zenana?'

The man left in a huff, threatening to inform the Nawab, and to bring some sepoys to the house. When Lado heard of what had happened, she came into the room and fell at Mother's feet, insisting that she leave immediately, lest her son-in-law brought us any trouble. She blessed me and my cousins, and left the house in tears. Poor Lado! She had been with us many years, and we had all come to like her. She had touched our hearts with her loyalty during our troubles.

In the evening, when Lala came home, he told us of what had befallen Lado. She had met her son-in-law in the city.

'Where have you been, Mother?' he had said. 'I have been searching for you everywhere. From where have you suddenly sprung up?'

'I am just returning from Fatehgarh,' she said.

'Why, Mother, what took you to Fatehgarh? And what has become of the *Angrezans* you were serving?'

'Now how am I to know what became of them?' replied Lado. 'They were all killed, I suppose. Someone saw Labadoor-Mem drowned in the Khannaut.'

The Nawab heard of the sudden reappearance of our old servant. He sent for her and had her closely questioned; but Lado maintained that she did not know what had happened to us.

The Nawab swore at her. 'This "dead one" tries to bandy words with me,' he said. 'She knows where they are, but will not tell. On my oath, I will have your head chopped off, unless you tell me everything you know about them. Do you hear?'

'My Lord!' answered Lado, trembling from head to foot, 'how can I tell you what I do not know myself? True, I fled with them from the burning house, but where they went afterwards, I do not know.'

'This she-devil!' swore the Nawab. 'She will be the cause of my committing a violent act. She evades the truth. All right, let her be dealt with according to her desserts.'

Two men rushed up, and, seizing Lado by the hair, held a naked sword across her throat. The poor woman writhed and wriggled in the grasp of her captors, protesting her innocence and begging for mercy.

'I swear by your head, my Lord, that I know nothing.'

'So you swear by my head, too?' raged the Nawab. 'Well, since you are not afraid even of the sword, I suppose you know nothing. Let her go.'

And poor Lado, half-dead through fright, was released and sent on her way.

ANOTHER NAWAB

ॐ

ON THE 24TH OF June there was a great beating of drums, and in the distance we heard the sound of fife and drum. We hadn't heard these familiar sounds since the day of the outbreak, and now we wondered what could be happening. There was much shouting on the road, and the trample of horses, and we waited impatiently for Lala to come home and satisfy our curiosity.

'A change of Nawabs today?' inquired Mother. 'How will it affect us?'

'It isn't possible to say as yet. Ghulam Qadar Khan is the same sort of man as his predecessor, and they come from the same family. Both of them were opposed to the Company's rule. There is this difference, though: whereas Qadar Ali was a dissolute character and ineffective in many ways, Ghulam Qadar has energy, and is said to be pious—but he, too, has expressed his determination to rid this land of all *Firangis* . . .

'When the Mutiny first broke out, he was in Oudh, where he had been inciting the rural population to throw off the foreign yoke. He would have acted in unison with Qadar Ali had they not already disagreed; for Ghulam Qadar was against the murder of women and children. However, Qadar Ali's counsels prevailed, and Ghulam Qadar withdrew for a while, to watch the course of events. Now several powerful landholders have thrown their lot in with him, including Nizam Ali Khan, Vittal Singh, Abdul Rauf, and even that ruffian, Javed Khan. Yesterday he entered Shahjahanpur and without any opposition took over the government. This morning the leading rebels attended the durbar of the new Nawab. And tonight the Nawab holds an entertainment.'

'Do you think he will trouble us, Lala?' asked Granny anxiously. 'What has he to gain by killing such harmless people as us?'

'I cannot say anything for certain, Bari-Bi,' said Lala. 'He might wish to popularize his reign by exterminating a few *kafirs* as his predecessor did. But there is a rumour in the city that he has been afflicted with some deep sorrow ...'

'What could it be?' asked Mother. 'Is his wife dead? Surely he can get another, especially now that he is the Nawab. And how can his grief affect us?'

'It could influence his actions,' said Lala. 'The rumour is that his daughter Zinat, a young and beautiful girl, has been abducted by a lover. Where she has been taken, no one knows.'

'And the lover?' asked Mother, displaying for a moment her habitual curiosity about other people's romantic affairs.

'They say that Farhat, one of Qadar Ali's sons, disappeared at the same time. They suspect that he has eloped with the girl.'

'Ah, I remember Farhat,' said Mother. 'A handsome young fellow who often passed in front of our house, showing off on a piebald nag. Still, what has all this to do with us?'

'I was coming to that, Mariam,' said Lala. 'No sooner had the Nawab taken his seat at the durbar, than some informers came to him with the story about Lado, and suggested that my house be searched for your family. Well, the Nawab wanted to know what had happened to Labadoor-Sahib who, he remarked, had always been a harmless and inoffensive man. When told that he had been killed along with the others in the church, the Nawab said, "So be it. Then we need not go out of our way to look for his women. I will have nothing to do with the murder of the innocent ...."'

'How far can we trust his present mood?' asked Mother.

'I was told by Nizam Ali Khan that the Nawab once gave his daughter a certain promise—that he would not lift his hand against the women and children of the *Firangis*. It sounds very unikely, I know. But I think Nizam Ali's information is usually reliable.'

'That is true,' said Mother. 'My husband knew him well. We had the lease of his compound for several years, and we paid the rent regularly.'

'Well, the Nawab likes him,' said Lala. 'He has given him orders to begin casting guns in his private armoury. If the Nawab sticks to men like Nizam Ali, public affairs will be handled more efficiently than they would have been under Qadar Ali Khan.'

*

We had all along been dependent upon Lala Ramjimal for our daily necessities and though Mother had a little money in her jewel box, which she had brought with her, she had to use it very sparingly.

One day, folding his hands before her, Lala said, 'Mariam, I ashamed to say it, but I have no money left. Business has been at a standstill, and the little money I had saved is all but finished.'

'Don't be upset, Lala,' said Mother, taking some leaf-gold from her jewel box and giving it to him. 'Take this gold to the bazaar, and sell it for whatever you can get.'

Lala was touched, and at the same time overjoyed at this unexpected help.

'I shall go to the bazaar immediately and see what I can get for it,' he said. 'And I have a suggestion, Mariam. Let us all go to Bareilly. I have my brother there, and some of your relatives are also there. We shall at least save on house rent, which I am paying here. If you agree, I will hire two carts which should accommodate all of us.'

We readily agreed to Lala's suggestion, and he walked off happily to the bazaar, unaware that his plans for our safety were shortly to go awry.

CAUGHT!

WE HAD BEEN WITH Lala almost a month, and this was to be our last day in his house.

We were, as usual, huddled together in one room, discussing our future prospects, when our attention was drawn to the sound of men's voices outside.

'Open the door!' shouted someone, and there was a loud banging on the front door.

We did not answer the summons, but cast nervous glances at each other. Lalain, who had been sitting with us, got up and left the room, and chained our door from the other side.

'Open up or we'll force your door in!' demanded the voice outside, and the banging now became more violent.

Finally, Ratna went to the front door and opened it, letting in some twenty to thirty men, all armed with swords and pistols. One of them, who had done all the shouting and seemed to be the leader, ordered the women to go up to the roof of the house, as he intended searching all the rooms for the fugitive *Firangis*. Lala's family had no alternative but to obey him, and they went up to the roof. The men now approached the door of our room, and we heard the wrench of the chain as it was drawn out. The leader, pushing the door open violently, entered the room with a naked sword in his hand.

'Where is Labadoor's daughter?' he demanded of Mother, gripping her by the arm and looking intently into her face. 'No, this is not her,' he said, dropping her hand and turning to look at me.

'This is the girl!' he exclaimed, taking me by the hand and dragging me away from Mother into the light of the courtyard. He held his uplifted sword in his right hand.

'No!' cried Mother in a tone of anguish, throwing herself in front of me. 'If you would take my daughter's life, take mine before hers, I beg of you by the sword of Ali!'

Her eyes were bloodshot, starting out of their sockets, and she presented a magnificent, and quite terrifying sight. I think she frightened me even more than the man with the raised sword; but I clung to her instinctively, and tried to wrest my arm from tha man's grasp. But so impressed was he by Mother's display that he dropped the point of his sword and in a gruff voice commanded us both to follow him quietly if we valued our lives. Granny sat wringing her hands in desperation, while the others remained huddled together in a corner, concealing Pilloo, the only boy, beneath their shawls. The man with the sword led Mother and me from the house, followed by his band of henchmen.

*

It was the end of June, and the monsoon rains had not yet arrived. It was getting on for noon, and the sun beat down mercilessly. The ground was hard and dry and dusty. Barefooted and bareheaded, we followed our captor without a murmur, like lambs going to slaughter. The others hemmed us in, all with drawn swords, their steel blades glistening in the sun. We had no idea where we were being taken, or what was in store for us.

After walking half a mile, during which our feet were blistered on the hot surface of the road, our captor halted under a tamarind tree, near a small mosque, and told us to rest. We told him we were thirsty, and some water was brought to us in a brass jug. A crowd of curious people had gathered around us.

'These are the *Firangans* who were hiding with the Lala! How miserable they look. But one is young—she has fine eyes! They are her mother's eyes—notice!'

A pir, a wandering hermit, who was in the group, touched our captor on the shoulder and said, 'Javed, you have taken away these unfortunates to amuse yourself. Give me your word of honour that you will not ill-treat or kill them.'

'So this is Javed Khan,' whispered Mother.

Javed Khan, his face still muffled, brought his sword to a slant before his face. 'I swear by my sword that I will neither kill nor ill-treat them!'

'Take care for your soul, Javed,' said the pir. 'You have taken an oath which no Pathan would break and still expect to survive. Let no harm come to these two, or you may expect a short lease of life!'

'Have no fear for that!' said Javed Khan, signalling us to rise.

We followed him as before, leaving the crowd of gazers behind, and taking the road that led into the narrow mohalla of Jalalnagar, the Pathan quarter of the city.

Passing down several lanes, we arrived at a small square, at one end of which a horse was tied. Javed Khan slapped the horse on the rump, and opening the door of his house, told us to enter. He came in behind us. In the courtyard, we saw a young woman sitting on a swing. She seemed astonished to see us.

'These are the *Firangans*,' said Javed Khan, closing the front door behind him and walking unconcernedly across the courtyard.

An elderly woman approached Mother.

'Don't be afraid,' she said. 'Sit down and rest a little.'

JAVED KHAN

WHEN JAVED KHAN RETURNED to his zenana after a wash and a change of clothes, he addressed his wife.

'What do you think of my *Firangans*? Didn't I say I would not rest until I found them? A lesser man would have given up the search long ago!' And chuckling, he sat down to his breakfast, which was served to him on a low, wooden platform.

His aunt, the elderly woman who had first welcomed us, and who was known as Kothiwali, spoke gently to Mother.

'Tell me,' she said, 'tell me something of your story. Who are you?'

'You see us for what we are,' replied Mother. 'Dependent on others, at the mercy of your relative who may kill us whenever it takes his fancy.'

'Who is going to take your miserable lives?' interrupted Javed Khan.

'No, you are safe while I am here,' said Kothiwali. 'You may speak to me without fear. What is your name, and that of the girl with you?'

'The girl is Khurshid, my only daughter. My name is Mariam, and my family is well known in Rampur, where my father was a minister to the Nawab.'

'Which Rampur?' asked Khan-Begum, Javed's wife.

'*Rohelon-ka-Rampur*,' replied Mother.

'Oh, *that* Rampur!' said Khan-Begum, evidently impressed by Mother's antecedents.

'This, my only child,' continued Mother bestowing an affectionate glance at me, 'is the offspring of an Englishman. He was massacred in the church, on the day the outbreak took place. So I am now a widow, and the child, fatherless. Our lives were saved through the kindness of Lala Ramjimal, and we were living at his house until your relative took us away by force. My mother and others of our family are still there. Only Allah knows what will become of us all, for there is no one left to protect us.'

Mother's feelings now overcame her, and she began weeping. This set me off too, and hiding my face in Mother's shawl, I began to sob.

Kothiwali was touched. She placed her hand on my head and said, 'Don't weep, child, don't weep,' in a sympathetic tone.

Mother wiped the tears from her eyes and looked up at the older woman. 'We are in great trouble, Pathani!' she said. 'Spare our lives and don't let us be dishonoured, I beg of you.'

Javed Khan, quite put out by all this weeping, now exclaimed, 'Put your mind at rest, good woman. No one will kill you, I can assure you. On the contrary, I have saved your daughter from dishonour at the hands of others. I intend to marry her honourably, whenever you will.'

*

The plate dropped from Javed Khan's wife's hand. He gave her a fierce look. 'Don't be such a fool, Qabil!' he said.

Before Mother could say anything, Kothiwali said, 'Javed, you should not have done this thing. These two are of good birth, and they are in distress. Look how faded and careworn they are! Be kind to them, I tell you, and do not insult them in their present condition.'

'Depend on it, Chachi,' he rplied. They will receive nothing but kindness from my hands. True, now they have fallen from their former greatness!'

'I should like to know how you became acquainted with them?' inquired Kothiwali. 'Is not your Khan-Begum as good a wife as any? Mark her fine nose!'

'Who says anything to the contrary? But, oh Chachi!' he exclaimed. 'How can I make you understand the fascination this girl exerted over me when she was in her father's house! The very first ime I saw her, I was struck by her beauty. She shone like Zohra, the morning star. Looking at her now, I realize the truth of the saying that a flower never looks so beautiful as when it is on its parent stem. Break it, and it withers in the hand. Would anyone believe that this poor creature is the same angelic one I saw only a month ago?'

I was full of resentment, but could say nothing and do nothing, except press closer to my mother, and look at Javed Khan with all the scorn I could muster. Khan-Begum, too, must have been seething with indignation; but she too was helpless, because Javed was well within his rights to think in terms of a second wife.

'The greater fool you, Javed, for depriving the child of her father, and breaking the flower from its stem before it had bloomed!' said Khan-Begum.

'What did you say, Qabil?' he asked sharply. 'No, don't repeat it again. The demon is only slumbering in my breast, and it will take little to rouse it.'

He game me a scorching look, and I could not take my eyes from his face; I was like a doomed bird, fascinated by the gaze of a rattlesnake. But Mother was staring at him as though she would plumb his dark soul to its innermost depths, and he quailed under her stern gaze.

'Don't put me down for a common murderer,' he said apologetically. 'If I have taken lives, they have been those of infidels, enemies of my people. I am deserving of praise rather than blame.'

'Now don't excite yourself,' said Kothiwali, coming to the rescue again. 'What I wanted to bring home to you is that if you are such an admirer of beauty, your Khan-Begum is neither ugly nor dark. I should have thought *Firangi* women had blue eyes and fair hair, but these poor things—how frightened they look!— would pass off as one of us!'

'All right, all right,' grumbled Javed Khan in a harsh voice. 'Don't carry on and on about Qabil's beauty, as if she ever possessed any. Let us drop the subject. But Chachi,' and his eyes softened as he glanced at me, 'you should have judged this girl at the time I first set eyes on her. She was like a rose touched by a breath of wind, a doe-like creature . . .'

'Will you not stop your rubbish?' interrupted Kothiwali. 'Look at her now, and tell me if she answers the same description.'

'*W'allah*! A change has come over them!' exclaimed Javed Khan wonderingly, becoming poetical again. 'She is not what she used to be. Within a month she has aged twenty years. When I seized the girl by her arm at the Lala's house, she was ready to faint. But oh, how can I describe the terror which seized me at the sight of her mother! Like an enraged tigress, whose side has been pierced by a barbed arrow, she hurled herself at me and presented her breast to my sword. I shall never forget the look she gave me as she thrust me away from the girl! I was awed, I was subdued. I was unmanned. The sword was ready to fall from my hand. Surely the blood of a hero runs in her veins! This is no ordinary female!' And bestowing a kindly glance on Mother, he exclaimed: 'A hundred mercies to thee, woman!'

GUESTS OF THE PATHAN

'I THINK YOU AND I will be good friends,' said Kothiwali to Mother. 'I already love your daughter. Come, *beti*, come nearer to me,' she said, caressing my head.

Javed Khan had finished his meal and had gone out into the courtyard, leaving his wife and aunt alone to eat with us. Though we were hungry and thirsty, we did not have the heart to eat much, with Granny's and cousin Anet's fate still unknown to us. But we took something, enough to keep up our strength, and when Javed Khan came in again, he seemed pleased that we had partaken of his food.

'Having tasted salt under my roof,' he said, 'you are no longer strangers in the house. You must make my house your home for the future.'

'It is very good of you to say so,' replied Mother. 'But there are others who are dependent on me, my mother and my niece, and without them everything I eat tastes bitter in my mouth.'

'Don't worry, they shall join you,' said Javed Khan. 'I had seen your daughter a long time before the outbreak, when I took a fancy to her. A ruffian had intended to carry her off before and would have done so had I not anticipated him. I have brought you here with the best of intentions. As soon as I have your consent, I propose to marry Khurshid, and will give her a wife's portion.'

'But how can you do that?' asked Mother. 'You have a wife already.'

'Well, what is there to prevent me having more wives than one? Our law allows it.'

'That may be,' rejoined Mother, 'but how can you, a Muslim, marry a Christian girl?'

'There is no reason why I may not,' replied Javed Khan. 'We Pathans can take a wife from any race or creed we please. And—' pausing as his wife let fall a petulant 'Oh!'—'I dare my wife to object to such a proceeding on my part. Did not my father take in a low-caste woman for her large, pretty eyes, the issue of that union being the brat, Saifullah—a plague on him!— and Kothiwali, whom you see here, was a low-caste Hindu who charmed my uncle out of his wits. So what harm can there be if I take a Christian for a wife?'

My mother had a quiver full of counter arguments, but the time was not favourable for argument; it was safer to dissemble.

'I trust you will not expect an immediate answer to your request,' she said. 'I have just lost my husband, and there is no one to guide or advise me. Let us speak again on this subject at some other time.'

'I am in no hurry,' said Javed Khan. 'A matter of such importance cannot be settled in a day. Take a week, good woman. And do not forget that this is no sudden infatuation on my part. The girl has been in my mind for months. I am not Javed if I let the opportunity pass me by. Be easy in your mind— there is no hurry . . .'

And he went out again into the courtyard.

*

All that had happened to us that morning, and Javed Khan's proposal of marriage, gave me food for thought for the rest of the day. A bed was put down for us in the veranda, and I lay down on my back, staring up at the ceiling where two small lizards darted about in search of flies. Mother was engrossed in a conversation with Kothiwali. Her perfect Urdu, her fine manners, and her high moral values, all took Kothiwali by storm. She was in raptures over Mother, and expressed every sympathy for us. She had come to Javed's house on a short visit, and did not fell like leaving.

'You must let Mariam come and spend a few days with me,' she said to her niece.

'And what is to become of her daughter?' replied Khan-Begum. 'Is she to be left here alone?'

'Of course not. She must come with her mother. And, Qabil, don't allow all this to upset you. Javed's head is a little befuddled nowadays, but he will be all right soon. As for these poor things, they are in no way to blame. You will come, Mariam, won't you?'

'With pleasure,' said Mother. 'If we are allowed to.'

*

We were worrying about Granny and the others when the sound of an altercation at the front door reached us. We recognized the voice of our friend and protector, Lala Ramjimal, who had tracked us down, and now insisted on seeing us.

'Khan Sahib!' we heard him say to Javed Khan. 'It was very wrong of you to enter my house during my absence and bring away my guests without my permission. Had I been there, you could only have done so by making your way over my dead body.'

'That is exactly why I came when you were not there,' replied Javed Khan. 'I had no wish to end your life.'

'I would not be a Mathur if I had not defended them. Well, what is done is done. I cannot force you to return them to my house. But let me be permitted to see if they need anything. I will also say goodbye to them.'

Mother went to the door and spoke to Lala, thanking him for taking the risk in coming to see us.

'What Vishnu ordered has come to pass,' said Lala resignedly. 'No skill of ours could have prevented it. But be comforted, for better days must lie ahead. I have brought your jewel box back for you.'

She took the jewel box from his hand, but did not bother to examine its contents, knowing that nothing would be missing.

'I have sold the gold you gave me,' said Lala, 'and I have brought the price of it—thirty rupees. I shall bring Bari-Bi and Nani to you this evening. The others can stay with me a little longer.'

'Oh, Lala!' said Mother. 'How are we to repay you for all your kindness?'

'I shall be repaid in time to come,' said Lala. 'But what is to become of your dogs?'

'Keep them, Lala, or do what you like with them. It is going to be difficult enough for us to look after ourselves.'

'True,' he said, 'I shall take them with me to Bareilly and keep them for you.'

He made a low bow to Mother and left us, and that was the last we saw of him.

*

We heard later that Lala had taken his family to Bareilly, along with our old servant, Dhani. We never knew what became of the dogs. That evening, Javed Khan had himself gone to Lala's house and brought away Granny and Anet, who were overjoyed to see us. According to the laws of hospitality, food was immediately put before them.

Our party of eight had now been thinned to four. Pilloo and his mother, and Champa, had been left at Lala's house, and we were not to know what became of them until some time afterwards. Javed Khan did not fancy introducing into his household a *Firangi* boy of fourteen. It was fortunate for Pilloo that he was left behind, otherwise he would surely have been killed by one of the cutthroats who lived in the mohalla near Javed's house.

PILLOO'S FATE

I**N ORDER TO PRESERVE** some sort of sequence, I must record what happened to the three members of our household who were left at Lala's house.

No sooner had he and Javed Khan left the house with Granny and cousin Anet, than it was beset again by another band of Pathans, headed by one Mangal Khan. He forced his way into the house, the Lala's womenfolk retired to the roof as before, and Pilloo, his mother, and Champa, their servant, shut themselves in their room.

'Where is the *Firangi* youth?' shouted Mangal Khan. 'Bring him out, so that we may deal with him as we have dealt with others of his kind.'

Seeing that there was no means of escape, Pilloo's mother came out, and falling at Mangal Khan's feet begged him to spare her son's life.

'*Your* son!' he said, eyeing her disbelievingly from head to foot, for she had a swarthy complexion. 'Let's see what sort of fellow he is.'

Pilloo now came out dressed fantastically, a perfect caricature of a Kayastha boy—pantaloons and shirt; no socks or shoes or headdress—all but his face and fair complexion, which could not be disguised.

'This fellow does not even reach my shoulders,' said Mangal Khan, standing over him. 'How old are you?' he asked sternly.

Pilloo was trembling all over with fright and was unable to answer; instead, he looked at his mother.

She folded her hands and replied, 'Your slave is not more than fourteen, Khan Sahib! I beg of you, spare his life for the Prophet's sake! Do what you like with me, but spare the boy.' And Pilloo's mother rained tears, and fell at his feet again.

The Pathan was moved by these repeated appeals to his feelings.

'Get up, woman!' he said. 'I can see the boy is young and harmless. Will both of you come with me? Remember, if you don't, there are others who will not be as soft-hearted as I.'

Lala's house was obviously no longer safe as a hiding-place, and Pilloo's mother agreed to accompany Mangal Khan. So off they were marched, together with Champa, to another mohalla inhabited chiefly by Pathans, where they were hospitably received at Mangal Khan's house.

Mangal Khan was at heart a generous man. After he had taken the fugitives under his roof, he showed them every kindness and consideration. He called Pilloo by his new name, Ghulam Husain, and his mother continued to be known as Ghulam Husain's mother. Champa, of course, remained Champa. She was a Rajput girl, and there was no mistaking her for anything else.

Pilloo and his mother continued to live under the protection of Mangal Khan. What their subsequent fortunes were we did not know until much later, many months after we had left Lala Ramjimal's house.

FURTHER ALARMS

IT WAS IN OUR interests to forget that we had European blood in our veins, and that there was any advantage in the return of the British to power. It was also necessary for us to *seem* to forget that the Christian God was our God, and we allowed it to be believed that we were Muslims. Kothiwali often offered to teach us the *Kalma*, but Mother would reply that she knew it already, which was perfectly true. When she was asked to attend prayers with the others, her excuse would be: 'How can we? Our clothes are unclean and we have no others.'

The only clothes we had were those acquired in Lala Ramjimal's house, and, on our third day in Javed's house, he seemed to notice them for the first time.

'Mariam,' he said. 'It won't do to wear such clothes in my house. You must get into a pyjama.'

'Where have I the means to make pyjamas?' asked Mother.

And the same day Javed went and bought some black chintz in the bazaar, and handed it over to Mother. She made us pyjamas and kurta-dupattas, cutting the material, while Anet and I did the sewing. Khan-Begum was astonished to find that Mother could cut so well, and that Anet and I were so adept with our needles.

Before we changed into our new clothes, Mother suggested that we be given facilities for bathing. I think we had not bathed for a month, for in Lala's house there was no water close at hand; his women folk would bathe every morning at the river, but it had been too dangerous for us to go out.

There was a well right in the middle of the courtyard of Javed Khan's house, and so it was quite possible for us to take a cold bath. Mother told Zeban, the female barber of the house, to draw water for us and help us bathe, and that she would reward this service with a payment of four pice—a pice per person—and Zeban was overjoyed at the prospect of this little windfall. She set up a couple of beds at right angles to one another in the courtyard, covering them with sheets to form a screen. Kothiwali had heard that we were going to change our clothes and bathe, and this being quite an event, she arrived at the house in a great fluster, determined to assist us in the mysteries of the bath.

It was the 2nd of July, a day memorable in our lives from a hygienic point of view.

Kothiwali offered to pour water over us with her own hands. To this, however, Mother strenuously objected. She pointed out that it was not customary among her people to be seen undressed by others, even by members of the same sex, and that she would not therefore, give Kothiwali the trouble.

Kothiwali was dismayed. 'But how can you take the sacred bath and be purified,' she urged, 'unless at least three tumblers of sanctified water are poured on you?'

Mother was ready with her reply. She said that each of us

knew the *Kalma,* and that doubtless we would remember the last three tumblers when we came to them. And this embarrassment being overcome, we had the satisfaction of washing our bodies with fresh water from the well, and afterwards, putting on our new clothes, which fitted us perfectly.

After this, we opened our hair to dry, and instantly there were loud exclamations of admiration from the women who were present. Such lovely long hair! And looking at my curls—my hair was not very long but quite wavy—exclaimed at my pretty *'ghungarwala.'* Mother and Granny did indeed have beautiful heads of hair. Granny's reached down to her heels; Mother's, to a little below the knees. Anet's hair, like mine, reached only to the waist, but it was very bushy, and when made into a plait, was as a fat woman's arm. As we sat about drying our hair, the women gazed at us with their mouths open. We explained that the family from which my mother came was distinguished for the long and bushy hair of its females.

We were also faced with the problem of oiling so much hair, and Khan-Begum asked us what oil we used. Mother said we used coconut oil, but no one knew where so much coconut oil could be had. So Khan-Begum gave a pice to Zeban, and had her fetch us some sweet oil from the bazaar. She also sent for a small fine-tooth comb made of horn. Granny got up and oiled and combed Mother's hair, while Mother dressed mine and Anet's, as well as Granny's.

*

Next morning we felt buoyant and refreshed. We busied ourselves in sewing a second suit of clothes, which we intended trying on after taking another bath the following Friday, the day of the week on which most Pathan women bathed.

At ten o'clock, Javed Khan received a visitor in the person of Sarfaraz Khan, his wife's brother-in-law. This man had been a constable in the police service, and had retired to his home on the outbreak of the Mutiny. In accordance with the costume of the time, he was armed with sword, pistol, knife and a double-barrelled gun. He appeared excited as he met Javed Khan at the door.

'You have brought some *Firangans* into the house, Javed?' he said. 'Wouldn't you like to show them to me?'

'You shall see them,' replied Javed, 'and be given the opportunity of appreciating my taste for the beautiful.'

With his hand on his pistol and a menacing look on his bearded face, Sarfaraz Khan strode into the veranda. Khan-Begum stood up and made him a salaam, and we did the same. He sat down on a cot, resting the butt of his gun on the ground, while with one hand he held the barrel—a typical Pathan attitude.

'So these are the *Firangans* who have made such a stir in the mohalla!' he observed.

Javed Khan had gone into the house, and Mother spoke up for us.

'What stir can we make?' she said. 'We are poor, helpless people.'

'And yet everyone is saying that you have come into this house to find a husband for your daughter, and that Javed Khan is going to marry her! Why have you brought trouble to this good woman?' he said, pointing towards Khan-Begum.

Though Mother was indignant at the insinuation, she restrained her feelings, and answered him quietly.

'What are you saying, brother? Surely you know that we would not have entered this house unless we had been compelled to. Javed Khan brought us here by force, from a house where we had received every kindness, in order to please himself. We are grateful for his hospitality, but as to marrying my daughter to him or anyone else, that is a matter which I am not in a position to discuss, and we are grateful to your brother for not forcing us to agree to his wishes.'

'And yet it is the talk of the mohalla,' said Sarfaraz Khan, 'that Javed intends marrying your daughter, and this talk has put Khan-Begum in a great state of mind!'

'In what way are we responsible for what people say?' replied

Mother. 'We would do anything to save Khan-Begum from unhappiness.'

Javed, who had overheard much of the conversation, now stamped in, looking quite ruffled.

'Brother, what is your motive in questioning this good woman and treating these people as though they were intruders? By my head, they are in no way to blame! It was I who brought them to my house, and only I am answerable for their actions.'

'Why have you brought trouble to your good wife?' asked Sarfaraz Khan. 'You have spoilt the good name of our family by your foolish conduct.'

'I know who has sent you here,' remarked Javed, folding his arms across his chest.

'Yes, Abdul Rauf has sent me here to take the women to the riverside. And there strike their heads off, in order that the fire raging in your wife's bosom may be quenched.'

'No one has the right to tell me what I should do in my own house,' said Javed fiercely, drawing himself up to his full height and towering over Sarfaraz Khan. 'If Abdul Rauf is wise, he will look to his own house and family, instead of prying into other people's affairs. I will have none of his interference. As to Qabil, she is a fool for talking too much to the neighbours. I shall have to restrict her liberty.'

The two enraged Pathans would have come to blows, or worse, had not Mother put herself forward again.

'As to cutting off our heads,' she said, 'you have the power, Khan Sahib, and we cannot resist. If it should be Allah's will that we die by your hand, let it be so. There is but one favour, however, that I would ask of you, and that is that you kill every one of us, without exception. I shall not allow you to kill one or two only!'

Sarfaraz Khan was touched, both by Mother's courage, and because she had spoken in the name of Allah. He warmed towards her, as others had done.

'Great is your faith, and great your spirit,' he said. 'Well, I wash my hands off of this business.' To have been sent on a fool's errand, and to be put off by the calm persuasiveness of a woman!'

'It was Allah's will,' said Javed. 'You will not be so foolish again. Why poison your heart on behalf of your relatives? It was their doing, I knew that all along.'

ANOTHER PROPOSAL

TWO OR THREE DAYS after the visit of Sarfaraz Khan, when we had taken our evening meal, Javed Khan entered the room and made himself comfortable on the low, wooden platform.

'Mariam, you promised to speak to me again on a certain subject which you know is close to my heart,' he said, addressing Mother. 'Now that you have had time to think it over, perhaps you can give me a definite answer.'

'What subject do you mean?' asked Mother, feigning ignorance.

'I mean my original proposal to marry your daughter.'

'I have hardly had time to argue the matter with myself,' said Mother, 'or to give it the attention it deserves. It was only the other day that your brother-in-law came here to kill us without a moment's notice. If we are likely to be killed even while under your protection, what use is there in discussing the subject of marriage? If I am to lose my life, my daughter's life must go too. She and I are inseparable. Someone like Sarfaraz may be on his way here even now!'

'Upon my head, you make me angry when you talk like that!' exclaimed Javed. 'I tell you that had he lifted his hand against either of you, he would have lost his own life. As long as you are under Javed's roof, there is not a man who would dare to raise his finger against you. I shall strike off the heads of half a dozen before a hair on my *Firangan*'s head can be touched.' And he gave me a look of such passion and ferocity, that I trembled with fright, and hid my face behind Mother's back.

He was terribly excited, and to calm him Mother said, 'I am sure you are strong enough to protect us. But why do you bring up this subject again?'

'Because it is always on my mind. Why delay it any longer?'

'If you knew our circumstances and the history of my family,' said Mother, 'you would see that I am not in a position to give her away.'

'Why so?' asked Javed.

'I have my brothers living. What shall I answer them when they find out that I have given you my daughter in marriage, and the girl is still only a child? And moreover, my husband's young brother is still alive. I have to consult them before I can decide anything.'

'That may be so,' said Javed. 'But they are not likely to question you, as in all probability they have been killed along with the other *Firangis*.'

'I hope not. But would it not be wiser to wait and make certain they are dead before we come to any definite decision?'

'I am an impatient man, Mariam, and life is not so long that I can wait an eternity to quench my desires. I have restrained myself out of respect for your wishes, and out of respect for you. But my desire to call your girl my wife grows stronger daily, and I am prepared to take any risk to have her for my own.'

'Suppose the English Government is restored to power—what shall we do then? Your life will be worth little, and with you dead, my daughter will be a widow at thirteen. Cannot you wait a few months, until we are certain as to who will remain master of this country?'

'True, if the English retook Shahjahanpur, they would show little mercy to the leaders of the revolt. They would hang me from the nearest tree. And no doubt you are hoping for their return, or you would not talk of such a possibility. But how many of them are left? Only a few thousand struggling to hold their own before the walls of Delhi, and they too will soon be disposed of, please God!'

'Then let Delhi decide our future,' said Mother, seizing at a straw. If the British army now besieging Delhi is destroyed, that will be the time to talk of such matters. Meanwhile, are we not your dependents and in your power? You have only to await the outcome of the war.'

'You point a long way off, Mariam, and seem to forget that I have the power to marry her against your will and the will of everyone else, including'—and he gave his wife a defiant look— 'the owner of a pair of jealous eyes now gazing at me!'

'Did I say you did not have that power?' asked Mother. 'If you take her by force, we have no power to resist. But if you were to wait until the British are driven from Delhi, my argument would no longer carry any weight. And by that time, my daughter would be more of an age for marriage.'

'It is fortunate for you that I am a man. No one shall take her away from Javed, and Javed's wife she shall be, and I will give her a handsome dowry. And if you were to take my advice, Mariam, you ought to take a husband as well and settle down again in life. You are still young.'

'Why would I marry now?'

'You should marry, if it be only to find a home of your own and bread with it.'

'Why would I marry?' asked Mother again. 'What would become of my girls?'

'Why, your daughter shall be mine,' said Javed brightly. 'And as for your niece, she too will fit in somewhere! She is not unattractive, you know!'

*

We did not speak much for the rest of the evening. Javed Khan settled himself before a hookah, puffing contentedly, blissfully unaware of the agitation he had set up in everyone's mind. No one spoke. Khan-Begum went about with a long face, and sighed whenever she looked at me. Mother, too, sighed when she looked at me, and Anet and I stared at each other in bewilderment.

As we rose to go to our part of the house, Khan-Begum seized

Mother's hand, and in a choking voice, whispered, 'Mariam, you are my mother. Do not help him to inflict greater torment on me than I have already suffered. Promise me that you won't give your daughter to him.'

Mother replied, 'Bibi, you have seen and heard everything that has happened. I am truly a dead one in the hands of the living. You distress yourself for nothing. If I have my way, he shall never get my consent. But will he wait for my consent?'

'Allah bless you!' exclaimed Khan-Begum. 'Your daughter deserves a better fate than to play second fiddle in this family. I will pray that your wishes are granted.'

*

I could not sleep much that night. The light from the full moon came through the high, barred window, and fell across the foot of the bed. I dozed a little, but the insistent call of the brain-fever bird kept waking me. I opened my eyes once, and saw Javed Khan standing in the doorway, the moonlight shining on his face. He stood there a long while, staring at me, and I was too afraid to move or call out. Then he turned and walked quietly away; and shivering with fright, I put my arms around Mother, and lay clinging to her for the remainder of the night.

On Show

When Khan-Begum had last visited her husband's sister, the latter had made her promise to come again soon; and on a Thursday, a servant came to her with a message, saying, 'Your sister sends her salaams, and wishes to know when you are going to fulfil your promise of calling on her?'

'Give my respects to my sister,' answered Khan-Begum, 'and tell her I cannot come now. There are some *Firangans* staying with us, brought into the house by my husband.'

Later, another messenger arrived with the suggestion that Khan-Begum take her guests along with her, as her relatives were most anxious to see them too. And so our hostess proposed that we accompany her to her sister Qamran's house the next morning. Four of us set out in one *meana*: Khan-Begum, Mother, Anet and myself. Granny was left behind.

A *meana* is something like a palanquin of old, but smaller, and used exclusively for the conveyance of women. It has short, stubby legs to rest on the ground, the floor is interlaced with string, and the top is covered with red curtains, hanging down the sides. The bearers fix two bamboo poles on either side, by which they lift the meana from the ground.

Supported by four perspiring bearers, we arrived at Qamran's house, where we were kindly received. Qamran had at first been prejudiced against us, but the report taken to her by Sarfaraz Khan had made her change her views. She was eager to make our acquaintance and pressed us to stay with her; and during the weeks to come, we were to be her showpieces, on display for those who wanted to see us.

Sarfaraz Khan had come to Javed's house with the intention of striking off our heads, but Mother's charm had baffled him and won him over. Returning home, he had said, 'Who can lift his hand against such harmless things? The girl is like a frightened doe, and the mother—she is a perfect nightingale!' And so, among those who came to see us at Qamran's house was Sarfaraz Khan's wife, Hashmat. She, too, fell a victim to Mother's charm. 'Oh sister!' she exclaimed to Khan-Begum. 'My husband was quite right in his opinion of them. Mariam's lips, like the bee, distil nothing but honey.'

As for Qamran herself, her soft, sympathetic nature was roused by the story of our bereavement and our trials. Her large, pretty black eyes would fill with tears as she listened to Mother, and once she placed her head on Mother's shoulder and sobbed aloud.

She was about thirty-five, and on the verge of becoming stout; but she had fine features and a clear complexion. We were told that when she was dressed for her marriage, her father passed by, and was so struck by her beauty, that he exclaimed: 'Couldn't we have reserved so much beauty for someone who did not have to go out of our family!'

Qamran's husband, a much older man, was a cavalry lieutenant in the army at Bhopal. At their first meeting, she had felt a repugnance for his person. She repelled his advances and would not allow him even to touch her, with the result that her mother and others began to believe that she was in love with a jinn, or spirit. It suited her to encourage them in this belief. Her husband was disgusted, and returned to his cavalry regiment, but continued to keep her supplied with funds. Eventually, through the good offices of mutual friends, they were reconciled, and were blessed with a daughter, whom they named Badran.

Badran's beauty was different from her mother's. At the time we saw her she was sixteen or seventeen; she was slightly darker than her mother, and her eyes, though large, lacked the liquid softness which gave such serenity to Qamran's face. But a pink birthmark on her left cheek gave her an interesting face. She did not have her mother's liveliness or inquiring nature, and we did not see much of her.

*

Qamran had heard of our skill with the needle. She had made up her mind to make a present to her sister-in-law's small son, and asked us if we would help make the kurta-topi, which would consist of miniature trousers, coat and cap. Mother offered to cut and sew them.

She gave the kurta, which was of purple cloth, a Moghlai neck; that is, it had one opening, buttoning to the side over the left shoulder. It was finished off with gold lace round the edges, the sleeves and the neck. She also gave it a crescent-shaped, gold-embroidered band round the neck, and epaulettes on the shoulders. The trousers were made of rich, green satin, and also finished off with gold lace. The cap was made of the same stuff as the coat, so that it formed a kind of fillet, resting on the forehead. The three garments cost Qamran something like forty rupees—a sumptuous suit for a child!

Mother was pleased with the result of her work, and all who saw the suit were in raptures, and Qamran made Mother a present of a new set of bangles made of glass and enamelled blue.

*

We soon established ourselves as favourites in Qamran's house, and members of the household vied with each other in showing us kindness. Whereas they had formerly believed that, as *Firangi* women, we would be peeping out of doors and windows in order to be seen by men, without whose society European women were supposed to be unable to live, they were agreeably surprised to find that we delighted in hard work, that we loved needles and thread, and that, far from seeking the company of men, we did our best to avoid them.

'You are like one of us,' said Qamran to Mother one day. 'I would not exchange you for half a dozen women of my own race. Who could possibly ever tire of you?'

Politics seldom entered the four walls of the zenana—wars and deeds of violence were considered the prerogative of men. Seldom was any reference made to the disturbances that were taking place throughout the country, or to our own troubles. Only once was the even tenor of our lives disturbed, and that was due to the woman, Umda, who had taken a jealous dislike to us from the beginning.

I do not know in what way she was related to Qamran, but they addressed each other as 'sister', and Badran called her 'aunt'. She was a spiteful young woman, with a sharp, lashing tongue, very hostile towards all foreign races. She had been very displeased at our introduction into the family, always gave us angry looks, and never missed an opportunity to speak ill of us.

It pleased Umda to hear of the British reverses, and she was convinced that they would be swept from the walls of Delhi. Occasionally, she would leave aside generalities and give her attention to individuals.

Once Mother, Anet and I sat quietly together, sewing a pair of pyjamas for Badran, while Badran herself sat at the end of the veranda, whispering nonsense to her good-natured young husband, Hafizullah Khan. He, however, had his eyes on Umda, for he knew her well.

She began by changing the conversation with a contemptuous reference to the *Firangi* race, bringing up the old story of the hunger of European women for male company.

'Those wantons!' she said. 'They cannot live without the society of men.' 'Perhaps not, Chachi,' observed Hafizullah Khan from the other end of the veranda, 'and perhaps they are quite right in doing so. They have so much of male company that their appetite for it is probably less than yours. And then not all their men are opium eaters like your husband, who, beyond rolling in the dust like a pig, has little time for anything else.'

'That may be so,' she said haughtily, 'but what has it to do with *Firangi* women? You cannot deny that they enjoy laughing and joking with strange men, that they dance and sing, sometimes half-nude, with the arms of strange men round their waists. Then they retire into dark corners where they kiss and are kissed by men other than their husbands!'

Badran's bright eyes had grown wide with astonishment at this recital of the ways of the *Firangi* female.

'I did not know all that,' said Hafizullah Khan. 'From where do you obtain your deep knowledge, Chachi?'

'Never mind where,' she replied impatiently. 'It is true, what I have said, and that's why I say these *Firangans* will prove troublesome.'

'Now you are going too far, Chachi,' said Hafizullah. 'Upon my head, you are very careless in what you say. What charge can you bring against our guests here?'

'Well, when they first entered Javed's house, there was some excitement among the men in the neighbourhood.'

'Quite possibly,' said Hafizullah with sarcasm, 'your good husband was a little excited too, I suppose. Well, what came of it?'

'You are a funny boy, Hafiz!' she said mischievously, giving him a knowing wink in full sight of us. 'What are your intentions, eh?'

'You are behaving very stupidly today, Chachi!' said Hafizullah, growing impatient. 'What do you insinuate by that shake of your unbalanced head? I tell you again, be careful how you speak of Mariam and her daughter!'

'The boy stands as a champion of the white brood! Well, I have no patience with them.'

There was a pause in the contention. Mother, Anet and I had remained absolutely silent during this heated conversation; we were not in a position to say anything in our own defence, for we were in Qamran's house only on sufferance, and had no right to quarrel with anyone, and at the same time, we could not have improved on Hafizullah's performance.

Umda was bent on mischief and would not change the subject. 'My son has gone with the expedition. I hope and pray that he does not bring a *Firangi* female back with him.'

Hafizullah was ready for her. 'No doubt your son will perform deeds of great valour on his expedition, but considering that it is only a few refractory landowners that they have been sent to quell, I don't think there is any chance of his finding any *Firangans* to come back with.'

Before Umda could take up the cudgels again, Hafizullah got to his feet and told her that it was time she returned to her own house; that he did not intend sitting by to hear us abused by her. But Umda was determined to have the last word.

'Great is the power of prayer,' she said. 'I have advised Khan-Begum to take ashes in her hand, and blow them towards these women so that they might fly away like this.' And throwing a pinch of dust towards us, she mumbled something under her breath.

It was too much for Hafizullah Khan. He rushed at Umda and

dragged her out of the veranda. Then telling her to be gone, or he would be more rough with her, he returned and sat down near his wife, in a great rage.

THE RAINS

&

'IT DOES NOT SURPRISE me,' said Qamran, when she came home and heard of the quarrel between Umda and her son-in-law. 'Umda has too long and too venomous a tongue altogether. What business is it of hers that you should be my guests? She might have taken a lesson from you in patience and forbearance. Son!' she said, addressing Hafizullah. 'You need not have dragged her out. Nevertheless, it was noble of you to have taken the side of these unfortunate ones. Mariam, forgive her for her foolishness. She has only succeeded in giving the young an opportunity to jeer at her. In my house you will always be welcome.'

It was now the height of the rainy season, and heavy clouds were banking in the west. A breeze brought us the fresh scent of approaching rain, and presently we heard the patter of raindrops on the jasmine bushes that grew in the courtyard. It was the day of the monsoon festival observed throughout northern India by the womenfolk, who put on their most colourful costumes, and relax on innumerable swings, giving release to feelings of joy and abandon. Double ropes are suspended from a tree, and the ends are knotted together and made to hold narrow boards painted in gay colours. Two women stand facing each other, having taken each other's ropes by catching them between their toes. They begin to swing gently, gradually moving faster and higher, until they are just a brightly coloured blur against the green trees and grey skies. Sometimes, a small bed is fixed between the ropes, on which two or three can sit while two others move the swing, singing to them at the same time.

A swing having been put up from an old banyan tree that

grew just behind the house, Badran and Hashmat, both dressed in red from head to foot, climbed on to it. Anet and I swung them, while Gulabia, the servant-girl, sang. When they came down we had our turn, and I found it an exhilarating experience, riding through the air, watching the racing clouds above me at one moment, and Anet's dark curls below me at the next. Removed for a while from the world below, I felt again that life could be gay and wonderful.

*

Mother's memory was stored with an incredible amount of folklore, and she would sometimes astonish our hosts with her references to sprites and evil spirits. One day, Badran, having taken her bath, came out into the courtyard with her long hair lying open.

'My girl, you ought not to leave your hair open,' said Mother. 'It is better to make a knot in it.'

'But I have not yet oiled it,' said Badran. 'How can I put it up?'

'It is not wise to leave it open when you sit outside in the cool of the evening. There are aerial beings called jinns, who are easily attracted by long hair and pretty black eyes like yours,' said Mother.

Badran blushed, her mother and husband both being present; and Qamran smiled at the recollection of her own youthful waywardness, when she made everyone believe that she was the object of a jinn's passion.

'Do the jinns visit human beings?' asked Hafizullah Khan.

'So it is said,' said Mother. 'I have never seen a jinn myself, but I have noticed the effect they have on others.'

'Oh, please tell us what you have seen,' begged Qamran.

'There was once a lovely girl who had a wealth of black hair,' said Mother. 'Quite unexpectedly she became seriously ill, and in spite of every attention and the best medical advice, she grew worse every day. She became as thin as a whipping-post and lost all her beauty, with the exception of her hair, which remained beautiful and glossy until her dying day. Whenever she fell asleep, she would be tormented by dreams. A young jinn would appear to her, and tell her that he had fallen in love with her beautiful hair one evening as she was drying it after a bath, and that he intended to take her away. She was in great pain, yet in the midst of her sufferings her invisible tormentor never ceased to visit her; and though her body became shrivelled, there shone in her eyes an unearthly light; and when her body decayed and died, her gorgeous head of hair remained as beautiful as ever.'

'What a dreadful story!' said Badran, hurriedly tying another knot in her hair.

Conversation then turned upon different types of ghosts and spirits, and Qamran told us about the *Munjia*—the disembodied spirit of a Brahmin youth, who had died before his marriage— which is supposed to have its abode in a pipal tree. When the *Munjia* gets annoyed, it rushes out from the tree and upsets bullock-carts, *meanas* and even horse-driven carriages. Should anyone be passing beneath a lonely pipal tree at night, advised Qamran, one should not make the mistake of yawning without snapping one's fingers in front of one's mouth.

'If you don't remember to do this,' said Qamran, 'the *Munjia* will dash down your throat and completely ruin you.' Mother then launched into an account of the various types of ghosts she was acquainted with: the ghosts of immoral women—*churels*— who appear naked, with their feet facing backwards; ghosts with long front teeth, which suck human blood; and ghosts which take the form of animals. In some of the villages near Rampur (according to Mother), people have a means by which they can tell what form a departed person has taken in the next life. The ashes are placed in a basin and left outside at night, covered with a heavy lid. Next morning, a footprint can be seen in the ashes. It may be the footprint of a man or a bird or an elephant, according to the form taken by the departed spirit.

By ten o'clock we were feeling most reluctant to leave each other's company on the veranda. It did not make us feel any better to be told by Mother and Qamran to recite certain magical verses to keep away evil spirits. When I got into bed I couldn't lie still, but kept twisting and turning and looking at the walls for moving shadows. After some time, we heard a knocking on our door, and the voices of Badran and Hashmat. Getting up and opening it, we found them looking pale and anxious. Qamran had succeeded in frightening them, too.

'Are you all right, Khurshid?' they asked. 'Wouldn't you like to sleep in our room? It might be safer. Come, we'll help you to carry your bed across.'

'We are quite all right here,' protested Mother, but we were hustled along to the next room, as though a band of ghosts was conspiring against us. Khan-Begum had been absent during all this activity (though she had been present during the story-telling), and the first we heard of her was a loud cry. We ran towards the sound and found her emerging from our room.

'Mariam has disappeared!' she cried. 'Khurshid and Anet have gone too!'

And then, when she saw us coming running out of her own room, our hair loose and disordered, she gave another cry and fainted on the veranda.

White Pigeons

'You are bearing your troubles very well,' said Hafizullah to Mother one evening. 'You are so cheerful and patient, and you seem to look forward to the future with hope. And after all, what is the good of mourning for a past which can never return?'

'I doubt if there can be any improvement in their situation,' said Khan-Begum. 'Only yesterday the fakir was saying that the *Firangis* had been wiped off the face of the land.'

'I am not so sure of that,' remarked Hafizullah.

'Nor I,' said Qamran. 'The fact is, we do not get much news here.'

'Well, I can tell you something,' said Hafizullah. 'Though my uncle did boast the other day that there were no *Firangis* left, I overheard him whispering to Sarfaraz Khan that they were not yet totally extinct. The hills are full of them. My uncle was relating how Abdul Rauf Khan had gone on the morning of Id to pay his respects to Mian Sahib, the same fakir you speak of, and he was astounded by what the old man told him.'

'What was it?' urged Khan-Begum.

'Abdul Rauf said that Mian Sahib was in a strange mood. He cast off the white clothes which he had been wearing during the past three months and, very suddenly, and without apparent reason, put on a black robe. Abdul Rauf and the others had gone to him to ask that he pray for the defeat of the *Firangis* before Delhi, but what do you think he told them?'

Hafizullah paused dramatically, and both Qamran and Khan-Begum said at the same time, 'What did he tell them?'

'He told them that the restoration of the *Firangi* rule was as certain as the coming of doomsday. It would be another hundred years, he said, before the foreigners could be made to leave. "See, here they come!" he cried, pointing to the north where a flock of white pigeons could be seen hovering over the city. "They come flying like white pigeons which, when disturbed, fly away, and circle, and come down to rest again. White pigeons from the hills!" Abdul Rauf folded his hands and begged Mian Sahib to say no more. But the Mian is no respecter of persons, and his words are not to be taken lightly.'

*

Our stay with Qamran was drawing to a close. We had passed almost the entire rainy season in the company of her agreeable household, and time had passed swiftly. We could not have received greater kindness or sympathy than we had been given by Qamran, and her son-in-law, Hafizullah. Javed Khan had been several times to see us—or rather, to see his wife and sister. Once or twice he had pressed Qamran to shorten our stay, but she did not want us to leave, and kept us on the pretext that we were sewing some things for her, which were not quite ready. He did not press her too much, as he knew that having both his wife and us under his roof did not make things easier for him.

Though appointed by the Nawab to a military command, we did not hear that Javed had engaged in any new or daring enterprise. His sacking of the Rosa Rum Factory had been his chief exploit to date, and that too had been done more for personal gain than from any other motive. He had shown no enthusiasm for the massacre at Muhamdi, where a company of sepoys had finished off the few Europeans who had managed to get away from Shahjahanpur. Now he limited his services to attending the Nawab's receptions, and to keeping him informed of news from Delhi and the whereabouts of stray refugees and survivors like ourselves. We heard, for instance, of the hiding-place of the Redmans. A beggar woman happened to be passing before the house of the Redmans' old washerwoman, and stopping there to beg, recognized the tall, fair woman sitting in the yard.

'Who are you, eh?' she cackled. 'I know who you are! And where are your white husband and son?'

'Be off, *churel*!' said Mrs Redman. 'Go about your begging, and do not interfere with my affairs.'

Meanwhile the dhobi came home and, taking in the situation, told the beggar woman, 'How do you know she is a *Firangan*? She happens to be my sister-in-law.'

'Very fair for one of your caste!' said the old woman slyly.

'Ask any more questions and my washing-board will descend on your head!' threatened the dhobi. 'Be off, dead one!'

The beggar woman hobbled off, cursing both the dhobi's family and the Redmans, and made her way to Abdul Rauf Khan's house, where she informed him of what she had discovered. Abdul Rauf took his information to the Nawab, and suggested that he be permitted to capture the *Firangan*.

'That would be an adventure worthy of you,' said the amused Nawab. 'No doubt you would need an armed detachment to capture her. But I prefer not to hound these refugees, Khan Sahib. They have not done our cause any harm.' And he showed them the same forbearance that he had shown us.

*

The season of Moharram had come and gone. We did not even notice that it was over, for there were very few Shia families in Shahjahanpur, and the festival was not kept up with the same zeal that was shown in other towns. Unlike the Shia women, the Pathan women do not go into mourning during the ten days of fasting, nor do they remove their ornaments. Food and clothing were, however, sent to the nearest mosque to be distributed among the poor of the city.

Moharram over, it was decided that we should return to Javed Khan's house on Friday, the 4th of September.

THE IMPATIENCE OF JAVED KHAN

POOR KHAN-BEGUM WAS TO suffer many more pangs of jealousy before she could be done with us. On the same day that we returned to her house, Javed Khan took the opportunity to question Mother again, regarding her plans for my marriage.

'Tell me, Mariam, how much longer am I to wait?' he asked after dinner.

'What can I say?' sighed Mother. 'You ask me so often. I have already told you that I cannot give my daughter away without consulting my brothers. You had agreed to wait until the contest before Delhi was decided.'

'May the *Firangi* name perish, I say!' he exclaimed furiously. 'Surely your brothers have all been exterminated by now!' Then, his mood changing suddenly from anger to a brooding sullenness, he muttered to himself: 'Perhaps the fellow spoke the truth when he said, "Subedarji, will you reach Delhi at all?" For Ghansham Singh was not fated to set foot within the walls of the city. He fell at the Hindan bridge, when the *Firangi* army attacked the Bareilly brigade. He could not tell the King of our achievements here on the 31st of May. Well, I have done my part—and the sugar loaf solved my sherbet problem at Moharram. I would also have dealt well with that boy at Mangal Khan's, but the fool, Mangal, came between us and said he had adopted the boy as his own son. I never heard of a true believer adopting an infidel—a plague on them all!'

His face was dark and threatening as he went out of the house, and after a few minutes, we were startled by the screams of the boy Saifulla, Javed's half-brother, who had bumped into Javed in the lane and upon whom the Pathan was now venting his rage and frustration.

Javed Khan had stripped the boy to the waist, and taking out his horsewhip, had lashed the boy so severely, that the skin was actually torn from his back. Saifulla was laid up for several days, yelling from the pain which the festered parts gave him; but instead of softening toward him, Javed Khan threatened to repeat the flogging if the boy didn't stop groaning.

I have no doubt that it was Mother's disappointing answer that had driven Javed into a frenzy, and I suppose I should have been grateful that his passion had found an outlet on the back of his brother. Javed hated the boy for being the offspring of an illicit affair of his father's.

The same evening, Javed gave a further display of his savage disposition. Having inquired from the syce whether his horse had received its gram, and having been informed that Rupia, the servant-woman, had not yet ground it, he called the woman and demanded to know why the gram had not yet been ground.

'I was busy with other things,' she explained.

'Were you, you dead one?' he shouted fiercely and, seizing his whip again, laid it on her so violently, that she was literally made black and blue, and her torn and scanty clothes were cut to rags. She was bedridden for several days. Everyone in the house went about in apprehension, wondering what Javed's next outburst would be like, but Mother could not bear to hear the groans of the woman and the boy. She had Zeban fetch some ground turmeric, which she heated on the fire and applied to the bruises. She attended to them for three days until their wounds began to heal.

*

One day, Javed approached Mother again, and we were afraid there would be a repetition of his earlier display of temper; but he looked crestfallen, and was probably a little ashamed of his behaviour. He complained of having pains all over his body, and begged Mother to tell him of a remedy.

'You have been prescribing for those two wretches,' he said. 'Can't you give me something too?'

'What can I give you?' replied Mother. 'I am not a hakim. When I was in my senses I might have been able to think of something for your pain. You look very well, I must say.'

'I am not well,' said Javed. 'I cannot sit on my horse as well as usual. It is all due to my disregard for the wisdom of my betters: "Don't shoot on a Thursday." Last Thursday when I went out shooting, I saw a blackbuck and fired at it, but I missed, and instead, I hit a white pigeon sitting on a tomb. The pigeon flew into a bush, and I could not find it; but it must have been killed. I got nothing that day, and when I returned home in the evening, I felt exhausted and quite unable to use my limbs. I was as stiff as a dead one. Abdul Rauf was informed, and when he heard of what had happened he came to see me, very angry, because I had fired on the bird. "Pigeons," he said, "are people who come out of their graves on Thursdays for a little fresh air." Well, Abdul Rauf had me treated, shut me in a room, and eventually I came to myself. But I have this swelling on my face, where the dead one must have slapped me.'

His face did appear to be slightly swollen; but, before Mother could take a closer look, Javed started at the sound of music in the street. His face underwent a violent change and, taking his whip, he rushed out of the house.

There was a great deal of commotion outside, and then we heard the sound of someone shouting: 'Hai! Hai! Save me, I am being murdered!'

We all looked at each other in wonder, and Khan-Begum said, 'It must be that boy who passes this way sometimes, singing and playing love songs on his flute. My husband swore, by the soul of his dead father, to flog the fellow within an inch of his life if he caught him singing before this house.'

'But what harm is done by his singing?' asked Mother.

'None that I know of. But in a Pathan settlement, no one is allowed to sing or play any instrument in the streets. Music is supposed to excite all sorts of passions, and so it is discouraged.'

'Still, I do not see what right our protector has to assault another in the street merely because he is singing and playing his flute. Is Javed not afraid that he might have to answer to the Nawab for his high-handedness?'

Khan-Begum began to laugh. 'The Nawab?' she said. 'Of what are you thinking, Mariam? Why should the Nawab care about it?'

A Visit from Kothiwali

It was the 13th of September, a Sunday morning, when the family barber brought a message from Kothiwali for Javed Khan. 'Your Chachi send you her salaams, and says she intends to pay you a visit tomorrow.' To this Javed Khan sent the reply, 'It is my Chachi's house, let her come and throw the light of her presence on it.' Messages of this sort were always couched in extremely polite language.

The following morning Kothiwali arrived in her *meana*, attended by her servants. We were glad to see her again, as she was always so friendly.

'Now, Mariam, I have come to ask you to spend some time with me. I am seething with jealousy because you spent so much time at Qamran's house. Javed, you have no objection to my taking them with me?'

'It is all the same to me whether they stay here or go with you,' said Javed Khan with a shrug of his shoulders.

'Why so?' asked Kothiwali mischievously. 'I thought you were unhappy unless they were under your own roof?'

'True, but what good is it?' he said. 'My ambition was to possess the girl.'

'Well, she is in your possession now, isn't she?' said Kothiwali.

'Upon my head, you are exasperating!' exclaimed Javed. 'So far as her presence in my house goes, she is in my possession, but what of that? I would marry her today, if it were not for her mother's procrastinations! Sometimes it is: "I have not consulted my brothers," as if she had any brother left to consult. Sometimes it is: "Wait until the fighting before Delhi is over," as if, even when it is over, it will make any great difference to people like us. It is foolish to expect that the *Firangis* will be victorious. Have I not seen a score of them running for their lives pursued by one of our soldiers?'

'Perhaps, but it is not always like that,' said Kothiwali.

'I wonder why your sympathies are with them, Chachi?'

'Well, they have always been quite good to me,' she replied. 'When my husband was killed by his enemies, it was the Collector who came to my house to condole with me, and it was he who saw to it that our fields were not taken from us. True, that was a long time ago. But I have no reason to wish them ill. At the same time, don't think I wish to run down the cause you have made your own—the rebel cause, I mean.'

'The *rebel* cause! Why do you always call it the rebel cause, Chachi?' Javed Khan looked very upset. 'Rebels against whom? Against aliens! Are they not to be expelled from the land? To fight them is not rebellion, but a meritorious act, surely!'

'Maybe, if it doesn't involve the murder of innocent women and children. But see how the *Firangis* are holding out before Delhi!'

'Enough, Chachi. Say no more, or you will rouse the demon in me. Let us not anticipate events. Delhi still stands, and Bahadur Shah reigns!'

'Nevertheless, I would advise you to take Mariam's suggestion and wait until the siege is raised. Be cautious, Javed, in your designs on this girl.'

'I have need to be, no doubt, after hearing about the example set by the Kanpur girl.'

'Oh! And who was she?'

'The General's daughter. A girl still beautiful at the age of twenty. She was saved from the massacre by Jamadar Narsingh, one of the Nana Sahib's bodyguards, who would have liked to make her his wife. His intentions, like mine, were probably quite honourable, but Zerandaz Khan, another officer, stole the girl one night from the Jamadar's house, and treated her so savagely, that he roused in her all the pride and resentment of her race. For some time she concealed her feelings, but one night, when he was asleep, she drew his scimitar from under his pillow and plunged it into his breast. She then went and threw herself in a well. That was pluck and daring, wasn't it, Chachi? But,'— pointing at me, though looking away—'I have not even looked her full in the face, believe me!'

'Ah, you sly man!' said Kothiwali jestingly.

There was a pause at the end of which Kothiwali said, 'They may come with me, Javed, mayn't they? You are in a surly mood this morning.'

'Oh yes, take them with you,' he muttered sulkily. 'If they are happier with you, they may go with you.'

*

Seated in the same *meana* as Kothiwali, we were carried along to her house. I should really call it a mansion, because it was a large brick building with a high entrance and a spacious courtyard. There was also a set of glass-roofed chambers over the gateway, which the men used as retiring rooms; while the women's apartments were situated on the ground floor, and were cool and spacious.

The family consisted of Kothiwali, her daughter and two sons, one daughter-in-law, one son-in-law and innumerable grandchildren. Kothiwali was the widow of a landed proprietor in the district, and must have been about forty years old when we knew her. She was tall, with black hair and eyes, a large mouth, small teeth coloured black with *missi* and paan. She wore no trinkets except for a round silver bangle on each hand, and a plain silver ring on her right small finger. Her face was always cheerful, and she possessed great spirit. She commanded great respect from the rest of her community, who often came to consult her when in difficulty.

Mother soon became a favourite in the household, and so did Anet and I, but to a lesser degree. Kothiwali paid special attention to us. 'What quiet girls they are!' she would sometimes say. 'They never waste their time in idle talk.'

'Why not have the girls' ears and noses pierced?' she said to Mother one day.

'What would be the good when I have nothing to make them wear,' replied Mother.

The lobes of our ears were already pierced, and I was glad I did not have to submit to having my nose pierced as well.

'I am glad you did not submit to Javed's request for your daughter's hand in marriage,' said Kothiwali. 'Had she been my daughter, I would never have agreed. Javed is very inconstant.'

'It would have been an incongruous match,' said Mother.

'My poor husband could never have imagined that she would be sought for by a Pathan as his second wife!'

Kothiwali's elder son, Wajihullah Khan, came in and sat down while we were talking. He was a young man of twenty-five, a hafiz—one who knows the *Quran* by heart—and regular at his prayers: it was he who gave the call to prayer in the neighbouring mosque. He was fair, of medium height, and quiet and respectful in his manner.

His usual haunt was the bungalow over the gateway, where

he spent most of his time reading or playing chess—a game which is now losing much of its popularity. He came in with a friend named Kaddu Khan, a very handsome young man, who called Kothiwali Chachi. I think I recognized him as one of the band who had forced us to leave Lala Ramjimal's house. He was suffering from consumption in its first stage, and Wajihullah joined Kothiwali in begging Mother to prescribe something for him.

'I am not a doctor,' said Mother. 'I know the remedies for some minor ailments, but I very much doubt if I could help this boy.'

'No, do not refuse to do something for him,' urged Wajihullah. 'He is really a man of an adventurous spirit, though he has yet to gain fame for his achievements.'

'Do not make fun of the poor fellow,' said Kothiwali. 'He looks sufficiently depressed already.'

'No, I shall relate his worthy deeds to Mausi, before I ask her to give him something to improve his condition.'

Kaddu Khan now looked more dejected than ever and hung his handsome head in acute embarrassment.

'To begin with, Mausi, this is the gentleman who proposed to Nawab Qadar Ali to dig up the Christian graves for the treasure which, he was sure, was buried there.'

Kaddu Khan looked up and said, 'So I was made to believe. And the fox who gave me that information also told me that when a *Firangi* dies, two bags of money are buried with him.'

'And of course you believed that absurd story, and went about digging up their bones? Tell us what treasure you found!'

'We began digging at night,' said Kaddu Khan, deciding it would be better if he told the story himself. 'It was a moonlit night. There were three of us. I volunteered to go down into the grave and bring up anything valuable that I could find. To keep in touch with my comrades, we hammered a peg in the ground above and fastened a rope to it, and with its help, I slipped down. But imagine my horror when, instead of touching firm ground, I found myself hanging between heaven and earth! I let out a cry of distress. My comrades, instead of helping me out, thought the *Firangi* devils were after us, and instantly took to their heels, leaving me dangling over the grave.'

'A situation you had merited,' observed Wajihullah. 'But tell us how you got out.'

'I hung on to the rope and with a great deal of effort managed to raise myself to the bank. And now I tried to follow the example of my brave companions by making a run for it, but as I got up to do so, I felt a violent jerk around my waist and fell down again. Again I tried to get up and run, and again I was pulled to the ground. I was half-dead through fright, but I made one last lunge forward, and this time the wooden peg came up too, and I lost no time in taking to my heels. Chachi, that graveyard is full of *Firangi* devils!'

'What a thick-headed fellow you are!' said Wajihullah, enjoying himself immensely. 'One would think there would be some sense beneath that beautiful brow of yours. It was your waistband, Kaddu, that got hammered down with the peg. It left you dangling over the grave, and when you tried to run, it pulled you down again. It was only when you pulled the peg up that your cummerbund was loosened.'

Kothiwali and the rest of us had a good laugh at Kaddu Khan's discomfiture.

'It should serve as a lesson to you,' said Kothiwali, 'that all men are alike when the time comes to die. When you are dead would you like somebody to disturb your body in search of treasure? Treasure indeed! Even kings go empty-handed when they die. A child, when it is born, comes into the world with a closed fist, and the same hand lies open and flat at the time of death. We bring nothing into the world and we take nothing out!' At this juncture, Kaddu Khan's mother and sister joined us and, folding their hands to Mother, entreated her to do something for the youth.

They had conceived an exaggerated idea of Mother's powers of healing. All she told Kaddu to do was to take a dose of *khaksir* tea every six hours, and to abstain from acidic and hot food; and she told him to chew some fresh coconut every morning, drinking the juice as well. Kaddu Khan tried these simple remedies, and we heard that he eventually got better.

The Fall of Delhi

&

WE WERE SITTING IN the veranda with Kothiwali when there was a disturbance in the next porch, where most of the men were sitting. Javed Khan had just ridden up, and had whispered something in Sarfaraz Khan's ear. Sarfaraz got up immediately and came and whispered something to Kothiwali. As soon as he had gone, Kothiwali turned to Mother and said, 'Well, Mariam, Delhi has been taken by the *Firangis*. What great changes will take place now . . .'

Our hearts leapt at the news, and tears came to our eyes, for a British victory meant a release from our confinement and state of dependence; but Delhi was a far cry from Shahjahanpur, and we did not give any expression to our feelings.

On the contrary, Mother took Kothiwali's hand and said, 'May you have peace out of it, too, Pathani.'

'Javed Khan will look quite small now, won't he?' said Kothiwali merrily. Apparently the news did not affect her one way or the other; she dealt in individuals, not in communities. 'But he has good reason to be worried. The *Firangis* will have heavy scores to settle in this city.'

*

The next day the menfolk held a long discussion. Some spoke of fleeing the city, others suggested that it would be better to wait and watch the course of events.

Sarfaraz Khan: 'Though Delhi has fallen to the *Firangi* army, it will be a long time before a small town like ours can be reoccupied. Our soldiers, who have been driven from Delhi, will make a stand at some other important place. Lucknow perhaps, and it will be months before we see a *Firangi* uniform in Shahjahanpur. Do not be in a hurry to run away, unless, of course, you have special reasons to be afraid of an avenging army . . .'

Javed: 'True, very true, *bhai*, I have done nothing to be afraid of. Have I, now? It's fellows like Abdul Rauf, who served under the *Firangis* and then threw in their lot with the sepoys, that are sure to be hanged. As for me, I never did take salt with the *Firangis*. If it comes to the worst, I shall ride across the border into Nepal, or take service in the Gwalior brigade.'

Sarfaraz: 'Oh, I'm sure you will. But why leave the city at all if there is nothing to be afraid of?'

Hafizullah: 'I saw some of our men who had returned from Delhi. They were lucky to get away. They had on only their tattered tunics and shorts.'

'Did they say anything of the fighting in Delhi?' asked Sarfaraz Khan.

'They told me that our army was not able to make much impression on the *Angrez* lines entrenched on the Ridge. There were many sorties, and during the last one, only a few days before the city was stormed, our men performed great feats of valour, but they were repulsed and cut down to the last man. The *Firangis* lost many men, too, but the victory gave them great confidence. When their storming parties approached the walls and blew open the Kashmiri Gate, their leader, Nikalsein, was seen waving his handkerchief on the point of his sabre from an elevated site. A ball struck him, and he fell. But his men forced their way through the city at the point of the bayonet, and Delhi is in *Firangi* hands again.'

'And what became of the King?' inquired Sarfaraz.

'He was made a prisoner, and his sons, who fled with him, were shot.'

'And so much for the rebellion,' said Sarfaraz Khan philosophically. 'The city of Delhi was a garden of flowers, and now it is a ruined country; the stranger is not my enemy, nor is anyone my friend ...'

'Don't grow sentimental and poetic, Sarfaraz,' said Javed Khan irritably. 'Who was it who came to my house to kill certain people?'

'It was I,' said Sarfaraz. 'But did I kill anyone?'

BEHIND THE CURTAIN

IT WAS NOW WINTER, though the cold winds had not yet begun to blow. Mother sold two of the silver spoons from the jewel box which she had rescued from our burning house, and used the money to make quilts and some warm clothing to keep away the cold.

Ever since we had heard of the fall of Delhi, a change had come over our outlook and our expectations. We began to look forward to the time when Shahjahanpur would be reoccupied by the British—it would mean the end of our captivity which, though it had been made pleasant by Kothiwali and Qamran and their households, was not a state to which we could resign ourselves for ever; it would—we hoped—mean a reunion with other members of my mother's and father's families; and it would put an end to Javed Khan's plans to marry me. Our motives in hoping for the restoration of British authority were, therefore, entirely personal. We had, during the past months, come to understand much of the resentment against a foreign authority, and we saw that the continuation of that authority could only be an unhappy state of affairs for both sides; but for the time being it was in our interests to see it restored. Our lives depended on it.

But as yet there was no sign of the approach of British soldiers. We had no doubt that they would arrive sooner or later, but of course we did not speak on the subject, nor did we consider it prudent to show too great an interest in what was happening elsewhere. Of Kothiwali's sympathy we were sure, but we were afraid Javed Khan, in his defeat and frustration, might try to inflict some injury on us.

One day the mohalla sweeper, having taken ill, sent another girl to carry out her duties. The new girl recognized us as soon as she saw us, and a look of understanding passed between her and Mother. I remembered that she was called Mulia, and that she was the elder sister of a girl with whom I used to play when I was younger.

The latrine was the one place where we could manage any sort of privacy, and when Mulia went behind its curtain wall, Mother followed her.

'Mausi, you have no need to worry any more,' whispered Mulia. 'Delhi is taken, and your own people will be among us again. And I am to tell you that your brother is safe at Bharatpur. If you wish to send him a message, there is a person going on a pilgrimage to Mathura, and he will take your letter.'

Overjoyed at having met someone whom she knew and could trust, Mother agreed to make use of the messenger.

'But what am I to write the letter with?' she asked.

'Don't worry,' said Mulia. 'Tomorrow I will bring paper and pencil. Meet me here again.'

*

We did not betray our feelings at this fortunate meeting, not did anyone notice anything unusual about our behaviour. We did not even tell Anet or Granny about it, for fear that our hopes might be disappointed.

Next morning, keeping her promise, Mulia came again and waited for Mother behind the curtain wall. She handed her a scrap of paper and a small pencil, upon which Mother scribbled these words: 'I, Ruth, Anet, Mother, alive and well and hiding here. Do your best to take us away.'

She handed the note to Mulia, who slipped it into her bodice.

Mulia then slipped away, leaving us in a state of suppressed excitement.

*

It was early January, and we had been with Kothiwali for over three months. We had wanted for nothing but had, on the contrary, been treated with great kindness and consideration. We were rather disappointed when it was suggested that we should return to Javed Khan's house. He came himself and asked Kothiwali to let us go. Perhaps he still hoped that Mother might be persuaded to give her consent to my marriage— months had passed since the British had taken Delhi, but there were still no signs of their arrival in Shahjahanpur.

Khan-Begum was not exactly overjoyed at our return, and was still subject to fits of jealousy. There must have been a heated argument between her and Javed, because the morning after our arrival we heard him exclaiming to her angrily: 'I hate this constant nagging of yours.' She gave him some reply, which was followed by the slash of Javed's whip and a long silence.

He left the house without speaking to anyone, and only came back in the evening for his dinner. He asked Khan-Begum if she had anything to eat.

She replied: 'No, I am not hungry.'

'Then you had better sit down and eat,' he said, 'and don't put on any more of your airs.' She knew he was in a bad temper and had no wish to feel his whip again; so she did what he told her, though she remained glum and unfriendly until Kothiwali came and took us away again.

The Battle of Bichpuri

WE WERE NOW IN the middle of April 1858, and the hot winds of approaching summer brought the dust eddying into Kothiwali's veranda. The gulmohar tree outside the gate was aflame with scarlet flowers, and the mango trees were in blossom, promising fruit in abundance. The visits of Javed Khan to Kothiwali's house had of late become more frequent, and there were many whispered conversations between him and Kothiwali. We had no idea how we would fit in with their future plans should the British reoccupy Shahjahanpur.

One day Kothiwali received a visitor, a stranger whom we had not seen before. His name was Faizullah, and he too addressed Kothiwali as Chachi, though he was not related to her. He was a brash young man, and gave a vivid account of his experiences at Fatehgarh, from where he had just returned.

'So you were present at the battle of Bichpuri?' asked Kothiwali.

'Yes, Chachi,' he replied, 'and what a great battle it was! We fought the *Firangis* hand to hand, and made them feel the strength of our arms. I made a heap of the slain, and have brought with me a string of heads to present to the Nawab!'

'What a liar you are!' exclaimed Kothiwali.

'I swear by my head, Chachi!'

'How did a thin fellow like you manage to carry so many heads?'

'Why, I slung them over my saddle, and rode home in triumph.'

'And who was it who got the worst of the fight?'

'Why, the *kafirs*, of course, Chachi. We made a clean sweep of them,' and he passed the palm of his right hand over his left.

'Indeed!' said Kothiwali.

'There was not one man left, Chachi, so do you know what they did? 'They sent their women out to fight us!'

'This becomes more intriguing,' said Kothiwali. 'You are a gifted boy, Faizullah—you have a wonderful imagination! Tell us, what did their women look like?'

'Well, they were rather big for women. Some of them wore false beards and moustaches. But each one of them had a high skirt with a metal disc hanging down in front.' (It suddenly dawned on me that Faizullah was describing a Scots regiment of Highlanders.) 'Such horrid-looking women, I assure you. Of course, there was no question of fighting them. I don't lift my hand against women, and out of sheer disgust I left the camp and came away.'

'You did right,' said Kothiwali. 'But will you not show us one of the *Firangi* heads you obtained?'

'I would be delighted to, Chachi, but believe me, I have made a present of the whole string to the Nawab!'

Judging by the fact that Faizullah was safe at home instead of with a victorious army, we were fairly certain that they had been defeated by the British at Fatehgarh, and that it would not be long before Shahjahanpur was entered. This surmise was confirmed by Sarfaraz Khan who arrived at that moment and, giving Faizullah a look of scorn, said, 'So this warrior has been telling you of the *Firangi* heads he cut off! Is he able to tell us who cut off Nizam Ali Khan's head?'

This announcement produced quite a sensation, and Kothiwali jumped up, exclaiming: 'Nizam Ali killed! You don't mean it!'

Nizam Ali Khan was probably the Nawab's most valued official, a moderate and widely respected man. We had once had the lease of his compound, and had always found him courteous and friendly.

'But I do mean it,' said Sarfaraz. 'I have it on better authority than the chatter of this bragging lout. There is mourning in Nizam Ali's family, and both his sons have been wounded—one in the head, the other in the leg.'

Faizullah, abashed at being found out, sat gazing at the ground while his hands, which had been busy with the slings of his rifle, now lay motionless.

'The Nawab sent out a strong force under Nizam Ali with instructions to prevent the *Firangi* army from crossing the Ganga. But they were too slow and cumbrous, and the enemy had made two marches towards our city before Nizam Ali sighted them! The *Firangi* troops had just reached their camping ground when they noticed a cloud of dust rising on the horizon. Their scouts brought them the intelligence that the Nawab's army was marching upon them, and the cavalry was immediately ordered to remount and prepare for action. They attacked the Nawabi force before the latter had time to form, while the light guns raked them in the flank. Taken by surprise, our soldiers were demoralized. They were seized by panic, and broke and fled.'

'And what about Nizam Ali?' asked Kothiwali impatiently.

'He made a desperate attempt to keep his men together and to put up some sort of resistance, but his efforts were in vain. He could not bring any of his men together to make a stand. His gunners could not fire, as the fugitive soldiers surged from one part of the field to the other. Resolved not to survive this disgrace, Nizam Ali dismounted, and requested his servant to pass his sword through his body. But the servant would not. Then Nizam Ali rushed about madly and put his head into the mouth of a cannon, and ordered a gunner to apply a match and blow him to pieces. But the gunner refused. Poor Nizam Ali! He was about to stab himself with his poignard when the *Firangi* cavalry came thundering down like a torrent, sweeping all before them. A *sawar* belonging to De Kantzow's Horse recognized him—Nizam Ali's distinctive appearance could not be mistaken—and wheeling round, charged at him at full gallop and pinned him with his lance to the ground. And so ended the life of a man who possessed more determination and character than Abdul Rauf Khan, and who was the mainstay of the Nawab. With Nizam Ali gone, I doubt if the Nawab's government will last another week.'

'I am truly sorry to hear of his fate,' said Kothiwali with a sigh. 'But what became of his sons? You said that two of them were wounded.'

'Better that they had been killed by the side of their noble father. Why, they joined in the stampede and fled from the field of battle as fast as their horses could carry them, following the example of my friend Faizullah here. I have just left them beating their heads and yelling like old women over their fallen fortunes.'

'You are the bearer of serious news,' said Kothiwali. 'Unless I am very much mistaken, the *Firangi* army will soon be here. What will become of us, then?'

'They are marching this way, that is certain,' said Sarfaraz. 'There can be no doubt that the city will soon be reoccupied. We must think of how to save ourselves, because it is certain that they will order the city to be sacked, as was done at Delhi. It has become the custom now.'

'Allah forbid!' cried Kothiwali. 'Let us all meet this evening at my house and discuss measures for our safety. No time must be lost, because tomorrow the *Firangi* army is sure to be in the district, and the day after they will enter the city.'

And so Kothiwali, who had remained quietly at home all through the most violent stages of the revolt, now showed her qualities as a leader. She ordered these rough, disorderly men about as though they were children, and brought about a sense of organization where otherwise panic might have prevailed.

IN FLIGHT AGAIN

THAT EVENING KOTHIWALI SAID to Mother, 'Well, Mariam, the *Firangis* are coming. I am glad that you are with me. Should it be necessary for us to flee the city, you will come with us, won't you?'

'Yes,' said Mother, 'for how will they know us for what we are? We have no one among them who would receive and protect us. From our complexions and our clothes they would take us for Mohammedan women, and we will receive the same treatment as your women. No, for the present we are identified with you all, and we must go where you go.'

When it was decided by Kothiwali that she and her family should flee Shahjahanpur, it was agreed by everyone that the rendezvous would be Javed Khan's house. We left for his house that same evening. There was Kothiwali's family; Qamran's family; and a doctor and his family, whom we had never seen before. Including Javed and his family, there were about thirty persons gathered at his house that evening, the 28th of April

1858. It was almost a year since we had left our own burning house behind. Before long, Javed Khan's house would be burning too. It did not make any sense at all; but I suppose war never has made sense to ordinary individuals.

There was, of course, no sleeping that night, for meana after meana kept dropping in till late, and there were whispers and secret consultations. The decision arrived at was that we should make our flight in a northerly direction, as the British force was marching from the south. And so, early on the morning of the 29th, long before dawn, the *meanas* began to fill up.

We had expected to get a seat in one of the *meanas* but soon they were all full and there was no room left.

Javed Khan came up to us and said, 'Mariam, you had better get into the doctor's bullock-cart. You will be quite comfortable there.'

There was no other choice; and so the four of us—Granny, Mother, Anet and myself—took our seats in the cart. Beside us were the doctor's wife, her brothers' wives, and their children. The party set off at once, the men riding ahead on their horses, while the meana-bearers trotted along at a brisk pace, and our bullock-cart trundled along in the rear.

After about two hours we reached the village of Indarkha, some eight miles out of Shahjahanpur. The sun was up, and when we raised the cloth which formed the roof of our cart, we were astonished to find ourselves alone, for the *meanas* and horsemen had all disappeared. It seemed that our driver had taken a circuitous route, and we had been left well behind. And there we were, in a strange village, and with companions who were unknown to us.

The doctor inquired for a vacant house where we could rest, but there was none to be had. The villagers were quite indifferent to our plight, and told us that we could not put up in the village. But the doctor grew bold, and brought them round to the notion that it was their duty to accommodate us all, whoever we were. Finally they told him: 'There really is no vacant house in the village, but there is one thing you can do. At the southern end of the village, just opposite the big banyan tree, a new house is being built. It is not yet complete, but it is habitable. You may occupy it and remain in it for a short time.' And so we gladly got down from our cart and entered a mud structure which consisted of a line of rooms at one end, a courtyard in front, and a wall all round.

We were, in a way, the guests of the doctor and his wife, and they were very kind to us. He was a Bengali Muslim, and had belonged to the Shahjahanpur regiment, but had severed his connection with it when it had marched out to Bareilly on the 1st of June 1857. Renting a house in the city, he soon acquired a reputation for possessing a healing hand and his practice flourished.

*

The doctor's sisters-in-law now busied themselves with digging and setting up an oven. One of them lighted it and set a pot of dal on the fire, while the other kneaded flour and began to make chapattis.

That evening, after everyone had eaten, the doctor came in and sat down, and in very civil language asked Mother to tell him who she was and what her circumstances were. Mother told him our story, which aroused his sympathy and compassion.

'Do you think,' asked Mother, 'do you think that British authority will be restored again?'

'I do not know about the distant future,' he replied, 'but certainly their authority will be restored. But, I was going to say that now you are with us, I hope you will make yourself at home and command me in any way you please. We are all in the same boat at present, so let us help each other as best as we can.'

Mother was touched by his expression of goodwill, and we remained with him that night and the next day. Long after sunset, when everything was still and the noisy birds in the banyan tree were silent, the doctor came to Mother and said, 'Javed Khan has come and he wants to speak to you.'

'Why has he come?' asked Mother. 'What further business has he with us?'

'He seems most anxious to see you,' said the doctor. 'He cannot come in here, but you can speak to him at the door.'

Mother went out to meet Javed Khan and I, being curious, followed her and stood in the shadow of the wall.

'Mariam,' said Javed, 'I have come to say that the *Firangis* have reoccupied Shahjahanpur. You will not, of course, go to them, but don't forget the protection you have received from me.'

'I will not forget it,' said Mother. 'I am grateful to you for giving us shelter. And I will never forget the kindness shown to me by Kothiwali and Qamran.'

'I have only one request to make,' said Javed, uneasily shifting his weight from one foot to the other.

'Yes, what is it?' asked Mother.

'I know that the time has passed when I could speak of marrying your daughter,' he said. 'It is too late now to do anything about that. But will you permit me to see her once more, before I leave?'

'What good will that do?' began Mother; but impelled by some odd impulse, I stepped forward into the light and stood before Javed Khan.

He gazed at me in silence for about a minute, and for the first time I did not take my eyes away from his; then, without a smile or a word, he turned away and mounted his horse and rode away into the night.

THE FINAL JOURNEY

&

THE DOCTOR SPOKE TO Mother the next morning: 'I have heard that yesterday the British Army entered Shahjahanpur and that a civil government has already been established. Won't you go to them now that order has been restored?'

'A good suggestion,' said Mother, 'but whom will we know among them?'

The doctor said, 'You will be known at once by your voice,

your accent and your manner, and perhaps you will find that some of your own relatives have arrived and are looking for you.'

The doctor then went to the village elders and told them that Mother was a European lady who had escaped during the massacre, and that she and her family wished to go into Shahjahanpur. Now that civil authority had been restored, would anyone undertake to carry them into town on his cart?

'You are not telling us anything we don't know,' said the headman. 'As soon as they stepped down from your bullock-cart we knew who they were.'

'How did you know?' asked the doctor.

'You must take me for a pumpkin,' said the old man. 'Why, their very walk and their carriage indicated who they were. I marked their legs particularly. Those are not the feet, thought I, of women who go about barefoot. The way they trod gingerly on the hot sand was proof enough. So they want to return to Shahjahanpur, do they? Well, I, Gangaram, shall take them in my own cart, and will reach them to any spot in Shahjahanpur where they wish to go. Tomorrow, in the morning, I shall be ready.'

*

We put our few belongings together and the next day, at about ten, we got into Gangaram's bullock-cart and set out for Shahjahanpur.

Our journey was uneventful. We reached the town late in the afternoon, and asked Gangaram to take us to our old house, for we did not know where else we could go. As we halted before the ruins of our old house, Mr Redman came up and told Mother briefly of his own escape and his family's. He informed us that the British Commander-in-Chief had reoccupied the district, but had since then continued his march to Bareilly, leaving a small force under Colonel Hall to guard Shahjahanpur. He said the town was not quite safe yet, as the Maulvi of Faizabad was still in control of the eastern boundary of the district; and he advised us to take shelter in the quarters he was occupying with his family. Mother was reluctant to accept his invitation, but we were still homeless and without any male protection, and so we stopped for the night in the building in which the Redmans had taken shelter. Here we met a party of three men whom my uncle had sent from Bharatpur to escort us to him. One was a mounted orderly named Nasim Khan, and the other two were servants of the Maharaja of Bharatpur. We came to know that the note sent through Mulia had actually been delivered to my uncle, and he took immediate steps for our rescue. Mother wept to see the familiar handwriting of her brother, and to read his letter which was full of affection and anxiety for our welfare, and contained a pressing invitation to come to him at Bharatpur where, he said, she would find a home for the rest of her life.

This was on Sunday, the 3rd of May 1858. Next morning we were surprised to see Pilloo's mother arrive in our midst— without Pilloo! She looked so upset that we felt certain Pilloo had been killed; but when at last we got her to speak coherently, we discovered that Pilloo had decided to remain behind of his own accord! He had grown so attached to Mangal Khan that he refused to come away, and his mother had to leave without him, hoping he would relent and follow her. But he never did. He preferred the companionship of the Pathan, and continued to live with him and his family. We never did understand his behaviour.

*

While we were listening to Pilloo's mother's tale of woe, Mr Redman returned from a visit to Colonel Hall's camp and invited us all to sit down to breakfast. We had, however, scarcely eaten anything, when an alarm was raised that the rebel army, under the Maulvi of Faizabad, was crossing the Khannaut by the bridge of boats. Nasim Khan, my uncle's man, who had gone to bathe his horse at the river, came running back at the same time, with the report that the enemy had driven in the vedettes of the little force led by the Colonel, who had entrenched himself in the old jail. There was a smell of battle in the air. The sound of bugles, the neighing of horses, the clatter of riderless mounts dashing across the plain, the dull thump of guns, and the confused noise of men running in different directions; all these were unmistakable signs that a considerable force had attacked the small British garrison.

We had no time to lose if we were to save ourselves. Gangaram's cart was still at our disposal. Though Mr Redman assured Mother that there was no danger, she was determined to make for the countryside where she thought we would be safer. We all climbed into the cart: Granny, Mother, myself, Anet, Pilloo's mother, and Vicky, the Redmans' daughter. We were scarcely out of the compound gate when we heard shouts, and, amidst a cloud of dust, some ten or twelve troopers of the rebel cavalry came riding at full gallop, flourishing their sabres in the air, and surrounded our cart. We heard one of them say: 'Here are some of them, let us finish them off!' We expected that at any moment, they would tear the covering from over our heads and bury their shining blades in our bosoms. Little Vicky held her neck with both her hands, saying: 'Let us all put our hands round our necks so that only our fingers will be cut off and our heads will be safe!'

Everyone was unnerved except for Mother. With her eyes almost starting out of their sockets, her face haggard and lined after months of sorrow and uncertainty, she grasped the handle of her knife, while with her free hand she removed the covering and put out her head. Her expression was enough to frighten even these ruffians who were thirsting for our blood. They reined back.

'What do you want with us, young fellows?' said Mother. 'Is there anything unusual about seeing so many helpless females fleeing from the city to escape dishonour and death?'

They did not stop to hear any more. Believing us to be Muslim women escaping from the city, they turned about and tackled Nasim Khan, who was riding behind us. But he had the presence of mind to tell them that he was a soldier of the faith, and that the women in the cart were his relatives, leaving the city as the *Firangis* had occupied it.

After the troopers had gone, Gangaram came down from the cart, and folding his hands before Mother, exclaimed: 'Well done! You are weak in body, but you have the spirit of a goddess! I do not know of any other woman who could have dealt so well with those men.'

*

Our adventures did not end there. Scarcely had we started moving again when, with a heavy thud, the cart fell down on its side. The axle had broken. There was no possibility of repairing it on the spot. We had to push on somehow, if we did not wish to fall in with another detachment of the enemy. The whirring and crashing of shells, the rattle of musketry, and the shouts of soldiers could be distinctly heard. We got down from the cart and, bidding goodbye to Gangaram, began to walk. We had no idea where we were walking, but it was our intention to get as far away as possible from the fighting.

After an hour of walking under the hot sun, we met a number of baggage carts passing along the highway. They belonged to the British Army and were going, like ourselves, in the direction of Bareilly. One of the Sikh escorts saw us, and took pity on our condition. Mother had a high fever, and kept asking to be left alone by the wayside while we went on and found a place of safety. Nasim Khan dismounted and put her up on his horse, while he walked alongside, supporting Mother with his hands. At this moment another accident took place.

As Nasim Khan was dismounting, his pistol went off. This threw us all into panic once more.

Nasim Khan looked puzzled and turned round several times before he realized what had happened. 'Oh, how stupid of me!' he exclaimed. 'I had cocked it when we met the Maulvi's men. But, as usual, it goes off only when the enemy is out of sight!'

The Sikh soldiers burst into laughter, and we could not help joining in, though our own laughter was rather hysterical. Then the Sikhs offered us a lift in one of the baggage carts and Anet, Vicky and I gratefully accepted it, for we were completely tired out.

We journeyed on like this for another three or four miles until we reached a small village where we were offered shelter. As it was now afternoon, and there was no shelter in the baggage cart from the blazing sun, we were only too glad to accept the villagers' hospitality.

Two days later, having hired a cart, we proceeded towards the south and, avoiding the main highway, reached Fatehgarh after four days. There we joined up with Mr Redman's party; and Mother called on the Collector, who gave her some 'succour-money', which enabled us to continue our journey to Bharatpur in comparative comfort. Ten days later we were in the home of my uncle, where we found rest, shelter and comfort, until a rumour that a rebel force was about to cross the territory threw us all into a panic again. It was only a rumour. But the trials of the past year had made such an impression on my mind, that I was often to wake up terrified from nightmares in which I saw again those fierce swordsmen running through the little church, slashing at anyone who came in their way. However, our troubles were really over when we arrived at Bharatpur, and we settled down to a quiet and orderly life, though it was never to be the same again without my father.

We did not hear again of Lala Ramjimal and his family. We would have liked to thank him for his kindness to us, and for risking his own life in protecting us; but beyond the knowledge that he had settled with his family in Bareilly, we received no further news of him.

We heard that Kothiwali and Qamran and their families eventually returned to Shahjahanpur, after life had returned to normal. But Javed Khan disappeared and was never seen again. Perhaps he had escaped into Nepal. It is more probable that he was caught and hanged with some other rebels. Secretly, I have always hoped that he succeeded in escaping. Looking back on those months when we were his prisoners, I cannot help feeling a sneaking admiration for him. He was very wild and muddle-headed, and often cruel, but he was also very handsome and gallant, and there was in him a streak of nobility which he did his best to conceal.

NOTES

Pathans formed thirty per cent of the Muslim population of Shahjahanpur (Muslims forming twenty-three per cent of the entire population) according to the 1901 census. Most were cultivators, although many were landed proprietors of the district. (True Pathans are descendants of Afghan immigrants.) 'Their attitude during the Mutiny cost them dear, as many estates were forfeited for rebellion.' (*Gazetteer*)

Most of the rebel leaders were either killed or brought to trial, and in all cases their property was confiscated. Ghulam Qadir Khan died shortly after the reoccupation and his estates were seized.

'The number of Muslims whose services (to the British) were recognized was extremely small, as, apart from the two men who sheltered their European kinsman, Mr Maclean, in pargana Tilhar, the only persons recognized were Nasir Khan and Amir Ali of Shahjahanpur, who buried the bodies of the Englishmen murdered on the occasion of the outbreak, and Ghulam Husain, who saved the commissariat buildings from destruction and for some time protected several Hindus on the district staff.' (p. 150, *Gazetteer*, 1900)

'At Jalalabad, the tehsildar Ahmed Yar Khan at once showed his sympathy with the rebels by releasing several criminals under arrest. On the arrival of Ghulam Qadir at Shahjahanpur, the tehsildar was raised to the dignity of *nezim*, but his tyranny aroused the resistance of the Rajputs of Khandar and other villages.' (p. 248, *Gazetteer*)

'Mr Lemaistre, a clerk in the Collector's office, was killed in the church, and the fate of his daughter is unknown.' (*The Meerut Mofussilite*, 1858)

The city was populated by a large body of Afghans sent there by Bahadur Khan (a soldier of fortune in the service of Jehangir and later, Shahjahan), at that time serving beyond the Indus. The story goes that these Afghans belonged to fifty-two tribes and that each had its own mohalla, many quarters of the city to this day being named after Pathan clans ... the history of the town and of Bahadur Khan's family is told in an anonymous work called the *Shahjahanpurnama* or the *Anhar-ul-bahr*, written in 1839, and also in the *Akbar-i-Muhabbat* of Nawab Muhabbat Khan.

I first heard the story of Mariam and her daughter from my father, who was born in the Shahjahanpur military cantonment a few years after the Mutiny. That, and my interest in the accounts of those who had survived the 1857 uprising, took me to Shahjahanpur on a brief visit in the late 1960s. It was one of those small UP towns that had resisted change, and there were no high-rise buildings or blocks of flats to stifle the atmosphere. I found the old church of St Mary's without any difficulty, and beside it a memorial to those who were killed there on that fateful day. It was surrounded by a large, open parade ground, bordered by mango groves and a few old bungalows. It couldn't have been very different in Ruth Labadoor's time. The little River Khannaut was still crossed by a bridge of boats.

THE SENSUALIST

CHAPTER ONE

✧

When you hold him in your two hands, you should first
honour him duly and then devour him. You will find
him with flesh upon his bones, but leave him as the
remnants of a fish, which are spines and skin. But what
am I saying? Even when there is no flesh left, you shall
by no means cast the bones aside till you have cracked
them and sucked the marrow. He must be left incapable
of work, unable even to stumble, with wandering glances,
emptied, broken, finished . . .

Damodaragupta, The Lessons of a Bawd,
(8th century A.D.)

THIS RANGE IS BARE and rocky, with steep hillsides suddenly
rearing up in front of the tired, discouraged traveller. The grass
is short and almost colourless. An eagle circles high overhead
and the burning sun, striking through the rarefied atmosphere, is
reflected from the granite rocks. Waves of banded light shimmer
along the dusty mountain path. I walk alone and I am thirsty.

The last stream disappeared into the valley ten miles back, and
this region seems to be devoid of any kind of moisture. The
villages, the terraced fields, have been left behind. The pine
forests are a purple blanket on the next mountain. I have a long
way to go to reach the river and the town. I must have taken the
wrong path sometime back, but this doesn't worry me very
much. I have lost my way in the hills before and found it again

simply by following the line of a valley; but I will not reach the river tonight. It is already half-past three and the September sun is low in the sky.

I have a strong desire to sit down and rest but there is no shade anywhere except under the big boulders which look as though they might topple over at any moment. Huge lizards bask on the rocks, scuttling away at my approach. Where do they get their moisture? Some subterranean pocket of water must exist here to sustain these creatures, because except for the eagle, I find no other sign of life.

But this path must lead somewhere. There are no muletracks, no imprint of human feet to give me confidence, but no mountain path can exist without someone to wear down the sharp rocks and prevent the grass from growing. Someone, at some time, must pass this way, and beyond the next hill there should be a village and grass that is green; perhaps a lime tree with a patch of fragrant shade and a glass of sour curds and a draw at the hookah.

Even while I dream of it, I find a patch of emerald grass at my feet, and trickling through it a sliver of clear water. It comes from a rock in the hillside. Just below the rock the water runs into a small pool made by the human hand, and it is the overflow from this that runs across the path. I drink from the little pool and find the water cool and sweet. I splash my face and let the water run down my neck and arms. Then, looking up, I notice a cave high up on the hillside, with the narrowest of paths leading up to it. There will be shade there and a place to rest.

I clamber up the steep path. The dazzling sun leaps on me like a beast of prey, but I climb higher with the aid of rocks and tufts of grass. The sky turns round and round. Never has it looked so blue.

*

There is someone squatting, crouching at the entrance to the cave. As the sun is in my eyes, I cannot be sure if the creature is human or animal. It doesn't move. It is black and almost formless.

But as I come nearer, it takes the shape of a man.

He is naked except for a tightly wound loincloth. Long, matted hair falls below his shoulders. The ribs show through his chest. His skin has been burnt black by the sun and toughened into old leather by the dry wind that sweeps across the mountains. The eyes are bright black pinpoints in a cavernous face.

'It is some time since I had a visitor.' His voice is deep, sonorous.

I stare at this creature who looks like primitive man but speaks like an angel.

'I lost my way,' I explain.

'I had intended that you should. In a moment of weakness I felt a need for human company, and sent my thoughts abroad to confuse the mind of the first traveller who rounded the bend of the next mountain!'

'I was certainly confused. I hope you will be able to set me on the right path again.'

'All in good time. Will you not sit down here in the shade? I assure you that I am perfectly harmless. I am not even an eccentric, as you might think. For that matter, I am not even lonely. It was just a whim that made me desire your company. I hope you don't mind?'

'No.'

I do not know what to make of him as yet. Here is a recluse who has obviously spent a long time far from the haunts of men. I do not expect him to think or speak like other men. I realize that my norm is not his, and that, living entirely within himself, he must have attained dimensions of thought that are beyond my reach. The question that troubles me is, 'Can he harm me physically?' I am not afraid of the power of his thoughts, for I have confidence in my own.

He sits in the dust, and as there is no sign of anything resembling a comfortable seat, I drop to the ground, some five feet away from him. It is hot sitting there in the sun, but the only shade is inside the cave, and I do not feel inclined to enter that place. Besides, it will soon be evening and it will be cooler.

CHAPTER TWO

໖**&**

THE RECLUSE LOOKS AT me, sizing me up, and I recognize the eyes of one with hypnotic gifts. I look away from him, although I know that it is not necessary for hiin to look at me in order to enter my mind. This is purely a defensive reaction on my part. I can feel the weight of his consciousness and I am immediately aware that he bears no hostility towards me. No action or word of his can make me feel easier than the aura of hopelessness that emanates from his mind, communicating itself to me.

'I suppose you practise many austerities,' I say. 'I admire men who can withdraw from the world, from a life of the senses. But I am not sure that I would want to do the same.'

'You haven't had enough of the senses, perhaps.'

'Did you have too much?'

'Yes, but that was not the only reason ...' He gives me an enigmatic half-smile and I wonder, how long has he been here, and how old is he? It is impossible to tell from his appearance. He might have been here five years or an eternity.

'Perhaps you are hungry?' he asks.

'No. I ate at noon. I was very thirsty, but the spring at the bottom of the hill quenched my thirst. What do you get to eat here?'

'I eat very little. My existence is not entirely supernatural—not yet, anyway—and I must sustain this body of mine a little longer. But I have managed to destroy my former interest in food, and my body gets along quite well on the nourishment it receives. It is a question of conditioning, I suppose.'

'At some stage in your life you received formal education,' I observe.

'Oh yes, a fairly good education, although I never completed a single course. The learning I acquired has made it all the more difficult for me to accept this life. I love books. Therefore I do not keep books.'

'But why? Why give up what you love?'

'One can't give up some things and keep others. To reject the materialism of this life one must reject even the pleasures of the intellect. Otherwise, accept it fully—as I did once—and savour the delights of the senses to the full. Don't do things by half-measures. I never believed in the middle way, in moderation in all things. It never satisfied me. I took every pleasure there was to take, and then, satiated, I took my leave of the world and all that it meant to me.'

'With no regrets?'

'With every regret.'

'Then, I ask again—why?'

'I can give you a hundred answers to your question, and all of them would be right, and yet none of them would be right. For there is not one answer, but many.'

He rises to stretch himself. He does so with a single elastic movement, without the help of his hands. There is hardly any flesh between his skin and his bones, but his skin is as tough as buffalo-hide. He must be impervious to wind and weather.

He looks out over the bare rolling hills and the valley and at the silver river twisting across the distant plain like some mythological serpent. It is the great river we see, most sacred of rivers. To bathe in its waters is to wash away all sin.

'Have you come from Kapila?'

'I am on my way there.'

Kapila lies on the banks of the river where it emerges from a gorge in the mountains. It is an ancient city, much favoured by the sages of old.

'The stones by the river are beautifully smooth,' he says. 'Once, picking one up I took it between my hot hands, polishing it with care. I did not find it round enough, and I threw it far into the river so that the water might rub away its angles for a few thousand years longer. To me, as to a stone, a thousand years are but a day.'

He sinks to his haunches again and his long hair falls across his shoulders hiding his face from me. Although he has rejected the past, he cannot help brooding upon it. We cannot destroy our memories until we have succeeded in destroying ourselves.

'Are you comfortable?' he asks.

'Not very, but I did not expect to find comfort here.'

'There are some old rugs and skins inside.'

'I am all right. It is cool out here.'

'The nights are cold. You will sleep in the cave with me?'

'I should be on my way.'

'You cannot reach Kapila tonight. There is no shelter between this place and the river.'

I do not say anything. I have a feeling that the cave will not welcome me. It has about it an aura of damp and decay, the sweetness of a corpse soaked in scented water. But at the same time I feel that if this recluse really wants me to stay, I will find it difficult to resist his will. Those who live alone can be very strong. Having mastered their own minds (or gone mad in the attempt), they have little difficulty in mastering the minds of others.

I see the pine-tops dipping gently on the next mountain, and a little later I feel the evening breeze on my cheeks. I am still young, and a cool uplifting breeze always stirs me to the marrow. It is the best aphrodisiac in the world.

CHAPTER THREE

'THE BODY OF A woman,' he says, as though something of what I have been musing on has reached him, 'the body of a woman is an inexhaustible source of wonder and delight.'

I look at him with unfeigned surprise.

'Oh, of course I have finished with all that,' he says. 'That is obvious, isn't it? But, looking at me, you might get the impression that I have always been celibate. Nothing could be further from the truth. As a youth, I had an insatiable appetite for pleasure. It overrode all other considerations, I moved from one conquest to another in the single-minded pursuit of sexual pleasure. I suppose it was partly due to the woman servant who looked after me as a boy. She had some crazy idea that I was gifted with supernatural powers in these matters. She gave me strange potions and concoctions to drink!

'She was a big woman with broad hips and flesh buttocks that quivered at every stride. Early every morning, even before the sun was up, she took me down the steps to bathe in the cold waters of the river. There was hardly anyone about at that time. Her huge, heavy breasts smelling of musk brushed against my cheeks as she poured the powerful waters over my head. She held me firmly between her thighs and laved my back with her rough hands. Later, in the small courtyard of our house, she would massage my limbs with mustard oil and with her fingers she would press at the root of my penis, a sensation both painful and pleasurable.

'Sometimes, when my parents were away, she would make me lie down with her, lie down upon her naked and mountainous flesh, and she would take my mouth between her heavy lips and thrust her tongue against mine. This kissing was always pleasurable and I never tired of it. I was a merry monkey, full of good intentions, trying to satisfy an elephant!'

'Stop!' I say, unable to control my laughter. 'Why do you tell me all this?'

'I thought you wanted to hear my story.'

'Did I say so? Well, I didn't think you would be so explicit.'

'Would you like a more romantic tale?'

'No. Carry on. Just so you finish it quickly and let me go my way.'

'Would you hear more of this woman who instructed me in the hidden arts of pleasure?'

'If she is relevant . . .'

*

'Oh, but she is relevant. She was the sorceress who helped me become, not a god, but a satyr! There has been no romance in my life, no "falling in love" as you call it—except, perhaps, once, oh yes, once! From the beginning I was trained in the art of seduction, in the art of extracting from a woman all that she had to give— exhausting her, drawing on her hidden resources, feeding on her like a vampire, until she had nothing to give and was completely destroyed. Of course I did not reach this stage at that early age; but already at puberty, I was working towards it, I felt certain powers growing within me. It was power that I sought, not simply the appeasement of lust.

'A man who lived beside the river taught me to concentrate, to channelize my thoughts in such a way that I could gain a measure of mastery over the minds of others ... every day, for an hour, I sat cross-legged on a smooth earthen floor and gazed steadily at a small black phallus placed a few feet away from me. As I gazed upon the stone, it seemed to grow before me, swelling and throbbing, and I experienced the sensation of having discarded my own sack of a body to enter the substance of the stone. It was only momentary. A spider crawling over my foot brought me back to the reality of my material self. Many hours of concentration were to pass before I could ignore the movements of spiders or insects.

'At home I practised before a mirror, concentrating on the space between my eyebrows. This was strenuous at first, and a throbbing headache would often result. But after a few weeks I found I could stand before the glass for an indefinite period, concentrating on the space between my eyes.

'I concentrated on sounds. I could close my eyes, admit into my mind one sound—the tinkling of a bell, or the dip of a tap— and live with that sound, to the exclusion of all else. After some time, the tinkle would become the clanging of many great bells or the drip of the tap would be a thunderous waterfall. I had to be shaken out of the trances I had entered. My mother was worried about my strange behaviour. My father, whose many business interests absorbed his own sexual drive, could not be bothered. Only the woman servant, my mentor and aide, was pleased. Who was she and where did she come from? Nobody seemed to know. She had come to our house soon after I was born and had made herself so useful that my parents kept her even after I was long past my childhood. She had no children of her own but it was said that she had been married once, that her husband had died and left her very rich and that she had squandered her money on some obscure cult. The more orthodox did not recognize this cult and associated it with sorcery.'

'Well, it was sorcery of a kind.'

'Slowly I was developing my adolescent will to a point where I could impose it on others. I found it easier to do this when I closed my eyes. Then I could shut out all visual distractions and direct my thoughts towards the person I wished to influence. The first time I succeeded in doing this I thought it was purely accidental. Perhaps it was, that first time; but its success gave me confidence in my growing powers.

'It was a warm, languid afternoon and I felt the slow turning of desire as I lay on the string cot in the bedroom. Through the half-open door I could see our servant stretched out on her cot, her waist bare, her hair loose, her lips slightly parted, her eyes only half-closed. (Even when she was sound asleep, her eyes were never completely closed.) Desire welled up' within me. I longed for her harsh kisses and rough caresses. But nothing was possible with my mother present, and I found myself wishing that I could be so gifted with magic powers that I would be able to make people disappear (or appear) at will! This, I knew, could only be achieved after hundreds of years of training, and one had first to learn to live a hundred years! Our thoughts are so tame and timid to begin with that we seldom realize, until it is too late, what concentrated powers lie untapped in our minds. And for those who learn too quickly, there is madness . . .

'But I turned towards my mother, and closing my eyes, directed my thoughts at her, willing her to leave the room, the house—go anywhere, do anything, until I willed her back again. For five minutes I assaulted her in this way, and when I opened my eyes I found her staring at me with a rather bewildered expression.

'"What time is it?" I asked.

'She glanced at the small gold watch on her wrist and said, "It is only three ... Is there anything you want?"

'"No, but you asked me to remind you to go out at three o'clock." She had not made such a request but did not seem surprised at the suggestion. She got up slowly, stretched herself and went to the mirror to arrange her hair.

'"I have to go out at three," she said. "But I forget what I wanted ..."

'"You were to visit someone."

'"Yes, that's it. Thank you for reminding me. It's your cousin Samyukta's birthday. Would you like to accompany me? They are always asking about you."

'"No. I do not like them. Besides, I have a headache."

'"Then I will wake Mulia and tell her to press your forehead."

'"It's all right, Mother. I will wake her myself when you have gone. Let her sleep a little longer."

'Mulia had been awake for some time and she came to me as soon as my mother left the house and began pressing my forehead, rubbing her thumbs over my eyelids and then pressing gently down on my temples. I let her do this for some time. I did have a headache, due perhaps to the effort I had made in shifting my mother from the house! It soon went, however, thanks to Mulia's ministrations.

'The voluptuous creature soon stood before me in all her monstrous beauty, a feast for the eye, a mountain worthy of conquest. I have never understood the misguided attitude of most people to heavy, fleshy women, who are generally considered ugly. Surely, in the generous abundance of their flesh, their broad dips and curves and gradual inclines—bodies where the questing lover may wander freely and unhindered, where he can stop and rest, or turn a corner and discover some hidden recess—surely these magnificient women have a marked superiority over those of a more conventional build? They have so much more to offer!

'Why go into detail? The memory no longer excites me and

would only disturb your own peace of mind. I'm only trying to give you some idea of my development as a destructive force. Suffice it to say that my former governess was as thrilled as I at the achievement, and now declared herself to be my devoted paramour.

'Nor was it simply a matter of having qualified as a lover. The physical conquest was only half the victory. It could not have been achieved so completely without my having gained some command over her personality. Mulia had of course always intended that I should be hers. In spite of her imposing proportions, the strength of her arm and her delightful witchcraft, her instincts were truly feminine. She had sought to conquer me only in order that she might be conquered. I had yet to impose my will on someone who resisted it. I had yet to enslave someone who held me in hatred and contempt. That would be the real challenge—the conquest, the ego-destruction of someone who had so far remained inviolate!'

Chapter Four

'I MUST GO NOW,' I say. 'It is not yet dark. I can be at the river before ten o'clock.'

'I advise you to stay,' urges my 'host'. 'It is not safe to walk these hills at night.'

'I am not afraid of wild animals.'

'Nor should you be, by day. But at night who is to tell which is beast and which is demon? For the evil spirits of these mountains, chained to the rocks by day, move abroad at night.'

'Do they trouble you, then?'

'They do not trouble me. I am too powerful for any kind of spirit save one—the spirit of an innocent! But come inside, it is getting cold out here.'

'It is dark in the cave.'

'I have a lamp. You have nothing to fear if you are pure at heart. Have you ever destroyed the soul of another human?'

'No.'

'Then what have you to fear?'

'Those who destroy souls.'

'Ah! Then you need not fear me, because I destroyed my last soul, my own, a long time ago.'

It is cold but dry inside the cave, which extends for some twenty feet into the side of the mountain. I sit down on a goat-skin and watch the recluse making a fire at the entrance to the cave.

'I will prepare some food for you,' he says.

'No, don't bother. I am not hungry.'

'As you wish. But I will light the fire to keep the animals away. Sometimes I am visited by a leopard or a hyena.'

The fire throws a warm red glow over his emaciated frame, and for a moment or two, as his shadow leaps across the walls of the cave, he seems a little larger than life. When he turns to me, his body comes between me and the fire, and he is now a crouching black phantom, featureless, faceless, formless, who might at any moment leap upon me in the dark to suck the blood from my fingers and feet. But his voice, as always, reassures me.

'Do you mind if I talk?' he asks.

'Not at all. I have no desire to sleep.'

'Nor have I. When I sleep, I am defenceless. Then my mind is invaded by sirens and beautiful women with twisted feet, and young maidens covered with boils, and they ravish me and I am helpless against them. By day, I am master of my own mind, and remembered flesh cannot touch me.'

'So you have not entirely escaped the world you left behind.'

'It is another world that invades my soul. Sometimes I sit up into the early hours of the morning, so that I may avoid these visitations. For when they possess me, they drain me of all my strength, as I once drained others of their life-blood. But I will not trouble you with a tale of torment. I will tell you instead, of the powers I developed as a youth, and what use I put them to! Did I mention my cousin Samyukta?

'I did not like her and she did not like me. We bore each other hatred and malice—and that was enough to make us physically attractive to each other.

'She was a pretty girl, but coy and very aloof, and I resented her airs and graces. I was never much to look at, and whenever we were in the same room she behaved as though I did not exist, although she was perfectly aware of my presence. She did her best to humiliate me. If she said anything, it was to comment on the careless way in which I dressed. But I was indifferent to my appearance. People were not impressed with me until I spoke to them or until they came within the ambit of my questing mind. Once I was certain of my powers, I could dominate most individuals; but certain barriers had first to be broken down.

'Samyukta and I were of the same age, and at the time I am telling you about, we were seventeen or eighteen. Mulia now called me her young stallion. But cousin Samyukta, unaware of my gifts, treated me with contempt and laughed at me whenever we passed each other on the road.

'I had always looked away at her approach, and that had been my mistake. But my joustings with Mulia had given me a new confidence in the presence of women, and I knew that my cousin, for all her supercilious ways, was not very sure of herself. One day I saw her walking along the opposite pavement, accompanied by two girls, school friends. Before she could notice me, I crossed the road and was standing in her way. She gave a start, but before she could speak (and her words were to be avoided, for they were as poisoned barbs), I fixed her eye with mine and held her motionless, while her expression changed from scorn to bewilderment to fear. At that moment, I am sure she felt I was capable of doing her violence. Later when we grew intimate, she swore that during that unexpected encounter she had seen a small yellow flame spring up in my right eye. I remember that she went pale, and when I saw her colour change I knew I had gained the ascendancy. I was so thoroughly aroused that I had difficulty in restraining myself from touching her on the street, in the presence of her friends. When I stood aside to let them pass, the colour flooded back to Samyukta's face, and she went strutting up the street, head in the air, as though she had just given me the snub of a lifetime.

'I smiled inwardly and walked home to Mulia. I told her of my intentions. She was not jealous. Knowing that she possessed my heart, she was prepared for others to possess my flesh.

'"But how do we arrange this?" I asked. "How do we get her here?"

'"We do not get her here. You go there, prince."

'"But she has a mother and an aunt."

'"They go out together on Saturday mornings. And on Saturday mornings Samyukta does not go to school. She prepares the midday meal, while her mother and aunt relax in the bazaar."

'"You are well informed, Mulia."

'She gave me a look of slavish devotion, took my hand and put my fingers to her lips. "You will never tire of me, will you?"

'"I will tire of you when you are old."

'"Ah! At least you do not try to deceive me."

'"You are not to be deceived."

'"No, but I am happy that you have told me the truth. I will preserve my burden of a body for another five, perhaps ten years, for as long as you desire it, and then I will go away."

'The next day Samyukta and her mother visited us. I did not make my presence felt, but sat quietly in a corner of the room, while tea was served. The woman talked about other women, the price of vegetables and the horoscope of a certain young man who might be a suitable match for Samyukta. My cousin sat between her mother and mine, saying very little, but occasionally casting a glance in my direction. Outwardly, I paid no attention to her, but after some time I closed my eyes, and conjuring up a vision of her face, dwelt upon it for some time, turning my thoughts towards her, creating a flow of mental energy that I hoped would reach her in waves of telepathic power! My intention, of course, was to impose my will on her in such a way that she would be absolutely receptive when the right opportunity brought us together. I wanted to be sure of her response well in advance.

'When I opened my eyes, I gazed full upon Samyukta. Her eyes were drawn inexorably to mine, and for more than minute we gazed intensely at each other, until even our mothers could not help noticing.

'"Why are you staring so?" asked Samyukta's mother, who was facing her daughter and had her back to me.

'And my mother, who could not see Samyukta's face said, "Do not stare like that, my son. You frighten me."

'My mother, a nervous creature, had in fact grown afraid of me during the past year or two. She could sense certain changes taking place in me without being able to understand them. She knew that Mulia and I were very close, and while she was relieved that I did not make too many demands on her, she was uneasy because I went to the servant woman with my confidences. Already dominated by my father, my mother was not one to assert herself in any way. She was content to put away money for my "future" and to make occasional donations to the temples. She was certain that there was only one way into the hearts of the gods, and that was through the hands of the priests.

'And so, because my mother was frightened by my look, I turned my face to the window. A band of hermaphrodites was passing by in the street. Just then I longed to be one of them, the perfect synthesis of man and woman.

'Could Samyukta and I uniting lose our genders in each other and be as perfect as the hermaphrodites? For a few moments, perhaps; and then, uncoupled, we would lose ourselves again until guided by the itching of desire, we took refuge once more in each other's embrace.'

*

'When the confrontation did take place about a week later, it came as something of an anti-climax. She was no novice. There was no pearl to prise loose from its shell, no citadel to lay waste. Even so, it must have been a novel experience for her, because she did not expect an assault as fierce as mine. She swooned away before the hour was up. I waited until she opened her eyes, and then I assailed her again, until she moaned and scratched and bit. I had expected to stain her bed crimson with my lust. Instead it was she who drew blood. My arms and shoulders bore the wounds for weeks. Men have nothing to teach women. We can subdue women but we cannot teach them anything!

'Are you listening? Good. I am not trying to lecture you, nor do I wish to titillate you with an erotic tale. There is a principle contained in life that is more powerful than life itself. The body's rapture cannot be divorced from the rapture of the soul. It took me a long time to realize this. Certainly, at the age of eighteen, I had no thought for my soul. I believed in nothing, only love and its pleasures; and the strengthening of my mind and will was carried out with the object of gratifying my senses. I had no ambitions other than to glory in the delights that are there for all those who seek them—I was not interested in power or position. My father had money, and I was his only son. Therefore my first duty was to spend his fortune.

'My father, a man I hardly knew, had spent a lifetime in amassing wealth. He manufactured electric bulbs, shoe polish and a hair-darkening cream. (The same ingredients went into both polish and cream.) On those rare occasions when he entertained his friends, he liked to tell them about the struggles of his youth and how he hawked his wares on the streets of Delhi. Although he had never been to school, he was determined that his son should receive the best possible education. After I had taken my degree, he would send me to Oxford!

'The thought of spending half my life in college horrified me. I was determined to fail my exams in order that I might discourage my parents from sending me to college. My father had lakhs of rupees, and competent managers to run his factories. I would be quite happy to take the money and leave the factories in the capable hands of his managers—they would see to it that the business continued to bring in profits. I could see no point in hoarding wealth and believed it to be a son's first duty to spend money as fast as his father could make it.

'My mother seemed to think so too, because though she was frugal by nature, she tried to get me the money I needed for my clothes, rings, watches, entertainments and wines. She always gave me what I wanted, even if it meant dipping into her own allowance.

'My affair with cousin Samyukta was to last for over a year. But in the course of it I was to have several other adventures, some of them rather expensive. But I cannot dismiss Samyukta so quickly. She was a girl of some character, and when I look back on that wild and wilful time I realize that she had more to offer than most of the professional courtesans whom I visited from time to time. She did not give herself to me for mercenary reasons. I was a challenge to her own strong sensuous nature, and she matched my aggressive skills with her own passionate and fevered responses. She was one of those restless women whose physical demands can never be wholly satisfied. If I was with her, she was happy and satisfied; but if a few days passed and I could not visit her, she grew pensive, irritable, burning up in the fever of her own desire. We grew to like each other. That's strange, isn't it? Because we had never liked each other before.

'But of course there were a few other adventures.

'A youth of eighteen who suddenly finds himself a sexual warrior becomes quite rampant, and pursues his prey indiscriminately. Too indiscriminately for his own good. The pleasure houses of Kapila were few, and did not offer any very startling attractions. Most of the painted trollops were past their prime, and their patrons had first of all to be bemused with bhang or opium so that they did not look too closely at their battle-scarred partners.

'But there was one who was different . . .'

CHAPTER FIVE

&.

'ONE EVENING, I PUSHED open the door of an old house teetering over the riverbank, and looked into a narrow passage dimly lighted by a green paper lantern. From within came the sounds of flute and sitar. A curtain was drawn back and an old woman came towards me. She was a withered old crone who glanced at me with an enticing leer and led me to the top of a staircase where she took my money with a swooping, gull-like movement. She then led me into a small, dark room where I was able to make out a wide couch, raised just above the floor and decorated with a gay but tattered rug.

'"I will fetch Shankhini for you," she said. "You will be happy with her."

'My eyes gradually grew accustomed to the dim light, and I was able to see the girl who entered the room and closed and bolted the door behind her. She drew near with a composed and friendly manner, as if I was an old acquaintance. And in some ways I suppose I must have been, for to the prostitute, all men are one—unity in diversity!

'Except for a diaphanous wrap of silk and a narrow girdle, the girl was completely naked. She wore white jasmine blossoms in her black hair. She looked little more than a child, although her hips were graceful and well-rounded.

'"Shall I dance?" she asked. "Tell me what you would like me to do."

'"Dance," I said. I had been unprepared for her youthfulness.

'And so she danced beneath the greenish moon of the paper lantern, and the only sound was the soft fall of her feet upon the mat. The heavy door shut out the music downstairs, the street-cries, the hollow boom of the river. It was a dance without music, without sound, and I felt as though those small feet were dancing gently on my heart, on the very source of my life. When the dancing ceased the girl smiled at me with an expression simultaneously wise, childlike and passionate. Looking like a sleek green-gold cat in the light from the lantern, she subsided softly on to the couch beside me. She had been trained in the art of making love. And yet beneath it all lay an undercurrent of innocence. I think this was because she suffered from no feelings of guilt. She had been brought up to please men as though this was her sole duty in life. She had not known and did not seek any other kind of existence.

'She did not let a moment pass in which she did not seem to be giving herself. Her aspect was continually changing. She did not surrender even one of her secrets without giving me an inkling that another still remained to be disclosed.

'"Do you find me beautiful?" she asked. It was her stock question. And I gave her the expected answer: "You are the most beautiful girl I have ever seen."

'She smiled at me with her large, childlike eyes. Then her head came between me and the lantern, and her face seemed to be framed in a halo of green light.

'"Forget everything," she said. "Here there is no time, neither night nor day."

'"Let me do something for you," I said, feeling suddenly generous towards this girl. "Let me give you something."

'"I take nothing," she answered. "It is for the old woman to take. You must only tell me that I am beautiful and that I have made you happy."

'"You are very beautiful. You make me very happy."

'"I have heard it a hundred times. But I still like to hear it." And then, drawing close to me and gazing into my eyes she said, "You are very important to yourself, are you not?" She raised her hand to my brow, and tapping my temples with her painted fingers, said: "There is a cold fire there! It is stronger than all other flames, and seems brighter. It fights against the warmth of the heart, and will quench the fire of many hearts. So you must always move from one to another. What are you looking for? There is nothing to find. Forget everything. Love me, and forget!"'

*

'Forget? Can the mind forget? It was written by a sage of old: "Remember past deeds, O my mind, remember!" But the injunction is unnecessary, because we are remembering all the time—even when we say we have forgotten. And can the memory of past deeds really shape the nature of future deeds? Man cannot help but live in conformity with his nature; his subconscious is more powerful than his conscious mind, and he cannot deny his body until he removes himself from the scene of all physical activity. It is useless to struggle against one's nature. Some believe that there is salvation in struggle—they are merely showing that they do not know what salvation is.

'At first I sought to assuage my restlessness by communing with nature. I searched for truth in the rippling of streams and the rustling of leaves; in the blue heavens or the wilderness of the jungle; in the behaviour of men, beasts and plants; in the superabundance of sunshine that pours down in India. But our bodies germinate as the resurrections of nature. Each bubbling spring, swelling fruit or bursting blossom, reminded me that I too was part of this burgeoning process, so that it was not long before the throb in my loins was as tenderly painful as the unfolding of a rosebud.

'I am not trying to give you the impression that those years of youthful dissipation were interspersed with a vague searching for my inner self. Once again, I have anticipated . . . The search, if you can call it that, came later. I am merely trying to tell you how I came to be here. This cave is the end of all searching but before the search there was the indulgence, and the indulgence was a part of the process that brought me to this place.'

CHAPTER SIX

'AND MEANWHILE, I GREW in Mulia's love.

'She tended me as a gardener tends a favourite plant, giving it all the water and nourishment it needs. Special sweets were made for me. Ancient recipes were turned up, and sherbets of many hues and flavours were given to me morning, noon and night. I had given up asking what they contained. I left everything to Mulia. She tried each portion before passing it to me, to make sure that the brew was not too potent. I was convinced that one day I would find her lying dead on the floor, poisoned by one of her own concoctions.

'But I was not the sort of person who could give anything in return for love. As soon as I found someone growing tender towards me, I withdrew into myself, became remote and cold, so that the love that might have been mine was squandered in an empty void. I was determined to leave them with a feeling of insufficiency. Those who gave themselves to me suffered for it. I became cruel and callous towards them. Was it victory I wanted, or the chance to spurn victory? Samyukta was made to suffer in this way. But Mulia, twenty years older than me, was an exception. I seldom withheld my affections from her, I knew that she was wholly for me and with me. My wealth, strength, welfare and happiness were her sole concern. I was the ruling passion of her life and I knew that if I was taken from her, she would lose the impetus for living.

'Shankhini, the woman who lived by night, was in a different category altogether. All men had immersed themselves in her, and she could not be expected to love an individual man any more than a man could be expected to love her. But what was the mysterious attraction that drew me back to her again and again? She had no hold over me. And the old crone who ran the house, certain that I was enamoured with the lithe and boyish figure of this unusual girl, put the price up at every visit. I did not care, I could afford it—or rather my father could afford it. It even gave me a sensuous thrill to hand over the money to the old woman. Not that the old woman excited me in any way; she would have found it hard to arouse a camel! But the business of handing over the money in exchange for an hour or two of personal possession, ownership, of the girl who lived always in green shadows, was a thrill in itself.

'But would I ever be able to arouse her to any degree of rapture? Although I restrained myself, and took the time and trouble to create in her some crisis of response, she seemed incapable of reaching a state of ecstasy and abandonment. There had been too many men, she told me. Coupling with them had become a mechanical process, and there was no intensity or pleasurable sensation in it. She went through the motions, expertly and in order to satisfy those who had paid for the pastime, but she could not be expected to enjoy the game herself.'

*

'So perhaps she was a challenge to me, and that was why I went to her. I wanted to elicit from her a genuine, not a trained response. I think she preferred me to most of her customers, many of whom were pot-bellied businessmen whose overburdened waistlines gave their manhood a shrivelled aspect. Obesity is not conducive to effective love-making.

'It may seem strange, but I liked to talk to Shankhini. In those days, there were few to whom I could talk freely. Mulia was illiterate, and her talk was confined to practical affairs, my needs and bodily functions. She had no other interest outside her small world of service. My mother was old-fashioned and superstitious and so we had very little to say to each other. I hardly ever saw my father. Fellow students at school and college considered me a snob, a wealthy aristocrat, a privileged member of a feudal society. They envied me, and were a little afraid of me too, because unlike others from affluent families, I made no attempt to ingratiate myself with them. Had I lavished money on a few young men, I would soon have had a following, but I had no need of sycophants. I could live with myself, and within myself, provided there were always these women to bear the burden of my ego.

'Samyukta was intelligent, but there was no real meeting of our minds—the relationship was purely sensual in nature. I gave her the satisfaction she needed after she had exhausted herself intellectually. She was studying medicine, and had to work very hard. Whenever she stopped working, she wanted to stop thinking. I could supply no intellectual need, nor was that what she wanted. But when I moved within her, she cried with ecstasy, she was convulsed with joy; but afterwards she had little or nothing to say. She turned over, lay flat on her belly, and slept.

'And so in the evenings, as the lights were lit in the bazaar, and pilgrims placed little leaf-boats filled with rose petals on the waters of the river, I made my way to the tall old house with the green paper-lanterns and asked for Shankhini.

'She was not always available in the evenings. So I took to visiting her in the afternoons, when other men were busy earning a living.

'The old woman told Shankhini I paid well, and so she went out of her way to make me comfortable, to please me and to persuade me to come again. She did this as part of her duty; but it wasn't all commercial enterprise. As familiarity grew between us, we spent some time in talk. What did we have to say to each other? I don't remember much of it, but this strange girl had evolved a philosophy of her own to deal with the situation she found herself in. It was all a question of doing one's duty, she said. Death was a duty, just as much as life was just another way of dying.'

Chapter Seven

It HAS GROWN COLD in the cave. While my ascetic host has been talking, using me as his confessor, the fire has died down. Outside, a jackal complains loudly, and the wind grows restless and rushes up and down the hillside, seeking entry into the cave. But we are well protected by rocks and overhang, and when this twentieth-century cave-dweller adds more sticks to the embers, the flames shoot up again, and the warmth reaches out to me and I reach out to the warmth, move closer, get up and stretch my limbs and then sit down again, while the man's eyes follow me with a bright, probing look.

'So far,' I say, 'so far, you have not told me anything very startling about yourself. You did nothing that would account for your giving up the pleasures you have described. I envy you some of your exploits, but they are not in themselves extraordinary. Many young men have visited prostitutes and have even found sensitive souls among them. And many young men have sought to go through their father's money. Some have sunk by stages into a hell of squalor and have been quite happy wallowing in their own filth. You did not sink very low. Your obsessions were not those of the pervert or psychopath. You were perhaps slightly more obsessed with sex than most, but apart from that your sex life appears to have been remarkably normal! Many young men would have done the same, given the opportunity.'

'I made my opportunities. I imposed my will on others. I cared for no one but myself.'

'I concede that.'

'And I am not even halfway through the story.'

'Ah, well, in that case . . . I have no desire to sleep, and it isn't midnight yet. You were talking of Shankhini, the girl with the green-gold body.'

'Yes. She preserved a perfect body, almost as a challenge and a taunt to the shapeless creatures who came to her by day and by night. She gave them their money's worth like a true professional. She was well-versed in all the technicalities of love making. She gave her customers her body but not her soul. She could not love men. Her love went to another, a dark girl from the coast who was also owned by the old woman. One day, entering the room unannounced, I found them in each other's arms, tenderly kissing each other. When they saw me standing there, they drew apart, unhurriedly and without any sense of guilt. Without a glance at me, the dark girl left the room.

"'You should not have come in without calling or knocking," said Shankhini.

"'There was no one about, and your door wasn't locked. Where's the old lady?"

"'She had to go out to collect some money. Sit down, and I will prepare some tea for you."

'I stretched myself out on the couch and asked, "Who was the girl with you?"

"'My friend. Why, did you like her? Would you like to go to her?"

"'I hardly saw her . . .'"

"'She is very beautiful. If you would like to go to her, I will tell the old one."

"'All right. If you don't mind, that is."

"'Why should I mind? It is my business to persuade you to keep coming here. If you tire of one of us, there is always another."

"'I haven't tired of you. I do not even know you as yet. But I thought you would mind because you seemed to like the girl."

"'I love her, but that does not interfere with our work. Men like you will come and go. Nalini and I will still be here."

"'Men like me . . . Am I like other men?"

"'You want the same things, don't you?"

"'No. Most men only want to possess you physically, I want both your mind and your soul."

"'I do not have these things to offer you. I think, I feel, but I cannot share my thoughts and feelings with any man."

"'You can share them with Nalini?"

"'Here is the tea. Drink it, and tell me your pleasure."

'But after drinking the tea, I got up to go. "You are very irritable today," I said. "I will come again." She looked dismayed and urged me to stay. Perhaps she was afraid that I might not come again and that her mistress would be annoyed. The old woman was just outside the door.

"'He would like to see Nalini," said Shankhini.

"'No," I said. "Not today. Some other time."

'It was a frustrating day. Mulia was out shopping. Samyukta's house was full of people. It was as though, for a few hours, I had ceased to exist for them! Although I knew that they were completely unconscious of my restlessness, I harboured feelings of resentment towards them. I was being neglected! I suppose it's the lot of the only son to feel that way.

'I must have given you the impression that as a youth I was obsessed with sex to the exclusion of all else, and that I was devoid of finer feelings. It is true there was a time when I believed that although all men were born equal, some men turned out to be more virile than others!

'As for falling in love, I had no idea what it was about. Loving (I was told) is giving, but at the time I was interested only in taking.

'Have I given you the impression that my life was spent entirely in the company of women? I had not made friends at college, but then, I seldom attended college. I found the lectures boring and a waste of time. I had nothing against books and even read some poetry, but I did not want life second-hand, from books. Mine was not a reflective nature—not then, anyway—and I could not reconcile mental pursuits with the pursuit of physical delight. And what would be the use of a degree in the Arts if I was going to spend the rest of my life helping my father to manufacture electric bulbs?

'When my father asked me to go to Delhi on his behalf, to attend an industrial exhibition that was being held in the capital, I agreed to do so. It was my father's intention to get me involved in the business. I was not interested in industrial exhibitions but I felt like a change from my confined life in Kapila and I set out with a sense of impending adventure. I had no idea where the adventure, if it came, would lead me. My father had given me five hundred rupees, and I would follow my fancy in seeing where it would take me and what I could do with it.'

CHAPTER EIGHT

🐌

'My TRAIN RUSHED INTO the darkness, the carriage wheels beating out a steady rhythm on the rails. The bright lights of Kapila were swallowed up in the night, and new lights—dim and flickering—came into existence as we passed small villages. A star falls, a person dies. I used to wonder why I did not see more shooting stars, because in India someone is dying every minute. And then I realized that with someone being born every half-minute, falling stars must be in short supply.

'The people in the carriage were settling down, finding places for themselves. There were about fifty of us in that compartment sharing the same breathing space, sharing each other's sweaty odours.

'At four in the morning I woke from a fitful sleep to find the train at a standstill. There was no noise or movement on the platform outside. It was a very small station, and the train for some mysterious reason of its own had stopped there longer than usual, so that those in the train who had woken up had gone to sleep again, and those few who had been spending the night on the platform slept on as though nothing had happened. This was not their train.

'I watched them from the window. A very small boy was curled up in a large basket. His mother had stretched herself out on the platform beside him. A coolie slept on a platform bench. The tea-stall was untenanted. A dim light from the assistant stationmaster's office revealed a pair of sandalled feet propped up against a mountain of files. A bedraggled crow perched on the board which gave the station its name: Deoband. The crow cawed disconsolately, as if to imply that this dismal wayside station was none of its doing. And yet—Deoband!—the name struck a chord. Wasn't this, by tradition, the most ancient town in India?

'The engine hissed, sending waves of hot steam into the fresh early morning air. My shirt clung to me. We were all smelling of perspiration. There had been no rain for a month but the atmosphere was humid, there were clouds overhead, dark clouds burgeoning with moisture. Thunder blossomed in the air.

'The monsoon was going to break that day. I knew it, the birds knew it, the grass knew it. There was the smell of rain in the air. And the grass, the birds and I responded to this odour with the same sensuous longing. We would welcome the rain as a woman welcomes a lover's embrace, his kiss, the fierce, fresh thrust of his loins after a period of abstinence.

'Suddenly I felt the urge to get out of that stuffy, overcrowded compartment, away from the sweat and smoke and smells, away from the commonplaces of life, from the certainty of my destination and predestined future. I would be a free wanderer, the last in a world where even the poets had retreated into the sculleries of their minds.

'I knew where I was supposed to be going: Delhi. I knew what I was supposed to do there—take the fatal step towards respectability. To be respectable—what an adventure that would be! And this prospect of an ordered, organized life frightened me. I knew that I could not put it off forever, but perhaps it could be postponed. I had five hundred rupees in my vest pocket. It would provide me with freedom for two weeks, perhaps three if I was not too extravagant. Five hundred rupees; the smell of coming rain; and outside, an unknown town. The combination was too strong for my wayward spirit.

'I clambered over my fellow passengers, my suitcase striking heads, shoulders, backsides. Grunts and curses followed me to the door. And then the train began to move. I was seized with panic. If I didn't get off quickly, I would never get off. I would be frozen forever into a respectable bulb manufacturer!

'I flung the door open and tumbled on to the platform. My suitcase spun away, hit the corner of a bench, burst open. The crow flew off in alarm. A dog began barking.

'The train moved on to Delhi, carrying with it six hundred souls in bondage, while I stood alone on the platform, in temporary possession of my own soul.

'The suitcase, which never locked properly, was soon closed. I looked furtively around. The coolie was still asleep—obviously no one ever got off at Deoband at that hour—or he would have grabbed my insignificant burden, carried it for a distance of twenty feet, and charged me a rupee. I needed my rupees. I could no longer scatter them about at random or live on credit as I did in my home town.

'I walked quietly to the turnstile. There was no one there to ask me for my ticket. I walked out of the station and found myself in a wasteland of nondescript shacks—some of them labourers' huts, some warehouses, one or two of them uninviting tea shops. The scene was a dismal one, and if the train had still been at the station I would have returned to it and gone to Delhi. But so far in my defiance of the gods, I had done quite well, and it would have been admitting defeat to have returned to the station to hang around waiting for another train.

'By evening I was still disconsolately on a small hotel balcony overlooking the street, telling myself that I was a fool. For three hours nothing had happened to me, and now it looked as though nothing was going to happen. There was no Mulia to press my aching limbs, no Samyukta to ravish, no Shankhini to battle with my ego. My only acquisition was a headache from drinking too much of the local beer and sleeping too long under the electric fan.

'The camel had gone from across the street, but in its place was a buffalo. The traffic had increased, there were more people in the street. There were also more flies on the balcony, and one of them came buzzing into my half-empty glass in an effort to drown itself in what remained of my drink. It was a suicidal kind of evening. I rescued the fly from my glass, placed it gently on the balcony railing and watched it crawl groggily away. But my compassion was wasted. As the fly neared the wall, a gecko, chuckling greedily, swooped on the insect and gobbled it up.

'There was no one to talk to. The hotel manager was a moron, and the bearer's thoughts dwelt on the contents of my suitcase. A large drop of water hit the balcony railing, darkening the thick dust on the woodwork. A faint breeze sprang up, and again I felt the moisture, closer and warmer.

'Then the rain approached like a dark curtain. I could see it marching down the street, heavy and remorseless. It drummed on the corrugated tin roof and swept across the road and over the balcony. I sat there without moving, letting the train wet my sticky shirt and gritty hair.

'Outside, the street rapidly emptied. The crowd dissolved in the rain. Stray cows continued to rummage in dustbins, buses and tongas ploughed through the suddenly rushing water. A group of small boys, now gloriously naked, came romping along the street which was like a river in spate. When they came to a gutter choked with rain water, they plunged in, shouting their delight to whoever cared to listen. A garland of marigolds, swept from the steps of a temple, came floating down the middle of the road.

'The rain stopped as suddenly as it had begun. The day was dying, and the breeze remained cool and moist. In the brief twilight that followed, I was a witness to the great yearly flight of insects into the cool brief freedom of the night.

'It was the hour of the geckos. They had their reward for weeks of patient waiting. Plying their sticky pink tongues, they devoured insects as swiftly and methodically as Americans devour popcorn. For hours they crammed their stomachs, knowing that such a feast would not be theirs again. Throughout the entire hot season the insect world prepared for this flight out of darkness into light, and not one survived its bid for freedom.'

*

'I had walked the streets of the town for over three hours, and it was past midnight. Shop fronts were shuttered, the cinema was silent and deserted. The people living on either side of the narrow street could hear my footsteps, and I could hear their casual remarks, music, a burst of laughter.

'A three-quarter moon was up, shining through drifting,

breaking clouds and the roofs and awnings of the bazaar, still wet, glistened in the moonlight. From a few open windows fingers of light reached out into the night. Who could still be up? A shopkeeper going through his accounts, a college student preparing for his exams, a prostitute extricating herself from the arms of a paramour who had suddenly fallen asleep . . .

'Three stray dogs were romping in the middle of the road. It was their road now, and they abandoned themselves to a wild chase, almost knocking me down. A jackal slunk across the road, looking to right and left to make sure the dogs had gone. A field rat wriggled its way through a hole in a rotting plank, on its nightly foray among sacks of grain and pulses.

'As I passed along the deserted street under the shadow of the clock tower, I found a young man, or a boy (I couldn't tell which) sleeping in a small recess under a rickety wooden staircase. He was wearing nothing but a pair of torn, dirty shorts—his shirt, or what was left of it, had been rolled into a pillow. He was sleeping with his mouth open; his cheeks were hollow, and his body, which looked as though it had been strong and vigorous at one time, was emaciated.

'There was no corruption, no experience on his face. He looked quite vulnerable, although I suppose he had nothing much to lose in the material sense.

'I passed by, my head down, my thoughts elsewhere—that is how we of the towns and cities usually behave when we see a fellow human lying in the gutter.

'And then I stopped. It was almost as though the bright moonlight had stopped me. And I started myself with the question, "Why do I leave him there? And what am I doing here anyway?"

'I walked back to the shadows where the boy slept and looked at him again. He seemed a very heavy sleeper, the sort of person who can fall asleep anywhere, at any time, oblivious to all that goes on around him. I coughed loudly, but nothing happened; I whistled, but still he slept; I picked up an empty can and dropped it beside him, but the noise had no effect on the sleeper.

In his dreams he was elsewhere, moving among the spirit-haunted mountains, while his material body lay in this town. I found myself wishing that I could sleep like that—it was the sleep of one who was protected by his own innocence.

'I went down on my knees and touched the boy's shoulder. But he must have been touched often in his sleep. His lips moved slightly, but there was no alteration in the rhythm of his breathing.

'One arm was thrown back, and I noticed a scar under his armpit where the hair began. Looking at that scar, all the warnings of Mulia and my mother crowded in upon me—tales of crime by night, of assault and robbery. But when I looked again at the untroubled face, I saw nothing there to disturb me.

'And since he did not wake, and seemed comfortable, why did I not stand up and walk away and take the morning train to Delhi? I still do not know. Something was pressing me on, urging me to shake the boy out of his slumber.

'I took him by the shoulders and gave him a good shaking. He woke with a loud cry, as from a nightmare, and stared at me with something like terror. He sat up, cringing away, holding his hands before his face. But then, when he realized that I was a man and not the demon of his dream, his fear turned to indignation.

'"Who are you? What do you want?"

'"Nothing," I said, standing up and moving away. '"I did not see you there. I am sorry to wake you."

'I moved a few steps away, then stopped and looked back at the youth. He was still crouching on the steps, still staring at me, but he had lost both his fear and his anger, and he was only a little puzzled by this apparition in the middle of the night.

'"Haven't you anywhere to stay?"

'He shook his head.

'Perhaps the tone of voice I used gave him some confidence, because the hostility left his face and in its place I saw a glimmer of hope.

'I had committed myself. I could not pass on.

'"Do you want a job?" I asked.

'"No."

'"You have money?"

'"No."

'"Do you want some money?"

'"No, babuji."

'"Then what do you want?"

'"I want to go home."

'"Where is your home?"

'"In the hills."

'"Far away?"

'"Yes, babuji. In the Jalan hills."

'"And how much does it cost to get there?"

'"Twenty rupees."

'"And how much have you got?"

'"One rupee."

'He held his torn shirt in his hands. It was his only possession. I liked his open look, the way he returned mine without any attempt at evasion.

'"I'll see that you get home," I said. "On one condition."

'A shadow of doubt passed across his mobile face. (It was no mask, that face.)

'"Babuji—I have never done anything—anything shameful."

'"Shameful? You have not heard my condition. What did you think I was going to ask you to do—sleep with me?"

'He laughed and looked embarrassed.

'I said, "Don't be an ass. I have always taken my pleasure with women. Listen to my condition before you start getting nervous."

'He did not say anything but kept twisting his shirt in his hands—he was no longer looking me in the eye.

'"I was about to say that I'd help you to get home provided you took me with you. I would like to see your hills."

'His dark, sombre face lit up. He smiled like an angel. All the latent hospitality of his tribe welled up and burst through the barrier of his poverty.

'"Oh, I will take you to my home, babuji. I have nothing here, but in the hills I have a house, fields, a buffalo! Yes! I will take you to my home."

'No longer hesitating, he came to me, brimming over with a simple trust and joy. I could not betray that trust, nor could I fail to trust him. I was committed to a stranger in the night. I had sought him out deliberately, imposed my will on him and the consequences of the meeting would be entirely of my own making.

'And so there were two of us on that lonely street. The rain had held off just long enough for the encounter. Soon it began to drizzle.

'"We will go to my hotel," I said. "Have you anything to bring with you?"

'"Nothing," he said. "Yesterday I sold my shoes."

'"Never mind. Let us get some sleep while the night remains with us. Tomorrow, in the morning, we will leave this place. It has served its purpose, and now there is nothing to keep me here. Nothing to bring me back again."

'The boy lay on the mattress which I had removed from the bed and placed on the floor. His face was in darkness but the light from the veranda bulb fell across his legs. There was no escape from my father's bulbs! I lay flat on my belly on the string cot, while the ceiling-fan hummed in the moist air immediately above me.

'"Are you awake?" I called.

'"Yes," said the boy.

'"The mosquitoes make it difficult to sleep. So let us talk. Tell me, how do we get to your village?"

'"It is a difficult place to reach," he said.

'"Well, if it was easy to reach, there would be no point in my going there. Will we have to walk a lot? I have not done much walking."

'"We must walk about thirty miles. But first we must take a train or a bus. Later we walk."

'"Good. And now tell me your name."

'"Roop."

'"You have brothers and sisters?"

'"A brother, no sisters. My brother is younger than me and

goes to school. I never went to school. There was another brother, but he died—he was attacked by a leopard, and the wounds were so bad that he died after several days."

'After a brief silence, he asked, "Why do you wish to visit my home, babuji?"

'"Because it is far away. Because I am bored with my own home. I have a mother and father and servants, but I am bored with all of them."

'Roop was one of those people blessed with the gift of being able to sleep sweetly and soundly through cannon-fire and earthquake. Once he fell asleep, there was little that could wake him. The morning sun embraced him, moved lovingly over his dark gleaming body, touched his eyelids, settled on his untidy hair. Still he did not wake. He slept on as though drugged. I called him, I shouted, I reached out and shook him by the shoulder, but he did not stir. A fly settled on his lips, but although his mouth twitched, he did not open his eyes.

'"One of us will have to get up," I muttered, looking at my expensive smuggled watch which showed nine o'clock. "Otherwise we won't get anywhere today."

'And I wanted to get away as soon as possible. The urge to stop at Deoband had been strong, but the urge to move on was stronger. During the night I had dreamt of pine forests and mountain streams, pale pink flowers growing in the clefts of rocks and fair hill maidens bathing beneath pellucid waterfalls.

'I got up and sprinkled water on Roop's face. Nothing happened. I placed my foot on his broad heavy thigh and shook him vigorously. But he simply smiled. He was still dreaming— of a girl, perhaps; or possibly of the chicken we had eaten on returning to the hotel the previous night.

'I decided that I would have to use some more positive method of rousing Roop. Shaking him was of no use, slapping his face would have been impolite. So I compromised—held the water-jug over his head and kept pouring until he awoke, spluttering and shaking his head and greeting the day (and me) with foul language.

'An hour later—my purse considerably lightened by our short stay at the hotel—we were sitting in a bus and moving hopefully in the direction of the hills.'

CHAPTER NINE

❧

'IT HAD BEEN RAINING all morning, and whenever there were dips in the road, the bus sent up sprays of muddy water. Sometimes the rain came in at the windows and wet my shirt. But I did not close the window, it was too stuffy in the bus, and the reek of cigarettes and beedis added to my discomfort.

'Let us be grateful for neem trees. Their pods had fallen on the roadside, and these, bursting or being crushed against the wet earth by passing vehicles, emitted a powerful but pleasant odour which drifted in through the window on the breeze.

'The road was straight, but the bus was continually having to swerve or brake to avoid coming into collision with the slow and ponderous bullock-carts that came lumbering and creaking down the middle of the highway. In the fields, the ploughing had begun. Long wooden ploughs yoked between two bullocks raked crooked furrows in the softened earth. A heron stood on one leg in a rice field. An egret perched behind a buffalo's ear, searching there for tender insects.

'The buffaloes were of course in their element. With tanks and ditches overflowing, they did not have to search for muddy water in which to wallow through the long hot days. Some were already knee-deep among the water-lilies. Their dung, as always, was precious, and I remember the quaint spectacle of a farmer, realizing that one of his buffaloes was about to give forth riches, taking up his position behind the heaving beast and collecting a generous amount of dung in his arms, even as it fell. Hot and fresh it must have been! A second later, and this precious product would have been lost forever in the lily-pond.

'Yes, I remember that bus ride. Who remembers bus journeys? They are always so monotonous. But I remember that one, because it was a monsoon day and I was moving towards the unknown.

'The bus moved past a score of naked children romping in the rain; past a tonga-load of villagers, drenched but merry; past a young man with a dancing bear; past a sugar factory; past a railway crossing, mercifully open; past a dead cow, dense with vultures; past tiny huts and huge factory buildings.'

*

'I woke to what sounded like the din of a factory buzzer but was in fact the voice of a single cicada emerging from the lime tree near my bed. A faint light was breaking over the mountains. The morning air was quite chill, and I moved closer to Roop for warmth. We had slept out of doors, sharing the same bed.

'His mother and young brother, who slept indoors, had thought me a little strange for wanting to sleep outside. Most hill people prefer to sleep inside the small stuffy rooms of their rough stone houses, even when the nights are warm. It has something to do with their fear of the dark, their belief in demons and malignant spirits who dwell in trees or take possession of the bodies of leopards and sometimes humans. Roop told me that he had seen the ghost of a woman who had been at least ten feet tall, and whose feet faced backwards. His strong belief in demonlore made him reluctant to join me outside; at the same time, he did not want to have his guest spirited off in the night. It would have been impolite on his part to leave me to the tree-spirits. His natural sense of hospitality overcame his naturally superstitious nature, and he joined me on the cot in the bright moonlight. No electric bulbs in his village—I had escaped my father at last!

'Once Roop was asleep, he was immune to all the spirits of the dead, being even more comatose than a corpse. The shrieking cicada had no effect on him. He slept with abandon, one leg thrown over my thigh, an arm hanging down from the side of the bed, his head thrown back, his mouth open in disregard of his own warning that spirits enter people through the mouth.

'As the sky grew lighter, I could see through the pattern of glossy lime-leaves the outlines of the mountains as they strode away into an immensity of sky. I could see the small house, standing in the middle of its narrow terraced fields. I could see the other houses, standing a little apart from each other in their own bits of land.

'I could see trees and bushes, and a path leading up the hill to the deodar forest on the summit. A couple of fruit trees grew behind the house.

'The tops of the distant mountains suddenly lit up as the sun torched the snow peaks. A door banged open. The house was stirring. A cock belatedly welcomed the daylight and elsewhere in the village dogs were barking. A magpie flew with a whirring sound as it crossed the courtyard and then glided downhill. Everyone, everything—except Roop beside me—came to life.'

*

'I was conscious of being observed. There was no one behind me, no one at the foot of the bed. But there was a soft football close by. I closed my eyes, pretended I was asleep. When I opened them, I found myself gazing into light brown eyes flecked with green—the fair complexioned face of Roop's younger brother. He had been looking at me with considerable curiosity because the night before, when I arrived, it had been dark and he had not been able to see me properly.

'When I returned his gaze, he smiled. He did not resemble Roop Singh at all, except in the sturdiness of his physique. He looked sensitive, reserved. The smile was shy, self-protective.

"'Is it time for us to get up?"

'He shook his head. "No, you can sleep. I have to go to school."

"'Your school starts very early."

"'It is very far," he said. "Five miles." And then, anxious to avoid further questioning, he ran off.

'The sun was up. It slipped across the courtyard and into the newly ploughed field and ran over the tips of the young maize that had come up with the first rain. It was time to get up.

'Roop's mother was a strong, handsome widow of about thirty-five. Those with conventional notions of beauty would not have called her good-looking. Some would have thought her ugly. Huge silver earrings passed through the tops of her ears, turning them inwards, elongating them, twisting them out of their natural shape. Those huge, imprisoned ears were inclined to divert one's attention from the rest of her face. The forehead was narrow, but the eyes were large and attractive. The nose was a strong one, having withstood the weight of another large silver ring. She wore a silver bracelet and silver bangles clashed at her ankles. All her savings had gone into silver ornaments. It wasn't safe to wear or keep gold.

'Her voice was deep and resonant without actually being masculine in tone. She had strong hands, large heavy feet—she walked barefoot even on the rocky hillsides.

'Roop was rather afraid of her. The younger brother loved her deeply.

'She gave us a heavy breakfast of curds and black *mandwa* bread and hot sweet tea.

'She did not look directly at me, but all the time I felt that she was watching me.'

CHAPTER TEN

'I WAS TO BE enslaved by this woman in a way that no woman had ever been enslaved by me. As the days passed, I became aware of her strange and powerful matriarchal passion. It was not the passive worship of Mulia, but something quite different.

'Strangely enough, I had not at first thought of her in terms of passion. Her physique did not attract me. True, Mulia was strong too, but that was because she was heavy, a mountain of flesh; otherwise she was a soft, feminine creature. But there was no surplus flesh on this woman of the mountains. She was hard, even muscular. Her feet were longer and much broader than mine. Her legs, which I glimpsed whenever she climbed the steep path to the fields, were the legs of an athlete. She had strong arms and lifted sacks of grass or bags of grain with an ease and facility that would have been the envy of most men.

'There was nothing delicate or pretty about her, but her face was strong and handsome, and her eyes, although lacking tenderness, were expressive and of dark spiritual intensity. She laboured more like a pack-mule than a man, but there were powerful, unquenched fires smouldering within her.

'Three days passed before she spoke to me, and then it was to ask me if I felt tired. Roop and I had returned after a long walk to a famous waterfall. We came back very hungry and with our limbs aching from the effort of climbing up two steep valleys. His mother prepared tea for us and when she handed my glass to me, she looked straight into my eyes and asked, "Are you tired?"

'"Yes," I said. "Very tired."

'"Tomorrow you will rest."

'It rained heavily that night and all next morning.

'Only at noon did the clouds begin to break up and then the sun came through, gleaming gold on the green slopes. I remember a flock of parrots swooping low over the house, their wings flashing red and gold and blue. They settled in the oak trees. Roop Singh had gone to the next village, where there was a shop, to buy salt and soap.

'I walked through the fields till I came to a grassy slope. Then the sun seduced me, and I took off my clothes and lay stretched out on the grass. I fell asleep—for how long, I could not tell—but when I woke, I felt curiously relaxed, languid, even light-headed. I passed my hand over my forehead and felt something sticky; then, looking at my hand, I found it was covered with bright red blood.

'I sat up, and got the fright of my life. My entire body was covered with leeches.

'They had crawled on to me while I was sleeping, had fastened on to my succulent flesh—as you must know, the bite of the leech can hardly be felt—and had then proceeded to gorge themselves on my blood. I now had about thirty leeches on my face, arms, chest, belly, backside and legs. One or two had had their fill and fallen off, leaving tiny punctures from which the blood trickled freely. One particularly fat leech—it was about two inches long—was feeding near my navel. I tried to pull it away, but it was stuck fast.

'I remembered being told that it was a mistake to remove leeches by force. The bite sometimes became septic. They would fall away and dissolve if a little salt was applied.

'I sprang to my feet, gathered up my clothes, and ran naked through the ploughed field until I reached the house. Seeing no one about I rushed indoors, surprising Roop's mother who was lighting a fire.

'If she was surprised at my condition, she did not show it.

'"Look, mother of Roop," I said, addressing her directly for the first time. "I'm covered with leeches. Give me salt."

'She got up from the fire, came nearer to examine me (it was always dark indoors) and said, "There are too many. Come into the other room, I will remove them for you."

'Armed with a container of salt, she led me into the next room and then started applying salt to the leeches. One by one, they squirmed and twisted and fell off.

'As they fell, they burst open and my blood oozed out of their slowly dissolving bodies, staining the floor. Little rivulets of blood kept trickling down from the open wounds on my body, which took a long time to close up.

'"I must have a bath," I said.

'"No. Let the blood dry on you. Only then will the bleeding stop."

'So I sat down on the floor feeling rather foolish, while Roop's mother watched me gravely from their doorway. If only she'd smiled or laughed, I would not have felt so uneasy. But she watched me intently, her seemingly dispassionate gaze taking everything in.

'It was an unusual situation for me. I had been in the habit of gazing upon the attributes of women. Now the positions were reversed, and a woman, fully clad, was studying my anatomy. I felt defenceless, rather as though I was a male spider or scorpion about to be first mated and then devoured by the female.'

*

'She came to me that night. I had been feeling the humidity and slept on the veranda, while Roop, afraid of the early morning chill, slept indoors with his brother.

'I woke from a sound sleep to find someone lying beside me. Automatically, and from force to habit, I moved to one side. I stretched out an arm and my hand encountered those heavy earrings and twisted ears. Hastily, I drew my hand away; but I could not leave the bed. The woman's strong arms were around me, her powerful legs held me in a vice. Her breath, smelling of cloves, almost overpowered me.

'She did not attempt to kiss me. Kissing was obviously something foreign to her nature. But she began to stroke me with her large, rough hands; and aroused, I could not help but respond.

'This was a reversal of the usual role. She was active rather than passive in her attitude.

'Her breasts were huge pendulous things. Her arms and legs were much stronger than mine. Always proud of my virility, I now felt as though I would be inadequate for this woman who did not flinch, but who took me in her powerful arms and pressed upon me until I gasped for breath and wanted to cry for help.

'She did not give me any rest. She worked on me with her hands until I was roused again, and then she mastered me with complacent efficiency. Nothing seemed to happen to her. She could not be satisfied. She was some kind of vampire, a succubus—I swear to it—and she was determined to drain me of my last ounce of manhood.

'Only towards morning, when first light showed in the sky, did she leave me, returning to her own room. I lay limp and exhausted. I had done nothing to quench her passion and I knew that she could overpower me again at the first opportunity.'

CHAPTER ELEVEN

DURING OUR LONG VIGIL in the cave, the fire has gradually died down. It is about four in the morning, and a faint light appears on the snow of the Bandarpoonch massif. I am feeling cold; but with sunrise only two hours away, I am able to summon enough patience and fortitude to bear the gnawing discomfort that has crept over me.

'Well—and then what did you do?' I ask.

'I ran away. Oh, not immediately. That would not have been possible. She watched over me wherever I went. She fattened me up with chicken and gave me strange sherbets to revive my flagging virility. It was Mulia all over again, but I was not the man who had tamed Mulia. I was in the hands of a lioness, a woman far stronger, both mentally and physically, then Mulia had ever been. Whereas once I had imposed my will on others, I now found myself squirming under another's will. Roop's mother fed me on reviving herbs and fluids only in order that she might drain me of my strength. She was a *rakshasni* prepared to reduce me to skin and bone, to suck me dry!'

'And what of Roop—did he know what was happening?'

'He was too simple to comprehend. And he was too busy wenching with the village girls. He was a randy fellow, poor Roop. But the younger brother, he knew ... He would wake up in the night, and tossing about restlessly, he would hope to disturb us, to put an end to the ravishing of my body. But she was in no mood to be bothered by minor distractions.

'And yet, there was a tremendous innocence about the way in which this single-minded woman had stripped me of my manhood and pretensions. Hers was the overpowering innocence of the mountains—I was helpless before it, just a computer lover overpowered by natural forces. She was not a scheming woman. She sought to appease a basic hunger, and she did so without a civilized veneer, without the cover of sophisticated talk. We who have grown up in the cities cannot understand the innocence of mountain people, because we cannot understand the innocence of mountains, high places which have retained their power over the minds of men because they still remain aloof from the human presence, barely touched by human greed. In the cities it is easy to despise those who live in awe of the mountains, because in the cities there are vehicles and noise and lights to hold at bay that fear of the dark which is the beginning of religion; but on the far hills the darkness is still terrible.

'And mountain people still keep some of their primal innocence. It can be disconcerting to one who is accustomed to the corruption of the cities, but unaccustomed to the simple terror and solitude of the hills, I was used to being the ravisher. I was now being ravished.

'Had another man violated me, I would not have found it as humiliating as the experience of being violated by this unlettered woman with the heavy feet and long twisted ears. It was not only my manhood that she stripped; it was my beloved ego.

'Roop's younger brother helped me get away. He had been in sympathy with me from the first, had sensed my predicament, my helplessness.

'Roop's mother had the custody of my suitcase which was locked in the storeroom. Having no need of any money in the village—there was nothing to spend it on—I had kept my remaining cash, about three hundred rupees, in the suitcase. I knew I wouldn't get very far without any money, and I was equally certain that Roop's mother would not give it to me—she had no intention of letting me get away.

'When the boy asked me, "Will you walk with me to my school?", I almost said no. The pleasures of walking did not appeal to me just then. But something in his expression told me that his intentions went deeper than what his words implied. He was not asking me to accompany him, he was urging me to do so.

'Puzzled, I said I'd come. His mother did not try to restrain me—she was confident that I would be back.

'We took the path to the stream, then followed the watercourse for a mile or two until that path forked, one branch twisting up the mountain on our right, the other keeping to the stream and running straight up the valley.

'"I will leave you here," said the boy.

'"Don't you want me to come as far as the school?"

'He shook his head. "No. You should go now." He opened the satchel which contained his school books, and took out my wallet. "The money is all there," he said.

'I took the wallet and thanked him; then I offered him a hundred-rupee note.

'"That is not why I brought it," he said.

'He smiled and started climbing the steeper path. Where the path went round the hillside he turned and waved to me. Then he disappeared round the bend and went out of my life—my first and only friend.'

CHAPTER TWELVE

'SOON IT BEGAN TO rain. But I did not seek shelter. I walked ten miles in pouring rain until I reached the bus terminus. I was very tired when I got there and was tempted to spend the night in one of those seedy little hotels that spring up like mushrooms near every bus-stand; but I was afraid that Roop may have been sent after me, to try and persuade me to return. I caught the last bus to the plains, and the following day I was back in Kapila, secure among the anonymous thousands who throng the waterfront.

'My parents did not ask me too many questions. They were glad enough to see me back. At least, my mother was glad. She did not have long to live and I think she knew it. She had suckled and spoilt me and wanted to see me happy. My father would probably not have minded if I had disappeared for ever. He hadn't much confidence in me, and knew I would never be of any help to him in the business. I've no doubt he was furious with me for having wandered off on my own instead of going to Delhi, but to humour my mother, he said nothing. She thought I'd run away from home. Now that I was back, she was ready to indulge my every whim. Instead of getting less money, I was given more. And if I did not attend college, no questions were asked. No prodigal son ever had it better. And in this way young men are ruined for life.

'Although my mother adored me, under the delusion that I was a favourite of the gods, Mulia fussed over me more like a mother—or rather, like a brooding hen. Who would have thought that I was almost twenty . . .

'Strangely enough, I found that I had grown indifferent to Mulia. Had she changed, or had I? Had she grown older, flabbier, heavier, uglier—or was it that I now looked only for the ugliness instead of for the beauty? The strong odour of her body, which formerly had aroused me so easily, now failed to excite me. Instead I found myself disliking the odour. Strange, isn't it, how things that attract us become, after a period of time, the things that repel us . . .

'I spoke to Mulia as before, but I avoided being alone with her. If my mother went out, I found some excuse for going out too. Mulia was constantly seeking opportunities for being alone with me; I was ever alert, ready to slip away.

'Still, the confrontation had to come.

'I slept late one morning and did not know that my mother had gone out early. The air of September was warm and humid, and I lay on my bed in singlet and shorts, watching the lizards scuttle about on the walls. Then the door opened and Mulia entered the room.

'She had bathed, she had perfumed her hair and she looked quite magnificent as she stood there before me, with the sun from the open window slanting across her great quivering breasts. She lay down beside me and began to caress and stroke my limbs almost as though she worshipped my body. And although you may not believe it now, my body once had all the attributes of the perfect male physique. I was slim-waisted like a pipal leaf, with fine broad shoulders; and my thighs were like plantains, long and smooth and powerful. That was—how many years ago—five, ten, I don't remember . . . But it doesn't take long for a man to lose his vigour and freshness. Women and trees last longer.

'Anyway, to return to what I was saying, Mulia began caressing me, but I was totally unresponsive to her ministrations.

'"What is wrong?" she asked.

'"Nothing" I said. "I am unwell, that is all. I will be all right in a day or two."

'And I got up from the bed and went to the tap to refresh myself with a cold bath.

'That evening I bathed in the river. I felt listless and ill at ease, and perhaps I was hoping that the icy water would instil new life in me. Thousands bathed daily in the river. Each person sought his own cure, his own solutions, his own personal benediction; and that surging mass of human flesh appeared to me as one living entity, a shapeless jelly of throbbing amoeba, struggling for life on the banks of a timeless river. Was I a distinct and sacred individual, or was I just a part of the quivering jelly that sought cohesion in the swirling waters? And did help come from within or from without? Did it come from the mind, as my teacher once said, or was there really a potency, a magic, in the waters of the river? Bathing should be a rite, not a routine, I thought.

'Mulia was worried about me. She made me one of her concoctions, a bitter brew of *senna* leaves, rose petals, pomegranate-bark and laburnum seeds. The result was diarrhoea.

'I placed more reliance on Samyukta. A few hours with her, I thought, and I would soon be myself again. I had spent too much time with older women, and I needed the challenge of someone my own age. Or so I tried to convince myself.'

CHAPTER THIRTEEN

🐍

'SINCE MY RETURN, I had seen Samyukta occasionally but had not found an opportunity to be alone with her. Then one day her mother decided to visit a fair on the other side of the river, and Samyukta, pleading a headache, remained at home. I found her combing her long black hair in front of the mirror. I knew that she spent many hours at the mirror, and suspected that she was deeply in love with her own beauty.

'I began kissing her on her lips and throat, and presently she got up and undressed and came to bed with me. She had blossomed in the past year, and I think there were few women who could match her physical attractions. She had never failed to rouse me, to meet my challenge. She was prepared to do so now—even eager to please—for in pleasing me, homage would be paid to her own beauty.

'But something terrible had happened to me. My failure with Mulia was not a thing of the moment. There I was, lying beside a girl with whom at one time I had been brutal in my love making. And now, though there was no diminishing of desire, I found myself helpless, unable to take possession of her. For the first time in my life I found myself up against forces beyond my control. Fear crept over me. Had the woman of the hills completely destroyed my manhood? Or had my own body rebelled against me?

'The unfocussed stare of desire faded from Samyukta's eyes. She looked at me in surprise, and then in anger. My inadequacy was an insult to her beauty and womanhood. And she asked the same question that Mulia had asked: "What is wrong?"

'"I don't know," I said. "I must be ill. Or it's the evil eye."

'She got up and began to dress. She said nothing. But her silence was more eloquent than speech.

'"I'll come again," I said, "When I feel better."

'How pathetic it sounded!

'And of course she said nothing. After all, what was there to say? A woman can hide her frigidity, but a man's impotence is obvious.'

*

'I primed myself on strong country liquor, and when evening came on and the sun sank in the river, and night crept up to cover our imperfections, I walked unsteadily towards the house with the green lantern and made my way upstairs. Shankhini's door was open. I walked in, but she was not to be seen anywhere. Feeling giddy and sick, I stumbled into the bathroom and, supporting myself against the sink, began retching. Then, exhausted, I leant back against the wall. And while I stood there trying to pull myself together, I heard the voices of two people who had entered the room.

'One voice was Shankhini's—I recognized it immediately. The other was a man's voice.

'They spoke together for a few minutes, then the bed creaked under their combined weight. I couldn't resist moving to the bathroom door and looking through the curtains. The bathroom was in darkness, but Shankhini's bedroom was brightly lit. She lay on her bed, a fragile figure, while her guest for the night took his pleasure.

'The man, a stranger in town, had close-cropped grey hair, hollow cheeks and skinny legs; he must have been at least sixty. But he went about the whole business with all the verve and vigour of a young stallion.

'I watched in fear and fascination. Fear for myself, fascination at the old man. I had fancied myself the world's most accomplished lover. And there I stood, finished before I was thirty, while a man who was more than twice my age performed wonders on a bed. My ego was shattered. My self-esteem lay in the washbasin.

'There was a door leading from the bathroom to the passageway and, unable to face Shankhini, I departed ignominiously, stumbling into the street and being sick again on the pavement.'

CHAPTER FOURTEEN

THE CLEAR LIGHT OF a September dawn has spread across the mountains, and from outside the cave comes the call of the whistling-thrush, a song sweet and haunting, recalling for me a different kind of joy. But inside the cave it is dark and clammy, a home for those who despise the light—bats, rodents and hollow men.

All the awe I had at first felt for the recluse disappeared at the very moment that the sun came shouting over the hills. There is nothing more beautiful than daylight. I want to flee from the cave, from all within it. Renunciation? He has not renounced the world, he has hidden from it. And I wonder how many thousands there are like him—men who have run, not simply from the world but from themselves; men who, hating themselves, cannot bear to see their own reflections in the faces of other men.

He has produced a small chillum—a clay pipe—and filled it with the dried leaves of the cannabis plant.

'No wonder you eat so little,' I say.

'It is mental food I require. Those few or many years ago of which I have told you, when I thought that by strengthening my mental powers I might regain my manhood, I went again to the man who had taught me to concentrate, to bend others to my will. But he could do nothing for me. Perhaps he had lost his hypnotic powers in the same way that I had lost my physical powers—a failure of conservation!

'And yet this weed which grows all about me, has made life tolerable. It has so solaced me that in my fantasies I can experience all those sensual pleasures without my miserable body having to do anything! Surely that's an achievement—surely that's victory for mind over matter!'

'I wouldn't call it that,' I say, now ready to refute. 'If it's the plant that brings you mental ease, that makes it a victory of matter over mind. Surely the only victory comes when the mind is free.'

'Perhaps, perhaps. But nothing else, human or divine, could help me. I had only one talent, you know. Misuse a gift, and you destroy it. And when I lost mine, I turned my back on the world and all it stood for.'

'But the world isn't exclusively a place for the pursuit of sensual pleasure.'

'No. But I was a sensualist. There was nothing else I could pursue.'

*

Before I go, I ask him where I can find the woman who had stolen his manhood—the hill-woman who had overpowered him with her own much stronger sensuality.

'Why?' he asks. 'Do you wish to lose your manhood too?'

'No. I wish to regain it. Or rather, I wish to discover it. And only a woman who can give so much of herself can revive true passion in a man.'

'You are wrong. A woman of great passion can only diminish a man.'

'That is because you were in love with your ego, you were too concerned about your self-esteem. You took the love but spurned the lover. And so you had to lose both. I hope to find them yet . . .'

And I leave him in the cave with his cold thoughts, and the cold ashes of his dead fire and the cold corpse he still inhabits.

I leave my dead self in the cave and continue my search for the perfect stranger in the night.

A Handful of Nuts

CHAPTER ONE

꧁

IT WASN'T THE ROOM on the roof, but it was a large room with a balcony in front and a small verandah at the back. On the first floor of an old shopping complex, still known as Astley Hall, it faced the town's main road, although a walled-in driveway separated it from the street pavement. A neem tree grew in front of the building, and during the early rains, when the neem-pods fell and were crushed underfoot, they gave off a rich, pungent odour which I can never forget.

I had taken the room at the very modest rent of thirty-five rupees a month, payable in advance to the stout Punjabi widow who ran the provisions store downstairs. Her provisions ran to rice, lentils, spices and condiments, but I wasn't doing any cooking then, there wasn't time, so for a quick snack I'd cross the road and consume a couple of samosas or vegetable patties. Whenever I received a decent fee for a story, I'd treat myself to some sliced ham and a loaf of bread, and make myself ham sandwiches. If any of my friends were around, like Jai Shankar or William Matheson, they'd make short work of the ham sandwiches.

I don't think I ever went hungry, but I was certainly underweight and and undernourished, eating irregularly in cheap restaurants and dhabas and suffering frequent stomach upheavals. My four years in England had done nothing to improve my constitution, as there, too, I had lived largely on what was sold over the counter in snack-bars—baked beans on toast being the standard fare.

427

At the corner of the block, near the Orient Cinema, was a little restaurant called Komal's, run by a rotund Sikh gentleman who seldom left his seat near the window. Here I had a reasonably good lunch of dal, rice and a vegetable curry, for two or three rupees.

There were a few other regulars—a college teacher, a couple of salesmen and occasionally someone waiting for a film show to begin. William and Jai did not trail me to this place, as it was a little lowbrow for them (William being Swiss and Jai being Doon School); nor was it frequented much by students or children. It was lower middle-class, really; professional men who were still single and forced to eat in the town. I wasn't bothered by anyone here. And it suited me in other ways, because there was a news-stand close by and I could buy a paper or a magazine and skim through it before or after my meal. Determined as I was to making a living by writing, I had made it my duty to study every English language publication that found its way to Dehra (most of them did), to see which of them published short fiction. A surprisingly large number of magazines did publish short stories; the trouble was, the rates of payment were not very high, the average being about twenty-five rupees a story.

Ten stories a month would therefore fetch me two hundred and fifty rupees—just enough for me to get by!

After eating at Komal's, I made my way to the up-market Indiana for a cup of coffee, which was all I could afford there. Indiana was for the smart set. In the evenings it boasted a three-piece band, and you could dance if you had a partner, although dancing cheek to cheek went out with World War Two. From noon to three, Larry Gomes, a Dehra boy of Goan origin, tinkled on the piano, playing old favourites or new hits.

That spring morning, only one or two tables were occupied—by business people, who weren't listening to music—so Larry went through a couple of old numbers for my benefit, *September Song* and *I'll See You Again*. At twenty, I was very old-fashioned. Larry received three hundred rupees a month and a free lunch, so he was slightly better off than me. Also, his father owned a small music and record shop a short distance away.

While I was sipping my coffee and pondering upon my financial affairs (which were non-existent, as I had no finances), in walked the rich and baggy-eyed Maharani of Magador with her daughter Indu. I stood up to greet her and she gave me a gracious smile.

She knew that some five years previously, when I was in my last year at school, I had been infatuated with her daughter. She had even intercepted one of my love letters, but she had been quite sporting about it, and had told me that I wrote a nice letter. Now she knew that I was writing stories for magazines, and she said, 'We read your story in the *Weekly* last week. It was quite charming, didn't I say you'd make a good writer?' I blushed and thanked her, while Indu gave me a mischievous smile. She was still at college.

'You must come and see us someday,' said the Maharani and moved on majestically. Indu, small-boned and petite and dressed in something blue, looked more than ever like a butterfly; soft, delicate, flitting away just as you thought you could touch her.

They sat at a table in a corner, and I returned to my contemplation of the coffee-stains on the table-cloth. I had, of course, splashed my coffee all over the place.

Larry had observed my confusion, and guessing its cause, now played a very old tune which only Indu's mother would have recognized: 'I kiss your little bands, madame, I long to kiss your lips . . .'

On my way out, Larry caught my eye and winked at me. 'Next time I'll give you a tip,' I said.

'Save it for the waiter,' said Larry.

It was hot in the April sunshine, and I headed for my room, wishing I had a fan.

Stripping to vest and underwear, I lay down on the bed and stared at the ceiling. The ceiling stared back at me. I turned on my side and looked across the balcony, at the leaves of the neem tree. They were absolutely still. There was not even the promise of a breeze.

I dozed off, and dreamt of my princess, her deep dark eyes

and the tint of winter moonlight on her cheeks. I dreamt that I was bathing with her in a clear moonlit pool, while small fishes of gold and silver and mother-of-pearl slipped between our thighs. I laved her exquisite little body with the fresh spring water and placed a hibiscus flower between her golden breasts and another behind her ear. I was overcome with lust and threw myself upon her, only to discover that she had turned into a fish with silver scales.

I opened my eyes to find Sitaram, the washerman's son, sitting at the foot of my bed.

Sitaram must have been about sixteen, a skinny boy with large hands, large feet and large ears. He had loose sensual lips. An unprepossessing youth, whom I found irritating in the extreme; but as he lived with his parents in the quarters behind the flat, there was no avoiding him.

'How did you get in here?' I asked brusquely.

'The door was open.'

'That doesn't mean you can walk right in. What do you want?'

'Don't you have any clothes for washing? My father asked.'

'I wash my own clothes.'

'And sheets?' He studied the sheet I was lying on. 'Don't you wash your sheet? It is very dirty.'

'Well, it's the only one I've got. So buzz off.'

But he was already pulling the sheet out from under me. 'I'll wash it for you free. You are a nice man. My mother says you are *seeda-saada*, very innocent.'

'I am not innocent. And I need the sheet.'

'I will bring you another. I will lend it to you free. We get lots of sheets to wash. Yesterday six sheets came from the hospital. Some people were killed in a bus accident.'

'You mean the sheets came from the morgue—they were used to cover dead bodies? I don't want a sheet from the morgue.'

'But it is very clean. You know *khatmals* can't live on dead bodies. They like fresh blood.'

He went away with my sheet and came back five minutes later with a freshly-pressed bedsheet.

'Don't worry,' he said. 'It's not from the hospital.'

'Where is this one from?'

'Indiana Hotel. I will give them a hospital sheet in exchange.'

CHAPTER TWO

❦

THE GARDENS WERE BATHED in moonlight, as I walked down the narrow old roads of Dehra—I stopped near the Maharani's house and looked over the low wall. The lights were still on in some of the rooms. I waited for some time until I saw Indu come to a window. She had a book in her hand, so I guessed she'd been reading. Maybe if I sent her a poem, she'd read it. A poem about a small red virgin rose.

But it wouldn't bring me any money.

I walked back to the bazaar, to the bright lights of the cinemas and small eating houses. It was only eight o'clock. The street was still crowded. Nowadays it's traffic; then it was just full of people. And so you were constantly bumping into people you knew—or did not know ...

I was staring at a poster of Nimmi, sexiest of Indian actresses, when a hand descended on my shoulder, and I turned to see Jai Shankar, the genius from the Doon School, whose father owned the New Empire Cinema.

'Jalebis, Ruskin, jalebis,' he crooned. Although he was from a rich family, he never seemed to have any pocket money. And of course it's easier to borrow from a poor man than it is to borrow from a rich one! Why is that, I wonder? There was William Matheson, for instance, who lived in a posh boarding-house, but was always cadging small sums off me—to pay his laundry bill or assist in his consumption of Charminar cigarettes: without them he was a nervous wreck. And with Jai Shankar it was jalebis ...

'I haven't had a cheque for weeks,' I told him.

'What about the story you were writing for the BBC?'

'Well, I've just sent it to them.'

'And the novel you were writing?'

'I'm still writing it.'

'Jalebis will cost only two rupees.'

'Oh, all right . . .'

Jai Shankar stuffed himself with jalebis while I contented myself with a samosa. Jai wished to be an artist, poet and diarist, somewhat in the manner of Andre Gide, and had even given me a copy of Gide's *Fruits of the Earth* in an endeavour to influence me in the same direction. It is still with me today, forty years later, his spidery writing scrawling a message across the dancing angel drawn on the title-page. Our favourite books outlast our dreams . . .

Of course, after the jalebis I had to see Jai home. If I hadn't met him, someone else would have had to walk home with him. He was terrified of walking down the narrow lane to his house once darkness had fallen. There were no lights and the overhanging mango, neem and peepal trees made it a place of Stygian gloom. It was said that a woman had hanged herself from a mango tree on this very lane, and Jai was always in a dither lest he should see the lady dangling in front of him.

He kept a small pocket torch handy, but after leaving him at his gate I would have to return sans torch, for nothing could persuade him to part with it. On the way back, I would bump into other pedestrians who would be stumbling along the lane, guided by slivers of moonlight or the pale glimmer from someone's window.

Only the blind man carried a lamp.

'And what need have you of a light?' we asked.

'So that fools do not stumble against me in the dark.'

But I did not care for torchlight. I had taught myself to use whatever the night offered—moonlight, full and partial; starlight; the light from street lamps, from windows, from half-open doors. The night is beautiful, made ugly only by the searing headlights of cars.

When I got back to my room, the shops had closed and only the lights in Sitaram's quarters were on. His parents were quarrelling, and the entire neighbourhood could hear them. It was always like that. The husband was drunk and abusive; she refused to open the door for him, told him to go and sleep with a whore or, better still, a donkey. After some time he retreated into the dark.

I had no lights, as my landlady had neglected to pay the electricity bill for the past six months. But I did not mind the absence of light, although at times I would have liked an electric fan.

It meant, of course, that I could not type or even write by hand except when the full moon poured over the balcony. But I could always manage a few lines of poetry on a large white sheet of paper.

This sheet of paper is my garden,
These words my flowers.
I do not ask a miracle this night,
Other than you beside me in the bright
  moonlight.
Naked, entwined like the flowering vine . . .

And there I got stuck. The last lines always fox me, one reason why I shall never be a poet.

'And we cling to each other for a long, long time . . .' Shades of *September Song*?

In any case, I couldn't send it to Indu, as her mother would be sure to intercept the letter and read it first. The idea of her daughter clinging to me like a vine would not have appealed to the Maharani.

I would have to think of a more mundane method of making my feelings known.

CHAPTER THREE

THERE WAS SOME EXCITEMENT, as Stewart Granger, the British film actor, was in town.

Stewart Granger in Dehradun? Occasionally, a Bombay film star passed through, but this was the first time we were going to see a foreign star. We all knew what he looked like, of course. The Odeon and Orient cinemas had been showing British and American films since the days of the silent movies. Occasionally, they still showed 'silents', as their sound systems were antiquated and the projectors rattled a good deal, drowning the dialogue. This did not matter if the star was John Wayne (or even Stewart Granger) as their lines were quite predictable, but it made a difference if you were trying to listen to Nelson Eddy sing *At the Balalaika* or Hope and Crosby exchanging wisecracks.

We had assembled outside the Indiana and were discussing the phenomenon of having Stewart Granger in town. What was he doing here?

'Making a film, I suppose,' I ventured.

Suresh Mathur, the lawyer, demurred, 'What about? Nobody's written a book about Dehra, except you, Ruskin, and no one has read yours. Has someone bought the film rights?'

'No such luck. And besides, the hero is sixteen and Stewart Granger is thirty-six.'

'Doesn't matter. They'll change the story.'

'Not if I can help it.'

William Matheson had another theory.

'He's visiting his old aunt in Rajpur.'

'We never knew he had an aunt in Rajpur.'

'Nor did I. It's just a theory.'

'You and your theories. We'll ask the owner of Indiana. Stewart Granger is going to stay here, isn't he?'

Mr Kapoor of Indiana enlightened us. 'They're location-hunting for a shikar movie. It's called *Harry Black and the Tiger*.

'Stewart Granger is playing a black man?' asked William.

'No, no, that's an English surname.'

'English is a funny language,' said William, who believed in the superiority of the French tongue.

'We don't have any tigers left in these forests,' I said.

'They'll bring in a circus tiger and let it loose,' said Suresh.

'In the jungle, I hope,' said William. 'Or will they let it loose on Rajpur Road?'

'Preferably in the Town Hall,' said Suresh, who was having some trouble with the municipality over his house tax.

*

Stewart Granger did not disappoint.

At about two in the afternoon, the hottest part of the day, he arrived in an open Ford convertible, shirtless and vestless. He was in his prime then, in pretty good condition after playing opposite Ava Gardner in *Bhowani Junction*, and everyone remarked on his fine torso and general good looks. He made himself comfortable in a cool corner of the Indiana and proceeded to down several bottles of chilled beer, much to everyone's admiration. Larry Gomes, at the piano, started playing *Sweet Rosie O'Grady* until Granger, who wasn't Irish, stopped him and asked for something more modern. Larry obliged with *Goodnight Irene*, and Stewart, now into his third bottle of beer, began singing the refrain. At the next table, William, Suresh and I, trying to keep pace with the star's consumption of beer, joined in the chorus, and before long there was a mad sing-song in the restaurant.

The editor of the local paper, *The Doon Chronicle*, tried interviewing the star, but made little progress. Someone gave him an information and publicity sheet which did the rounds. It said Stewart Granger was born in 1913, and that he had black hair and brown eyes. He still had them—unless the hair was a toupe. It said his height was 6 feet 2 inches, and that he weighed 196 lbs. He looked every pound of it. It also said his youthful

ambition was to become a 'nerve specialist'. We looked at him
with renewed respect, although none of us was quite sure what
a 'nerve specialist' was supposed to do.

'We just get on your nerves,' said Mr Granger when asked,
and everyone laughed.

He tucked into his curry and rice with relish, downed another
beer and returned to his waiting car. A few good-natured jests,
a wave and a smile, and the star and his entourage drove off into
the foothills.

We heard, later, that they had decided to make the film in
Mysore, in distant south India.

No wonder it turned out to be a flop. Sorry, Stewart.

Two months later, Yul Brynner passed through but he didn't
cause the same excitement. We were getting used to film stars.
His film wasn't made in Dehra, either. They did it in Spain.
Another flop.

Chapter Four

WHY HAVE I CHOSEN to write about the twenty-first year of my
life?

Well, for one thing, it's often the most significant year in any
young person's life. A time for falling in love; a time to set about
making your dreams come true; a time to venture forth, to blaze
new trails, take risks, do your own thing, follow your star ...
And so it was with me.

I was just back after four years of living in the West; I had
found a publisher in London for my first novel; I was looking for
fresh fields and new laurels; and I wanted to prove that I could
succeed as a writer with my small home town in India as a base,
without having to live in London or Paris or New York.

In a couple of weeks' time it would be my twenty-first birthday,
and I was feeling good about it.

I had mentioned the date to someone—Suresh Mathur, I think—and before long I was being told by everyone I knew that I would have to celebrate the event in a big way, twenty-one being an age of great significance in a young man's life. To tell the truth I wasn't feeling very youthful. Komal's rich food, swimming in oil, was beginning to take its toll, and I spent a lot of time turning input into output, so to speak.

Finding me flat on my back, Sitaram sat down beside me on my bed and expressed his concern for my health. I was too weak to drive him away.

'Just a stomach upset,' I said. 'It will pass off. You can go.'

'I will bring you some curds—very good for the stomach when you have the *dast*—when you are in full flow.'

'I took some tablets.'

'Medicine no good. Take curds.'

Seeing that he was serious, I gave him two rupees and he went off somewhere and returned after ten minutes with a bowl of curds. I found it quite refreshing, and he promised to bring more that evening. Then he said: 'So you will be. twenty-one soon. A big party.'

'How did you know?' I asked, for I certainly hadn't mentioned it to him.

'Sitaram knows everything!'

'How did you find out?'

'I heard them talking in the Indiana, as I collected the table-cloths for washing. Will you have the party in Indiana?'

'No, no, I can't afford it.'

'Have it here then. I will help you.'

'Let's see . . .'

'How many people will you call for the tea-party?'

'I don't know. Most of them are demanding beer—it's expensive.'

'Give them *kachi*, they make it in our village behind the police lines. I'll bring a jerry-can for you. It's very cheap and very strong. Big *nasha*!'

'How do you know? Do you drink it?'

'I never drink. My father drinks enough for everyone.'

'Well, I can't give it to my guests.'

'Who will come?'

I gave some consideration to my potential guest list. There'd be Jai Shankar demanding jalebis and beer, a sickening combination! And William Matheson wanting French toast, I supposed. (Was French toast eaten by the French? It seemed very English, somehow.) And Suresh Mathur wanting something stronger than beer. (After two whiskeys, he claimed that he had discovered the fourth dimension.) And there were my young Sikh friends from the Dilaram Bazaar, who would be happy with lots to eat. And perhaps Larry Gomes would drop in.

Dare I invite the Maharani and Indu? Would they fit in with the rest of the mob? Perhaps I could invite them to a separate tea-party at the Indiana. Cream-rolls and cucumber sandwiches.

And where would the money come from for all these celebrations? My bank balance stood at a little over three hundred rupees—enough to pay the rent and the food bill at Komal's and make myself a new pair of trousers. The pair I'd bought on the Mile End Road in London, two years previously, were now very baggy and had a shine on the seat. The other pair, made of non-shrink material, got smaller at every wash. I had given them to a tailor to turn into a pair of shorts.

Sitaram, of course, was willing to lend me any number of trousers provided I wasn't fussy about who the owners were, and gave them back in time for them to be washed and pressed again before being delivered to their rightful owners. I did, on an occasion, borrow a pair made of a nice checked material, and was standing outside the Indiana, chatting to the owner, when I realized that he was staring hard at the trousers.

'I have a pair just like yours,' he remarked.

'It shows you have good taste,' I said, and gave Sitaram an earful when I got back to the flat.

'I can't trust you with other people's trousers!' I shouted. 'Couldn't you have lent me a pair belonging to someone who lives far from here?'

He was genuinely contrite. 'I was looking for the right size,' he said. 'Would you like to try a dhoti? You will look good in a dhoti. Or a lungi. There's a purple lungi here, it belongs to a sub-inspector of police.'

'A purple lungi? The police are human, after all.'

*

Yes, money talks—and it's usually saying goodbye.

A freelance writer can't tell what he's going to make from one month to the next. This uncertainty is part of the charm of the writing life, but it can also make for some nail-biting finishes when it comes to paying the rent, the food bill at Komal's, postage on my articles and correspondence, typing paper, toothpaste, socks, shaving soap, candles (there was no light in my room) and other necessities. And friends like William Matheson and Suresh Mathur (the only out-of-work lawyer I have ever known) did not make it any easier for me.

William, though Swiss, had served in the French Foreign Legion, and had been on the run in Vietnam along with the French administration and army once the Vietnamese had decided they'd had enough of the *Marseillaise*. The French are not known for their military prowess, although they would like to think otherwise.

William had drifted into Dehra as the assistant to a German newspaper correspondent, Von Radloff, who based his dispatches on the Indian papers and sent them out with a New Delhi dateline. Dehra was a little cooler than Delhi, and it was still pretty in parts. You could lead a pleasant life there, if you had an income.

William and Radloff fell out, and William decided he'd set up on his own as a correspondent. But there weren't many takers for his articles in Europe, and his debts were mounting. He continued to live in an expensive guest house whose owner, an unusually tolerant landlord, reminded him one day that he was five months in arrears.

William took to turning up at my room around the same time as the postman, to see if I'd received any cheques or international money orders.

'Only pounds,' I told him one day. 'No French or Swiss francs. How could I possibly aspire to a French publisher?'

'Pounds will do. I owe my Sardarji about five thousand rupees.'

'Well, you'll have to keep owing him. My twelve pounds from the *Young Elizabethan* won't do much for you.'

The *Young Elizabethan* was a classy British children's magazine, edited by Kaye Webb and Pat Campbell. A number of my early stories found a home between its covers. Alas, like many other good things, it vanished a couple of years later. But in that golden year of my debut it was one of my mainstays.

'Why don't you look for cheaper accommodation?' I asked William.

'I have to keep up appearances. How can the correspondent of the Franco-German press live in a hovel like yours?'

'Well, suit yourself,' I said. 'I hope you get some money soon.'

All the same, I lent him two hundred rupees, and of course never saw it again. Would I have enough for my birthday party? That was now the burning question.

CHAPTER FIVE

&

EARLY ONE MORNING I decided I'd take a long cycle ride out of the town's precincts. I'd read all about the dawn coming up like thunder, but had never really got up early enough to witness it. I asked Sitaram to do me a favour and wake me at six. He woke me at five. It was just getting light. As I dressed, the colour of the sky changed from ultramarine to a clear shade of lavender, and then the sun came up gloriously naked.

I had borrowed a cycle from my landlady—it was occasionally

used by her son or servant to deliver purchases to favoured customers—and I rode off down the Rajpur Road in a rather wobbly, zig-zag manner, as it was about five years since I had ridden a cycle. I was careful; I did not want to end up a cripple like Denton Welch, the sensitive author of *A Voice in the Clouds*, whose idyllic country cycle-ride had ended in disaster and tragedy.

Dehra's traffic is horrific today, but there was not much of it then, and at six in the morning the roads were deserted. In any case, I was soon out of the town and then I reached the tea-gardens. I stopped at a small wayside teashop for refreshment and while I was about to dip a hard bun in my tea, a familiar shadow fell across the table, and I looked up to see Sitaram grinning at me. I'd forgotten—he too had a cycle.

Dear friend and familiar! I did not know whether to be pleased or angry.

'My cycle is faster than yours,' he said.

'Well, then carry on riding it to Rishikesh. I'll try to keep up with you.'

He laughed. 'You can't escape me that way, writer-sahib. I'm hungry.'

'Have something, then.'

'We will practise for your birthday.' And he helped himself to a boiled egg, two buns and a sponge cake that looked as though it had been in the shop for a couple of years. If Sitaram can digest that, I thought, then he's a true survivor.

'Where are you going?' he asked, as I prepared to mount my cycle.

'Anywhere,' I said. 'As far as I feel like going.'

'Come, I will show you roads that you have never seen before.'

Were these prophetic words? Was I to discover new paths and new meanings courtesy the washerman's son?

'Lead on, light of my life,' I said, and he beamed and set off at a good speed so that I had trouble keeping up with him.

He left the main road, and took a bumpy, dusty path through

a bamboo-grove. It was a fairly broad path and we could cycle side by side. It led out of the bamboo grove into an extensive tea-garden, then turned and twisted before petering out beside a small canal.

We rested our cycles against the trunk of a mango tree, and as we did so, a flock of green parrots, disturbed by our presence, flew out from the tree, circling the area and making a good deal of noise. In India, the land of the loudspeaker, even the birds have learnt to shout in order to be heard.

The parrots finally settled on another tree. The mangoes were beginning to form, but many would be bruised by the birds before they could fully ripen.

A kingfisher dived low over the canal and came up with a little gleaming fish.

'Too tiny for us,' I said, 'or we might have caught a few.'

'We'll eat fish tikkas in the bazaar on our way back,' said Sitaram, a pragmatic person.

While Sitaram went exploring the canal banks, I sat down and rested my back against the bole of the mango tree.

A sensation of great peace stole over me. I felt in complete empathy with my surroundings—the gurgle of the canal water, the trees, the parrots, the bark of the tree, the warmth of the sun, the softness of the faint breeze, the caterpillar on the grass near my feet, the grass itself, each blade . . . And I knew that if I always remained close to these things, growing things, the natural world, life would come alive for me, and I would be able to write as long as I lived.

Optimism surged through me, and I began singing an old song of Nelson Eddy's, a Vincent Huyman composition—

When you are down and out,
Lift up your head and shout—
It's going to be a great day!

Across the canal, moving through some wild babul trees, a dim figure seemed to be approaching. It wasn't the boy, it wasn't a stranger, it was someone I knew. Though he remained dim, I was soon able to recognize my father's face and form.

He stood there, smiling, and the song died on my lips.

But perhaps it was the song that had brought him back for a few seconds. He had always liked Nelson Eddy, collected his records. Where were they now? Where were the songs of old? The past has served us well; we must preserve all that was good in it.

As I stood up and raised my hand in greeting, the figure faded away.

My dear, dear father. How much I had loved him. And I had been only ten when he had been snatched away. Now he had given me a sign that he was still with me, would always be with me . . .

There was a great splashing close by, and I looked down to see that Sitaram was in the water. I hadn't even noticed him slip off his clothes and jump into the canal.

He beckoned to me to join him, and after a moment's hesitation, I decided to do so. Sitaram and I romped around in the waist-deep water for quite some time. He was a beautiful glistening chocolate colour in the late morning sunshine. I would have to get into the open more often; I felt pale and washed out.

After some time I climbed the opposite bank and walked to the place where I had seen my father approaching. But there was no sign that anyone had been there. Not even a footprint.

CHAPTER SIX

IT WAS MID-AFTERNOON WHEN we cycled back to the town. Siesta-time for many, but some brave souls were playing cricket on a vacant lot. There were spacious bungalows in the Dalanwala area; they had lawns and well-kept gardens. Dehra's establishment lived here. As did the Maharani of Magador, whose name-plate caught my eye as we rode slowly past the gate. I got off my cycle and stood at the kerb, looking over the garden wall.

'What are you looking at?' asked Sitaram, dismounting beside me.

'I want to invite the Maharani's daughter to my birthday party. But I don't suppose her mother will allow her to come.'

'Invite the mother too,' said Sitaram.

'Brilliant!' I said. 'Hit two Ranis with one stone.'

'Two birds in hand!' added Sitaram, who remembered his English proverbs from Class Seven. 'And look, there is one in the bushes!'

He pointed towards a hedge of hibiscus, where Indu was at work pruning the branches. Our voices had carried across the garden, and she looked up and stared at us for a few seconds before recognizing me. She walked slowly across the grass and stopped on the other side of the low wall, smiling faintly, looking from me to Sitaram and back to me.

'Hello,' she said. 'Where have you been cycling?'

'Oh, all over the place. Across the canal and into the fields like Hemingway. Now we're on our way home. Sitaram lives next door to me. When I saw your place, I thought I'd stop and say hello. Is your mother at home?'

'Yes, she's resting. Do you want to see her?'

'Er, no. Well, sure, but I won't disturb her. What I wanted to say was—if you're free on the 19th, come and join me and my friends for tea. It's my birthday, my twenty-first.'

'How nice. But my mother won't let me go alone.'

'The invitation includes her. If she comes, will you?'

'I'll ask her.'

I looked into her eyes. Deep brown, rather mischievous eyes. Were they responding to my look of gentle adoration? Or were they just amused because I was so self-conscious, so gauche? I could write stories, earn a living, converse with people from all walks of life, ride a bicycle, play football, climb trees, put back a few drinks, walk for miles without tiring, play with babies, charm grandmothers, impress fathers; but when it came to making an impression on the opposite sex, I was sadly out of depth, a complete dunce. It was I, not Indu, who had to hide the blushes . . .

Even in London, two years earlier, when I had tried to prove my manhood by going to a prostitute in Leicester Square, everything had gone wrong. She had looked quite attractive under the street light where she had accosted me—or had I accosted her? But when she took me up to her room and exposed her flabby legs and thighs, I was repelled, mainly because she was suffering badly from varicose veins. You linger over your *Playboy* centre spreads, and then you go out and find your first woman, and she has varicose veins! I gave the unfortunate lady her fee and fled. But the smell of her powder and paint wouldn't leave my coat—my only coat—and I had to live with this failure for days!

The experience convinced me that I was more suited to romantic dalliance than sexual conquests, and that the latter would follow naturally from the former. My intentions towards Indu were perfectly honourable, although I couldn't see her mother accepting me into the royal fold. But perhaps one day when fame and fortune were mine (soon, I hoped!) Indu would give up her protected existence and come and live with me in a house by the sea or a villa on some tropical isle. I made up these lines on the spot, but held back from reciting them:

With the bougainvillaea in her hair
And blossoms on her breasts
My lips would search between her thighs for
    honeydew's caress . . .

As Indu gazed into my eyes, I said, quite boldly and to my own surprise, 'I have to kiss you one of these days, Indu.'

'Why not today?'

She was offering me her cheek, and that's where I started, but then she let me kiss her on her lips, and it was so sweet and intoxicating that when I felt someone pressing my hand I was sure it was Indu. I returned the pressure, then realized that Indu was on the other side of the wall, still holding the hedge-cutters. I'd quite forgotten Sitaram's presence. The pressure of his hand increased; I turned to look at him and he nodded approvingly.

Indu had drawn away from the wall just as her mother's voice carried to us across the garden: 'Who are you talking to, Indu? Is it someone we know?'

'Just a college student!' Indu called back, and then, waving, walked slowly in the direction of the verandah. She turned once and said, 'I'll come to the party, mother too!'

And I was left with Sitaram holding my hand.

'Only one thing missing,' he said.

'What's that?'

'Filmi music.'

*

There was filmi music in full measure when we got to the Orient Cinema, where they were showing *Mr and Mrs 55* starring Madhubala, who was everybody's heart-throb that year. Sitaram insisted that I return my bicycle and join him in the cheap seats, which I did, almost passing out from the aromatic *beedi* smoke that filled the hall. The Orient had once shown English films, and I remembered seeing an early British comedy, *The Ghost of St. Michael's* (with Will Hay), when I was a boy. The front of the cinema, facing the parade-ground, was decorated with a bas-relief of dancers, designed by Sudhir Khastgir, art master at the Doon School, and they certainly lent character to the building— the rest of its character was fast disintegrating. But I enjoyed watching the crowd at the cinema. For me, the audience was always more interesting than the performers.

All I remember of the film was that Sitaram got very restless whenever Madhubala appeared on the screen. He would whistle along with the tongawallahs and squeeze my arm or other parts of my anatomy to indicate that he was really turned on by his favourite screen heroine. A good thing Madhubala wasn't coming to town, or there'd have been a riot; but for some time there had been a rumour that Prem Nath, a successful male star, would be visiting Dehra, and my landlady had been quite excited at the prospect. But Sitaram was not turned on by Prem Nath. It was Madhubala or nothing.

After the film, while wending our way through the bazaar, we were accosted by Jai Shankar, who walked with us to the Frontier Sweet Shop, where hot fresh jalebis were being dished out to the evening's first customers.

'Your turn to pay,' I said.

'Next time, next time,' promised the pride of the Doon School.

'I'm broke,' I said.

'Your friend must have some money.'

It turned out that Sitaram did possess a few crumpled notes, which he thrust into my hand.

'What does your friend do?' asked Jai.

'He's in the garment business,' I said.

Jai looked at Sitaram with renewed respect. When he'd had his fill of jalebis he insisted on showing us his new painting. So we walked home with him along his haunted alley, and he took us into his studio and proudly displayed a painting of a purple lady, very long in the arms and legs, and somewhat flat-chested.

'Well, what do you think?' asked Jai, standing back and looking at his bizarre creation with an affectionate eye.

'Are you doing it for your school founder's day?' I asked innocently.

'No, nudes aren't permitted. But you should see my study of angels in flight. It won the first prize!'

'Well, if you give this one a halo and wings, it could be an angel.'

Jai turned from me in disgust and asked Sitaram for his opinion.

Sitaram stared at the painting quizzically and said, 'She must have given all her clothes for washing.'

'There speaks the garment manufacturer,' I put in.

'The breasts could be bigger,' added Sitaram, as an afterthought.

'Maybe I will enlarge the breasts,' conceded Jai, with a thoughtful nod.

'Not too much,' I said. 'Large breasts are going out of fashion.'

'Why's that?' '

'Too many males have them.'

Jai saw us to the door, but not down the dark alley; he never took it alone. All his life he was to be afraid of being alone in the dark. Well, we all have our phobias. To this day, I won't use a lift or escalator unless I have company.

Sitaram and I walked back quite comfortably in the dark. He linked his fingers with mine and broke into song, a little off-key; he was no Saigal or Rafi. We cut across the *maidaan*, and a quarter-moon kept us company. I was overcome by a feeling of tranquility, a love for all the world, and wondered if it had something to do with the vision of my father earlier in the day.

As we climbed the steps to the landing that separated my rooms from Sitaram's quarters, we could hear his parents' voices raised in their nightly recriminations. His mother was a virago, no doubt; and his father was a drunk who gambled away most of his earnings. For Sitaram it was a trap from which there was only one escape. And he voiced my thought.

'I'll leave home one of these days,' he said.

'Well, tonight you can stay with me.'

I'd said it without any forethought, simply on an impulse. He followed me into my room, without bothering to inform his parents that he was back.

My landlady's large double-bed provided plenty of space for both of us. She hadn't used it since her husband's death, some six or seven years previously. And it was unlikely that she would be using it again.

CHAPTER SEVEN

SOMEONE WAS GETTING MARRIED, and the wedding band, brought up on military marches, unwittingly broke into the *Funeral March*. And they played loud enough to wake the dead.

After a medley of Souza marches, they switched to Hindi film tunes, and Sitaram came in, flung his arms around and shattered my ear-drums with Talat Mehmood's latest love ballad. I responded with the *Volga Boatmen* in my best Nelson Eddy manner, and my landlady came running out of her shop downstairs wanting to know if the washerman had strangled his wife or vice-versa.

Anyway, it was to be a week of celebrations . . .

When I opened my eyes next day, it was to find a bright red geranium staring me in the face, accompanied by the aromatic odour of a crushed geranium leaf. Sitaram was thrusting a potted geranium at me and wishing me a happy birthday. I brushed a caterpillar from my pillow and sat up. Wordsworthian though I was in principle, I wasn't prepared for nature red in tooth and claw.

I picked up the caterpillar on its leaf and dropped it outside. 'Come back when you're a butterfly,' I said.

Sitaram had taken his morning bath and looked very fresh and spry. Unfortunately, he had doused his head with some jasmine-scented hair oil, and the room was reeking of it. Already a bee was buzzing around him.

'Thank you for the present,' I said. 'I've always wanted a geranium.

'I wanted to bring a rose-bush but the pot was too heavy.'

'Never mind. Geraniums do better on verandahs.'

I placed the pot in a sunny corner of the small balcony, and it certainly did something for the place. There's nothing like a red geranium for bringing a balcony to life.

While we were about to plan the day's festivities, a stranger walked through my open door (one day, I'd have to shut it), and declared himself the inventor of a new flush-toilet which, he said, would revolutionize the sanitary habits of the town. We were still living in the thunderbox era, and only the very rich could afford Western-style lavatories. My visitor showed me diagrams of a seat which, he said, combined the best of East and West. You could squat on it, Indian-style, without putting too much strain on your abdominal muscles, and if you used water to wash your bottom, there was a little sprinkler attached which, correctly aimed, would do that job for you. It was comfortable, efficient, safe. Your effluent would be stored in a little tank, which could be detached when full, and emptied—where? He hadn't got around to that problem as yet, but he assured me that his invention had a great future.

'But why are you telling me all this?' I asked, 'I can't afford a fancy toilet-seat.'

'No, no, I don't expect you to buy one.'

'You mean I should demonstrate?'

'Not at all. But you are a writer, I hear. I want a name for my new toilet-seat. Can you help?'

'Why not call it the Sit-Safe?' I suggested.

'The Sit-Safe! How wonderful. Young Mr Bond, let me show my gratitude with a small present.' And he thrust a ten-rupee note into my hand and left the room before I could protest. 'It's definitely my birthday,' I said. 'Complete strangers walk in and give me money.'

'We can see three films with that,' said Sitaram.

'Or buy three bottles of beer,' I said.

But there were no more windfalls that morning, and I had to go to the old Allahabad Bank—where my grandmother had kept her savings until they had dwindled away—and withdraw one hundred rupees.

'Can you tell me my balance?' I asked Mr Jain, the elderly clerk who remembered my maternal grandmother.

'Two hundred and fifty rupees,' he said with a smile. 'Try to save something!'

I emerged into the hot sunshine and stood on the steps of the bank, where I had stood as a small boy some fifteen years back, waiting for Granny to finish her work—I think she had been the only one in the family to put some money by for a rainy day— but these had been rainy days for her son and daughters and various fickle relatives who were always battening off her. Her own needs were few. She lived in one room of her house, leaving the rest of it for the family to use. When she died, the house was sold so that her children could once more go their impecunious ways.

I had no relatives to support, but here was William Matheson waiting for me under the old peepal tree. His hands were shaking.

'What's wrong?' I asked.

'Haven't had a cigarette for a week. Come on, buy me a packet of Charminar.'

*

Sitaram went out and bought samosas and jalebis and little cakes with icing made from solidified ghee. I fetched a few bottles of beer, some orangeades and lemonades and a syrupy cold drink called Vimto which was all the rage then. My landlady, hearing that I was throwing a party, sent me pakoras made with green chillies.

The party, when it happened, was something of an anticlimax:

Jai Shankar turned up promptly and ate all the jalebis.

William arrived with Suresh Mathur, finished the beer and demanded more.

Nobody paid much attention to Sitaram, he seemed so much at home. Caste didn't count for much in a fairly modern town, as Dehra was in those days. In any case, from the way Sitaram was strutting around, acting as though he owned the place, it was generally presumed that he was the landlady's son. He brought up a second relay of the lady's pakoras, hotter than the first lot, and they arrived just as the Maharani and Indu appeared in the doorway.

'Happy birthday, dear boy,' boomed the Maharani and seized the largest chilli pakora. Indu appeared behind her and gave me a box wrapped in gold and silver cellophane. I put it on my desk and hoped it contained chocolates, not studs and a tie-pin.

The chilli pakoras did not take long to violate the Maharani's taste-buds.

'Water, water!' she cried, and seeing the bathroom door open, made a dash for the tap.

Alas, the bathroom was the least attractive aspect of my flat.

It had yet to be equipped with anything resembling the newly-invented Sit-Safe. But the lid of the thunderbox was fortunately down, as this particular safe hadn't been emptied for a couple of days. It was crowned by a rusty old tin mug. On the wall hung a towel that had seen better days. The remnants of a cake of Lifebuoy soap stood near a cracked washbasin. A lonely cockroach gave the Maharani a welcoming genuflection.

Taking all this in at a glance, she backed out, holding her hand to her mouth.

'Try a Vimto,' said William, holding out a bottle gone warm and sticky.

'A glass of beer?' asked Jai Shankar.

The Maharani grabbed a glass of beer and swallowed it in one long gulp. She came up gasping, gave me a reproachful look—as though the chilli pakora had been intended for her—and said, 'Must go now. Just stopped by to greet you. Thank you very much—you must come to Indu's birthday party. Next year.'

Next year seemed a long way off.

'Thank you for the present,' I said.

And then they were gone, and I was left to entertain my cronies.

Suresh Mathur was demanding something stronger than beer, and as I felt that way myself, we trooped off to the Royal Cafe; all of us, except Sitaram, who had better things to do.

After two rounds of drinks, I'd gone through what remained of my money. And so I left William and Suresh to cadge drinks off one of the latter's clients, while I bid Jai Shankar goodbye on the edge of the parade-ground. As it was still light, I did not have to see him home.

Some workmen were out on the parade-ground, digging holes for tent-pegs.

Two children were discussing the coming attraction.

'The circus is coming!'

'Is it big?'

'It's the biggest! Tigers, elephants, horses, chimpanzees! Tight-rope walkers, acrobats, strong men . . .'

'Is there a clown?'

'There has to be a clown. How can you have a circus without a clown?'

I hurried home to tell Sitaram about the circus. It would make a change from the cinema. The room had been tidied up, and the Maharani's present stood on my desk, still in its wrapper.

'Let's see what's inside,' I said, tearing open the packet.

It was a small box of nuts—almonds, pistachios, cashew nuts, along with a few dried figs.

'Just a handful of nuts,' said Sitaram, sampling a fig and screwing up his face.

I tried an almond, found it was bitter and spat it out.

'Must have saved them from her wedding day,' said Sitaram.

'Appropriate in a way,' I said. 'Nuts for a bunch of nuts.'

CHAPTER EIGHT

LINES WRITTEN ON A hot summer's night:

On hot summer nights I dream
Of you beside me, near a mountain stream
Cool in our bed of ferns we lie,
Lost in our loving, as the world slips by.

I tried to picture Indu in my arms, the two of us watching the moon come over the mountains. But her face kept dissolving and turning into her mother's. This transition from dream to nightmare kept me from sleeping. Sitaram slept peacefully at the edge of the bed, immune to the mosquitoes that came in like squadrons of dive-bombers. It was much too hot for any body contact, but even then, the sheets were soaked with perspiration.

Tired of his parents' quarrels, and his father's constant threat of turning him out if he did not start contributing towards the family's earnings, Sitaram was practically living with me. I had been on my own for the past five years and had grown used to a form of solitary confinement. I don't think I could have shared my life with an intellectual companion. William and Jai Shankar were stimulating company in the Indiana or Royal Cafe, but I doubt if I would have enjoyed waking up to their argumentative presences first thing every morning. William disagreed with everything I wrote or said; I was too sentimental, too whimsical, too descriptive. He was probably right, but I preferred to write in the manner that gave me the maximum amount of enjoyment. There was more give and take with Jai, but I knew he'd be writing a thousand words to my hundred, and this would have been a little disconcerting to a lazy writer.

Sitaram made no demands on my intellect. He left me to my writing-pad and typewriter. As a physical presence, he was acceptable and grew more interesting by the day. He ran small errands for me, accompanied me on the bicycle-rides which often took us past the Maharani's house. And he took an interest in converting the small balcony into a garden—so much so, that my landlady began complaining that water was seeping through the floor and dripping on to the flour sacks in her ration shop.

The red geranium was joined by a cerise one, and I wondered where it had come from, until I heard the Indiana proprietor complaining that one of his pots was missing.

A potted rose-plant, neglected by Suresh Mathur (who neglected his clients with much the same single-minded carelessness) was appropriated and saved from a slow and lingering death. Subjected to cigarette butts, the remnants of drinks and half-eaten meals, it looked as though it would never produce a rose. So it made the journey from Suresh's verandah to mine without protest from its owner (since he was oblivious of its presence) and under Sitaram's ministrations soon perked up and put forth new leaves and a bud.

My landlady had thrown out a wounded succulent, and this too found a home on the balcony, along with a sickly asparagus-fern left with me by William.

A plant hospital, no less!

Coming up the steps one evening, I was struck by the sweet smell of *raat-ki-rani*, Queen of the Night, and I was puzzled by its presence because I knew there was none growing on our balcony or anywhere else in the vicinity. In front of the building stood a neem tree, and a mango tree, the last survivor of the mango grove that had occupied this area before it was cleared away for a shopping block. There were no shrubs around—they would not have survived the traffic or the press of people. Only potted plants occupied the shopfronts and verandah-spaces. And yet there was that distinct smell of raat-ki-rani, growing stronger all the time.

Halfway up the steps, I looked up, and saw my father standing at the top of the steps, in the half-light of a neighbouring window. He was looking at me the way he had done that day near the canal—with affection and a smile playing on his lips— and at first I stood still, surprised by happiness. Then, waves of love and the old companionship sweeping over me, I advanced up the steps; but when I reached the top, the vision faded and I stood there alone, the sweet smell of raat-ki-rani still with me, but no one else, no sound but the distant shunting of an engine.

This was the second time I'd seen my father, or rather his apparition, and I did not know if it portended anything, or if it was just that he wanted to see me again, was trying to cross the gulf between our different worlds, the worlds of yesterday, today and tomorrow.

Alone on the balcony, looking down at the badly-lit street, I indulged in a bout of nostalgia, recalling boyhood days when my father was my only companion—in the RAF tent outside Delhi, with the hot winds of May and June swirling outside; then the cool evening walks in Chotta Shimla, on the road to Bishop Cotton School; and earlier, exploring the beach at Jamnagar, picking up and storing away different kinds of seashells.

I still had one with me—a smooth round shell which must have belonged to a periwinkle. I put it to my ear and heard the hum of the ocean, the siren song of the sea. I knew that one day I would have to choose between the sea and the mountains, but for the moment it was this little sub-tropical valley, hot and humid, patiently waiting for the monsoon rains . . .

*

The mango trees were sweet with blossom. 'My love is like a red, red rose,' sang Robbie Burns, while John Clare, another poet of the countryside, declared: 'My love is like a bean-field in blossom.' In India, sweethearts used to meet in the mango-groves at blossom time. They don't do that any more. Mango-groves are no longer private places. Better a dark corner of the Indiana, with Larry Gomes playing old melodies on his piano . . .

I walked down to A.N. John's saloon for a haircut, but couldn't get anywhere near the entrance. An excited but good-natured crowd had taken up most of the narrow road as well as a resident's front garden.

'What's happening?' I asked a man who was selling candyfloss.

'Dilip Kumar is inside. He's having a haircut.'

Dilip Kumar! The most popular male star of the silver screen! 'But what's he doing in Dehra?' I asked.

The candyfloss-seller looked at me as though I was a cretin. 'I just told you—having a haircut.'

I moved on to where the owner of the bicycle-hire shop was standing. 'What's Dilip Kumar doing in town?' I asked. He shrugged. 'Don't know. Must be something to do with the circus.'

'Is he the ringmaster for the circus?' asked a little boy in a pyjama suit.

'Of course not,' said the pigtailed girl beside him. 'The circus won't be able to pay him enough.'

'Maybe he owns the circus,' said the little boy.

'It belongs to a friend of his,' said a tongawallah with a knowing air. 'He's come for the opening night.'

Whatever the reasons for Dilip Kumar's presence in Dehra, it was agreed by all that he was in A.N. John's, having a haircut. There was only one way out of A.N. John's and that was by the front door. There were a couple of windows on either side, but the crowd had them well covered.

Finally the star emerged; beaming, waving to people, looking very handsome indeed in a white bush shirt and neatly pressed silvery grey trousers. There was a nice open look about him. No histrionics. No impatience to get away. He was the ordinary guy who'd made good.

Where was Sitaram? Why wasn't my star-struck friend in the crowd? I found him later, watching the circus tents go up, but by then Dilip Kumar was on his way to Delhi. He hadn't come for the circus at all. He'd been visiting his young friend Nandu Jauhar at the Savoy in neighbouring Mussoorie.

Chapter Nine

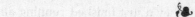

The circus opened on time, and the parade-ground became a fairy land of lights and music. This happened only once in every five years when the Great Gemini Circus came to town. This particular circus toured every town, large and small, throughout the length and breadth of India, so naturally it took some time for it to return to scenes of past triumphs; and by the time it did so, some of the acts had changed, younger performers had taken the place of some of the older ones, and a new generation of horses, tigers and elephants were on display. So, in effect, it was a brand new circus in Dehra, with only a few familiar faces in the ring or on the trapeze.

The senior clown was an old-timer who'd been to Dehra before, and he welcomed the audience with a flattering little speech which was cut short when one of the prancing ponies farted full in his face. Was this accident or design? We in the audience couldn't tell, but we laughed all the same.

A circus does bring all kinds of people together under the one tent-top. The popular stands were of course packed, but the more expensive seats were also occupied. I caught sight of Indu and her mother. They were accompanied by someone who looked like the Prince of Purkazi. I looked again, and came to the conclusion that it was indeed the Prince of Purkazi. A pang of jealously assailed me. What was the eligible young prince doing in the company of my princess? Why wasn't he playing cricket for India or the minor counties, or preferably on some distant field in east UP where bottles and orange-peels would be showered down on the players? Could the Maharani be scheming to get him married to her daughter? The dreadful thought crossed my mind.

He was handsome, he was becoming famous, he was royalty. And he probably owned race-horses.

But not the ones in the circus-ring. They looked reasonably well-fed, and they were obedient; but they weren't of racing stock. A gentle canter around the ring had them snorting and heaving at the flanks as though they'd just finished running all the way from Meerut, their last stop.

Dear Nergis Dalal was watching them with her eagle eye. She was just starting out on her campaign for the SPCA, with particular reference to circus animals, and she had her notebook and fountain-pen poised and ready for action. Nergis, then in her thirties, had come into prominence after winning a newspaper short story contest, and her articles and middles were now appearing quite regularly in the national press. She knew William Matheson and disapproved of him, for he was known to move around in a pony trap. She knew Suresh Mathur and disapproved of him; he had shot his neighbour's Dobermann for howling beneath his window all night. She disapproved of the Indiana owner for serving up partridges at Christmas. And did she disapprove of me? Not yet. But I could sense her looking my way to see if I was enjoying the show. That would have gone against me. So I pretended to look bored; then turned towards her with a resigned look and threw my arms up in the air in a sort of world-weary gesture. 'I'm here for the same reasons as you,' was what it meant, and I must have succeeded, because she gave me a friendly nod. Quite a decent sort, Nergis.

There were several other acquaintances strewn about the audience, including a pale straw-haired boy called Tom Alter, who had managed to secure Dilip Kumar's autograph earlier that day. Tom was the son of American missionaries, but his heart was in Hindi movies and already he was nursing an ambition to be a film star.

William and Jai were absent. They felt the circus was just a little below their intellectual brows. Jai said he had a painting to finish, and William was writing a long article on one of the country's Five-Year Plans—don't ask me which one ... At the time a writer named Khushwant Singh was editing a magazine called *Yojana*, which was all about Five-Year Plans, and he had asked William to do the article. I'd offered the editor an article on punch and its five ingredients—spirit, lemon or lime juice, spice, sugar and rose water—but had been politely turned down. Mr Singh liked his Scotch, but punch was not within the purview of the Five-Year Plan.

To return to the circus ... The trapeze artistes (from Kerala) were very good. The girl on the tight rope (from Andhra) was scintillating in her skin-tight, blue-sequinned costume. The lady lion-tamer (from Tamil Nadu) was daunting, although her lion did look a bit scruffy. The talent seemed to come largely from the south, so that it did not surprise me when the band broke into that lovely Strauss waltz, *Roses of the South*.

The ringmaster came from Bengal. He had a snappy whip, and its sound, as it whistled through the air, was sufficient to command obedience from snarling tigers, prancing ponies and dancing bears. He did not actually touch anyone with it. The whistle of the whip was sufficient.

Sitaram, who sat beside me looking like Sabu in *The Thief of Baghdad*, was enthralled by all he saw. This was his first circus, and every single act and individual performance had his complete attention. His face was suffused with delighted anticipation. He gasped when the trapeze artistes flew through the air. He laughed at the clown's antics. He sang to the tunes the band played, and he whistled (along with the rowdier sections of the audience) when those alluring southern beauties stood upright on their cantering, wheeling ponies—oh, to be a pony!

Oh, to be a pony
With a girl upon my rump,
And I'll take you round the ring, my dear,
Without a single bump.

Not one of my best efforts, but it came to me on the spur of the moment and I said it out loud for the benefit of Sitaram.

'Nice song,' he said. 'I like the one on the second pony. Isn't she beautiful?'

'Stunning,' I agreed. 'I like the sparkle in her eyes.'

'Sparkling eyes are for the poets,' said Sitaram, always bringing me back to earth. 'I like her thighs. Say something about her thighs, poet.'

'Her thighs are like melons—' I began.

'Not melons! I hate melons. They grow all over the *dhobi-ghat*.'

'Sorry, friend. Like half-moons? You like moons?'

'Yes. And her lips?'

'Like rosebuds.'

'Rosebuds. Good. And her breasts?'

'Well, in the frilled costume she's wearing, they look like cabbages.'

Sitaram pinched my thigh, fiercely, so that it hurt. But he wasn't angry. His gaze followed the girl on the pony until she, along with the others in the act, made their exit from the ring.

There were a number of other interesting acts—a dare-devil motor-cyclist riding through a ring of fire, the lady-wrestler taking on a rather somnolent bear and three tigers forming a sort of pyramid atop a revolving platform—but Sitaram was only half-attentive, his thoughts still being with the beautiful, dark, pink-sequinned girl on her white pony.

On the way home he held my hand and sighed.

'I have to go again tomorrow,' he said. 'You'll lend me the money won't you? I have to see that girl again.'

CHAPTER TEN

FOR A COUPLE OF weeks Sitaram was busy with the circus, and I did not see much of him. When he wasn't watching the evening performance, he was there in the mornings, hanging round the circus tents, trying to strike up an acquaintance with the ring-hands or minor performers. Most of the artistes and performers were staying in cheap hotels near the railway station. Sitaram appointed himself an unofficial messenger boy, and as he was familiar with every corner of the town, the circus people found him quite useful. He told them where they could get their clothes stitched or repaired, dry-cleaned or laundered; he guided them to the best eating-places, cheap but substantial restaurants such as Komal's or Chacha-da-Hotel (no Indiana or Royal Cafe for the circus crew); posted their letters home; found them barbers and masseurs; brought them newspapers. He was even able to get a copy of the *Madras Mail* for the lady lion-tamer.

Late one night (it must have been after the night show was over) he woke me from a deep dreamless sleep and without any preamble stuffed a laddoo into my mouth. Laddoos are not my favourite sweetmeat, and certainly not in bed at midnight, when the crumbs on the bedsheet were likely to attract an army of ants. While I was still choking on the laddoo, he gave me his good news.

'I've got a job at the circus!'

'What, as assistant to the clown?'

'No, not yet. But the manager likes me. He's made me his office boy. Two hundred rupees a month!'

'Almost as much as I make—but I suppose you'll be running around at all hours. And have you met the girl you liked—the dark girl on the white pony?'

'I have spoken to her. She smiles whenever she sees me. I have spoken to all the girls. They are very nice—especially the ones from the south.'

'Well, you're luckier than I am with girls.'

'Would you like to meet the lady wrestler?'

'The one who wrestles with the bear every night? After that, would she have any time for mere men?'

'They say she's in love with the ringmaster, Mr Victor. He uses his whip if she gets too rough.'

'I don't want to have anything to do with lady wrestlers, lions, bears or whips. Now let me go to sleep. I have to write a story in the morning. Something romantic.'

'What are you calling it?'

'"The Night Train at Deoli." Now go to sleep.'

He leant over and gave me a quick sharp bite on the cheek. I yelped.

'What's that supposed to be?' I demanded.

'That's how tigers make love,' he said, and vanished into the night.

*

The monsoon was only a fortnight away, we were told, and we were all looking forward to some relief from the hot and dusty days of June. Sometimes the nights were even more unbearable, as squadrons of mosquitoes came zooming across the eastern Doon. In those days the eastern Doon was more malarious than the western, probably because it was low-lying in parts and there was more still water in drains and pools. Wild boar and swamp deer abounded.

But it was now mango-time, and this was one of the compensations of summer. I kept a bucket filled with mangoes and dipped into it frequently during the day. So did Jai Shankar, William, Suresh Mathur and others who came by.

One of my more interesting visitors was a writer called G.V. Desani who had, a few years earlier, written a comic novel called *All About H. Hatterr*. I suspect that the character of Hatterr was based on Desani himself, for he was an eccentric individual who told me that he slept in a coffin.

'Do you carry it around with you?' I asked, over a coffee at Indiana.

'No, hotels won't allow me to bring it into the lobby, let alone my room. Hotel managers have a morbid fear of death, haven't they?'

'A coffin should make a good coffee-table. We'll put it to the owner of the Indiana.'

'Trains are fussy too. You can't have it in your compartment, and in the brake-van it gets smashed. Mine's an expensive mahogany coffin, lined with velvet.'

'I wish you many comfortable years sleeping in it. Do you intend being buried in it too?'

'No, I shall be cremated like any other good Hindu. But I may *will* the coffin to a good Christian friend. Would you like it?'

'I rather fancy being cremated myself. I'm not a very successful Christian. A pagan all my life. Maybe I'll get religious when I'm older.'

Mr Desani then told me that he was nominating his own novel for the Nobel Prize, and would I sign a petition that was to be presented to the Nobel Prize Committee extolling the merits of his book? Gladly, I said; always ready to help a good cause. And did I know of any other authors or patrons of literature who might sign? I told him there was Nergis Dalal; and William Matheson, an eminent Swiss Journalist; and old Mrs D' Souza who did a gardening column for *Eve's Weekly*; and Holdsworth, at the Doon School—he'd climbed Kamet with Frank Smythe, and had written an account for the journal of the Bombay Natural History Society—and of course there was Jai Shankar who was keeping a diary in the manner of Stendhal; and wasn't Suresh Mathur planning to write a PhD on P.G. Wodehouse? I gave their names and addresses to the celebrated author, and even added that of the inventor of the Sit-Safe. After all, hadn't he encouraged this young writer by commissioning him to write a brochure for his toilet-seat?

Mr Desani produced his own brochure, with quotes from reviewers and writers who had praised his work. I signed his petition and allowed him to pay for the coffee.

As I walked through the swing doors of the Indiana, Indu and her mother walked in. It was too late for me to turn back. I bowed like the gentleman my grandmother had always wanted me to be, and held the door for them, while they breezed in to the restaurant. Larry Gomes was playing *Smoke Gets in Your Eyes* with a wistful expression.

Chapter Eleven

Lady Wart of Worcester, Lady Tryiton and the Earl of Stopwater, the Hon. Robin Crazier, Mr and Mrs Paddy Snott-Noble, the Earl and Countess of Lost Marbles and General Sir Peter de l'Orange-Peel . . .

These were only some of the gracious names that graced the pages of the Doon Club's guest and membership register at the turn of the century, when the town was the favourite retiring place for the English aristocracy. So well did the Club look after its members that most of them remained permanently in Dehra, to be buried in the Chandernagar cemetery just off the Hardwar Road.

My own ancestors were not aristocracy. Dad's father came to India as an eighteen-year-old soldier in a Scots Regiment, a contemporary of Kipling's 'Soldiers Three'—Privates Othenis, Mulvaney and Learoyd. He married an orphaned girl who had been brought up on an indigo plantation at Motihari in Bihar. My maternal grandfather worked in the Indian Railways, as a foreman in the railway workshops at some god-forsaken railway junction in central India. He married a statuesque, strong-willed lady who had also grown up in India. Dad was born in the Shahjahanpur military camp; my mother in Karachi. So although my forebears were, for the most part, European, I was third generation India-born. The expression, 'Anglo-Indian', has come to mean so many things—British settler, Old Koi-Hai, Colonel

Curry or Captain Chapatti, or simply Eurasian—that I don't use it very often. Indian is good enough for me. I may have relatives scattered around the world, but I have no great interest in meeting them. My feet are firmly planted in Ganges soil.

Grandfather (of the Railways) retired in Dehradun (or Deyrah Dhoon, as it was spelt in the old days) and built a sturdy bungalow on the Old Survey Road. Sadly, it was sold at the time of Independence when most of his children decided to quit the country. After my father's death, my mother married a Punjabi gentleman and so I stayed on in India, except for that brief sojourn in England and the Channel Islands. I'd come back to Dehra to find that even mother and stepfather had left, but it was still home, and in the cemetery there were several relatives including Grandfather and Great-grandmother. If I sat on their graves, I felt I owned a bit of property. Not a bungalow or even a vegetable patch, but a few feet of well-nourished sod. There were even marigolds flowering at the edges of the graves. And a little blue everlasting that I have always associated with Dehra. It grows in ditches, on vacant plots, in neglected gardens, along footpaths, on the edges of fields, behind lime-kilns, wherever there is a bit of wasteland. Call it a weed if you like, but I have every respect for a plant that will survive the onslaught of brick, cement, petrol fumes, grazing cows and goats, heat and cold (for it flowers almost all the year round) and overflowing sewage. As long as that little flowering weed is still around, there is hope for both man and nature.

A feeling of tranquility and peace always pervaded my being when I entered the cemetery. Were my long-gone relatives pleased by my presence there? I did not see them in any form, but then, cemeteries are the last place for departed souls to hang around in. Given a chance, they would rather be among the living, near those they cared for or in places where they were happy. I have never been convinced by ghost stories in which the tormented spirit revisits the scene of some ghastly tragedy. Why on earth (or why in heaven) should they want to relive an unpleasant experience?

My maternal grandfather, by my mother's account, was a man with a sly sense of humour who often discomfited his relatives by introducing into their homes odd creatures who refused to go away. Hence the tiny Jharipani bat released into Aunt Mabel's bedroom, or the hedgehog slipped between his brother Major Clerke's bedsheets. A cousin, Mrs Blanchette, found her house swarming with white rats, while a neighbour received a gift of a parcel of papayas—and in their midst, a bright green and yellow chameleon.

And so, when I was within some fifty to sixty feet of Grandfather's grave, I was not in the least surprised to see a full-grown tiger stretched out on his tombstones apparently enjoying the shade of the magnolia tree which grew beside it.

Was this a manifestation of the tiger cub he'd kept when I was a child? Did the ghosts of long-dead tigers enjoy visiting old haunts? Live tigers certainly did, and when this one stirred, yawned and twitched its tail, I decided I wouldn't stay to find out if it was a phantom tiger or a real one.

Beating a hasty retreat to the watchman's quarters near the lych-gate, I noticed that a large, well-fed and very real goat was tethered to one of the old tombstones (Colonel Ponsonby of Her Majesty's Dragoons), and I concluded that the tiger had already spotted it and was simply building up an appetite before lunch.

'There's a tiger on Grandfather's grave,' I called out to the watchman, who was checking out his cabbage patch. (And healthy cabbages they were, too.)

The watchman was a bit deaf and assumed that I was complaining about some member of his family, as they were in the habit of grinding their masalas on the smoother gravestones.

'It's that boy Masood,' he said. 'I'll get after him with a stick.' And picking up his lathi, he made for the grave.

A yell, a roar, and the watchman was back and out of the lych-gate before me.

'Send for the police, sahib,' he shouted. 'It's one of the circus tigers. It must have escaped!'

Chapter Twelve

Sincerely hoping that Sitaram had not been in the way of the escaping tiger, I made for the circus tents on the parade-ground. There was no show in progress. It was about noon, and everyone appeared to be resting. If a tiger was missing, no one seemed to be aware of it.

'Where's Sitaram?' I asked one of the hands.

'Helping to wash down the ponies,' he replied.

But he wasn't in the pony enclosure. So I made my way to the rear, where there was a cage housing a lion (looking rather sleepy, after its late-night bout with the lady lion-tamer), another cage housing a tiger (looking ready to bite my head off) and another cage with its door open—empty!

Someone came up behind me, whistling cheerfully. It was Sitaram.

'Do you like the tigers?' he asked.

'There's only one here. There are three in the show, aren't there?'

'Of course, I helped feed them this morning.'

'Well, one of them's gone for a walk. Someone must have unlocked the door. If it's the same tiger I saw in the cemetery, I think it's looking for another meal—or maybe just dessert!'

Sitaram ran back into the tent, yelling for the trainer and the ringmaster. And then, of course, there was commotion. For no one had noticed the tiger slipping away. It must have made off through the bamboo-grove at the edge of the parade-ground, through the Forest Rangers College (well-wooded then), circled the police lines and entered the cemetery. By now it could have been anywhere.

It was, in fact, walking right down the middle of Dehra's main road, causing the first hold-up in traffic since Pandit Nehru's last visit to the town. Mr Nehru would have fancied the notion; he was keen on tigers. But the citizens of Dehra took no chances.

They scattered at the noble beast's approach. The Delhi bus came to a grinding halt, while tonga-ponies, never known to move faster than a brisk trot, broke into a gallop that would have done them proud at the Bangalore Races.

The only creature that failed to move was a large bull (the one that someimes blocked the approach to my steps) sitting in the middle of the road, forming a traffic island of its own. It did not move for cars, buses, tongas and trucks. Why budge for a mere tiger?

And the tiger, having been fed on butcher's meat for most of its life, now disdained the living thing (since the bull refused to be stalked) and headed instead for the back entrance to the Indiana's kitchens.

There was a general exodus from the Indiana. William Matheson, who had been regaling his friends with tales of his exploits in the Foreign Legion, did not hang around either; he made for the comparative safety of my flat. Larry Gomes stopped in the middle of playing the *Anniversary Waltz*, and fox-trotted out of the restaurant. The owner of the Indiana rushed into the street and collided with the owner of the Royal Cafe. Both swore at each other in choice Pashtu—they were originally from Peshawar. Swami Aiyar, a Doon School boy with ambitions of being a newspaper correspondent, buttonholed me near my landlady's shop and asked me if I knew Jim Corbett's telephone number in Haldwani.

'But he only shoots man-eaters,' I protested.

'Well, they're saying three people have already been eaten in the bazaar.'

'Ridiculous. No self-respecting tiger would go for a three-course meal.'

'All the same, people are in danger.'

'So, we'll send for Jim Corbett. Aurora of the Green Bookshop should have his number.'

Mr Aurora was better informed than either of us. He told us that Jim Corbett had settled in Kenya several years ago.

Swami looked dismayed. 'I thought he loved India so much that he refused to leave.'

'You're confusing him with Jack Gibson of the Mayo School,' I said.

At this point the tiger came through the swing doors of the Indiana and started crossing the road. Suresh Mathur was driving slowly down Rajpur Road in his 1936 Hillman. He'd been up half the night, drinking and playing cards, and he had a terrible hangover. He was now heading for the Royal Cafe, convinced that only a chilled beer could help him recover. When he saw the tiger, his reflexes—never very good—failed him completely, and he drove his car onto the pavement and into the plate-glass window of Bhai Dhian Singh's Wine and Liquor Shop. Suresh looked quite happy among the broken rum bottles. The heady aroma of XXX Rosa Rum, awash on the shopping verandah, was too much for a couple of old topers, who began to mop up the liquor with their handkerchiefs. Suresh would have done the same had he been conscious.

We carried him into the deserted Indiana and sent for Dr Sharma.

'Nothing much wrong with him,' said the doctor, 'but he looks anaemic,' and proceeded to give him an injection of vitamin B12. This was Dr Sharma's favourite remedy for anyone who was ailing. He was a great believer in vitamins.

I don't know if the B12 did Suresh any good, but the jab of the needle woke him up, and he looked around, blinked up at me and said, 'Thought I saw a tiger. Could do with a drink, old boy.'

'I'll stand you a beer,' I said. 'But you'll have to pay the bill at Bhai Dhian's. And your car needs repairs.'

'And this injection costs five rupees,' said Dr Sharma.

'Beer is the same price. I'll stand you one too.'

So we settled down in the Indiana and finished several bottles of beer, Dr Sharma expounding all the time on the miracle of Vitamin B12, while Suresh told me that he knew now what it felt like to enter the fourth dimension.

The tiger was soon forgotten, and when I walked back to my room a couple of hours later and found the postman waiting for me with a twenty-five rupee money-order from *Sainik Samachar* (the Armed Forces' weekly magazine), I tipped him five rupees and put the rest aside for a rainy day—which, hopefully, would be the morrow, as monsoon clouds had been advancing from the south.

They say that those with a clear conscience usually sleep well. I have always done a lot of sleeping, especially in the afternoons, and have never been unduly disturbed by pangs of conscience, for I haven't deprived any man of his money, his wife or his song.

I kicked off my chappals and lay down and allowed my mind to dwell on my favourite Mexican proverb: 'How sweet it is to do nothing, and afterwards to rest!'

I hoped the tiger had found a shady spot for his afternoon siesta. With goodwill towards one and all, I drifted into a deep sleep and woke only in the early evening, to the sound of distant thunder.

CHAPTER THIRTEEN

THE TIGER PADDED SILENTLY but purposefully past the Dilaram Bazaar, paying no attention to the screaming and shouting of the little gesticulating creatures who fled at his approach. He'd seen them every night at the circus—all in search of excitement, provided there was no risk attached to it!

Walking down from the other end of the Dilaram Road was a tiger of another sort—sub-Inspector Sher ('Tiger') Singh, in charge of the local police outpost. 'Tiger Singh' was feeling on the top of the world. His little thana was notorious for beating up suspected criminals, and he'd had a satisfying night supervising the third-degree interrogation of three young suspects in a case of theft. None of them had broken down and confessed, but 'Tiger' had the pleasure (and what was it if not a pleasure, an appeal to his senses?) of kicking one youth senseless, blackening the eyes of another and fracturing the ankle and shinbone of the third. The damage done, they had been ejected into the street with a warning to keep their noses clean in the future.

These young men could have saved themselves from physical injury had they disbursed a couple of hundred rupees to the sub-inspector and his cohorts, but they were unemployed and without friends of substance; so, beaten and humiliated, they crawled home as best they could. 'Tiger' Singh liked the money he sometimes picked up from suspects and the relatives of petty offenders; but many years in the service had brought out the sadistic side to his nature, and now he took a certain pleasure in seeing noses broken and teeth knocked out. He claimed that he could extract teeth without anaesthesia, and would do the job free for those who could not afford dentists' bills. There were no takers.

Today he strutted along the pavement, twirling his moustaches with one hand and pulling up his trousers with the other. For he was a well-fed gentleman, whose belly protruded above his belt. He had a constant struggle keeping his trousers, along with his heavy revolver holster, from slipping to the ground. Had he not been in the direct path of the tiger, he would have been ignored. But he chose to stand frozen to the ground, really too terrified to reach for his gun or even hitch up his trousers.

The tiger slapped him to the ground, picked him up by his fat neck and dragged him into the lantana bushes. Sher Singh let out one despairing cry, which turned into a gurgle as the blood spurted from his throat.

The tiger did not eat humans. Their flesh was unappetizing, acceptable only to the lame or ageing beasts who could no longer hunt. True, the circus tiger had almost forgotten how to hunt, but his instincts told him that more succulent repasts could be found in the depths of the forest. And the forest was close at hand (or so it was in those days), so he abandoned the dead policeman, who would have made a more suitable meal for vultures had not his colleagues come and taken him away.

The autopsy report said, 'Killed by wild tiger,' which was

inaccurate in that the tiger was tame, but it was the only extenuating remark ever made about the sub-inspector. His family received a pension and lived fairly happily ever after.

Neither the tiger nor the S.I. was familiar with the Laws of Karma, or Emerson's Law of Compensation, but they appeared to have been working all the same.

*

As the tiger sought its freedom in the forest, the clouds that had gathered over the foothills finally gave way under their burden of moisture. The first rain of the monsoon descended upon the hills, the valley, the town. In minutes, a two-month layer of dust was washed away from trees, rooftops and pavements. The rain swept across the streets of Dehra, sending people scattering for shelter. Umbrellas unfolded for the first time in months. A gust of wind shook the circus tent. The old lion, scenting the rain on the wind, sat up in its cage and gave a great roar of delight. The ponies shook their manes, an elephant trumpeted. One of the dwarves, who had been making love to the lady-wrestler, now did so with greater abandon. The ravished lady squealed with pleasure; for it has to be said that the dwarf was undersized in every department but one, and in that one area few could surpass him.

The rain swept over the railway yards, washing the soot and dust from the carriages and engines. It brought freshness and new life to the tea-gardens and sugarcane fields. Even earthworms responded to the cool dampening of their environment and stretched sensuously in the soft mud.

Mud! Buffaloes wallowed in it; children romped in it; frogs broke into antiphonal chants. Glorious, squelchy mud. Hateful for the rest of the year, but wonderfully inviting on the first day of the monsoon. A large amount got washed down from the loose eroded soil of the foothills, so that the streams and canals were soon clogged, silted up and flooded their banks.

The mango and litchi trees were washed clean. Sal and shisham shook in the wind. Peepal leaves danced. The roots of the banyan drank up the good rain. The neem gave out its heady fragrance. Squirrels ran for shelter into the embracing branches of Krishna's buttercup. Parrots made merry in the guava groves.

I walked home through the rain. Home, did I say? Yes, my small flat was becoming a home, what with Sitaram and his geraniums upstairs, my landlady below and other familiars in the neighbourhood. Even the geckos on the wall were now recognizable, each acquiring an identity and personality of its own. Sitaram had trained one of them to take food from his fingers. At first he had stuck a bit of meat at the end of a long thin stick. The lizard had snapped up this morsel. Then, every day, he had shortened the stick until the lizard, growing in confidence, took his snack from the short end of the stick and finally from the boy's fingers. I hadn't got around to feeding the wall lizards. One of them had fallen with a plop on my forehead in the middle of the night, and my landlady told me of how a whole family had been poisoned when a gecko had fallen into a cooking pot and been served up with a mixed vegetable curry.

A neighbour, who worked for Madras Coffee House, told me that down south there were a number of omens connected with the fall of the wall lizard, especially if it dropped on some part of your body. He told me that I'd been fortunate that the lizard fell on my forehead, but had it fallen on my tummy I'd have been in for a period of bad luck. But I wasn't taking any chances. The lizards could have all the snacks they wanted from Sitaram, but I wasn't going to encourage any familiarity.

Now, happy to get my clothes wet with the first monsoon shower, I ran up the steps to my rooms, but found them empty. Then Sitaram's voice, raised in song, wafted down to me from the rooftop. I climbed up to the roof by means of an old iron ladder that was always fixed there, and found him on the flat roof, prancing about in the nude.

'Come and join me,' he shouted. 'It is good to dance in the first monsoon shower.'

'You can be seen from the roofs across the road,' I said.

'Never mind. Don't you think I'm the sexiest man of 1955?'

'I shall look forward to seeing you in 1956,' I said, and retreated below.

Chapter Fourteen

I~T~ WAS STILL 1955, and the middle of the monsoon, when Sitaram decided to throw his lot in with the circus and leave Dehra. Those roses of the south had a lot to do with it. I wasn't sure if he was in love with one of the pony-riders, or with the girl on the flying trapeze.

Perhaps both of them; perhaps all of them. He was at an age when his sexual energies had to be directed somewhere, and those beautiful dusky circus girls were certainly more approachable, and more glamorous, than the coy college girls we saw every day.

'So you're going to desert me,' I said, when he told me of his plans.

'Only for a few months. I'll see the country this way.'

'Once with the circus, always with the circus.'

'Well, you have your Indu.'

'I don't. I hear she's getting engaged to that cricket-playing princeling. I hate all cricketers!'

'You're better-looking.'

'But I'm not a prince. I haven't any money, and I don't play cricket. Well, I played a little at school, but they always made me twelfth man, which meant carrying out the drinks like a waiter. What a stupid game!'

'I agree. Football is better.'

'More manly. But not as glamorous.'

Sitaram pondered a while, and then gave me the benefit of his wisdom.

'To win Indu you must win her mother.'

'And how do I do that? She's a dragon.'

'Well, you must pretend you like dragons.'

*

I was sitting in the Indiana, having my coffee, when Indu's mother walked in. She was alone. (Indu was probably with her prince, learning to bowl under-arm). I said good morning and asked her if she'd like to join me for a cup of coffee. To my surprise, she assented. Larry Gomes was playing *Love is a Many-Splendoured Thing*, and the Maharani was just a bit dreamy-eyed and probably a little sloshed too. But she wasn't in any way attractive. Her eyes were baggy (did she drink?) and her skin was coarse (too many skin lotions?) and her chin was developing a dewlap. Would Indu look like her one day?

She drank her coffee and asked me if I would like a drive. On the assumption that she would be driving me to her house, I thanked her and followed her out of the restaurant, while Larry Gomes looked anxiously at me over his spectacles and broke into the *Funeral March*.

CHAPTER FIFTEEN

WELL, IT WAS VERY nearly my funeral.

Have you ever made love to a dragon—and a scaly one at that? How could a monster like the Maharani have produced a beautiful, tender, vivacious, electrifying girl like Indu? It was like making a succulent dish from a pumpkin, a bitter gourd and a spent cucumber.

The Maharani had denied me the dish, but she was prepared to give me the ingredients.

She drove me to her home in her smart little Sunbeam-Talbot, and no sooner was I settled on her sofa, with a glass of Carew's

Gin in my hand, than I found my free hand encased in a fold of crocodile skin—*her* hand!

A shudder ran down my spine. She mistook the shudder for a shiver of excitement, and started playing with the lobe of my ear. My ear got caught between two of her gold bangles and was almost wrenched off as I jerked my head away. Gin was spilt on my trousers, and I put the glass down on a sidetable. As I did so, the Maharani cuddled up to me, and I discovered that the sofa wasn't really large enough for both of us. Also, one was inclined to sink deeper into the upholstery, making a quick escape very difficult.

It had never occured to me that this badly-preserved Christmas pudding could be of an amorous disposition. I had always thought of middle-aged mothers as having gone beyond the pursuit of carnal pleasures. But not this one!

She tried to set me at my ease.

'I'm a child psychologist, you know.'

'But I'm twenty-one.'

'All the better to *treat* you, my dear.'

'Your Highness,' I began.

'Don't Highness me, darling. My pet name is Liz.'

'As in lizard?'

'Cheeky! After Queen Elizabeth.' And she gave me a sharp pinch on the thigh. 'You write poetry, don't you? Recite one of your poems.'

'You need moonlight and roses.'

'I prefer sunshine and cactii.'

'Well, here's a funny one.' I was anxious to please her without succumbing to her blandishments and advances. So I recited my latest limerick.

There was a fat man in Lucknow
Who swallowed six plates of pillau,
When his belly went bust
(As distended, it must)
His buttons rained down upon Mhow.

She clapped her hands and shrieked with delight. 'Buttons, buttons!' And she made a grab for mine. (We weren't using zips in those days.)

I tried to get up from the sofa, but she pulled me down again.

'You deserve a reward,' she said, producing a lump of barley-sugar from a box on the side-table. 'This came all the way from Calcutta. Open your mouth.'

Dutifully I opened my mouth. But instead of popping the sweet in, she planted her lips on mine, large lips like suction pumps, and thrust her long lizard-like tongue down my throat. Her crocodile fingers were all over me, and even if my buttons did not reach Mhow, they must have landed on Mussoorie.

What can you do in such a situation? Not much, really. You just let the more active partner take over—in this case, the rich Maharani of Magador. She certainly knew how to get you worked up. After a hesitant start, all I had to do was imagine that I was another crocodile. I slid into her quivering orifice, and my virginity was at an end.

Afterwards I was rewarded with more barley-sugar and Turkish coffee.

She offered to drop me home, but I said I would walk. Physically I felt great, but I wanted to put my head in order. My thoughts were in whirl. How could I be the Maharani's lover while I was in love with her daughter? Love lyrics for Indu, and limericks for her mother?

'There's no justice anywhere,' I said aloud, in my best William Brown manner. "T'isn't fair.' And then, as Popeye would have said, 'It's disgustipating!'

And as I closed the gate and stepped onto the sidewalk, who should appear but Indu, riding pillion on her cricketing prince's Triumph motor-bike. At the sight of him my feelings of guilt evaporated. And looking at Indu, smiling insincerely at me, I began to see points of resemblance between her and her mother. Would she be like the Maharani in twenty years' time? I had never seen her father (the late deceased Maharaja of Magador) but fervently hoped that he had been as goodlooking as his portraits suggested and that Indu had taken after him.

I gave her and her escort a polite bow (part of my grandmother's influence, no doubt) and set off at a dignified pace in the direction of the bazaar. A car would never be mine, but at least my legs wouldn't atrophy from disuse. Hadn't this very cricketing legend suffered from several torn ligaments in the course of his short career? Chasing cricket balls is a certain way to get a hernia, I said to myself, and then turned my thoughts to the composition of a new limerick in honour of the lady who had just tormented me into becoming her lover. There was no Amnesty International in those days; I had to defend myself in my own way. So I composed the following lines:

> They called her the Queen of the Nile,
> For she walked like a fat crocodile.
> But she said, 'You young bugger,
> I'll make you my *mugger,*'
> And took me to bed with a smile.

CHAPTER SIXTEEN

WE ALL NEED ONE friend in whom to confide—to whom we can confess our misdemeanours, look for sympathy in times of trouble. Sitaram was my only intimate, and he listened with bated breath while I gave him a hair-raising account of my seduction by royalty. But he wasn't sympathetic. His first response was the following succinct remark:

'Congratulations, *ullu ka pattha.*'

'Why the heady compliment?' I asked.

'Because you cannot escape her now. She'll suck you dry.'

'A succubus, forsooth!'

'Don't use fancy language—you know what I mean. When an older woman gets hold of a young man, she doesn't let him go until he's quite useless to her or anyone else! You'd better join the circus with me.'

'And what do I do in the circus? Feed the animals?'

'They need someone for giving massage.'

'I've always fancied myself as a masseur. Whom do I get to massage—the acrobats, the dancing-girls, the trapeze artistes?'

'The elephants. They lie down and you massage their legs. And backsides.'

'I'll stick to the Maharani,' I said. 'Her skin has the same sort of texture, but there's not so much of it.'

'Well, please yourself . . . See, I've brought you a pretty tree. Will you look after it while I'm away?'

It was a red oleander in a pot. It was just coming into flower. We placed it on the balcony beside the rose bush and the geraniums. There were several geraniums now—white, cerise, salmon-pink and bright red—and they were all in flower, making quite a display on the sunny verandah.

'I'll look after them,' I said. 'As long as the landlady doesn't turn me out. The rent is overdue.'

'Don't lend money to your friends. Especially that Swiss fellow. He owes money everywhere—hasn't even paid my parents for two months' washing. One of these days he'll just go away—and your money with him. There is nothing to keep him here.'

'There is nothing to keep *me* here.'

'This is where you belong, where you grew up. You will always be here.'

It was where I had grown up—my mother's, her parents' home—but I had always been happier with my father, sharing a wartime tent with him on the outskirts of Delhi or Karachi; visiting the ruins of Old Delhi—Humayun's Tomb, the Purana Killa, the Kashmiri Gate; going to the cinema with him to see the beautiful skating legend Sonja Henie in *Sun Valley Serenade*, Nelson Eddy singing *Volga Boatmen* and *Ride, Cossack, Ride* in *Balalaika*, Carmen Miranda swinging her hips *Down Argentine Way*, and Hope and Crosby *On the Road to Zanzibar* or *Morocco* or *Singapore*; rickshaw-rides in Shimla; ice-creams at Davico's; comics—*Film Fun* and *Hotspur* . . . And those colourful postcards he used to send me once a week. At school, the distribution of the post was always something to look forward to.

But I must also have inherited a great deal of my mother's sensuality, her unconventional attitude to life, her stubborn insistence on doing things that respectable people did not approve of . . . Traits that she probably got from her father, a convivial character, who mingled with all and shocked not a few.

I'm sure my mother was quite a handful for my poor father, bookish and intellectual, who did so want her to be a 'lady'. But this was something that went against her nature. She liked to drink and swear a bit. The ladies of the Dehra Benevolent Society did not approve. Nor did they approve of my mother going to church without a hat! This was considered the height of irreverence in those days. There were remonstrances and anguished letters of protest from other (always female) members of the Congregation.

As a result, my mother stopped going to church, and I never picked up the habit. Her sisters, with the exception of the eldest, Enid, were conventional types who found and kept conventional husbands. Aunt Enid, though married to a doctor, distributed her favours on a first-come, first-served basis; she wasn't particular about the cut of your trousers as long as there was something in them. She liked having a good time, and in those war years there was no shortage of Allied troops prepared to make her their mascot. She had a daughter, Sally, who was my age and a bit of a tomboy. Sally and I wrestled in Granny's flowerbeds and took a spirited interest in each other's anatomy. We were only six or seven, and it was all innocent play—or arrested foreplay, I suppose. We sucked each other's lollipops, and this gave us as great a thrill as anything else we did.

Growing up in fairly unfettered fashion, I was quite at ease with Sitaram, another free soul. I was not so sure about the Maharani, although I suspect Aunt Enid would have approved of her. Would she pursue me with relentless abandon, as Sitaram feared, or would she already be looking for other conquests? If she was anything like Aunt E, it would be the latter.

CHAPTER SEVENTEEN

❦

THE CIRCUS TENTS WERE being dismantled and the parade-ground was comparatively silent again. Some boys kicked a football around. Others flew kites. The monsoon season is kite-flying time, for it's not too windy, and the moist aircurrents are just right for keeping a kite aloft.

In the old part of the Dhamawalla bazaar, there used to be a kite-shop (it was still there five years ago, when I revisited the area), and, taking a circuitous way home, I stopped at the shop and bought a large pink kite. I thought Sitaram would enjoy flying it from the rooftop when he wasn't dancing in the rain. But when I got home, I found he had gone. His parents told me he had left in a hurry, as most of the circus people had taken the afternoon train to Amritsar. He had taken his clothes and a cracked bathroom mirror, nothing else, and yet the flat seemed strangely empty and forlorn without him. The plants on the balcony were poignant reminders of his presence.

I thought of giving the kite to my landlady's son, but I knew him for a destructive brat who'd put his fist through at the first opportunity, so I hung it on a nail on the bedroom wall, and thought it looked rather splendid there, better than a Picasso although perhaps not in the same class as one of Jai Shankar's angels.

As I stood back, admiring it, there was a loud knocking at my door (as in the knocking at the gate in Macbeth, portending deeds of darkness) and I turned to open it, wondering why I had bothered to close it in the first place (I seldom did), when something about the knocking—its tone, its texture—made me hesitate.

There are knocks of all kinds—hesitant knocks, confident knocks, friendly knocks, good-news knocks, bad-news knocks, tax-collector's knocks (exultant, these!), policemen's knocks (peremptory, business-like), drunkard's knocks (slow and deliberate), the landlady's knock (you could tell she owned the place) and children's knocks (loud thumps halfway down the door).

I had come to recognize different kinds of knocks, but this one, was unfamiliar. It was a possessive kind of knock, gloating, sensual, bold and arrogant. I stood a chair on a table, then balanced myself on the chair and peered down through the half-open skylight.

It was Indu's mother. Her perfume nearly knocked me off the chair. Her bosom heaved with passion and expectancy, her eyes glinted like a hyaena's and her crocodile hands were encased in white gloves!

I withdrew quietly and tiptoed back across the room and out on the balcony. On the next balcony, my neighbour's maidservant was hanging out some washing.

'For God's sake,' I told her. 'That woman out front, banging on my door. Go and tell her I'm not at home!'

'Who is she?'

'A *rakshasni*, if you want to know.'

'Then I'm not going near her!'

'All right, can you let me out through your flat? Is there anyone at home?'

'No, but come quickly. Can you climb over the partition?'

The partition did not look as if it would take my weight, so I climbed over the balcony wall and, clinging to it, moved slowly along the ledge till I got to my neighbour's balcony. The maidservant helped me over. Such nice hands she had! How could a working girl have such lovely hands while a lady of royal lineage had crocodile-skin hands? It was the Law of Compensation, I suppose; Mother Nature looking after her own.

'What's your name?' I whispered, as she led me through her employer's flat and out to the back stairs.

'Radha,' she said, her smile lighting up the gloom.

'Rather you than that rakshasni outside!' I gave her hand a squeeze and said, 'I'll see you again,' then took off down the stairs as though a swarm of bees was after me.

My landlady's son's bicycle was standing in the verandah. I decided to borrow it for a couple of hours.

I rode vigorously until I was out of the town, and then I took a narrow unmetalled road through the sal forest on the Hardwar road. I thought I would be safe there, but it wasn't long before I heard the menacing purr of the Maharani's Sunbeam-Talbot. Looking over my shoulder, I saw it bumping along in a cloud of dust. It was like a chase-scene in a Hitchcock film, and I was Cary Grant about to be machinegunned from a low-flying aircraft. I saw another narrow trail to the right, and swerved off the road, only to find myself parting company with the bicycle and somersaulting into some lantana bushes. There was a screech of brakes, a car door shot open and the rich Maharani of Magador was bounding towards me like a man-eating tigress.

'Jim Corbett, where are you?' I called feebly.

'He's in Kenya, you fool,' said the tigress, as she engulfed me and swallowed me whole.

Chapter Eighteen

A CHANGE OF AIR was needed. What with the attentions of the Maharani, the borrowings of William, the loss of Indu and the absence of Sitaram, I wasn't doing much writing. My bank balance was very low. I had also developed a throat infection, probably as a result of having that rasping lizard's tongue slide down my throat. Anyone else would have bitten it off!

There was the sum of two hundred and seventy rupees in the bank. Always prudent, I withdrew two hundred and fifty and left twenty rupees for my last supper. Then I packed a bag, and left my keys with the landlady with the entreaty that she tell no one in Dehra of my whereabouts and took the bus to Rishikesh.

Rishikesh was then little more than a village, scattered along the banks of the Ganga where it cut through the foothills. There were a few ashrams and temples, a tiny bazaar and a police outpost. The saffron-robed sadhus and ascetics outnumbered the rest of the population.

There had been a break in the rains, and I spent a night sleeping on the sands sloping down to the river. The next night it did rain, and I moved to a bench on the small railway platform. I could have stayed in one of the two ashrams, but I had no pretensions to religion of any kind, and was not inclined to become an acolyte to some holy man. Kim had his Lama, the braying Beatles had their Master and others have had their gurus and godmen, but I have always been stubborn and thick-headed enough to want to remain my own man—just myself, warts and all, singing my own song. Nobody's *chela*, nobody's camp-follower.

Let nature reign, let freedom sing! . . .

And, so, on the third morning of my voluntary exile from the fleshpots of Dehra, I strode up river, taking a well-worn path which led to the shrines in the higher mountains. I was not seeking salvation or enlightenment; I wished merely to come to terms with myself and my situation.

Should I stay on in Dehra, or should I strike out for richer pastures—Delhi or Bombay perhaps? Or should I return to London and my desk in the Thomas Cook office? Oh, for the life of a clerk! Or I could give English tuitions, I supposed. Except that everyone seemed to know English. What about French? I'd picked up a French patois in the Channel Islands. It wasn't the real thing, but who would know the difference?

I practised a few lines, reciting aloud to myself:

Jeune femme au rendezvous.
(Waiting for her lover.)
Oh, Oui! Il va venir
(Oh, yes, he is coming!)
Enfin je le verrai!
(Finally I shall see him!)
Pourquoi je attends?
(What am I waiting for?)

Roll up, folks. Learn how to make love in French! I could see my flat overflowing with students from all over Dehra and beyond. But how was I to keep the Maharani from attending?

The future looked rather empty as I trudged forlornly up the mountain trail. What I really needed just then was a good companion—someone to confide in, someone with whom to share life's little problems. No wonder people get married! An admirable institution, marriage. But who'd marry an indigent writer, with twenty rupees in the bank and no prospects in a land where English was on the way out. (I was not to know that English would be 'in' again, thirty years later.) No self-respecting girl really wants to share the proverbial attic with a down-and-out writer; least of all the princess Indu from Magador. I was pretty sure her mother would let me stay in the garage—but for how long? She was the sort who tired pretty quickly of her playthings.

I should have taken my cricket more seriously, I told myself. Must dress better. Put on the old school tie.

This depressing thought in mind, I found myself standing on the middle of a small wooden bridge that crossed one of the swift mountain streams that fed the great river. No, I wasn't thinking of hurling myself on the rocks below. The thought would have terrified me! I'm the sort who clings to life no matter how strong the temptation is to leave it. But absent-mindedly I leant against the wooden railing of the bridge. The wood was rotten and gave way immediately.

I fell some thirty feet, fortunately into the middle of the stream where the water was fairly deep. I did not strike any rocks. But the current was swift and carried me along with it. I could swim a little (thank God for those two years in the Channel Islands), and as I'd lost my chappals in my fall, I swam and drifted with the current, even though my clothes were an encumbrance. The breast-stroke seemed the best in those turbulent waters, but ahead I saw a greater turbulence and knew I was approaching rapids and, possibly, a waterfall. That would have spelt the end of a promising young writer.

So I tried desperately to reach the riverbank on my right. I got my hands on a smooth rock but was pulled away by the current. Then I clutched at the branch of a dead tree that had fallen into the stream. I held fast; but I did not have the strength to pull myself out of the water.

Looking up I saw my father standing on the grassy bank. He was smiling at me in the way he had done that lazy afternoon at the canal. Was he beckoning to me to join him in the next world, or urging me to make a bid to continue for a while in this one?

I made a special effort—yes, I was a stouthearted boy—heaved myself out of the water and climbed along the waterlogged tree-trunk until I sank into ferns and soft grass.

I looked up again, but the vision had gone. The air was scented with wild roses and magnolia.

> You may break, you may shatter
> the vase if you will,
> But the scent of the roses will linger
> there still.

CHAPTER NINETEEN

BACK TO SLEEPY DEHRA, somnolent in the hot afternoon sun and humid from the recent rain. Dragonflies hovered over the canals. Mosquitoes bred in still waters, multiplying their own species and putting a brake on ours. Someone at the bus stand told me that the Maharani was down with malaria; as a result I walked through the bazaar with a spring in my step, even though my cheap new chappals were cutting into the flesh between my toes. Underfoot, the neem-pods gave out their refreshing though pungent odour. This was home, even though it did not offer fame or riches.

As I approached Astley Hall, I saw a kite flying from the roof of my flat. The landlady's son had probably got hold of it. It darted about, pirouetted, made extravagant nose-dives, recovered and went through teasing little acrobatic sallies, as though it had a life of its own. A pink kite against a turquoise-blue sky.

It was definitely my kite. How dare my landlady presume I had no need for it! I hurried to the stairs, stepping into cowdung as I went and consoling myself with the thought that stepping into fresh cow-dung was considered lucky, at least according to Sitaram's mother.

And perhaps it was, because, as I took the narrow stairway to the flat roof, who should I find up there but Sitaram himself, flying my kite without a care in the world.

When he saw me, he tied the kite-string to a chimney-stack and ran up and gave me a tight hug and bit me on the cheek.

'Why aren't you with the circus?' I asked.

'Left the circus,' he said, and we sat down on the parapet and exchanged news.

'What made you leave so suddenly? You were ready to follow those circus-girls wherever they went.'

'They are all in Ambala. There's a big parade-ground there. But it was too hot. Much hotter than Dehra.'

'Is that why you left—because of the heat?'

'Well, there was also this tiger that escaped.'

'But it escaped in Dehra! Don't tell me it returned to the circus?'

'No, no! This was the other tiger. It got out of its cage, somehow.'

'Not again! Did *you* have anything to do with it?'

'Of course not. I hadn't been near it since early that morning.'

'Someone must have left the cage open. Or failed to close it properly.'

'Must have been Mr Victor, the ringmaster. Anyway, when he tried to drive it back into the cage, it sprang on him and took his arm off. He's in hospital.'

'And the tiger?'

'It ran into the sugarcane fields. No one saw it again.'

'So the circus has lost two tigers and the ringmaster his arm. Has the lion escaped too, since you've been there?'

'No, the lion's too old. Besides, it's deeply in love with the lady-wrestler.'

'I thought that was the dwarf.'

'They both love her.'

I gave up. I had a sneaking suspicion that he'd had something to do with the escape of the tiger, but he managed to convince me that he'd come back (a) because of the heat, and (b) because he missed me. In that order. Had it been the other way round, I wouldn't have believed him.

I collected my keys from the landlady (Sitaram had got into the flat through the skylight, anxious to find clues to my whereabouts), and she gave me a couple of letters. One of them contained a cheque from the *Weekly*, with a note from its editor, C.R. Mandy, saying he would be happy to serialize my novel, *The Room on the Roof*. The cheque was for seven hundred rupees.

'We're rich!' I shouted, showing Sitaram the cheque. 'Well, for two or three months, at least ... See, I told you I'd be a successful writer some day!'

'Will there be more cheques?'

'As long as I keep writing.'

'Then sit down and write.' He pulled a chair up for me and forced me to sit in front of my desk.

'Not now, you ass. I'll start tomorrow.'

'No, *today*!'

And so, to make him happy, I wrote a new limerick:

There was a young fellow called Ram

Who set up a frantic alarm,

For he'd let loose a tiger,

Two bears and a liger,

Who bit off the ringmaster's arm.

'What's a liger?'

'A cross between a lion and a lady-wrestler.'

'Write more about me.'

'Tomorrow. Now let's go out and celebrate.'

We went to one of the sweetshops near the bazaar and ate jalebis. Jai Shankar found us there and we ate more jalebis.

Then, walking down Rajpur Road, we met William Matheson, who said he was badly in need of a drink. So we took him to the Royal Cafe, where we found Suresh Mathur expounding on the fourth dimension. There were a great many drinks, and everyone got drunk. Suresh Mathur so forgot himself that he signed the chit for the drinks.

It was late evening when we rolled into the Indiana for dinner. Larry Gomes played *Roll Out the Barrel* and joined us for a beer.

I couldn't write the next day because I had a terrible hangover. But I started again the following day, and I have been writing ever since.

EPILOGUE

THE FRIENDLY READER KNOWS that I have continued scribbling away for forty years, but he (or she) might well be interested in knowing what happened to the other nuts described in the foregoing pages.

Unlike her mother, Indu grew old quite gracefully. She did not marry the Purkazi prince, as the Maharani had hoped; and this was just as well, for his nose was permanently disfigured by a bump-ball hurled at him by a West Indies paceman. He retired shortly afterward and became a sports journalist known for his bitter diatribes against his fellow cricketers and fast bowlers in particular. Indu married a hotelier in Mauritius where she spends most of her time.

The Maharani of Magador went quite potty in her declining years, took to the bottle and became convinced that she'd been Mae West in a previous incarnation. Whenever she saw a good-looking man approaching, she welcomed him with the line, 'Is that a gun in your pocket, or are you just happy to see me?'

I met her a few months before she died. She was sitting at the bar of a well-know club in New Delhi, and when I greeted her deferentially, she looked me up and down speculatively and said, 'You're that writer chap, Bunskin Ronde, aren't you? Tried to seduce me when I was a girl!'

William Matheson returned to Switzerland, where he inherited a fortune from his father and lived the good life for a number of years; but he never returned the money he'd borrowed from me.

Suresh Mathur went to practise law in the neighbouring hill station of Mussoorie, a resort that at close quarters looked as though it had been hammered out of old biscuit-tins. It is prettier at night when darkness hides the scars on its cardboard hillsides. Suresh had one too many Vodka Marys, and finally entered the fourth dimension.

Jai Shankar went to Oxford, where he painted a mural for his college dining-room. Apparently the boat-crew did not like it and dumped him in the Thames near Tilbury. He gave up art when one of his models sued him for exhibiting a painting in which he had shown her with three breasts. He now lives in Paris and writes poems in French.

And what of dear Sitaram?

No, he did not enter his father's profession. He remained with me for another year, and then, at the age of eighteen, decided to try his luck in Mumbai, then Bombay. He went to work for a well-known actress, who liked his winning ways and got him a small part in one of her films. After that, he went from strength to strength and by the time he was in his thirties he was one of the most popular stars of the Indian screen. He wrote to me a couple of times and asked me to come and stay with him; but I felt shy of his success and stayed away. The bright lights, whether in the circus or on the film-sets, were not for me. The writer's art is a lonely one.

Of course Sitaram became famous under another, assumed name, and I am sure, dear reader, that you would like to know his identity. But I have promised to keep it a secret, and so we must leave it at that. But I'll give you a few clues: he doesn't sing, though he dances; he can't act but he has a sexy smile; and although the hair on his head is jet-black, the hair on his torso is now quite grey. But most of them are a bit like that, aren't they?